## DEFIANCE AND DESIRE

"You must understand that I'm not accustomed to speaking of such things to a man," Meg began, slowly raising her eyes to Ransom's. "But . . . well, becoming someone's mistress implies that there would be . . ." Constraint overcame her and she paused, fearing that she was about to begin stuttering like a schoolgirl. The impatient expression that crossed Ransom's face caused her to hurry on. ". . . intimacies between them . . . and . . ."

Ransom's firm lips twisted upward in a smile as he displayed enjoyment of her embarrassment. "And . . . ?"

She forced herself to keep meeting his eyes, bracing herself for his reaction. "And I simply don't think I could stand to be . . . to be touched by an *Englishman.*" She shuddered involuntarily.

Instead of the burst of anger she'd anticipated, something more like determination came into Ransom's eyes.

"I think you're a liar," he said in a low tone.

"What!"

"Yes, that's precisely what I think." Before she could move out of reach, his hands clamped around her arms and he jerked her into a hard embrace. "I think," he murmured, looking down into her distinctly shocked gaze, "that you don't have the slightest aversion to my touch. And I can prove it."

He bent his head to hers, and when she would have cried out in protest, his mouth covered hers, effectively silencing her as he pursued a fiery kiss that seemed to go on and on.

# SCOTNEY ST. JAMES

# HIGHLAND HEARTS

ZEBRA BOOKS
KENSINGTON PUBLISHING CORP.

*This book is gratefully dedicated to my friend Sandy Kennedy, who dragged me whining and complaining into the Computer Age. Her expertise and willingness to help have been invaluable—I couldn't have made it without her!*

ZEBRA BOOKS

are published by

Kensington Publishing Corp.
475 Park Avenue South
New York, NY 10016



First Printing: February, 1993

Printed in the United States of America

# Chapter One

*March 1770*
*Devon, England*

Ransom St. Claire had two choices.

Three, actually, if he cared to count the gallows outside Barnstaple gaol.

But since he didn't relish that particular option, he was left with the remaining two. He could go to Scotland as his king had ordered, or he could become a fugitive.

Either way, obedient or outlaw, it was very likely he would never see Rogue's Run again.

Ransom's hands tightened on the stone railing before him. He stood on the balcony of his country manor, looking out over the bay below. The magnificent Devon coastline rolled away in both directions, and off in the distance to his left stood the huge, jagged rocks of Hartland Point, made blue by the ocean mist.

Ransom lifted his face to the strong breeze and felt the bracing sting of seaspray against his skin. The March sun was warm upon his hands, and the ivy that curled around them was already showing the pale green of new growth. It was his favorite time of year at Rogue's Run—how in God's name was he going to leave all this behind?

Sighing, he bowed his head, bringing into his line of sight the small group of red-coated horsemen gathered on the front lawn. The soldiers were waiting, watching him with an intense curiosity. Most likely, they had laid down various wagers on whether he would calmly deliver himself into their hands or slip out the back way and disappear. Apparently, several of them had fully expected him to be gone by the time they arrived, and the fact that he wasn't seemed to confound them. It had, he realized, only made them increasingly suspicious. His reputation was such that now they probably expected him to make his escape in some more flamboyant manner. Damned if the idea wasn't tempting . . .

He moved his gaze from the soldiers back to the sun-sparkled bay, deliberately reminding himself of one more reason he had to submit to the punishment being meted out to him. A sleek, two-masted ship rode atop the waves, tugging restlessly at its moorings. If ever he wanted to feel the deck heave beneath his feet or hear the wind snapping through her sails again, he must make the hated journey to Scotland and carry out his duties there. King George had confiscated both his ship and his home, and neither would be returned to him until all the conditions of his so-called sentence had been met. And, he silently acknowledged, met they would be, one way or another.

But submission did not set well with Ransom, and the taste of defeat was the bitterest of medicines. He reckoned it was a medicine that could kill as easily as cure.

He left the balcony then, reentering the house through doors of leaded glass which he secured behind him. For a moment, he surveyed the room where he stood. It was his own bedchamber, a pleasant sanctuary of dark wood paneling and heavy, masculine furnishings. These had always been his quarters, even when the house had still belonged to his grandmother and he'd come to visit as a lad. He'd enjoyed seeing the ocean from the windows, loved leaving the doors open to admit the wild, salty wind. His earliest desire to build and outfit his own ship had been born in this very room, as had, later, his daring scheme to do something to help the impoverished citizens of Rogue's Run village.

And this was where, three weeks ago, he'd been awakened from a sound sleep and arrested in the name of King George

III, ruler of England and all her colonies. Crimes against the Crown were not to be tolerated, the writ of arrest had proclaimed—not even when committed by men of good and noble family.

Ransom made a last, methodical check of the desk in the corner. He'd already gone through it more than once, but he wanted to be absolutely certain there was nothing in it to incriminate any of his felonious colleagues. Satisfied that little remained but a few harmless personal correspondences, he closed the desk without bothering to lock it. A canvas seabag rested on the floor next to the bed, and he hoisted it to his shoulder with ease. Then, after a final glance, he left the room.

A wide walnut staircase curved downward to the stone-flagged front hall below. As he descended, a sleek black cat slipped from the shadows to follow him. When Ransom turned to speak to the animal, he caught a glimpse of his own reflection in a long, beveled mirror: a big man dressed in a coat of ebony leather. The same coat, he recalled, that he'd been wearing the rainy afternoon in London when he'd been taken before the king. His eyes narrowed as he became lost in recollection . . .

The soldiers who'd arrested him in Devon had not subdued him with manacles. He was a gentleman, after all, and expected to react with dignity to a summons from his sovereign. That he did, but all the while he was riding toward London, his agile mind was busy with excuses and alibis. He'd been taken into custody after being named a pirate and smuggler, so there was no doubt George had substantial proof of his recent activities. Denial might be useless, but surely there was some other approach to the problem.

They had arrived at the royal estate at Windsor in late afternoon, and Ransom had immediately been ushered in to his audience with the king. George III of England was in the conservatory pruning the miniature roses he loved to grow. His pudgy face was flushed from the humidity in the room, his fleshy lips pressed into a firm line of disapproval. Ransom didn't know if the emotion was directed toward him or the thorny plants, but he assumed it would not be long before he knew without doubt.

He knelt in obeisance and waited for the king to speak.

There was a long, awkward moment before George tore his attention from the roses and addressed Ransom. "I vow, Ransom," he finally said, "you've been trying my patience since you were eighteen years old."

Ransom verified the statement by keeping silent.

"If you wished to see how far you could push me before I took action," George continued, brushing dirt from his soft, dimpled hands, "you have done so."

"Yes, sire."

"God's teeth, will you get off your knees," the king snapped. "And dispense with that false humility. I know you too well to be duped by such an attitude."

Ransom rose to his feet, surprised by the barest hint of levity that lingered just behind the other man's words. Perhaps matters weren't as black as he'd first thought.

"Aren't you concerned about what course of action I intend to pursue?" George casually inquired. "After all, piracy is a serious crime."

"I have only been *accused* of piracy," Ransom pointed out. "I assumed the charge would have to be proven."

George waved a negligent hand. "If that is your wish, naturally I would be happy to provide evidence and bring forth witnesses. But, dear boy, I can assure you that many of those witnesses might be reluctant to testify against you. They would most certainly have to be . . . well, coerced, shall we say?" Now his tone was devoid of all humor.

"Torture?" muttered Ransom, thinking of the villagers who had been his accomplices. "I thought England was finished with such things."

"Not when the situation warrants it. And, Ransom, I think you realize that if my men have proof of your recent activities, they can also confirm the names of those who've been aiding and abetting you. Something tells me you wouldn't want to see those people incarcerated."

Ransom was careful to keep a tight rein on his feelings. He could not afford to let dismay or anger show on his face. His only hope was to appear impassive, to bluff his way through. "I have always acted on my own. Even if I were engaged in piracy, it would be the same."

"Come now," the king chided. "What about the crew on your brigantine?"

"They take my orders, of course, and could hardly be held responsible for a crime you believe I have committed."

"And the villagers? The ones who receive and hide the goods your men smuggle ashore?"

Ransom's gaze remained steady, but beneath the soft leather coat, he was beginning to sweat. Obviously, George understood a great deal about the business being conducted at Rogue's Run. "I'm afraid I don't know of any such villagers, Your Majesty."

"You are a pirate and a smuggler—I have little doubt you are a liar as well."

The fact that he *was* lying didn't prevent Ransom from experiencing anger at the king's words, but he clenched his hands at his sides and said nothing, continuing to stare calmly at the shorter man. Although only thirty-two, George III looked older. He was already inclined to stoutness, and because of his propensity for wearing old clothes and gardening, he had more the look of a farmer than an authoritative ruler. But just because he had the appearance of a commoner did not mean he was unaware of the extent of his power.

"You've been a thorn in my side for too long, and I've decided to put an end to your brazen lawlessness—one way or another. I won't have it, do you hear?" The monarch pointed a dirt-stained finger at Ransom. "It's past time you started exhibiting a bit of loyalty to your sovereign."

Ransom's mouth curved in a mirthless smile. "I'm a St. Claire. Can you doubt my loyalty?"

"Apparently, any litter can spawn a cur."

At the sound of a different, albeit familiar, voice, Ransom spun about. "Father?" he drawled. "What are you doing here?"

"Trying to come to terms with the shame of learning my second son is a traitor to everything I hold dear—king, country, family."

Ransom faced the man he knew was an older version of himself. The dark auburn hair was streaked with gray, and the green eyes had lost some of their keenness, but the resemblance was evident nonetheless. Both shared the same rangy physique, the same stubborn set of jaw . . . and, as had been demonstrated many times, the same swift temper.

"You, too, condemn me without a hearing?"

"As an advisor to His Majesty, I am privy to all information that reaches him. There can be no doubt that you are guilty of the charges leveled at you." The Duke of Rosswell eyed his son sternly. "Now we must concern ourselves with your punishment."

"Without a trial?" Ransom protested. "There's no justice in that."

"Traitors aren't allowed the privilege of justice," George put in.

"Nor," added the duke, "are they usually fortunate enough to receive clemency at the hands of their king. If you are wise, son, you will keep silent and be grateful that His Majesty counts the St. Claire family among his friends."

George bent to sniff a stem of small, scarlet roses. "Your father refers to my decision to let you choose your own sentence. And the sentence, I might add, of your ship's crew."

"Choose a sentence?" Ransom looked from one man to the other, unease curling around his spine. What game were they playing?

"Indeed." George straightened. "You have three choices, Ransom. Death, imprisonment, or a sojourn in Scotland."

"Scotland?"

"Ah, somehow I sensed you would dismiss the first two choices as unsatisfactory." George gave him a cold smile. "As for Scotland . . . well, your presence there could somewhat mitigate your crime."

"I don't understand," Ransom began.

"It would seem that I am blessed with the most contentious

subjects in history," George stated, heaving a weary sigh. "The colonists in the New World are threatening to revolt; the Highlands are filled with heathen rebels. And I needn't tell you that even here in England there are those who seek to overturn my rule." He favored Ransom with a harsh glare, making it obvious that the young man was known to be one of the latter. "Neither I nor my soldiers can be in all places at all times," he went on. "Therefore, I am reduced to sending deputies into some of the more inaccessible areas. Wolfcrag is such a place."

"Wolfcrag, Your Majesty?" Ransom queried. Although he had never heard the name before, he surmised it was going to be very relevant to his future.

"It's a castle on the west coast of Scotland," George explained. "It was once rather impressive and, so I'm told, could be again. The trouble is, it's located in the midst of a settlement of longtime rebels."

"Wolfcrag once belonged to an outlaw named Revan MacLinn," Ransom's father said. "He and his clan were driven into hiding nearly fifteen years ago, but it seems the local people have complete faith he will return and lead them against the English. Especially now that the government has agreed to the removal of crofters to make more land available for grazing livestock."

"And I cannot risk any organization of these dissidents," George broke in. "All rebellion in the north must be put down immediately. Before it can become a real threat."

"I don't see what I can do about that," Ransom commented dryly. "I have no army—"

"You won't need an army," the king assured him. "Your task is simply to take up residence at Wolfcrag and befriend the locals. Give them employment, let them learn to trust you. Once they see the English aren't ruthless invaders, perhaps talk of insurrection will cease."

"How is giving them employment going to win them over?"

"They'll see that those who cooperate with me will be given

asylum within Wolfcrag itself—the rest will be without land or homes."

"But won't there only be positions for a handful of men?"

"Oh," demurred George with a tight smile, "did I neglect to mention that Wolfcrag is in ruins? I should think it would take a goodly number of workers to restore it to its former glory."

"Ruins?" Ransom choked. "You're sending me to a ruined castle?"

"Would you prefer the gallows?" his father asked quietly.

"Or a damp, moldy cell in the Tower?" George chimed in. "Ransom, my boy, I am doing you the courtesy of sparing your life—and the lives of your crew. Surely you would not expect me to let the lot of you off without some small retribution?"

"And how long is this . . . retribution to last?"

"Only as long as it takes you to rebuild and refurnish the castle to my satisfaction. And to subdue those who hold a grudge against my reign." George rolled his slightly bulbous eyes upward in thought. "With any luck, a year or two at the most."

"Two years?"

"Not long in the life of a young man. Now, I'll give you a moment to consider." The king picked up a watering can and strolled away to a box of flowers well out of earshot. Ransom stared after him in disbelief.

"But what's to happen to my home?" he murmured. "My businesses? The people who depend on me?"

"You should have thought of those things before you defied the law," the duke exclaimed.

"The law is wrong," Ransom declared fiercely. "Taxes are too damned high, wages too low. Men resort to crime out of necessity, and well you know it."

"But you are of wealthy stock," his father pointed out. "What need do you have to rob the Crown? To steal and smuggle goods into Devon and cheat the government out of its rightful monies?"

"I've seen how the poor have to live . . . Or should I say *ex-*

*ist?* Most of them are so destitute they barely have food to eat or clothes to wear." Ransom began pacing back and forth on the pathway that ran between the beds of roses. "Is it so wrong for them to want more for themselves and their children?"

" 'Tis not our concern," the Duke of Rosswell argued. "We have a duty to the government."

Ransom turned to face his father. "Don't you think we have a responsibility toward the people whose families have lived and worked on our land for generations?"

"Why? We've given them a place to live, jobs to work at . . . my God, what else should they expect? Give them more and they'll only turn on you . . ."

"Can you possibly believe that?" Ransom raged. "Do you mean you'd deprive men of a decent life simply to . . . to keep them in their place? To safeguard your own indulgent style of living? Can you actually abide being such a leech, growing bloated on the blood of unfortunates?"

"Enough!" roared the duke. Eyes narrowed in anger, he drew back one hand and struck his son across the face. "Do not dare to speak to me in that manner."

Ransom flinched slightly but did not move. Despite the murderous rage that suddenly burned within him, he sought no retaliation against the older man. He endured his father's tirade with stony silence.

"Why must you always be so intractable? Just once, couldn't you manage to adjust to the society in which you live?" He tightened his mouth in disgust. "Look at you—you even dress like a ruffian. And that earring you affect is nothing short of heathen."

"Yes, I know . . ."

"Thank God your brother Edmund was my firstborn. He, at least, knows his place, his duty to the St. Claires." The duke shook his head. "No, you'll never be another Edmund."

"Nor would I want to be," Ransom said softly. "Two coats cut from the same cloth are enough."

The duke's face reddened. "And I suppose you are proud that you so favor your mother? It was her influence that caused you to turn out as you have. You're a wild, trouble-making dreamer just like her—and like her, you'll never see old age. Mayhap it would be best to hang you now and save someone else the trouble later."

At that point, the two men became aware that George was once again within hearing. "I doubt you mean that, old friend," he said. "Let's save the gallows as an option to be entertained should Ransom fail in his mission to Scotland. But who knows? Perhaps a year of deprivation in the far north will be something of a redemption for him. They say Spartan living can do that for a man."

The duke inclined his head. "As always, I defer to your judgment, Your Majesty."

"Very well." The king waved a hand, summoning the soldiers who waited in the doorway. "These men will accompany you back to Devon, Ransom. You and your crew will have two weeks to gather your belongings and get your affairs into order. At that time, another small contingency of soldiers will arrive to escort you to Wolfcrag. I know I can count on your full cooperation . . ."

Ransom bowed his head, lest George catch sight of the sudden elation he was feeling. If they were not to be guarded any more closely than that, they could surely find a means of avoiding the journey to Scotland.

". . . but just to insure it," George continued, "I'll be taking control of both your estate and your ship."

Ransom felt the blood drain from his face. "You're confiscating my property?"

"You've confiscated a rather large share of mine from time to time." George chuckled. "Don't look so alarmed. It's customary for a felon's property to be appropriated. But you're more fortunate than most—you'll have a chance to win yours back." His smile was placid. "By the way, I've had papers drawn up giving you legal ownership of Wolfcrag Castle, so if you fail in your mission, it will simply mean that we are exchanging properties."

Ransom struggled against the profanities he wanted to utter, fought back the tide of violence that threatened to sweep over him. He wanted to wail in anguish, to smash the glass walls of the hot-house—rip the blossoms from every rose bush in sight. He was enraged, he was . . . afraid.

Rogue's Run was the only secure home he had ever known, the only place he could escape the loneliness and unhappiness that had plagued him since childhood. If he lost that, he'd have lost everything that mattered to him.

"Well, Ransom, let's not delay further," the king said. "What is your decision?"

Ransom realized he did not have the luxury of truly speaking his mind, of cursing the king and his own interfering father as he wanted. He was in a position where the best course of action was compliance, however sorely it galled him. A year, even two, in the cold, desolate Highlands would be hell . . . but it was his only choice if he wished to retain ownership of his land.

"Very well, sire," he murmured, sinking to his knees again. "I will do as you command."

George touched his shoulder lightly. "On your feet, then, and take my advice. Go to Scotland and work to restore Wolfcrag Castle. Then, next time you contemplate treason, think long and hard, for you will not receive leniency again. Do you understand?"

Ransom rose to his full height. His jaws were clenched so tightly his answer had to be forced. "Yes, Your Majesty."

"Be off with you now. My men are waiting."

"Sire, I've no need of an escort. I would prefer to ride back to Devon alone."

"How can I be assured you will present yourself for the journey to Scotland in a fortnight?"

"You've made my choices very clear, sir. I will be ready at the appointed time."

"Excellent . . . if I have your word on it."

"You have my word . . . and it can be trusted. I am, after all, a St. Claire." With one last, scornful look at his father, Ransom strode from the room.

* * *

He had ridden like a hell-haunted demon all the way back to his country estate, trying to exorcise the crippling anger from his brain. And he had ridden the same way every day since, up and down the long, curving beach below Rogue's Run, stopping often to sit and gaze up at his home, implanting its image within his memory. The anger had not abated, but it had settled into a kind of frustrated resentment. At least he'd had the opportunity to meet with his accomplices and warn them to lay low until his return from the north. And he'd had time to remove all physical evidence from his property and put his papers into order.

Now there was nothing left to do but leave.

Ransom broke free of his reverie and looked about him. He couldn't remain there, staring into a mirror, forever. The soldiers were growing restless; it was time to go.

With the cat at his heels, he walked briefly through each of the downstairs rooms, saying a silent farewell to possessions he treasured. He knew Fletcher, his first mate, had assembled the crew and that they would be waiting outside with the king's men. In addition, the staff that ran his home had gathered on the lawn to say their goodbyes. Still, he lingered as long as he dared, dreading the moment of departure.

He paused in the front hallway to take down a small watercolor painting of Rogue's Run and slip it into his seabag. It might prove a comfort in the dreary months ahead. Then, after one last look, he wrenched open the front door and walked through, closing it quietly behind him.

*April 1770*
*Carraig Isle, Scotland*

Meg MacLinn pulled her cloak about her and huddled deeper into the shelter of the boulder. No matter that it was storming; she couldn't have stayed in the cottage a moment longer. There was too much noise, too much confusion—too much incessant female chatter.

Ever since Ailsa and her mother had arrived to start preparations for Ailsa's upcoming wedding, there had been no peace or quiet in the MacLinn household. Each afternoon the village women gathered to bake or sew, and the men fled to the fields or went fishing or, on days like today, congregated at the public house. Meg despised baking and sewing—and, in truth, was vastly untalented at both—but her stepmother fussed if she spent time hunting or fishing with the men. And the world would no doubt come to an end if she ever set foot inside the tavern.

Meg sighed as she watched the rain fall silently, to be swallowed up by the rough waters of the Inner Sound. The bleak, barren scene suited her mood of the past week. She only wished she knew what had caused this pall of gloom to descend upon her.

With brutal self-honesty, she questioned whether her despondency was actually jealousy brought about by the flurry of activity surrounding Ailsa's wedding. She didn't think so.

They'd been companions since childhood, but even they had realized the difference in their characters. Ailsa was sweet, pretty, biddable . . . and usually scared half-silly by Meg's wild schemes—or *adventures,* as Meg chose to call them. On the other hand, Meg should have been a lad. She disdained proper behavior and had a distinctly hoydenish air about her, despite her stepmother's patient guidance. Pledging herself to some man was the last thing she desired. It made no difference that their friend Rob had grown to manhood following her and Ailsa about, indulging them in their mischief, protecting them when it went amiss. Or that of all the men she knew—with the exception of her father—Rob was the only one she could abide for more than a few hours at a time. Most males seemed to be vain, strutting peacocks, spreading their feathers to win a female whom they then proceeded to dominate and mistreat. No, she wasn't envious of her friend, even though, at the advanced age of twenty-two years, Meg knew she would soon be considered a hopeless spinster.

*So be it,* she mused. Something told her life would be more peaceful that way. Thus, whatever was disturbing her, it had nothing to do with Rob and Ailsa's upcoming wedding.

A solitary figure emerged from the misty rain, and Meg observed a man strolling along the water's edge, oblivious to the weather. She knew it was her father because of his unusual height and the broad structure of his shoulders, but as he drew nearer, she could make out his features and discern the contemplative expression on his handsome face.

Meg had been told all her life how much she looked like her father, and, in truth, it was a matter of pride with her. They both possessed midnight-black hair and smoky eyes, although Revan MacLinn's had an odd topaz hue, while her own were plain gray. No one ever told Meg she resembled her dark-haired and dark-eyed mother, and that suited her. She felt no closeness to her mother, had barely mourned her death so many years ago. Sometimes she questioned whether anyone ever thought of her mother anymore, but knew they must, for the woman's treachery had changed the lives of the Clan MacLinn beyond all imagining.

Meg watched as her father came to a halt and stood staring out at the sound and at the line of blue hills beyond. Just a few miles away lay the mainland of Scotland—Scotland, the home he loved and had been forced to leave. She wondered if he was thinking of Wolfcrag Castle and missing life there, as she herself so often did. Revan MacLinn was not an unhappy man, despite the fact that he was ill suited for existence on this small, cramped island with its moors and bogs and thatched-roofed cottages. He belonged to the rugged, rocky hills of the Highlands, to the savage land that engendered such majestic fortresses as Wolfcrag.

Narrowing her eyes as though trying to see across the miles that separated Carraig Island from the west coast of Scotland, Meg envisioned her family's ancestral home, pictured it crouching like a dangerous beast ready to spring. Its huge stone walls, its towers and battlements, had meant security to her, to all of them, and had allowed the MacLinns to live in the old manner, even though the Highland ways had been forbidden by the English king.

Following the Battle of Culloden, where the government

troops had ruthlessly slaughtered entire clans in an effort to subdue them, their heritage had virtually been destroyed. Scotsmen were denied the right to wear tartan, own weapons, or observe the centuries-old traditions they held dear. No longer were they allowed to play the bagpipes or perform the intricate Highland dances.

Revan MacLinn, himself too young to fight at Culloden, had lost his father and two brothers there, and had been endowed with a legacy of rage and hatred against all things English. Gathering his shattered clan around him, he had retreated to Wolfcrag and shut out the rest of the world, flouting the law and living as he pleased. That had only been possible because of the castle's inaccessibility. Hidden among the rocks and ravines of an isolated coast, Wolfcrag was impossible to breach. Impossible, that is, until one spurned and angry woman betrayed her entire clan in order to exact revenge on the man who no longer wanted her.

Meg closed her eyes and leaned her head against the rock behind her. Memories of her traitorous mother never failed to bring her shame. It amazed her that the petty emotions of a single person could wreak so much havoc, create so much loss and pain. Although fifteen years had passed, the events of that last day at Wolfcrag remained firm in her mind.

Meg had been seven years old, frightened and confused. She would always recall the horror she'd felt upon learning that her own mother had plotted with the enemy, had actually opened the castle gates to them while the men of the clan were away. She remembered the terrifying sound of the battering ram crashing against the front doors as she was being herded into a secret passageway with the women and other children; she would never forget cowering there, arms clasped about her pet dogs, her breath tight in her chest as she attempted to be absolutely silent. Later she learned that they had been saved only because her mother's collaborators had killed the traitorous woman before they'd realized the castle's inhabitants had gone into hiding.

Though they did not succeed in destroying the clan or capturing their chieftain, the English soldiers left the castle in ruins. They broke the windows, scarred the beautiful wood and plaster, burned what they could, and stole the valuables. Knowing any hope of a future at Wolfcrag was gone, Revan and his men rescued the women and children, then made their escape by sea, sailing into the western isles, where they built a new life for themselves.

They were safe there, and happy, and the name Wolfcrag was seldom mentioned these days. But there were times when Meg knew her father's thoughts returned to Scotland and the ruined castle where he'd been born and raised. She knew of his wish to go back and rebuild it, and in her own heart she prayed he would someday have the chance to do just that. When that day came, she would be proudly at his side. To live at Wolfcrag again had become *her* dream as well.

Her gaze drifted back to her approaching father. The red and black plaid draped over his shoulders made a splash of bright color in the rain-washed landscape. He had never forsaken the tartan, but wore it with fierce defiance. Even on this rocky island, he was the MacLinn, an outlawed chieftain who would never let his people forget their heritage.

With sudden insight, Meg sensed the reason for the melancholy lurking beneath his restlessness. No doubt the current wedding preparations had made him aware that another generation had reached adulthood in exile, that their children could conceivably grow up never having seen their rightful homeland.

She was stricken with guilt, knowing the blame lay with her mother. Somehow, at least in her own mind, she felt accountable as well. Although no one had ever spoken to her with accusation, she had long ago accepted a certain amount of responsibility. The years were passing, and her father's restlessness had become her own. There had to be something she could do to help the MacLinns reclaim what they had lost.

Meg rose, leaving the shelter of the rocks. For a long moment she stood, poised, staring across the water toward Scotland. Then she ran to meet her father.

"Meg," he cried, his somber face lighting. "What are you doing out in this weather?"

"You know I love storms," she answered, linking an arm with his. "Besides, I wanted to walk with you."

She could feel the soft rain against her face as she smiled up at him.

*One day, Father,* she vowed silently, *I'll get Wolfcrag back for you. One day soon . . .*

# Chapter Two

*May 1770*
*Scotland*

The ghost had returned.

From his position at the window high in the ruined castle, Ransom looked down at the moonlit beach and saw the wraithlike figure of a woman gazing up at him.

No, not at him, he realized—but at the castle itself. Her eyes were dark smudges in a colorless face, and though he could not see them clearly, he sensed they moved slowly, deliberately over the rough exterior of Wolfcrag Castle. So diligently did she study it that it seemed she was committing each stone, each line of the battlements, to memory.

Ransom wondered who she was and, more importantly, where she had come from. Despite his birth in the West Country of England, he was not a particularly superstitious man. He did not believe, as his companions did, that she was a ghost. It was his opinion that she was decidedly flesh and blood, but her sudden appearance intrigued him nonetheless. She had not simply materialized from the fog, he knew, because there was only gray and churning ocean behind her. And she wasn't a resident of the castle, for there were no women at Wolfcrag.

They had seen her there last night, but only briefly—in that wrenchingly lonely time of evening the Scots referred to as the *gloaming.* When Fletcher, his manservant, had pointed her out, Ransom had moved to the window, candle in hand. Apparently having spied the wavering light, the woman seemed to freeze in place for a long moment before backing away into the misty darkness. But somehow Ransom had known she would return.

He was glad his men were in the next room, gaming. Were they to see the supposed ghost again, who knew what kind of hue and cry would go up. They were nervous enough just staying in the dank and eerie stronghold.

This time the woman was bolder, or perhaps she wasn't yet aware that he was watching her. She came out of the shadows and began walking toward the base of the castle. With each step she took, thick fog swirled around her, obscuring her figure. To Ransom, it looked as though she was gliding . . . spectral and unearthly. A wry smile pulled at his mouth. Maybe he was wrong. Maybe she was a ghost after all.

He leaned closer to the cold glass and peered down at her. Human or not, it would appear that she was bent on gaining entrance to Wolfcrag.

His mood lightened considerably. Even if she was a creature straight from the maws of Hell, at least she'd be a distraction. And at this point Ransom St. Claire would welcome anything that lessened his deadly boredom.

"Fletcher!" he boomed. "Get in here, you scurvy sea dog!"

In a matter of seconds, the short, balding first mate was at the door.

"What is it, Cap'n?"

"We've got a guest," replied Ransom, with a crooked smile. "Go down to the tunnel and meet her—then bring her to me."

Meg pulled her plaid shawl tightly about her head and shoulders. The night was cold and damp . . . and threatening, somehow. She knew that what she was doing was foolish, possibly even dangerous, but she could no more turn her back and walk away now than she could have flown over the parapets of the stark and empty shell of the castle looming above her.

Since seeing that candle in the window the night before, she had been driven by a terrible urgency to learn who dared to inhabit Wolfcrag. He was a damned imposter, whoever he was! The castle had been built by the MacLinns, and had never been intended to house anyone but members of that once proud clan.

*Still proud,* she thought. *But with a bit less to boast of these days.*

The sand crunched beneath her feet as she moved cautiously across the small crescent of beach. Somewhere ahead of her, in the inky blackness at the base of the castle, lay the entrance to a tunnel that snaked inward to the bowels of Wolfcrag. She wished for a lantern, but knew it would be too risky. She couldn't afford to let the enemy know she was there, so she would simply have to rely on good fortune and memory.

Memory? It had been fifteen long years since she had last set foot in the secret tunnel—and then she and her family had been fleeing Wolfcrag. Even in her wildest imaginings she had never envisioned herself returning in such a clandestine manner. During the years of exile, it had been her dream to come back in triumph, head held high. But to manage that, it would have been necessary for her father and his kinsmen to have received a pardon from the old King George . . . an unlikely situation at best. And now that king was long since dead and another Hanoverian sat on the throne of England. As priggish and pragmatic as his father, George III was not much inclined to pardon Scottish rebels.

Meg paused and raised her head to sniff the cool, moist air. Having spent the majority of her young life in Scotland's western isles, she was accustomed to the smell of the sea, but tonight there was something different about its usual tangy aroma. It took her a few seconds to realize what the difference was—the sea air smelled not only of brine, but also of vegetation. Here on the mainland the seaspray took on the verdancy of bracken and heather. Her heart quickened. She had set foot on the soil of her true homeland for the first time in more than a decade! She had, in every sense of the words, come home.

With that thought, her resolve to discover the interloper in her father's castle deepened, and she began moving forward again.

"Hsst, Meg!" came a harsh voice behind her. "Where in the devil are ye?"

Meg halted and turned. "I'm here, Robbie—keep your voice down."

"Listen, lass, ye'll not do this." The tall, thin man who emerged from the mist reached out a hand and clasped her arm. " 'Tis too dangerous." The speckled hound accompanying him jumped against Meg's skirts, marking the black wool with sandy paw prints.

"Down, King," she insisted firmly before turning back to the man. "Do you think I could leave now, knowing there are strangers in the castle?"

"Damn, I should never have brought ye here in the first place." He groaned. "I must have been daft to let ye cajole me so."

Meg had to smile. "Admit it—you wanted to see Wolfcrag as much as I did."

"Aye, but I had not dreamed of this . . . this madness. Leave it go and let's get out of here."

"I can't walk away now, Rob, and you know it." She patted his hand reassuringly. "But I promise to be careful. I just want to slip inside through the tunnel and perhaps overhear something that will give me a clue as to who it is that has invaded our home."

"Ye don't mean to enter the castle? Ye won't go further than the end of the passageway?"

Meg withdrew her hand, tucking it behind her back so that he might not see her crossed fingers. "I promise," she lied. "If I hear nothing from the tunnel, I will give up."

"Very well, then. Let's be on our way."

Meg was not surprised that he intended to join her—Robbie might fuss and fume, but he had been staunchly by her side in every adventure they'd experienced since childhood. And she could almost wager that he was aware of her blatant falsehood but knew the uselessness of arguing with her.

"The entrance to the tunnel should be close by," Meg murmured, her hands searching blindly in front of her. "Blast it, why does it have to be so dark?" Although a hazy moon floated high in the sky, its light was now blocked by the castle itself.

"Look," said Rob, touching her shoulder. "There's the outcropping of rock that marks the opening."

Despite the darkness, it seemed almost like yesterday when they had squeezed past the malformed rock, and their feet found the relatively smooth slate floor of the secret passageway. Arms outstretched, they could touch either side, and thus they guided themselves through the impenetrable blackness.

There were no sounds to be heard except for the ever more distant rush of the ocean and the slow, insidious dripping of water down the rock walls. That and their own breathing, harsh with excitement.

"It can't be much farther," Meg whispered when she felt the floor beneath her feet angle upward. "We must be under the main stairway now."

"Eight or ten more feet . . ."

Abruptly, her groping hand met the damp coldness of a stone wall and Meg stopped, her heart pounding. "This is it—we've reached the end."

They waited, listening.

"What do ye propose to do now, lass?" asked Rob. "There's not a sound to be heard from here."

"I'll have to open the door. No one will notice . . ."

Before he could protest, she found the turn stone and gave it a twist. With a rusty creak, a section of the wall began to move inwardly, flooding the tunnel with weak light.

"I'll just step out and have a—oh!" Two strong hands seized Meg's arms, and she was dragged out of the passageway and into the once elegant Banqueting Hall of Wolfcrag Castle.

"I've got her," gasped Fletcher, holding a struggling Meg.

"Is she a . . . a ghost?" gulped a second man, making the sign of the cross. A third one hung back even further, eyes bulging.

"More apt to be a witch," Meg's captor panted, dodging her frantic kick. "Ransom told us she was real, didn't he?"

"Who are you?" blazed Meg. "Ouch! Let me go!"

Rob dashed from the tunnel, bent on rescue.

"Blimey, she's not alone. Get him, Yates! Beale!"

"Run, Robbie!"

Unfortunately, it was too late for the confused Scotsman to do anything. The man called Yates placed a well-aimed tap on Robbie's temple with the short wooden club he carried. Uttering an astonished grunt, Rob keeled over and lay still.

"Rob!" At the sound of Meg's horrified cry, the dog began to bark, the noise magnified many times in the narrow confines of the tunnel.

"Jesus, she's brought all the hounds of Hell with her!" cried Beale, looking on.

"Get a pistol!" shouted Yates, backing away.

Just then, the lone puppy crept out of the passage, his skinny tail wagging uncertainly. He immediately ran to Meg, cowering near her skirts and whining. She soothed him with a whisper. *"Thà, a ghaolaich.* Yes, that's a good fellow."

Relieved laughter broke out among the men when they saw the animal. "All the hounds of Hell, eh?" chortled the short one.

Rob stirred and moaned.

"At least you didn't kill him," snapped Meg, wrenching one arm free of her captor's grip. "But you didn't have to treat him so roughly!" Garnering every bit of strength she possessed, she doubled her fist and swung it into the laughing man's midsection.

*"Whoof!"* he gasped, staggering backward and clutching his stomach. "The little harpy struck me."

Meg drew back her arm for a second attack, but Yates raised his club. "I wouldn't if I was you, missy. It don't matter to this stick none that yer a female."

Meg straightened to her full height. "Oh, a curse on you and your stick," she flared.

The man gasped and turned pale. "Gor, she *is* a witch!"

"Then perhaps you'd better take care," said the man who

had first seized Meg, still grinning despite his discomfiture.

Yates groaned, flinging the club he held across the room. It clattered against the wall and rolled away into the shadows. "Oh, you're a vicious one, you are!" he ground out, towering over Meg. "I demand that you remove that curse right now."

Meg eyed him warily, intrigued by her unexpected advantage. Finally she shrugged in apparent indifference and knelt beside Rob. "You have nothing to worry about as long as Robbie recovers," she announced. "When he is himself again, I will remove the curse."

"What were the two of you doing sneaking around here anyway?" the shorter man asked, and for the first time his strange accent registered in Meg's confused mind.

"My God," she said, rising to her feet. "You're English! Who are you?"

"Exactly what the owner of this castle would like to ask *you*."

Meg stiffened. "The owner? I'll have you know that my . . . that I am the owner of this castle."

Beale threw back his head and laughed. He was a big man, shabbily dressed and none too clean. "By God, that's a rare un! Ransom'll be interested in hearing that story, eh, Fletcher?"

"Indeed. No doubt he'll find it most amusing." Fletcher sighed and fixed Meg with a stern glare. "However, my guess is that they're common vandals—though what sort of idiot thief takes his wife and pet along when he goes out to ransack, I couldn't say," he added sarcastically.

Meg shot him a venomous look. "Rob is not a thief . . . and I'm not his wife. As for the dog, King belongs to me and goes everywhere I do."

"King?" chuckled Beale. "A grand name for that scrawny mutt."

"I rather think it's the other way 'round," she said sweetly. "After all, he is named for England's King George."

Fletcher bristled. "You're speaking treason, girl, and we won't have any of that in this household."

"You might be surprised at how much treason has been spoken here," Meg retorted, but the very thought made her bite off any further words and look around.

The Banqueting Hall was a travesty of the room she remembered so well from her childhood. Odd how often she had thought of it during the years of exile in the islands. Perhaps because it had been the scene for the happiest time of her life in Wolfcrag—the festive holiday season of that last winter before the English had come and driven them away.

Remembering, she squinted her eyes against harsh reality and saw again the hundreds of candles, the bright warmth of red-and-black tartan covering the long tables. She could smell the scent of pine, the freshness of holly leaves—and hear again the soul-stirring strains of an old Jacobite ballad. She blinked and bit her lower lip in consternation. Now the room was bare, the MacLinn arms above the cold fireplace hacked and gashed by enemy sabers. The high, arched windows had been broken, and the night wind howled and keened through the hall. Birds had nested in the rafters, and the scarred stone floor was filthy with their droppings. Meg swallowed deeply. Never had she imagined it would look like this.

The man named Fletcher cleared his throat. "Uh . . . I think you'd better come with me now, miss. The master wishes to speak to you."

"Yes," she said softly, "I should like to speak to him as well."

"Beale, get our friend there on his feet and bring him along. Yates, find your stick and search out the tunnel. Make sure there aren't any others."

Holding his lantern high, Fletcher led the way out of the banqueting room and across the Great Hall. In the flaring shadows, it, too, looked to be in shambles. And it was cold, so terribly cold. Meg shuddered and hunched her shoulders within her shawl. Spring could be a misery in Scotland, its dampness seeping right into one's very bones.

She trailed her hand along the banister of the central staircase and winced as she felt the roughness of the wood beneath her fingers. The mark of the enemy looters was everywhere, and her contempt for the English nearly choked her. She realized that for the last fifteen years, the fires of hatred had only been banked. Now that she was reminded of all that the English had done to her clansmen, her hatred had begun to flame anew.

They paused outside a room on the second floor and Fletcher pounded on the door. "I've got the woman, Ran. Do you want to see her now?"

"Send her in," boomed a resonant voice, filled with easy command.

"The dog'll have to stay out here," Fletcher said. "I don't think Satan would like him very much."

*Satan?* Meg thought. *What manner of man am I about to meet.*

She entered the room, followed by the men. Her first impression was that this bedchamber had been restored to some kind of order. There was glass in the windows and a huge, roaring fire in the fireplace. A table and chairs stood near the hearth, and in the far corner was a curtained bed.

Meg glanced about with interest. At least he had picked a bedroom that had belonged to one of the lesser clan officers; she wasn't sure what her reaction might have been had she found the enemy comfortably ensconced within her father's old room.

Her attention was captured by the heavy silence in the chamber, and her gaze shifted from its contemplation of the furnishings to the man who stood quietly by.

Meg's breath fluttered in her throat. He was frightening, but undeniably magnificent.

Dressed in a white shirt with full sleeves, snug black trousers, and a pair of black knee boots, he lounged against the fireplace, his posture casual. Cradled in one arm was the biggest black cat Meg had ever seen, and the sight of the man's lean fingers stroking the animal's head mesmerized her for a long moment. When she eventually forced her eyes upward, they came to rest on the gold medallion revealed by the open collar of his shirt. Warmed by the firelight, the medallion lay against a wide chest, which was covered by an abundance of dark hair. Meg stared unabashedly until she detected a low rumble of laughter and saw that same chest rise and fall in amusement.

Stung by her own lack of sophistication, she raised angry eyes and studied his face. It was tanned and angular, marred, in her opinion, only by the insolent smile that revealed strong, white teeth. His eyes were shadowed by long, thick lashes, but could their expression be seen, Meg was certain it would be filled with further levity at her situation. That he was enjoying himself was evident in every line of his face and body.

Her hands flexed impatiently as she thought longingly of burying them in the thick curliness of his dark auburn hair and yanking with all her strength. She could almost laugh herself, thinking of the swiftness with which his arrogant smile would fade.

The shine of the medallion about his neck was reflected in the gleam of an earring worn in his left ear. Meg's lips parted in astonishment as she became aware that the earring was actually a small gold fishhook. She had never known a man who wore such pagan jewelry—it didn't seem quite respectable somehow. He appeared to be a rogue, or a pirate. She narrowed her eyes and made another survey. Yes, he definitely had an aura of danger and disdain about him. He might, Meg surmised, serve his king, but she could almost sense his contempt for law and order.

Surprisingly enough, it made her respect him more. She who had been raised among outlaws deemed it easier to deal with a man who might skirt the edges of propriety than with one who was morally upright, prudent, and prissy.

Apparently, her intense scrutiny had begun to unnerve the man, for he finally broke the silence.

"May I take it that you like what you see?" he observed imperiously. Behind her, one of the men snickered.

"If you wish," Meg replied. "The truth is, I was curious to see what the enemy looked like."

"And?"

She straightened her shoulders, bracing herself for the violent reaction she expected. "You seem very much like any other thief."

For an instant he looked furious, but then his expression

cleared and he threw back his head and shouted in laughter. Meg's shocked eyes were drawn to his muscular throat, to the beguiling glint of firelight in his coppery hair. His laugh was deeply mellow and, for some obscure reason, filled her with unrestrained wrath.

"I see nothing humorous in the situation," she said. "Why have you taken over my home?"

His laughter faded swiftly. "What the devil are you talking about?"

Meg gestured at the room around them. "You have made yourself comfortable here. Do you mind telling me why you've seen fit to move into a castle that belongs to someone else?"

"It was my right to inhabit this . . . castle, as you wish to call it, because it belongs to me."

"You are a liar!" she cried angrily.

Ransom's lips thinned, but he calmly turned to lift the cat he held onto the mantel, where it settled with a world-weary sigh. "You know," Ransom said, facing Meg again, "if you were a man, I'd be inclined to run you through for saying such a thing."

Meg smiled sweetly. "Oh? I'm sorry that my words seem less offensive coming from a female. I didn't intend them to be anything other than insulting."

Ransom came closer to her, but she stood her ground, refusing to lower her eyes.

"How is it that you're not afraid of me?" he asked softly. "Most women would be throwing themselves at my feet, tearfully pleading for mercy."

"You are in the Highlands now – here we do not beg." Meg flicked a contemptuous look at him. "Nor do I feel the need for your clemency. You are, after all, the one at fault. Perhaps you should be pleading for my forgiveness."

"You're an insolent little wench, aren't you?" he growled.

"Be warned, my lord," interjected Beale. "The woman is a witch. She put a curse on Yates. And," he added, "we heard her speaking in the Devil's own tongue."

Meg stared straight at the man and murmured, *"Rag-mhéirleach nan cearc."*

Beale yelped. "Make her quit using that evil talk. She'll curse us all before she's through."

" 'Twas no curse, you coward," said Meg. "I merely implied that you were a sly thief of hens. Appropriate, don't you think?"

"I ain't no thief," Beale countered. "It wasn't me caught sneaking into someone else's house."

Meg sniffed haughtily.

"If I'm not mistaken," Ransom interrupted, "the lady is speaking Gaelic. Of course, there are those who think that *is* the Devil's own language." He chuckled. "And what have we here?" He lifted the tartan shawl from her shoulders and held it high for all to see. "It seems to me that the Scottish tartan was proscribed—forbidden."

"Give that back," cried Meg, snatching the shawl from his fingers. "It belongs to me."

"I find this all very interesting," mused Ransom. "We discover you creeping into our midst under cover of night, wearing tartan and spewing Gaelic curses . . ." He turned to his men. "Fellows, I think we have a wee Highland rebel on our hands."

Rob groaned aloud at the words, drawing Ransom's attention.

"And who is this?" Ransom asked. "Your husband? A brother?"

"No."

"Ah, your lover?"

"That is none of your business," replied Meg. "What difference could it possibly make if he's my lover . . . or my brother?"

Ransom grinned. "I doubt you could have bullied a brother into abandoning common sense to bring you here. No, he must have the misfortune of being your husband or sweetheart."

"What do you intend to do with us?" Rob demanded.

"That depends . . ."

"On what?" asked Meg. "We've broken no law."

"I can't be certain of that until you have explained what you're doing here."

"Tell him, Meg," Rob said softly. "Once he sees that our purpose was innocent enough, he'll not detain us."

"So your name is Meg?" Ransom inquired.

"I suppose it won't do any harm to tell you who I am," Meg said. "I am Margaret MacLinn. I once lived in this castle."

Behind her, Fletcher whistled sharply. "Blimey, Ran. She must be kin to the outlaw MacLinn."

Meg swiveled about to stare at him. "All the MacLinns are outlaws," she said calmly. "Which one did you mean?"

"The clan chieftain. Revan MacLinn, I believe his name was," Fletcher replied. "We've heard many a tale about the fellow."

"Do you know him?" inquired Ransom.

Made hesitant by his sudden interest, Meg cast a quick glance at Rob. Instinct told her it would be to her advantage not to elaborate. "Aye," she finally answered.

"And how do you know him?" Ransom persisted.

The last thing she wanted was to lead the English to her father once more. Her mother had done it the first time, and Meg would rather die than have history repeat itself. Revan MacLinn had been safe for over a dozen years; she intended to see that he remained that way.

"He was my father," she replied.

"Was?" echoed Ransom.

"Yes, he was killed by the damned English," she retorted, her chin jerking upward in a defiant motion.

Ransom chose to ignore her profanity. "We had not heard he was killed."

"It was a well-guarded secret for a long time . . ."

"I see." Ransom arched a brow. "So . . . the famous Scottish outlaw was your father?" he murmured. "No wonder your manners are somewhat lacking."

"My manners are no more imperfect than your own," she said stiffly.

"How so?"

"You keep us standing here awaiting your pleasure. Either toss us in the dungeon or release us."

"Is it nostalgia, then, that leads to your desire to see the dungeon?"

"I didn't say I had any desire to see the dungeon. I simply wish that you would decide what you are to do with us . . . then do it."

"Still no pleas? No begging?"

*"Never."*

Ransom St. Claire couldn't quite suppress the flare of admiration he felt for the slender woman standing before him. He had known men who in similar situations had blubbered like babes, but this Highland lass truly seemed to have no fear of him. There was more apprehension visible in the thin face and tensed shoulders of the man with her than she herself had exhibited since entering his chamber. At first, Ransom thought that that could simply be an indication the man had more sense than the woman, but he didn't believe that such was the case. No, she seemed to possess the inborn courage of a warrior, and somehow that intrigued him.

Ransom studied her carefully, realizing that he had never seen such a woman. She was nothing like the ladies he had met in English drawing rooms. She was neither pale nor retiring, and though it was obvious she had been raised with some degree of civility, her demeanor made it clear that she would not let propriety get in her way. Never had he seen a female so forthright in expressing her views—Meg MacLinn would not stoop to seductive guile. Even though, he suddenly realized, her looks were such that she could easily resort to that age-old tactic.

Hers was a wild beauty—a natural beauty not obtained by hours in front of a mirror. Her hair was as black as a night in Hell, tangled and blown, flowing freely down her back. Her eyes were the same stormy gray as the Scottish seas—and at times filled with the same intense chilliness. Her heart-shaped face was touched with a faint honey-colored glow, a healthiness that spoke of time spent outdoors. She was slightly above average in height, though still small by comparison to his own large physique, and he sensed that her figure would be revealed as nicely rounded if it were not so well hidden by the ugly black dress and the voluminous tartan.

He glanced again at the man called Rob, thinking it was too bad about the girl's association with him. He seemed far too mild-mannered and ineffectual to handle such a firebrand. Well, that was, as she had said, none of his concern . . .

"Now that I know you are an outlaw's spawn," Ransom said carefully, "I think I shall hold you for questioning. My suspicions have been aroused, and I want to know what you were seeking here."

"I merely wanted a look at my old home," Meg explained. "I thought that—"

Just then, there was a loud rapping, and the door to the chamber was thrown open to admit Yates. "I searched the tunnel and there ain't no one else with 'em," he said.

Meg's hound came bounding into the room behind him, eagerly looking for his mistress. As he spied her, he gave his long ears a hearty shake and barked joyously.

*"Meeeeoooooooowwww!"*

The cat that had been quietly resting on the mantelpiece was transformed into a spitting, hissing ball of fur that launched itself off the mantel and into Ransom St. Claire's arms. Frightened by the unexpected noise, the dog began to bark more shrilly, causing the cat to claw its way up onto its master's shoulder.

"Jesus Christ!" swore Ransom, flinching as the sharp claws dug into his unprotected chest. "Where did that animal come from?"

"He belongs to her," Beale said, nodding toward Meg. "It's the witch's dog. Gor, she's tryin' to kill you!"

"Fletcher," Ransom roared, "get this cat off me . . . and then take that hound out of here."

"You won't hurt him," Meg cried, stating it as a command and not a request.

The look on Ransom's face was not altogether reassuring, but Yates led the dog away with a not unkind hand and Meg relaxed, prepared to enjoy the spectacle of the short manservant standing on tiptoe to forcibly remove the cat from the Englishman's shoulder.

"God, that hurts like sin," Ransom muttered, strong teeth clenched.

Meg clasped her hands behind her back and allowed herself a tiny, self-satisfied smile. It was apparent that her amusement was not wasted on Ransom, for as soon as the cat had been removed to the top of a tall armoire, he turned a dark scowl on her.

"I believe I'd like to speak to the lady . . . alone. Fletcher, go prepare us some supper. Beale, take the Scotsman into the next room and keep a guard with him."

"No, I'll not go," said Rob. "I'll not leave Meg alone with ye."

"You will, sonny," smirked Beale. "Mark my words. There's others here that would enjoy a chance to subdue you."

"Go on, Rob," Meg said quietly. "I'm not afraid of him. I'll be all right."

"But lass—"

"Beale!" barked Ransom. "Get him out of here."

"Aye, Cap'n. Be glad to."

With that, the brawny man seized Rob and began shoving him from the room. Ransom followed them, closing the studded door when Rob would have made further protestations.

"There," he said, sliding a heavy bolt lock into place. "That leaves just the two of us. Now we can talk."

He turned to find Meg standing close behind him, her wide gray eyes the color of a winter sky. In her small but capable hand was a short, deadly-looking Highland dirk—and the tip of its razor-sharp blade was aimed directly at his throat.

"Oh, damnation," he muttered in disgust. "I'll admit I was bored, but all I ever asked for was a simple diversion."

# Chapter Three

Ransom St. Claire didn't like having his back against the wall, and he most certainly didn't like it being put there by the bedraggled snippet of a female who stood before him. He could only be grateful his men had already exited the chamber and were not around to be entertained by the spectacle.

"You're beginning to try my patience," he announced in quiet tones. "I've exercised restraint despite the fact you were caught spying, but I can hardly believe you'd expect me to stand by and let you threaten me with that nasty little weapon."

"You're attempting to detain me," she pointed out.

"None too successfully at the moment." His natural sense of the ridiculous restored, Ransom allowed himself a small chuckle.

"Don't laugh at me," Meg admonished. "I couldn't possibly fail to recognize the danger to myself and Rob."

"At the moment, it doesn't seem that you're the one at risk."

Meg's fingers curled more tightly about the dirk, as if to reassure herself of her advantage. "There'll be no risk if you let us go."

"I'll do that gladly—just put away the damned knife."

"How do I know I can trust you?" Meg asked, keeping the dagger steadily at his throat.

"You don't," he said, and before she knew what he was doing, his strong-fingered hand had closed over her wrist in a numbing grip. He gave her hand a quick shake and the knife clattered to the stone floor.

"You unscrupulous . . . sneak," she stormed, wrenching her hand from his grasp.

Ransom laughed harshly. "Can you blame me for trying to preserve my own neck? Besides, if anyone's a sneak, it's you."

"It is not!"

Meg made a sudden, unexpected dive for the knife. With a startled curse, Ransom flung himself after her, his body bearing hers to the floor with a muffled thud. Facedown, Meg cried out in anger and pain as he sprawled atop her, his hands clasping her wrists, his legs entwining with hers through the thin layer of petticoats she wore.

"Get off me," she gasped.

"Not until you give me your word you'll behave yourself."

Meg writhed beneath him, furious at the ease with which he subdued her.

"Lie still," he commanded, beginning to breathe a bit more heavily himself. He had the notion that he'd cornered a wildcat. "Do you have any more weapons?"

"I'd never tell you if I did," she managed to say.

"Don't think I won't find out for myself . . ." He shifted his weight, resting one arm across her back and freeing the other for the search. Reaching behind him for the hem of her gown, he brushed it aside and brazenly ran his hand up the length of her leg. Meg squirmed, nearly choking with rage.

*"Smàlaidh mi an t-eanchainn asad!"* she sputtered.

"I know I'll . . . rest . . . easier . . . not knowing what you just . . . said." Ransom's fingers continued their bold foray until they located the leather scabbard he'd fully anticipated finding strapped to her thigh. "Now . . . is there another?" he muttered.

As he fumbled beneath her skirts, his fingertips grazing the soft, warm flesh of her legs, Ransom became aware that a feeling of excitement had begun to flare deep inside him. The earthy scent of heather and rough-made soap rose about him, insinuating its way below the surface of his anger and determination. That and the thrashing of the feminine form beneath him was causing his body to rebel against its recent lengthy bout of celibacy. His jaw tightened as he made a swift and final search.

Satisfied that Meg carried no further weapons, he removed his hand from beneath her skirts and took the restraining arm from her back. He leaned away from her, balancing on his knees as he straddled her body. "Now," he demanded, "will you behave?"

Meg vented her wrath by pounding her fists on the floor. Then she twisted about to confront him, yet another Gaelic curse issuing from her lips. As she caught sight of his arrogant smile, she uttered a low, enraged scream and sprang toward him, her hands curled into claws that groped for his eyes.

Instantly, Ransom closed his legs, trapping her neatly between them as he grasped her wrists and forced them behind her back. The action pulled her close to his chest, bringing their faces to within inches of each other.

"You little hellcat," he rasped, drawing a deep breath. "I ought to . . ." His words trailed away as he gazed into her wide gray eyes. There was still no fear in them, only the dawning of sudden caution.

Meg lay absolutely motionless. She was aware that she might have placed herself in a precarious position, and that the man she was dealing with could prove more menacing than she'd ever imagined. The faintest tingle of alarm crept along her spine as she stared back at him.

*What in God's name am I to do now?* she wondered, noticing that Ransom's eyes had grown dark and heavy-lidded, his gaze uncomfortably heated as it traveled from hers downward to rest on her mouth. A muscle twitched in the man's tightly held jaw, and he swallowed deeply. It seemed to Meg that he had moved imperceptibly closer. With a tiny sound that unfortunately resembled the frightened mewing of a kitten, she drew as far away from him as she could, the first stirrings of fear blossoming as she felt his hands loosen their grip and slide along her arms to her elbows. His touch was almost a caress . . .

There was an unexpected rapping at the door, and a muffled voice choked out, "Captain, open up. I . . . I need to talk to you."

"What is it, Beale?" Ransom asked, his tone wavering between impatience and relief.

"Let me in," Beale insisted. "It's important."

With a last rueful look at Meg, Ransom got to his feet and pulled her to hers. Then, stooping to retrieve the dagger, he crossed the room to throw open the door.

Beale pushed his way inside the room, followed by Rob MacLinn, brandishing a dirk of his own.

"Sorry, Cap'n," muttered the shamefaced man, "but he caught me off guard."

Again, Ransom's laughter—albeit edged with disgust—filled the chamber. "By all the gods, we were naive to think we had the better of these two! Next time we decide to entertain Highlanders, we'd be well advised to disarm them first."

Rob cast Meg a questioning look when he noticed the dagger in Ransom's hand. She scowled. "I've become too civilized, Robbie," she said sadly. "I allowed my attention to waver just for an instant and this chortling son-of-a-badger took my weapon."

"Dinna fash yerself ," Rob said softly. "I can slice up the both of them, if need be."

"I didn't think we were in any danger," Meg pointed out. "But he . . ." She nodded her head in Ransom's direction, and a look of chagrin came over her face. "I don't even know his name," she muttered, as if that somehow made the matter even more unforgivable.

"Ransom St. Claire, lately of Rogue's Run in Devon," Ransom readily supplied. "And you're in no danger. I merely want to talk to you."

"About what?" Rob's suspicion was as evident as Meg's had been.

"I'd like some information. And in exchange I'm offering a good meal and a night's lodging."

Rob's frown deepened. "A night's lodging?"

"Yes. I would think shelter from the elements would be a

pleasant respite." Ransom eyed him with interest. "I gather your home is at some distance. Where would you spend the night if you did not remain here?"

Rob and Meg exchanged looks, then Rob shrugged.

"On the beach, I suppose. It's where we slept last night. With a fire, 'tis comfortable enough."

Ransom turned his intense gaze on Meg and she chafed beneath his speculation. She knew as surely as if he'd said the words aloud that he was wondering what sort of loose woman roamed the countryside alone with a man, spending nights in such haphazard conditions. She raised her chin and put a touch of ice in her voice.

"I have no information to give you."

"Not even for roasted beef and potatoes?" Ransom queried. "It's Tuesday, and Fletcher always serves beef on Tuesday."

Meg could feel her stomach lurch in anticipation of a satisfying meal. The dry oatcakes and lukewarm water she and Rob had dined on earlier in the day were much in need of company. But even more compelling was the opportunity to wander unimpeded through her old home. Ransom St. Claire's offer was tempting.

"There's still no guarantee we can trust you," she managed to say.

"My word as a gentleman is all I can tender," Ransom stated.

Meg's face plainly showed her disgust. "And do you think we'd pay heed to the word of an Englishman?"

"It doesn't matter," Ransom said flatly, obviously making an effort to contain his temper. "You'll be staying."

Without warning, he swung his arm and knocked the dirk from Rob's hand. At the same instant, Beale gave the Scotsman a shove that sent him reeling backward against the stone wall. Then he bent to seize the dagger and place the blade of it against Rob's neck. Stunned, Rob could only look at Meg, his acute sense of failure obvious.

"Now," said Ransom with an air of finality, "have you left your belongings somewhere? Since you'll be our guests for a few days, I'd be glad to send a man for them."

"But you can't keep us here," cried Meg. "We're expected at home. If we don't return, someone will come looking for us."

"Forgive me if I don't believe you," Ransom said dryly. "Something tells me this castle is the last place anyone would expect you to be."

Meg couldn't restrain the guilty glance she threw Rob, and her face flamed at Ransom's accurate assessment. After a long moment, she shrugged.

"Our valises are hidden in a small cave down the beach near where we left our boat . . ."

Later, when the bags had been found and brought to the castle, Meg was left alone in the bedchamber to refresh herself before the evening meal. Angered that she had been locked in, the first thing she did was to make a thorough survey of the room, seeking some means of escape. There appeared to be none. The chamber boasted several windows, but all of them looked out over the rocky beach below. Too far to climb down, too far even to attempt the fashioning of a rope. The only door was stout, bolted on the outside; there were no convenient secret passages.

With a defeated sigh, Meg abandoned the search. It would seem that, for the time being at least, she was the devil Englishman's prisoner. The only thing she could do was take the meal he offered and hope to bluff her way through the interrogation. Until she found out why the foreigners were in her father's castle, she was not going to divulge anything that might incriminate her family. If she answered his questions with the proper amount of guile, he might not suspect she was lying.

By the time Ransom returned to his bedchamber, a number of significant changes had been made.

Fletcher, the only other with a key to the room, had already been there to place the table in front of the fire and set it for dinner. Ransom noticed he had used a linen cloth for the first time since they had come to Scotland. Two fat wax tapers burned in polished silver holders on either side of a gleaming bowl of fruit. Wryly, he mused that the old hoarder had never offered fruit before.

The biggest change, however, involved Meg. She was standing at a pair of tall, arched windows and looking down at the beach.

"You saw me down there, didn't you?" she asked without turning.

"Yes, that's why I had my men waiting for you."

Meg wheeled about to face him. "But how did you know about the tunnel?"

Ransom was so astounded by the change in her that he had difficulty framing a reply. Even when she'd been wearing the damp and muddied black gown, her hair straggling down her back, he'd been aware that she possessed a wild, untamed sort of beauty. But he had not realized how that beauty could be enhanced by the donning of a clean dress and the expedient use of a hairbrush. The woman standing before him now was nothing less than exquisite.

"Actually," he began, "we had been told the stories of your clan's escape to the islands west of Wolfcrag. It seemed logical that there had to be another way out of this castle—a way unknown to most people."

"So you hunted until you found it?"

"Yes. And the search enlivened the first week I spent in this miserable place. Nothing since has been that entertaining." He cleared his throat. "Not, that is, until your arrival. Did you know my men took you for a ghost?"

"I thought they had marked me as a witch."

"Well . . . that, too. Frankly, they weren't certain what to make of you."

And, in truth, neither was he.

Meg had dressed in a plain woolen gown that was the same soft blue-gray color as the mountains on the distant islands that could be glimpsed from the ramparts of Wolfcrag Castle—the islands where, apparently, she had made her home. The hue of her clothing was repeated in her eyes, making them bluer and less stormy than earlier. Her hair had been brushed and pulled high in back, tied with a blue ribbon whose streamers tangled in the fall of lustrous curls. Without the shawl, Ransom could see, her figure was slender and well formed, as he had guessed it would be. But he had not foreseen that she would move with such grace, such inborn regality. Being a chieftain's daughter might mean nothing politically these days, but her bearing was surely inborn, a trait that harked back to the time when the chief of a clan was looked upon as royalty.

"Well," Meg said tartly, "I'm not a ghost. And I'm not really a witch either, though there are times when it would be most convenient." Her expression was less guarded, and she seemed more at ease in her surroundings. As she talked, her eyes restlessly roamed around the room, as if memorizing every corner. Ransom wondered if she had kinfolk who would be waiting to hear a detailed account of her visit. His curiosity began to stir.

"Be seated," he said, gesturing toward the table. "We might as well get on with the questioning."

Meg slipped into a chair, arranging her skirts carefully—again amazing him that every sign of the hoyden had vanished.

"I want to know," Ransom prodded, "what you hoped to find at Wolfcrag?"

"I lived here for the first seven years of my life. I wished to see the castle again . . . it was a whim, nothing more."

"But didn't you think that such a whim might be dangerous?"

Meg's gaze was cool. "No."

A tap at the door and the entrance of Fletcher carrying a large tray stopped Ransom's questions for the moment.

"Your dinner, Cap'n," Fletcher announced, setting the tray on a sideboard and sweeping a cloth off the plates it contained.

"But there are only two—what about the others?" Meg asked. "Aren't they joining us?"

"Oh, no, ma'am. The men and me will eat in the next room."

"What about Rob?"

"Don't worry," Fletcher assured her. "Your friend will be fed."

Meg sneaked a look at Ransom, who seemed intent on opening the bottle of wine Fletcher had handed him. Her instincts told her she was safe enough alone with him, that he was no ordinary villain. Trouble was, those same instincts had led her into this situation in the first place. Perhaps she had, as her stepmother often predicted, finally taken leave of her good senses.

"Wouldn't it be possible for . . . for us all to dine together?" she asked. "I'd like to see for myself that Rob comes to no harm."

At the hint of unease in her tone, Ransom glanced up. "He'll be fine—unless, of course, you refuse to tell me what I want to know. In that case, my men will have the opportunity to question him." He removed the cork from the wine bottle. "And I assume you'd want to spare your friend their zealousness."

"Is that a threat?" she muttered.

"Consider it one, if you like."

"Why don't you simply ask your damned questions?" Meg blazed. "Why this . . . this farce of a meal?"

"Perhaps I'm merely eager for a dinner companion," suggested Ransom. "Meals have been dull affairs since coming north to this dismal pile of rubble."

Meg's head went up. "I resent hearing my ancestral home referred to as a pile of rubble!"

Ransom shrugged but offered no apology as he gestured for Fletcher to depart. When the door had closed behind the other man, he said, "Help yourself to your dinner."

Meg wanted to be indifferent to the meal before her, but it smelled so wonderful that her mouth began to water. She picked up her fork and prodded the nicely browned cut of meat on her plate. It promised to be excellent, tender and juicy, and she looked for a knife to slice it.

"Hand me your plate," Ransom instructed, "and I'll cut the beef for you. It doesn't seem prudent to trust you with yet another dagger."

Meg contemplated refusal, for it galled her to be treated like a child, but her hunger won out, and she passed him her dinner with an ungracious grimace. Hiding his own smile, he took up the knife Fletcher had laid upon his plate and cut the meat into pieces.

Just then, the black cat vacated its place on the wardrobe and leaped down onto the table, landing with a soft thud. Startled, Meg jumped, but the animal calmly ignored her and made his way to Ransom. He lay down a few inches from his master's heavily laden plate and waited patiently. Ransom handed Meg's dinner back to her, then cut a few small pieces from his own roast beef and offered them, one at a time, to the cat.

"I hope you don't mind Satan," Ransom said, one eyebrow quirked upward in question. "I understand most females don't care for animals on the dinner table . . . live ones, that is. But it's a habit I've gotten into since coming here."

"I don't mind the cat," answered Meg, plainly implying that the animal's company was preferable to his.

Satan took the last morsel of beef and began cleaning his paws with delicate efficiency.

"Why don't you tell me about yourself while we eat?" Ransom commented. "It could save us some time."

"There's nothing much to tell," she hedged, filling her mouth and chewing slowly.

"Don't be modest. I have a feeling there's a great deal I need to know about you and your companion."

"Such as?"

"Such as where you came from . . . how you got here."

"I could ask you the same thing," Meg pointed out. "I take it that you're a seaman, and yet where is your ship? Rob and I didn't see it anchored nearby."

Ransom grew still, his eyebrows drawn together to give him a fierce look. "No, she's back home in Devon. I was privileged to travel overland to this remote corner of the world."

Meg's fork stopped halfway to her mouth. The bitter sarcasm in his voice surprised her. "Why did you come here at all?" she ventured. "You don't seem fond of Scotland."

"How can you say that? I love the hostile people, the endless, dreary rain, and fog so thick it can choke a grown man."

"It's springtime," Meg began. "The weather isn't at its best—"

"God forbid I should ever have to spend a winter here." Ransom shuddered and reached for his wine glass. "It can't be healthy for a man to be stuck up here, shut away from the world."

"You know," Meg said with affront, "this *is* the world to many people."

"Not to me," he stated flatly. "Not to a Devon man."

"And is Devon that different from Scotland?"

"In my mind, there is all the difference between Heaven and Hell."

"Then why did you leave there?"

"I was ordered to leave," he replied shortly. "Sent to this place as a punishment, if you will."

"Punishment for what?" Meg's wide eyes met his over the rim of her wineglass.

His laugh was harsh. "I was . . . well, engaged in activities that were slightly outside the law."

"What sort of activities?" Clearly more interested, Meg set the goblet aside.

The black cat yawned, giving the impression he had heard the story too many times already. With a faint purring rumble, he settled himself in the center of the tablecloth and proceeded to have a nap. "I was arrested for smuggling and piracy," Ransom stated.

*"Fuigh!"* Meg exclaimed. "I thought you looked like a pirate."

"My father and King George weren't precisely thrilled about it. In fact, they seemed to consider it something of a disgrace."

"And you?" Meg asked.

Ransom frowned. "A man always believes he has the noblest of reasons for doing what he does. Actually, smuggling provides a livelihood for the villagers near Rogue's Run. As a young boy, I saw my friends involved in aiding their fathers—I even helped a time or two." He shook his head. "But I could never condone the wrecking, so in the end I decided to become a pirate. Removing highly overtaxed perfume and brandy from the hulls of foreign ships was a lucrative way to earn a living . . . and to help the village."

"Did you never kill anyone?"

"For perfume or brandy? Hardly! As a matter of fact, I like to think my piracy saved lives. Once I started sharing booty with the villagers, they agreed to stop the wrecking."

"But when you were caught, why did they send you to Scotland? I mean, shouldn't they have hanged you or something?"

"Are all Highland ladies as sympathetic as you?" he asked, skewering a slice of parsnip on his fork.

"It doesn't matter—you're here, so they obviously didn't mete out justice in that manner."

"Justice? Sometimes I think I'd rather have swung from the gibbet than been buried alive here on the back side of civilization. Of course, I assume they were being magnanimous when they decided to bend the law on my behalf."

"Why would the king bend the law, as you put it?"

"For my father's sake, not mine. They're old friends, you see."

"Then your father is someone of consequence?"

"He's the Duke of Rosswell . . . and, more importantly, a lifelong friend of the king's."

"I see. No doubt that means he's wealthy as well. Tell me, why didn't your father simply use his own money to aid the villagers?"

"Obviously, you don't know much about the landed gentry. Wealth that was his by right of birth was not meant to be squandered on half-starving peasants."

"He didn't think they should be helped?"

"Oh, he had no quarrel with them being helped. He just didn't think that it was his duty to do so."

"I see." Meg studied him. "Do you hold a title?"

Ransom grinned wickedly. "Thief. Ne'er-do-well. Wastrel.

At least those are my father's favorite ones. All of the more meaningful titles will go to my older brother, Edmund St. Claire. I'm a second son, you see."

"But still a lord," Meg pointed out. "That should count for something."

"Indeed. It counts for the fact that I own Rogue's Run, one of the finest manor houses in Devon. It came into the family through my mother's people and passed to me upon her death. Being a lord means little to me, but ownership of that estate is all-important."

Meg picked up her fork again. "At least that explains your surly mood . . ."

"Surly?"

"Well, you have to admit you haven't shown much enthusiasm for Scotland. Now I understand why. You miss England. When will you return?"

"Not soon enough to suit me," Ransom grumbled. "As punishment for my crimes, I have been given this . . ." He dropped his fork and gestured at the room around them. ". . . this decaying pile of stones and told to rebuild it."

"You're going to rebuild Wolfcrag?"

"Don't look so pleased. I said I was given that duty . . . I didn't say it was possible."

"But it *is* possible," Meg cried, leaning forward in her excitement. "Only the inside was destroyed. All the outer walls are intact."

Ransom was suddenly aware of how the candlelight reflected in her wide eyes, gilding the gray with a faint shine of gold. His statement seemed to have fired some response from deep within her. Exhilaration was evident in every line of her body as she leaned closer and said, "Wolfcrag was magnificent once—it can be that way again."

Ransom pushed away from the table and lurched out of his chair to pace back and forth across the room. "Yes, of course it could," he snapped, "if the task was undertaken by someone who gave a damn about the place. But I'm not that man! I've been sent on a fool's errand with inadequate supplies and a handful of men who could work ten years and see no progress."

"But you can hire others to help," declared Meg. "There are still workers in the area who know carpentry and—"

"The locals won't even speak to us," stated Ransom. "We've been treated as though we had the plague since we got here."

"That's because you're English. You can't really blame those poor people, not after the way your government has treated them."

"But that's not my fight either," ground out Ransom. "I want no part of their politics. I want no part of anything this godforsaken country has to offer."

Meg fell silent, strangely hurt. How ironic that this man who had been given Wolfcrag outright neither wanted it nor saw any merit in its reconstruction. What one might sacrifice his life for was handed to another who was without gratitude or appreciation. At best, life was unfair, but moments like this made her think it was damnably painful.

After a few seconds of watching Ransom pace, Meg made a comment. "Since the castle was given to you by the king, I imagine it would be a breach of etiquette to sell it, but why not rent it to someone else? Someone who would care about restoring it?"

"You don't understand," he said, turning to stare at her. "This place is my punishment, not a reward. The king has ordered me to remain in Scotland until the castle has been renovated and the locals won over to the English cause. To assure my cooperation, he is holding both my ship and my home in Devon. They won't be returned to me until he is satisfied I have met my end of the bargain he struck with my father."

"And you've reason to believe you might not be able to complete the task," Meg murmured. "In which case you'll never see your home again."

Ransom moved back across the room to stand by her chair. "Quite right. And it's a bitter draft."

Meg had not yet grown accustomed to his great height, nor the gleam of the gold earring he wore, but she felt she was beginning to comprehend something of what drove the man.

"I know what you mean," she said quietly. "And the irony of it all is that that is precisely how my father feels . . . felt about this place. This castle was built by MacLinns, and for two centuries none but MacLinns resided here. When the English massacred the clans at the Battle of Culloden over twenty years ago, my father's father and two older brothers were slain. A grieving mother and Wolfcrag Castle were all he had left." Meg looked about. "Oh, yes, I can understand why a man's home can be the most important thing in the world to him."

Ransom looked down at her. "And did it remain the most important thing to him?"

Meg's unexpected smile was soft, lighting her face. "Only until Cathryn and Alex came along."

Ransom tilted his head to one side. "And who might Cathryn and Alex be?"

"Cathryn is my stepmother," she explained. "And Alex is my half-brother—Cathryn and my father's son. He's nearly fifteen now."

"Good Lord," Ransom swore. "Do you mean to tell me you have a stepmother and that she allowed you to make this idiotic jaunt back here?"

Meg's smile faded. "Do you know, you have a way of irritating me beyond belief? Of course Cathryn didn't allow me to come here! In fact, she knows nothing of it. I . . . well, if you must know, I lied to her. She thinks I'm spending a few days with an old friend."

"And so, while you and your young man are cavorting about in strange places, risking your fool necks, the poor woman thinks you're safe at a friend's house?"

"Cathryn would have all your fine red hair pulled out by its roots if she heard you refer to her as 'poor woman,' " Meg snapped. "That implies helplessness, and there's nothing helpless about Cathryn."

Ransom considered her. "And I suppose you're a great deal like her?"

"That would please me, I assure you."

"Did you have enough to eat?" Ransom asked abruptly.

"Yes," answered Meg, grateful for the change of topic. "I'm impressed with Fletcher's capabilities. Has he been with you long?"

"Ten years," Ransom replied. "Since my first sea journey. Good God!" His disgust was evident as he dropped into the chair opposite hers. "I've just realized the game you're playing. Here I've been chattering away like a schoolboy . . . when *you* were supposed to be answering the damned questions!"

It infuriated him that he had practically bared his soul to this woman who made no pretense of being other than the enemy. It had been years since he had talked so freely about himself. She, on the other hand, had revealed nothing of importance. Where had his ruthless examination gone wrong?

Meg bit her lips as she studied her hands, which were twisted together in her lap. What had happened to her? She hadn't planned on uttering a single syllable of the truth, and she had blurted out all sorts of details about her father's life. He'd have been infuriated by her loose tongue had he been there!

"Enough meaningless conversation," Ransom declared. "I can only excuse myself because it has been hellishly lonely here, but I won't forget what I'm about from now on. I want to know why you came to Wolfcrag."

"I've already told you."

"And you expect me to accept that you were merely having a look around? For sentiment's sake?" Restless, he stood up. Hands on his hips, he glared fiercely at her. "I think you're lying."

"Then you tell me why you think I've come here," she spat.

"To make contact with the local rebels."

"Local . . . ? What are you talking about?" Meg shook her head in amazement. "Rebels?"

"Yes, indeed. The king mentioned them—how they're waiting for Revan MacLinn to return and lead them against the English. Are you his messenger?"

"Don't be ridiculous. He's—" Meg broke off and glanced up at him, her eyes wide. "He's dead, as I've told you. There's no way he can return to lead a rebellion."

"Then what about you? Or your friend Rob? Have you any notions of treason or treachery?"

"You must be mad if you think so."

"Where does your clan reside?"

"I'd never tell you that!"

"How far from here?"

Meg remained mute, shaking her head from side to side.

"If, as you say, your father is dead, who heads the clan now?"

She shrugged. "No one."

"Who sent you here?"

"No one."

"What local people do you know?"

"None."

Ransom placed his hands on the arms of her chair and leaned close to her. "I don't want to resort to violence," he warned. "Are you going to answer my questions or not?"

"When I do give you an answer," she reminded him, "you don't believe me."

Ransom seized her upper arms and dragged her from the chair. His face close to hers, he admonished, "I could force you to talk. Is that how this interview is going to have to be conducted?"

Meg swallowed deeply, praying he wouldn't detect her fright. Given his strength and the fact that he could call in his men at any time, she knew he had the advantage. Her only hope was to keep him from realizing she knew that. Her bravado was all she had left.

"I've told you what I can. If you feel you have to resort to . . . to torture, then do so."

Ransom clenched his teeth, and his fingers tightened painfully on her arms. For a second, Meg thought he was angry enough to strike her, but then he simply pushed her back into the chair and turned away from her. Rubbing the nape of his neck with one hand, he heaved a weary sigh.

"I'll give you one more chance to reconsider," he said. "If, in the morning"—he turned to look at her—"you give me the information I wish to know, you can go free. If not . . . matters won't go well with you. Do you understand?"

Meg kept her face immobile. "I understand."

"Good." He started toward the door. "You'll sleep here tonight."

"But . . . where will you. . . ?"

"Don't worry," he responded with a short laugh. "I plan to sleep in the taproom, with a keg of ale to keep me warm."

Meg was distinctly relieved. "What's to happen to Rob?"

"Forget your lover," he advised. "You'd best be concerned about yourself."

He went out and slammed the door after him, locking it securely.

Meg eased back into the comfortable chair and, after a few moments, kicked off her slippers and held her stockinged feet up to the fire. She had only a few hours to come up with a scheme to extricate herself and Rob from this absurd dilemma. But spending the preceding night on the beach had been something less than enjoyable, so she meant to make the most of Ransom St. Claire's hospitality while she had the opportunity.

In the meantime, she'd think of something. She had to—there was no other choice.

# Chapter Four

Lying in the soft, warm bed in the pirate's chamber, Meg was content in a way she had not been in a long time. The fire crackled on the hearth and cast dancing shadows on the high, beamed ceiling. Outside the wind moaned, rattling the glass and filling her with remembered pleasure. How she had missed the eternal winds of the Highlands!

Despite the fact that she was virtually a prisoner, she felt safe and protected, nestled in the arms of her ancestral home for the first time in many years. Her immediate worries faded—King George, the hound, lay across her feet, snoring softly, and Fletcher had assured her that Rob was being well taken care of. As she drifted toward sleep, she renewed her vow that no matter how long it took, she was going to find a way to give her father's castle back to him.

"What do you intend to do with the wench?" Fletcher was asking as he drew a mug of ale and set it before his captain. "It's doubtful she knows anything of rebellion."

Ransom leaned back in his chair and propped his feet on the crude table before him. "You think not?" He chuckled, then took a drink of the foaming brew. "She probably knows more of such things than you or I ever will."

"She's too young, Ran. Surely you can't believe she'd have any part of stirring up the locals?"

"There's no doubt she's been raised on hatred for the English." Ransom took another long swallow. "She hasn't seemed overfond of any of us, now has she?"

Fletcher grinned. "No, I can't say that she has." His expression sobered. "But just because she can spit and claw doesn't mean she could actually condone a bloody revolution."

Ransom swung his long legs off the table and leaned forward in his chair. "Have you forgotten how quick she and her man were to draw knives on us? Do you think they'd have hesitated to spill our blood if they'd had the chance?"

"I think that had they wanted violence, you and Beale would both be dead right now," Fletcher stated primly. "It's my opinion you overcame them simply because they were trying to get out of the situation in the best way they could without hurting you or themselves." He nodded wisely. "From what I hear, no Highland man ever gives up as easy as Rob did."

"So you think he chose to be subdued?"

"Aye, to keep Meg safe. He probably reckoned that she'd be in less danger if the pair of them cooperated. At least until they found out what you really want with them."

"Did Rob offer any explanation as to why they were sniffing around Wolfcrag?" Ransom asked. "I can't imagine why a sane man would risk his woman's life in such a way."

Fletcher dropped into the chair opposite Ransom. "That's just it, Cap'n. Looks like Meg was telling the truth when she said they weren't sweethearts. From what Rob told me, he's married to someone else—a friend of Meg's."

Ransom's green eyes flashed with ill-concealed interest. "Then why in the name of everything that's holy is the man dragging her all over the country? For God's sake, they slept together on the beach last night!"

Fletcher's laugh boomed out. "Obviously, the Scots don't exercise the same social rules as the English. And I don't believe they *slept together* in quite the way you're implying."

"How do you know?"

"Rob told me. He seemed anxious to volunteer that much. I guess he doesn't want us to think Meg's a loose woman."

"I'd say that bit of information is more important to him

than to her," Ransom commented. "I could swear that she doesn't care what we think."

"Exactly. That's why Rob tried to straighten it all out. For some reason, he doesn't want us to believe ill of her."

"The outlaw's daughter? No, that would never do."

Ignoring Ransom's sarcasm, Fletcher asked, "Do you want to hear his explanation?"

"Very well. Proceed."

"Rob says the MacLinns are scattered throughout several different islands in the Inner Hebrides, and that his bride had to travel some distance to his village for their wedding. A few weeks afterwards, they accompanied her mother back home, and because they were going to stay on for a short visit, Meg joined them. It was while they were in the other village that she persuaded Rob to bring her here for a look at Wolfcrag."

"To his deep regret, no doubt," muttered Ransom.

"No doubt," agreed Fletcher. "But you see, they really weren't bent on mischief. Meg wheedled, like women do when they want their own way. Even Rob's wife thought it was a good idea."

"She must be a trusting soul."

"The three of them have been friends since they were children. Coming to Wolfcrag was an escapade, that's all. Besides, the MacLinn chieftain is dead—it's unlikely they'd be planning a rebellion without leadership."

Ransom's scowl was fierce, drawing his deeply auburn brows together. "Perhaps you're right, Fletcher."

The other man studied him for a few seconds, then said, "Why so sour, Cap'n? I thought you'd be glad to hear what the lad had to say. Especially since it's plain there's no real need to hold them . . ."

"Oh, it's comforting to know we don't have to prepare for an immediate invasion of vengeful Scots," declared Ransom wryly. "But I have to confess that it rankles to know you got more truth out of Rob MacLinn in ten minutes than I did in an entire evening with the girl."

"Closemouthed, is she?" Fletcher reached for the empty mug, but Ransom waved him away.

"I've had enough," he affirmed. "I can see that I'm going to have to keep my wits about me if I'm to deal with the woman." He preferred not to mention that Meg had turned the tables on him during supper—that she had had him answering questions, while she remained nearly as secretive as ever.

"No need to deal with her now, Ran. Send her home in the morning."

"I don't know, Fletcher," Ransom said. "Something tells me we shouldn't be so hasty."

Fletcher coughed lightly. "And could that somethin' be a pair of pretty gray eyes? I've seen the way you've been watching the lass, and I don't like it. She isn't Clarice, you know."

Ransom pounded his fist against the table, rattling the glasses. "No, she's not, damn your eyes!"

"Then surely you can't be thinking—"

"What I might or might not be thinking is none of your business."

"But Cap'n . . ."

"Leave it, Fletcher."

Although the older man's disapproval was evident in the pugnacious tilt of his chin, he abruptly fell silent. Ransom nodded, then gave him a slow, crooked smile.

"Don't work yourself into a frenzy," he chided. "I haven't really decided what I should do about Miss MacLinn." Ransom stood, stretching and yawning. "But I intend to give it some serious thought." He winked at his first mate. "Some *very* serious thought."

The next morning, Meg was awakened by shouts from the courtyard below. She sat up in bed and looked about, momentarily confused by her surroundings. As she remembered where she was, the urgent need for escape reasserted itself. She threw back the covers and got out of bed, dashing barefoot into the small garderobe. When she came out of the privy, she dressed hastily, putting on the blue gown she had worn the evening before.

As she folded her nightgown and tucked it back inside the

valise, she wondered what Ransom St. Claire's mood would be today. It seemed foolish to hope he would suddenly change his mind and release her. As long as he believed she had information he wanted, he would hold her there and, as he had promised, his methods of extracting that information might prove increasingly forceful.

All she could do was wait until he chose to make an appearance. There was no way to escape from the room, not even if she managed to pick the lock on the door—because the door was bolted on the outside. Silently, she cursed her lack of a weapon.

Meg was cold and hungry. She tossed some wood on the fire, then looked around the room, wondering how to pass the time until someone came for her. As her eyes fell upon the rumpled bed, an idea presented itself.

Before the more practical side of her nature had a chance to analyze the scheme, her impulsiveness took over. Swiftly, she bundled the feather pillows together and shaped them to look as much like a human body as possible, carefully arranging the bedcovers over them. She stood back and viewed her handiwork with a critical eye. It was a child's trick, but if St. Claire didn't pause to examine the scene too long before rushing into the room, surely it could fool him momentarily.

She put her valise against the wall next to the door, then set about finding the best hiding place for herself. She decided to crouch beside the huge oak armoire, hoping the early morning shadows would shield her from sight for the few minutes crucial to her plan. Now, if only someone would venture up the stairs to check on her . . .

She didn't have long to wait. Soon there was a general stirring up and down the hallway outside. She heard the sound of cheerful whistling and the low rumble of men's voices. She detected the approach of booted feet, then someone knocked loudly, the noise echoed by the sudden, sharp pounding of her heart. Taking a deep breath, Meg summoned all her dramatic ability and moaned loudly as she positioned herself beside the wardrobe, the hound huddled next to her.

The knock was repeated, followed immediately by the grating of the key in the lock. Meg let another pain-filled groan issue from her lips and, hand over her mouth, called out feebly, "Who's there?"

The door was shoved open and a tall figure strode into the room. Damn, it *would* be the pirate himself who came to fetch her . . .

Meg hardly dared to breathe as the man moved toward the bed. "Meg?" he queried. "Is anything wrong? Are you sick?"

As his hand reached toward the quilted coverlet over the heap of pillows, Meg's own cold fingers closed over the handle of her valise and she gathered courage for her intended flight.

"Meg, answer me—what's wrong?"

Knowing she dared not delay another second, Meg, the dog at her heels, scurried around the corner of the armoire, slipping through the half-open door and pulling it shut behind her. She dropped the valise, for it took both hands and all her strength to shoot the heavy bolt on the outside. As the bolt slid into place, the harsh metallic sound it made masked a shout of outraged anger from inside the bedchamber. With a quick look around to make certain she was unobserved, she grabbed the valise and flew down the corridor. She had to find the room where they were holding Rob. It wasn't going to be easy to set him free, but she had to try.

"Open this door!" Ransom yelled, pummeling the unyielding wood with his fists. "I'm warning you, you Scottish witch—when I get my hands on you . . ."

Meg closed her ears to his threats. She knew all too well the price of failure, and she couldn't let that deter her now. She tried the door to the first room she came to, but found only an empty, ruined chamber. Moving with purpose, she crossed to the next door and grasped the latch. It opened easily enough, but when she poked her head inside, she was dismayed to see Rob sitting at a table playing cards with the big man named Beale. With a joyous bark, King bounded across the room to him. Rob, eyes wide with shock, started to his feet.

"Meg!" he cried. "My God, what are ye doing, lass?"

Beale shoved him back into his chair with one brawny arm. "Sit, man. I'll handle this." He drew a knife from his belt and brandished it at Meg. "Now, missy, what are you doin' here? How'd you get out . . . ?"

Meg didn't wait to hear the rest of his question. She ducked back out of the room, slamming the door shut behind her. Unfortunately, it hadn't been fitted with a bolt lock, so she could only secure the latch and leave her valise on the threshold, in an effort to impede the man's progress. She dashed off down the hallway, away from the main staircase and into the shadows surrounding the set of steps located in the corner tower. She was glancing back down the hall, trying to decide which way to go, when she heard Beale's noisy exit from the room where he had been guarding Rob.

Pressed against the wall, Meg watched as the man tripped over her bag and went sprawling. His howl of rage brought a smile to her lips, a smile that died abruptly as she saw Fletcher appear on the stairs beyond. When he ran to Beale's aid, Meg knew it was only a matter of seconds before the two would release Ransom. She didn't like having to run farther into the castle when the front doors were only the distance of the stairs away, but she realized she'd never get past Beale and Fletcher. She'd have to take her chances hiding in the upper regions of Wolfcrag, making her way back down later with as much stealth as possible. There must be a hundred places she could conceal herself, places that would surely come back to her as she explored the floors above.

But she hadn't counted on the barrenness of the rooms. Having just spent the night in a comfortably furnished bedchamber, she had forgotten the total destruction of the rest of the castle. The lack of draperies and furniture made concealment difficult. It also left closets and garderobes as the most likely hiding places, and meant, therefore, they would be the first places searched. And if she kept climbing, she'd come to the roof . . . with nowhere to go from there.

She paused, leaning against the wall to rest and try to force her mind to slow down and think rationally. There must be somewhere to hide. She could hear barks and shouts from the floor below, and she knew she didn't have long to deliberate. Frantically, she looked about, praying for a revelation. It appeared—in the shape of the arched door that led into the old nursery.

Meg hurried through the door and into the room she had last seen as a child. It was cold in the nursery and so damp that moss had begun to grow along the cracks in the plastered walls. Her flight forgotten, she stood and stared about her.

She had not expected the sight of her former playroom to be so painful. The scattered debris of smashed toys and charred schoolbooks was still strewn down the length of the room. Jagged shards of glass littered the floor, making her fingers fairly itch to find a broom and sweep the chamber clean.

She had spent hours before the fire, playing with her dolls or sharing picnics with her father and Cathryn. In this room, her father had read to her on long winter evenings, and Cathryn had started teaching her to read and write.

Meg sighed and ran a hand across the scarred mantel. Would it ever look the same? Could it ever again be a warm and welcoming room, filled with laughing children and sleeping dogs?

Just then she heard footsteps on the stairs outside, followed by Ransom's voice.

"Fletcher," he was saying, "you and Beale go on up to the next floor. Yates and I will search the rooms on this one."

Frantically, Meg whirled about, looking for a hiding place. The old toy cupboard leaned drunkenly against one wall, and she ran for it. She had barely slipped behind its doors when she heard someone enter the nursery, boots scuffing through the dust and debris on the floor.

Meg found herself in the midst of an odd jumble of balls and blocks and games. Apparently, the invaders had not taken time to rifle through the contents of the cupboard. It was a blessing, she knew, for it was almost a certainty that whoever was in the room would look inside. If something came to hand that she could use as a weapon, it might improve her chances of escaping capture. Crouching in the depths of the cupboard, she quietly began sifting through the objects on either side of her, searching for the most likely armament. When her fingers touched a curved wooden surface, she knew she was grasping one of the shinty sticks that the older boys had used in the rough-and-tumble game once played on the beach behind the castle. Wielded properly, it could be a very adequate war club.

Meg sensed movement in the room beyond, and every instinct warned her that her pursuer was approaching her hiding place. It had been too much to hope that he would merely scan the room and decide she wasn't there. Meg drew a deep breath and held it, her heart hammering in her breast.

She heard the faint scrape of a leather sole against the stone floor, then a sudden splintering crash. Whoever was out there must have kicked or tossed aside some piece of broken furniture . . .

For a moment she was hurtled back in time—back to the winter day when her home had been overrun by the enemy. She would never forget the horrible sounds of that morning: the pounding of the battering rams against the castle doors, the horrible shriek of rending wood, the clank of weapons . . . the bloodthirsty cries of the invaders. She had hidden with the others, her heart beating rapidly, her mind filled with silent prayers.

Since then she had harbored a dislike for dark, enclosed places—as well as a determination never again to fear anything or anyone. She couldn't simply cower in this closet and wait to be discovered.

With no further thought, she tossed open the doors to the cupboard and, shouting the battle cry she had heard her father and brother use when playing at combat, leaped forth, brandishing her weapon.

"Jesus!" gasped Ransom, falling back beneath her unexpected attack. Meg swung the shinty stick, catching him on the shoulder.

"Damn it," he roared, reaching for the stick. "Give me that thing before you—"

With all her might, she swung the curved club again, this time striking him on the side of the head. With a groan, he crumpled to the floor and lay still.

"Oh, my God," she breathed, horrified that she might have

killed the man. Shuddering, she tossed the stick aside and fled. Just as she reached the door, she heard Yates's shouted query.

"Is somethin' wrong, Cap'n? Do ye need help?"

The man was close, too close for her to make it through the door to safety. She spun about, seeking another place to hide in the room behind her. There was nothing . . .

Suddenly her gaze fell upon the massive fireplace and she was recalling the summer day she and Ailsa had climbed to the roof inside its crowstepped interior. She had received a memorable scolding for that foolish prank, but now, perhaps, that incident from childhood would stand her in good stead. St. Claire's men would never realize that inside the huge fireplace were steps that led all the way to the top of the castle—steps that had been designed as a means of escape back in Wolfcrag's more perilous past.

Gathering her skirts, she raced across the floor and scuttled into the fireplace, heedless of the pile of charred wood and ashes that still remained from so long ago. Shielding her eyes from the light drift of soot, Meg peered upward into the gloom, satisfied to see a square of blue sky in the distance. She'd climb the two stories to the roof and, once there, decide on the best way to slip back down to the lower floors. If nothing else, she could crouch on the roof until darkness and then reenter the castle when Ransom and his men had abandoned the search.

*That is,* she thought ruefully, *if I haven't murdered the man.*

The stone steps were nearly vertical, making it necessary to proceed as though she were climbing a ladder. She raised her hands over her head to feel the way, even as her feet were clambering onto the lower stones. Dust, cobwebs, and powdery soot threatened to choke her, and she soon found herself dragging in deep breaths of air and holding them as she maneuvered ever higher into the chimney.

Her pent-up breath was expelled in a shocked gasp as she heard a shout from below.

"Come back here, do you hear me?"

It was him . . . Ransom! He wasn't dead after all—just

mad as sin, if his tone was any indication. Meg began climbing faster, mentally cursing her long, cumbersome skirts.

"Did you think I wouldn't find you?" Ransom yelled, his voice echoing as he stepped into the fireplace below. "Well, your footprints in the dust made it easy enough. Now, if I have to come after you, I will, but you can make that easy, too, and climb back down here."

Meg raised her head and looked upward, gaining new strength from the glimpse of sky. If only she could get to the top before he realized where the staircase led, she still might have a chance to avoid capture. Surely Ransom and his men had had no occasion to be on the roof, which meant they should be ignorant of the various hiding places it contained.

"All right, if that's the way you want it," Ransom bellowed, "I'm coming after you."

Meg's throat constricted as she glanced down and saw him on the first steps. Could she outdistance him? He'd be stronger, and unhampered by silly feminine clothing. She bit her lower lip and renewed her efforts—she wouldn't give up, of that she was certain.

The fireplace chimney narrowed, and Meg could no longer look up or down. She concentrated on thoughts of the freedom that awaited her. After only a few more steps, she began to struggle against the feeling of being enclosed in a dark place. Her breathing became labored, and her chest hurt with the exertion of drawing the stale air into her lungs. She felt the seeds of panic spring to life within her, uncoiling throughout her body, weakening her arms and legs. She clung to the blackened stone, eyes closed, heart pounding, fighting for rationality. If she gave in to blind terror, she'd never escape Ransom St. Claire . . . and the man had a score to settle with her now. She had nearly killed him with the shinty stick, and he'd be anxious for revenge.

Meg forced her eyes open, focusing on the rough stone surface no more than a foot away from her face. The sight gave her new courage. If she could just climb another dozen steps or so, she'd be able to escape Ransom—he'd be too large to squeeze into the narrowed shaft. Two hundred years ago, when the castle had been built, men were smaller. Few of them ever attained the height or breadth of the pirate from Devon.

Smiling again, Meg raised her hand, seeking purchase on the stones above. At that instant, warm fingers closed about her ankle, and a startled shriek was wrenched from her throat.

Ransom gripped her legs, effectively stopping any upward movement on her part. She clutched the steps before her, but he was too strong, and she felt herself being pulled down. Had the fireplace been any wider at that point, she knew she would have fallen. As it was, her descent was halted only by the barrier formed by his body.

Meg stiffened as his hands encircled her waist and drew her downward into the wider part of the chimney. Helpless against his strength, she soon found herself hugging the steps to which she clung, his body wedged in behind her.

"I told you it would be simpler if you came back down on your own," he growled, his breath heated as it stirred the tendrils of hair around her ear. Something in his low voice was menacing, sending a tingle of alarm all the way down her spine. She shivered in response and felt his quiet chuckle.

"Damn you," she whispered, angered that she was, once again, the cause of his amusement. With waning energy, she twisted her body, throwing back her head and kicking out with one heel, catching him off guard. Her head banged against his chest; her heel caught his shin. Ransom nearly lost his footing, and for an instant the scrabble of his boot upon the stone was loud in the confined space.

"Don't try that again," he warned. "Not unless you want both of us to end up with broken necks . . ."

He tightened his hold on her, and Meg found herself flattened against the steps. The rather painful crush of the unyielding stone didn't disturb her nearly as much as the unfamiliar feel of a man's body pressed along the entire length of hers. They were so close she could discern the well-developed muscles of his chest, the granite curve of his rib cage, the strong, rapid beat of his heart. Lower, she was humiliatingly aware of the hard press of his hips, and of the long legs that entrapped her own. She had never been treated in such a way—no other man she'd ever known would have dared such liberties.

"Get away from me," she hissed.

"Will you be sensible and climb down on your own?" he asked.

She clamped her mouth shut, refusing to give him an answer, even though she knew she had no choice in the matter.

"Will you do as I say?" he prodded.

Stubbornly, she kept silent, and after a moment his big hand closed over her shoulder. "Answer me," he insisted. "Are you going to behave yourself?"

Infuriated by her impotence, Meg bent her elbow and jabbed him in the ribs, momentarily gratified by his grunt of pain. But just as suddenly as she had lashed out at him, he retaliated, and Meg felt her body swinging out into empty space, supported only by Ransom's arm encircling her waist like a band of steel. In an effort to scramble back to safety, she kicked her legs and flailed her arms, bringing forth his roar of displeasure.

"Be still!" he commanded.

"Put me down," she panted, her eyes locked with morbid fascination on the square of hearth far beneath them.

"It's a long drop," he warned.

"I meant . . . put me back on the steps . . ." Her breath was severely restricted by his hold, yet she found her hands clenching his arm, thankful for its strength. "I'll . . . I'll do as you say."

"I don't trust you," he said flatly. "I think we'll proceed like this. It seems the best way to assure your cooperation."

Meg fumed, but knew she was at his mercy. The situation was fraught with danger, and her protestations and struggles would only make it worse. She quickly decided she'd rather rely on the hated Englishman than die for her foolishness. But she'd never tell him so . . .

Ransom felt the subtle relaxation of the woman he held and, with an inward smile, recognized it as the only sign of submission she'd give him. Slowly, he started back down the steps, bringing Meg to rest against his hip to help brace her.

She remained still, but he could feel her slightly ragged breathing. Again, he admired her courage—reckless and foolhardy as it might be. He wondered what it would take to make her stoop to using the ordinary womanly wiles. Any other female he'd ever known would have attempted to buy her freedom with a kiss or the promise of a few moments of passion, but not Meg MacLinn. She preferred to fight for her release, whether by fashioning a weapon from a child's toy or scaling a straight wall. He had a horrible suspicion that had she made it to the roof of the castle, she'd have flung herself over the edge rather than risk falling into his hands again.

Well, like it or not, she was in his hands now . . . and he fully intended to gain some compromise from her before setting her free again. If the thought hadn't already been in his mind, those several seconds when they'd been pressed together on the stairway would have put it there. She was a soft, sweet-smelling woman, and he had thoroughly enjoyed the feel of her body beneath his. The fact that she had an angelic face but the temperament of a demon from Hell only seemed to further intrigue him. For the past weeks, his life had been curiously flat and empty. Now every instinct told him that the Fates had sent this woman to enliven his existence.

Meg, literally dangling in thin air, couldn't remember when she had ever felt as helpless as she did at that moment. She was bent at the waist, legs trailing awkwardly, hair streaming forward over her face. Whether she wanted to be or not, she was completely dependent upon the man who held her. Even the slightest shifting of her weight could cause a false step, and they might both be dashed to the flagstones below. It was not at all the sort of way she would choose to meet her end. She had left her home with a lie on her lips . . . if her family found out the truth, their memory of her would be irrevocably tarnished.

*Why,* she silently berated herself, *do I get into these stupid predicaments? Why couldn't I be docile and obedient like Ailsa? Or calm and sensible like Cathryn?*

She occupied her mind by listing the qualities she intended to cultivate from then on. She was going to strive to become more mature, more discerning . . . more cautious. She would think once, then twice, before entering into any more adventures! It was past time for her to grow up and accept her responsibilities. She was through flitting off on selfish, senseless missions. Just let her and Rob get out of Wolfcrag Castle, and she'd swear never to leave her home on Carraig again.

Unbelievably, Meg's toes struck solid stone. Pushing her hair from her eyes, she looked down to see the ash-covered hearth beneath her feet. Though she was now standing upright, Ransom kept his arm about her waist. With a twist of her head, Meg flung back her hair and stepped away from him. She knew she should thank him for possibly saving her life, but before she could form the words, a shout drifted down from above.

"Everythin' all right, Cap'n?"

"Yes, Yates—we're on the ground again."

Meg looked up the long chimney and saw that the square of sky was nearly obliterated by a man's head. It was obvious that even had she managed to elude Ransom, Yates would have been waiting for her. The English devil was one step ahead of her, no matter which way she turned. She heaved a sigh of disgust and, for the briefest second, considered giving in. Let him do as he pleased, she was too tired and defeated to care any more.

"You should see yourself," Ransom said, laughter edging his words. "You're covered with soot, your hair's a rat's nest . . ."

Meg's chin shot up. "You're no great prize, either," she retorted, even though some stubborn something inside her insisted upon observing how damnably attractive he looked with just a smudge of soot on one lean jaw, his darkly auburn hair in disarray. There was a trickle of blood in front of his left ear from where she had hit him with the shinty stick. But, she noticed, he didn't even have the decency to breathe heavily, despite the wound or the strenuous downward climb with her hanging from his arm.

"What are you thinking?" Ransom asked softly and unexpectedly.

Meg blinked, then answered honestly for once. "I was thinking that you can't be human."

"Oh, but I am, I assure you." His laugh was as soft as his voice had been. "Very human."

He took a step toward her and Meg backed away, leaving the cavernous fireplace to move into the empty, echoing nursery.

There was such a look of intent in his eyes that Meg faltered. "I . . . I don't know what you're talking about," she breathed.

"Don't run away from me again, Meg," he remarked. "It's time we settled our differences."

"I . . . agree." She couldn't help but wonder what he had in mind now. She didn't believe for an instant that he was going to forget his injury and the danger she'd put them in as easily as all that.

"You claim you sneaked into my castle just to have a look at your old home," Ransom went on. "Isn't that correct?"

"Aye . . ."

Ransom's teeth flashed whitely as he favored her with a smile. "So, in light of your wish to spend time in Wolfcrag, I've decided to offer you a position here."

Meg drew herself up to her full height, her eyes sparking fire. "I'll have you know that I'm a chieftain's daughter! How could you dare think I'd want to work as your maidservant? Or is it a cook you need?"

Ransom laughed outright, entertained by her indignation. "Actually," he replied, "there is something I need a great deal more than either a maid or cook. I'm asking you to stay on as my mistress."

# Chapter Five

Meg felt the blood drain from her face.

"Your . . . mistress?" she repeated.

"Don't look so horrified," Ransom said. "I thought you'd be flattered by the idea."

"Why, you're insufferable! Why would I be flattered?"

"Well . . ." For an instant, he was at a loss. "It's not something I've asked many women."

"For which we can all be grateful, I'm sure," Meg snapped.

"You've taken offense?"

"Indeed I have! I consider your offer the worst kind of insult."

The broad-shouldered man seemed taken aback, his bold confidence obviously shaken. Meg suspected he'd never been refused by a woman before.

"Why should you ask me anyway?" she questioned. "I mean . . . you hardly know me. And you've done nothing but shout at me since I came here."

"That's true enough. However, I find you an interesting distraction. You're pretty . . . and you amuse me. What more reason would I need?"

"Perhaps none, but let me assure you—I wouldn't have you."

"Oh?" Ransom knotted his fists, planting them on his narrow hips. He glared down at Meg. "You're a fine one to be so choosy. I'd be willing to wager you haven't gotten many such proposals."

"And thank the heavens for it." Meg glared right back at him. "The men I know are gentlemen."

"And of course they'd prefer ladies," he remarked.

Meg scowled. "What I meant was that if anyone had ever been senseless enough to suggest such a thing, my father . . . uh, his kin would have dismembered the blackguard."

With a swift mood change, Ransom grinned. "Ah . . . dismemberment. That is something I'd rather avoid."

"Then end this silliness and let me go home."

"You'd rather return home than see Wolfcrag restored?" he inquired.

"I would, if staying here means becoming your . . ."

"Mistress?" he prompted.

Meg nodded. "Yes."

"You find the prospect distasteful?"

"Extremely."

His grin faltered somewhat and his expression grew perplexed. "Why?"

"I could grow old and gray recounting the reasons," she retorted.

"Has no one ever taught you to curb your tongue?" he queried, running a hand through his already untidy hair in exasperation. "It isn't wise for you to be so insolent—especially when you are still entirely at my mercy."

Knowing that he was right, Meg merely shrugged, determined not to show the prickle of anxiety his words caused her. "I . . . look, I appreciate your offer, but I cannot accept it. My stepmother is expecting me home any day now . . ."

Ransom's handsome face was contorted by an angry glower. "You appreciate my offer?" he echoed. *"Appreciate?"*

"Perhaps that was a poor choice of words," Meg stammered, at a loss as to how to extricate herself from this absurd conversation. She took a cautious step backward, and, to her dismay, he followed, remaining close enough for her to see all too clearly the vexation in his green eyes. Plainly, he didn't care for maidenly refusals. "What I meant," she hurried on, "is that I . . . well . . ."

"I have no doubt that what you said was exactly what you meant."

Meg smiled weakly. "Aye, I suppose so," she said in a small voice. "And now, if you don't mind, I should like to clean up . . ."

"Oh, but I do mind," he responded. "I'd like for you to specify the qualities that you feel make me unsuited as a paramour."

"A . . . paramour?" Meg couldn't control the smile that pulled at her mouth. The word had such a prim sound to it that it was difficult to apply it to the bold and prepossessing man standing over her. Ransom's frown deepened.

"Very well," he barked, *"lover!"*

Meg's smile died and she turned her gaze away from his heated one, letting it rove over the interior of the nursery. Casually, she commented, "This room is in disastrous condition. Do you suppose it can ever be restored?"

"Don't avoid the question." Ransom's voice was a thunder of sound, reverberating hollowly against the walls. "I want to know what's wrong with me."

"All right," Meg shouted back. "You're arrogant and . . . and ill-tempered . . ."

"This coming from the most obstinate, sharp-tongued female it has ever been my misfortune to meet?"

"Oh—*fuigh!* Name-calling isn't going to help matters," Meg stated, and began walking rapidly toward the door.

"Where do you think you're going?" he demanded.

"I should like to find some water with which to wash."

"You can't leave this chamber until I dismiss you. You're my prisoner, damn it!" He stalked toward her. "And, I might add, in some danger of having to answer for your unbelievably childish exploits this morning."

Meg refused to meet his eyes. "I simply wanted to go home," she said with dignity. "That's still all I want."

"So you're refusing to even consider—"

The door opened and Fletcher stuck his balding head inside. "I've sent Yates to the kitchen to fetch some hot water for you, lass. Beale is returning your valise to your room."

"Thank you," Meg replied. "That's very kind."

Then, not giving Ransom the opportunity to say anything further, Meg swept past both him and the amused first mate and entered the hallway. As she hastened down its shadowed length, she heard Ransom's parting words.

"Twenty minutes! I'll give you twenty minutes to refresh yourself . . . and then we're going to resume this discussion. Fletcher, bring us some breakfast . . ."

Meg estimated that it was precisely twenty minutes later that Ransom's imperious knock sounded at the door. Without waiting for an invitation, he strode into the bedchamber and stood observing her. His thickly curling hair had been tamed, and there was no longer any blood staining his temple. His stance was that of a man who fully expected a battle.

Meg sighed. There was no point in prolonging matters. The two of them had to come to some sort of agreement. She and Rob had been gone long enough. If they weren't to cause Ailsa and the others undue alarm, they needed to depart for the islands soon. Somehow she had to make Ransom realize that it was impossible to stay at Wolfcrag, even if she wanted to—which she definitely did not. Not as the man's mistress, anyway. He'd had incredible gall to suggest it.

Still, watching him cross the floor toward her, seeing him move with such authority and purpose, she couldn't deny that many women would have been thrilled by the opportunity to share his bed. He was pleasing to look at, and excitingly different from most other men because of his obvious lack of interest in the conventions. Females, fools that they were, ofttimes adored males of wild and untameable natures. Ransom St. Claire seemed made for a woman who wanted to sacrifice her heart—and, very likely, her soul—to his devilish charms. Thankfully, she wasn't that woman.

"Fletcher will be here shortly with our meal," Ransom said, stepping up to the fire and holding out his hands to its warmth. "It has started to rain outside and the day has turned dreary."

"Rob and I don't need to postpone our leave-taking because of a little rain," Meg informed him.

"So you're determined to go, then?" He quietly appraised her for a few long moments, during which she stood, uncomfortably aware of his curious gaze sweeping over her freshly brushed hair, her clean face, the black wool gown she'd donned once again.

"Aye, I should like to." She cleared her throat and ventured, "Unless, of course, I'm still being considered a prisoner."

He shook his head. "No, I won't hold you against your will."

"You won't?" Her surprise was evident.

"There's no need—not after your friend Rob told us what we wanted to know."

Meg's hand flew to her throat. "What did you do to Rob?"

"Calm yourself, we didn't hurt the man. He volunteered enough information to let us know the two of you weren't bent on rebellion."

"He . . . volunteered information?" she half whispered, her mind busy trying to catalog the facts Rob might or might not have told them.

"Yes, but there is one additional thing I want to know."

Meg felt a ripple of alarm course through her. Had Rob told them about her father? "And what would that be?" she asked.

"Why did you go to such effort to sneak into Wolfcrag," Ransom challenged, "when you'd refuse an honest offer to stay here?"

Relieved that he hadn't brought up the subject of the MacLinn chieftain, Meg said the first thing that came into her head. "Only a man would think your offer honest."

"And what would a woman think it?"

"I've already told you—it's an insult. And completely degrading."

"An opinion you inherited from your stepmother, I take it."

Meg flashed him a severe look. "She wouldn't approve, if that's what you mean."

"Would it make any difference to you if I told you she'd be welcome here, also?"

"Cathryn? Come here to live?"

He shrugged. "I just thought you might be more willing to stay if I allowed you to invite some of your family here. Your young half brother would be welcome as well."

"I . . . I . . . no, that really wouldn't be possible," Meg murmured, alarmed by the mere idea of even broaching such a plan to Cathryn. Besides, there was her father to consider . . . and she could only imagine his wrath if she asked permission to live in a state of sin with any man, let alone a stranger who must be counted as one of the enemy.

"I'd consider taking responsibility for them as a part of our bargain," he countered.

"Bargain?"

"Yes." He grinned. "Surely you don't think I'd expect to gain all the benefits?"

Meg blushed and glanced away.

Ransom put a finger to the curve of her jaw and gently turned her face back to him. His voice grew more intimate. "I swear there'd be plenty of benefits for you, too, Meg. Shall I enumerate them?"

"No," she cried quickly, wrenching away from the lingering touch of his hand. "No . . . I don't want to hear them. I mean, there's no reason to continue this discussion. I cannot stay here."

"Are you afraid of me?" he queried softly.

"Of course not."

"Then why leave?"

"My family will grow worried about me . . ."

"We could send them a message."

"My stepmother would never agree to my . . . staying."

"Not even if it enabled you to return a few of the MacLinns to their ancestral home?" He rocked forward on his heels, looking most pleased with himself. "Think of it, the outlaw's son could some back to his heritage . . ."

"As it stands, Wolfcrag is not exactly desirable."

"No, but it will be improved with time. At least, that is my hope."

New worry began to crease Meg's forehead. He had answered each of her arguments with quiet reason; he fully intended to wear her down. She would have to come up with some excuse he could not turn aside, something he was powerless to refute.

"What is it?" he asked. "Is there another problem?"

"Well, actually there is," she agreed.

"What?"

"I don't know how to tell you."

"Just say it," he suggested. "I doubt it can be as damning as all that."

"You must understand that I'm not accustomed to speaking of such things to a man," she started, slowly raising her eyes to his. "But . . . well, becoming someone's mistress implies that there would be . . ." Constraint overcame her and she paused, fearing that she was about to begin stuttering like a schoolgirl. The impatient expression that crossed Ransom's face caused her to hurry on. ". . . intimacies between them . . . and . . ."

Ransom's firm lips twisted upward in a smile as he displayed enjoyment of her embarrassment. "And . . . ?"

She forced herself to keep meeting his eyes, bracing herself for his reaction. "And I simply don't think I could stand to be . . . to be touched by an *Englishman.*" She shuddered involuntarily.

Instead of the burst of anger she'd anticipated, something more like determination came into his eyes.

"I think you're a liar," he said in low tones.

"What!"

"Yes, that's precisely what I think." Before she could move out of reach, his hands clamped around her arms and he jerked her into a hard embrace. "I think," he murmured, looking down into her distinctly shocked gaze, "that you don't have the slightest aversion to my touch. And I can prove it."

He bent his head to hers, and when she would have cried

out in protest, his mouth covered hers, effectively silencing her.

As Meg struggled, his hold tightened. Her hands were flattened against his chest as he slipped one arm about her waist and molded her to his body. His other hand slid upward along her spine to capture the back of her head in its grasp. He held her prisoner in this way while he pursued a fiery kiss that seemed to go on and on.

Having immobilized his prey, Ransom was content to gentle the kiss somewhat, and after a moment of blinding rage, Meg began to register exactly what was happening to her. His mouth was wide and warm and commanding, and not nearly as unpleasant as she would have imagined.

The kiss was alternately fierce and coaxing, as if Ransom was spurred by frustration—as if he couldn't make up his mind whether it was to be pleasure or punishment. While his lips remained hard and unyielding, Meg felt her backbone stiffen in protest, but her initial objection faded when the pressure of his kiss lightened. Suddenly, unexpectedly, she found herself nearly melting against him. The smooth rub of his lips upon hers was so seductive that her knees weakened measurably, and her fingers clutched desperately at his chest as she fought the sensation of sliding downward to lie in a heap at his feet.

The very notion was like the jab of an elbow, and it rudely brought her back to her senses. Ransom St. Claire was her enemy, hazardous to her in untold ways—and she could ill afford to let him prolong such a moment. He had crudely suggested she become his mistress, and had then proceeded to treat her like a dockside strumpet. She had to find some means of reminding him of her identity. She was no lightskirt to be subjected to his lusty whims. She was the only daughter of a clan chieftain, a lady of some importance in this part of the world.

Summoning the last of her waning strength, she pushed against the hard warmth of his massive chest, leaning her body as far from him as his inflexible clasp would allow.

Aware of her withdrawal, Ransom raised his head to look

at her. He was thoroughly distracted, his eyes shadowed by dark emotion. He dragged in an unsteady breath, almost as if he sought composure, but then his gaze fell once more to her moist, faintly swollen mouth. With a murmured growl, he bent toward her again, the lowering of thickly lashed eyelids doing little to shield her from the blatant intent that flared in his eyes.

"Don't!" Meg warned frantically, knowing she had to do something—anything—to turn his attention from this increasingly intimate diversion. "Don't touch me again!"

She slipped one arm free and swung it in an attempt to slap him, but he ducked, easily avoiding her.

"Admit you liked it," he demanded.

"I didn't! I hated it!"

"No, I think you're angry because I proved my point," he taunted, dodging yet another blow. Livid, Meg struggled to release her other arm, but he grappled with her, subduing her with infuriating ease.

"Well, well, well. What have we here?"

The man who spoke stood in the doorway of the bedchamber staring at Meg and Ransom. As their startled attention centered on him, his mud-speckled face lit up with a huge smile.

"Ransom, you rutting swine!" he said in a low, incredulous voice. Then, louder, he boomed, "Why you . . . filthy . . . lying . . . *whining* . . . rutting swine!"

"Who is this—?" Meg began.

"Invite me in, you horny coxswain!" the man demanded. "I want to hear what you have to say for yourself."

"Good morning, Dickson," Ransom said calmly as he set Meg aside. "Do you mind explaining what in thunderation you're doing here? Besides making an ass of yourself, that is."

The man named Dickson grinned. "Hellfire, when your first mate sent me up here to find you, he neglected to tell me you'd be busy!" He turned back to Meg and favored her with a gallant bow. "Won't you introduce me to this charming lady?"

*Charming? Far too tame a word,* Ransom reasoned, as he

glanced at Meg. Standing there in her rumpled black gown, her equally black hair tumbling wildly about her shoulders and down her back, she was one of the most contradictory women he'd known in his lifetime. Her mouth was soft and rosy, her smile tentative and confused. But her gray eyes were still sparking with anger, and if a stranger hadn't entered the room, Ransom suspected she would have continued her incensed attack.

He found himself wanting to deny Dickson an introduction, though he knew his friend would never stand for that. "This is Meg MacLinn. Meg, this unexpected visitor is Hale Dickson, from London."

"How do you do?" Meg murmured.

"Not as well as Ransom, obviously," Dickson said with a broad smile. He came forward to claim Meg's hand, kissing it in courtly style.

"Now," Ransom growled impatiently at Dickson, "how in the name of St. Elmo did you get here? And what do you want?"

"Is that any way to welcome me?" Dickson inquired, smiling blandly. "Somehow, I expected you to be a bit more hospitable."

Ransom had the discomfiting feeling that the man had read his mind . . . and had interpreted his mood as one of jealousy.

"You creep in unannounced and expect us to greet you with open arms?" Ransom thundered.

"Not open, precisely," drawled Dickson, still grinning. "Especially when your arms were so delightfully occupied."

Exasperated, Ransom had to laugh. "I can't for the life of me say why, but Lord, it's good to see you, you mangy sheep's stomach."

The two men clasped hands and slapped each other on the back. Then Dickson turned to Meg. "I'm pleased to meet you, Miss MacLinn. And I beg your forgiveness of my buffoonery. I was so taken aback to find such a lovely female in Ransom's company that my manners deserted me. He wrote that there were no pretty women in Scotland, you see."

Ransom grimaced. "I can scarcely believe this gabbling hen is the man I used to call friend."

"And will again," Dickson assured him, "once you've fed me some breakfast and listened to the news I bring from London."

"Ah, something of interest, I take it?"

"I think you will find my news of extreme interest," Dickson replied. "I can hardly wait to see your face when you hear. But first, I want to get out of these mud-stained clothes and fill my lank belly."

"As you wish," Ransom said. "Fletcher will be bringing up a hot meal in a few moments."

"And you, Miss MacLinn," inquired Dickson. "You'll be joining us, won't you?"

"I wouldn't want to intrude on your visit."

"Never fear," commented Dickson with a chuckle. "Ran and I are such good friends, your presence may be needed just to keep us from each other's throats."

By the time breakfast was served in Ransom St. Claire's bedchamber, Hale Dickson had shed his heavy cloak and washed his face. He was dressed much the same as Ransom, in a white, open-throated shirt and dark trousers. His hair and eyes were brown, his complexion ruddy, and his stature only slightly less imposing than Ransom's. He smiled a great deal, seeming constantly on the verge of laughter. Meg quickly decided it would be impossible not to like the man.

Dickson had come into the room carrying small hemp bags in either hand; these he dropped on the table in front of Ransom.

"Gold, you lucky whoreson," he said, beaming. "I still can't believe I'm obediently turning it over to you."

"Where did it come from?" asked Ransom, peering into one of the bags.

"When your escort returned to London and reported to King George what sad shape this place was in, he decided to release some of your own money to you—to repair the castle, of course." Dickson wagged a playful finger at his friend. "All of it to be spent on restoring the castle, mind you. Not a shilling to be wasted for fun or frolic."

"No chance of that," grumbled Ransom. "There's no fun or frolic to be had in these parts."

Dickson's eyes twinkled as they darted toward Meg. "Is that so?"

"I, for one," groused Ransom, "find no fun in building and farming. It's a hellishly unpleasant prospect, in fact."

"Ah, yes," agreed Dickson. "You'd much prefer to be at the helm of your ship, sailing into the teeth of the wind, wouldn't you?"

"You're damned right I would."

"Mayhap you will be again . . . as soon as you've accomplished your task here."

The look Ransom cast around the room was doubtful. "I am of the opinion that by the time I've managed to make this castle livable again, I'll be too old and infirm to maneuver a gangplank."

Dickson favored Meg with a wink. "I swear, Ran, despite your good fortune in having such a lovely companion, you sound very self-pitying. Tell me, how did it happen that the two of you met?"

Ransom merely frowned, lending his attention to the plates of coddled eggs and ham with crisp, curling edges that Fletcher was serving. But since it was obvious Hale Dickson was enormously curious about Meg's presence in the castle, she gave him a somewhat sketchy account of her arrival, the details of which seemed to satisfy, if disappoint, him.

"So you are strangers, then?" Dickson cocked his head in Ransom's direction. "A pity, I must say. For a time, finding Meg here made me doubt the letters you've sent to London, Ran."

"It's true enough that there are no women at Wolfcrag."

Dickson's eyes gleamed wickedly. "A sad state of affairs that, I am happy to inform you, is about to be rectified."

"What do you mean?"

"Before I left court, I overheard a casual remark that I think you will find of interest."

"Yes?"

"Ransom, my boy, you are soon to be blessed with the company of a whole bevy of females, among them a certain blonde lady you once referred to as the most beautiful woman in the world—"

"Clarice is coming here?" Ransom's dark eyebrows drew together in a fierce scowl.

Meg folded and unfolded the linen napkin she held, watching the play of emotion on the handsome face of the man across from her. She found it noteworthy that Ransom had known immediately just which beautiful woman his friend had referred to. That was significant, no doubt. But if he admired the mysterious Clarice, why did he seem so opposed to her visit to his new home?

Hale Dickson's own face had grown more somber and he leaned forward to speak earnestly. "Rumor has it that our good sovereign has decided upon the final measure of your punishment. He has come to the conclusion that nothing will settle you down like marriage—"

"Marriage? Good God! Why do I sense my father's hand in this?" Ransom muttered.

"Not only your father's, but Clarice's as well," Dickson said.

"What in blazing hell are you saying, Hale?"

"George has agreed to a marriage between you and Clarice. She and her mother and aunts are on their way here to—"

Ransom leaped from his chair so rapidly that it tipped backward, crashing on the stone floor and startling the cat who lay sleeping in the center of the table. "By God, I won't do it!" he shouted, flinging his napkin aside and striding off across the room.

Meg flashed a puzzled look at Dickson, but his eyes followed the other man, concern etched on his features.

"It's not as if you . . . don't know Clarice," Dickson hazarded.

"Are you attempting a jest?" thundered Ransom, whirling to face Dickson.

"No, it's just that . . . well, it doesn't seem that you have much choice in the matter."

"I won't do it," Ransom repeated, his voice calmer. "The king may have confiscated my ship, my home—he may have seen fit to send me to this bleak hole—but he will not, by God, tell me who to marry."

"The contracts are already drawn up," Dickson informed him. "And the marriage would have been accomplished by proxy had not Clarice insisted she wanted to see and speak with you first. I think she hopes to . . . well, to clear the air, perhaps."

"If she plans to win me over with her . . . charms," Ransom said sarcastically, "she is going to be surprised. I've been down that road before, and it's one I won't willingly travel again."

"But how can you refuse the king's bidding?" Dickson asked quietly.

"I tell you, Hale, I've bowed my head for the last time." Ransom glared at his friend. "If George is trying to test my limits, he has done it with this latest piece of nonsense. If he persists in this . . . this so-called marriage, then I'll simply disappear into the western isles." He turned his head to gaze at Meg. "It has been done before, has it not?"

She nodded uncertainly. "So I have heard," she murmured.

"You'd be an outlaw," Dickson commented.

"I'm an outlaw now," Ransom stated.

"But you could never go home . . ."

"I'm not so sure I'd want to, if Clarice Howard is to be waiting by the fire."

"You didn't feel that way six months ago," Dickson reminded him.

"A great deal has happened since then. No, Dickson, I won't do it."

"But, Ran—"

"I find myself in the mood for a gallop along the beach," Ransom said abruptly. "Care to join me?"

"Not me, thanks," answered Dickson. "I spent the night on a horse—I'd prefer a soft bed right now."

"Very well, I'll inform Fletcher."

"Uh . . . could I join you?" Meg was as surprised by her question as Ransom seemed to be.

"You?"

"I'd like to see something of the countryside before I leave Wolfcrag."

"But it's raining," Ransom pointed out.

"I don't care. I'd like to go . . . that is, if you don't mind my company."

"If you choose to risk my somewhat uncertain temper, then come along." Ransom clapped a hand on Dickson's shoulder. "Thanks for coming all this way, Dickson . . . and thanks for the warning. I appreciate it. Get some rest and we'll talk later."

He fairly stomped from the room, leaving Meg to snatch up her tartan shawl and run after him. As she followed him down the dusty staircase, it suddenly occurred to her that now that she had his permission to leave, she was growing ever more reluctant to see the last of Wolfcrag Castle. Idly, she wondered if her attitude had anything to do with Hale Dickson's news. Soon the empty, echoing chambers of the MacLinn stronghold would be overrun by even more usurpers—among them the beautiful Clarice Howard, who seemingly couldn't wait to become the next lady of the castle.

# Chapter Six

Meg felt as exhilarated as the seven-year-old child she had been the last time she'd ridden through the front gates of Wolfcrag. Astride a surefooted pony, she crossed the newly repaired drawbridge, reveling in the chill wind, the blowing mist, and the breathtakingly beautiful view of the craggy ravine below. The island where she had been living was lovely, but so *tame* compared to the mainland's rugged coastline.

Ransom was ahead of her, mounted on a chestnut stallion. He had put on a wool seaman's coat, but his head was bare—and even with the absence of the sun, his hair was the same deep red color as the horse he rode.

After crossing the bridge, Ransom guided his mount down the weed-choked lane that led toward the beach. Meg twisted in the saddle to look back at the castle, seeing it rear up against the gray backdrop of ocean. It was a sight she had not seen since the days she and Cathryn had ridden down this very road. Except for the broken windows, Wolfcrag looked exactly as it had in her childhood, and for two hundred years before that. Had the walls been pulled down, a successful renovation might have been out of the question, but as it was, Meg had every reason to believe the castle could be restored to its former glory.

A sudden, nearly unbearable excitement took possession of her, and she thought her heart could burst from the sheer wonderful agony of hope she felt. Not knowing how else to deal with such overwhelming emotion, she spurred her horse into a gallop. As she overtook and passed Ransom, she shouted a challenge, her words wrenched away by the wind.

"I'll race you to the bend in the road from where you can see Castle Island!"

Jolted from his gloomy reverie, Ransom watched her ride past. She was obviously skilled at horseback riding, but she rode astride instead of sidesaddle. It didn't seem to bother her at all that a good deal of leg encased in thin, knitted stockings was showing, or that her hair had come unbound and was streaming out behind her. She bent low over the horse's neck, one hand entwined in its mane, her lips close to its ear as she murmured encouragement. He knew the place of which she had spoken—it wasn't far, and he was content to allow her a goodly headstart. The short-legged hill pony she rode could never outrun his own stallion.

When he judged he had given her enough distance, he urged his horse forward. The animal's strong legs covered the ground in long, sure strides, scattering sand and filling the air with the thunderous pounding of hoofs. Meg gave the mare her head, but at the last moment the bigger horse overtook and passed them, and she reined in seconds after Ransom. Breathless and laughing, she looked anything but vanquished.

"I should have demanded a mount equal to your own," she cried. "Then we'd have had a fair race."

"Ladies don't ride stallions," Ransom retorted. "They ride docile little mares . . . and conduct themselves properly."

Meg tipped her chin upward. "Did I forget to mention that I am rarely ladylike?"

"Mmmm."

A sea bird shrieked against the wind. Wheeling in midair, it followed its companions into the crumbling and broken ruins of a small castle situated on a scrap of island lying just offshore.

Ransom's eyes were also drawn to the island. "Tell me," he said, "do you know what those ruins used to be? Or who lived there?"

"Surely. My father told me the story many times. Before

he was born, the castle was a beautiful home, owned by one of his kinsmen. When the man's beloved wife died, he grieved until he went insane and threw himself from the highest tower." The breeze tangled Meg's hair, as she studied the pile of stones. "No one has lived there since because it's haunted."

"Haunted, is it?" Ransom's tone was amused.

"Do you doubt it?"

"I don't hold with tales of ghosts or goblins. Or hauntings. In fact, I find it difficult to believe that any man could go insane over the loss of a *wife.*"

Meg gave him a sharp look. "You seem bitter where marriage is concerned," she commented wryly. "Am I to assume you have some objection to the state of matrimony?"

"It's not a condition I would wish upon myself."

"Obviously."

"I sense that you are fairly bursting with questions, Miss MacLinn. Would you care to ask me one or two?"

"Yes, I would. Tell me about . . . Clarice. Why are you so opposed to marriage to her? I mean, you think she is beautiful . . . so that must mean you at least know her."

"I know her very well indeed."

"Another friend of your family's?" she asked with some asperity.

"Yes. There's that, of course . . ." He seemed unconcerned as his gaze continued to roam over the ocean before him. "But she was also my mistress for more than a year."

Meg gasped. She hadn't known that young ladies of good family were ever anyone's mistresses. "Oh . . . well then, I understand."

"What do you understand?"

"Why you don't wish to marry her." Meg studied her hands, which were still entwined in the mare's shaggy mane. "Even if you . . . loved her."

"Enlighten me," he said.

"Men don't marry their mistresses," Meg stated firmly. Then, with a quick lift of her chin, she sneaked a glance at the man beside her.

Ransom pulled his gaze away from the ruins and back to Meg. He concentrated on the tiny frown that wrinkled her forehead and made her look so earnest . . . and so young.

"What prompts you to say that?" he queried.

"I have never known it to be so. My . . . my own mother was my father's mistress, never his wife."

Ransom sensed the deep regret behind her words and was surprised at his own feeling of empathy. "And you blamed your father that this was so?"

"No . . . not that. My mother was not worthy of him, actually."

Ransom half turned in his saddle, his interest snared by the simple statement. "What do you mean?"

Meg shifted her eyes back to the island beyond, to the gray-shrouded ruins. "It would seem there are different sorts of women in this world," she finally said. "Those whom men marry, and those who are best suited to be mistresses."

A harsh laugh burst forth from Ransom's throat. "If you're right—and you probably are—then Clarice is definitely the latter."

Meg shot him a startled look. "Why do you say that?"

"For two years before I met her," he answered, "she was my older brother's lover. When he married, she came to me. I didn't know of her relationship with Edmund—it was only later that I learned of it and knew she must have sought me out as a means of staying close to him."

"So you believe she is still in love with your brother?"

"Whom she loves or does not love is no concern of mine." His mouth tightened. "But I will not take someone else's cast-off as a wife, regardless of what His Majesty says."

"What will you do?"

"I haven't yet decided." He bunched the reins in his fist. "But I won't be cowed. If I choose to disobey the king's orders this time, there won't be anyone but me to bear his wrath."

"And before?"

"Before, he was able to use my crew and the people on my lands to convince me that submission was my wisest course."

"But what about Clarice herself?"

"Have you forgotten that I came on this outing to forget all that?"

"No, but—"

"Let's ride on to the deserted fishing village," he suddenly suggested, signaling an end to the discussion.

*So,* Meg thought, *he does love the woman . . . and it troubles him to talk about it.*

"All right, I'd like that," she said. "I haven't seen it in years."

*Still,* her musing continued, *if he loves her, why isn't he more pleased that she's coming here?*

Stubborn pride—of course! Had she ever known a male without it? Ransom might love Clarice Howard, but he was afraid she still loved his brother. And that hurt his pride. In the two days Meg had known him, she'd been witness to his conceit more than once. A handsome man, he was clearly accustomed to having females abide by his every wish. What a blow to his vanity that the one he wanted above all others might prefer someone else.

Meg couldn't deny a tiny smile. Ransom St. Claire's king had branded him pirate and outlaw, but, in truth, he was only a petulant little boy!

They rode in silence, the light rain falling about them like a faint silver curtain. The fresh, grassy smell of wet bracken crushed beneath the horses' hoofs mingled with the salty tang of the sea, creating poignant memories of happier days. Meg thought of her father, wishing he could be there, that there was some way to bring him home to experience all that she was feeling.

A short while later, as they drew nearer the abandoned village, she could see the chimneys of the fishermen's deserted cottages, and her mood grew somber again. Her own clansmen had lived there, driven out by the same English soldiers who had attacked Wolfcrag. Most of the villagers had fled with her immediate family and were still living with them on the offshore islands.

An air of sadness and neglect lay over the little town, and Meg was surprised at the emotion she felt. As a child, she had accompanied her father here, had run barefoot along the dusty streets, laughing and playing with the other children. Now the village looked as if it had been thoroughly ransacked, then burned. Meg's lips thinned into a straight line as she recalled the foul deeds done there by the English. It shamed her to think she had forgotten them long enough to enjoy herself in the company of the enemy.

A dog barked and Ransom and Meg exchanged startled looks.

"Why would there be a dog here?" she asked.

"Perhaps a stray . . ."

"Perhaps." But Meg was not swayed. Highlanders took better care of their animals than that. She guided her horse down a narrow street, peering into the fire-blackened interiors of the cottages she passed.

At the end of the street, she caught sight of the dog as it slunk through the rain and disappeared into one of the broken hovels. "There he goes," she muttered, slipping from her horse.

"What do you intend to do?" Ransom asked warily.

"See if he's all right. He might be hurt . . . Or hungry."

"He could be rabid . . ."

Meg waved a negligent hand and continued on her way. Ransom started to forbid her to enter the hut, but a sudden vision of Clarice's reaction to a stray animal stopped him. A *lady* would no doubt have stayed on her horse, too horrified to think of risking injury. He found he was curious to see what this unpredictable Scotswoman would do. Wryly, he imagined that she would rescue the dog, insist on taking it back to Wolfcrag, and, in the meantime, manage to persuade him he needed to start a kennel of his own.

"Ransom," she said quietly from the cottage doorway, "come here."

"Why?"

She looked back at him. "There's something here I think you should see."

Ransom dismounted, and for the first time Meg saw that he was armed. One hand swept the tail of his coat aside to reveal a pistol tucked into the waistband of his trousers.

As he joined her in the doorway, she said, "I don't think you'll be needing a weapon—they look harmless enough."

Huddled in one corner of the dark and dirty cottage was a young woman and two children. One of the small boys was attempting to quiet the dog; the other watched them with huge, frightened eyes.

"What the devil?" swore Ransom. "Who are these people and where did they come from?"

Meg repeated his question, speaking in Gaelic. A wan smile lighted the woman's face and she made a soft reply. Meg turned back to Ransom.

"She says they were driven out of their home—that her husband died last month and the landlord wouldn't spare them a cottage any longer."

"Why did they come here, for God's sake?"

Meg relayed that question as well. When the woman had given her an answer, Meg said, "Because the others were here."

"What others?"

Meg gave him a severe look. "Do you mean to tell me you knew nothing of the burnings?"

His puzzled, half-angry expression told her he did not.

"Your neighbor has been systematically putting people out of their homes so that he might use the land to raise sheep. Surely you've heard of it."

"I knew your father's land had been deeded over to a man named Spottiswoode. I was not aware that the tenants were being evicted."

"Well, they are—and it seems they have no place to go but here." Meg spoke to the woman again, and this time the boys nodded vigorously in response.

"They say they are hungry," she said to Ransom. "Would it be permissible if I told them to go up to the castle for a meal?"

Ransom looked grim, but he had missed no detail of the children's thinness, nor the forlorn demeanor of their mother.

"I suppose it would be all right. We can't leave them to starve."

"And may I tell them that you'll speak to Spottiswoode on their behalf?"

"Me? What business is it of mine? I have no influence over the man."

Meg uttered several sentences to the woman, causing her to glance at Ransom with visible surprise, then smile in relief. Ransom tried to restrain his sudden suspicion. "What did you tell her?" he asked.

"I simply told her that you were afraid of the landlord, but that perhaps I could speak to him."

"By all the flames of hell," he exclaimed. "I think you may be a witch after all. You know damned good and well that I'm not afraid of the man."

"No, I don't know that." Meg's gaze was direct. "Perhaps you would care to demonstrate your courage by speaking to him."

Ransom heaved a gusty sigh, making the two boys giggle softly. Meg made another speech in Gaelic, using animated gestures and reassuring nods of her head.

"Now what have you told them?"

"Only that you've agreed to intercede on their behalf."

"I can't promise anything . . ."

"Yes, I know. But at least you'll be making the effort."

"How on earth did I get drawn into this?"

"It's no more than any decent man would do," Meg insisted.

"But I'm not a decent man," he argued. "I've already told you, I'm a thief and a smuggler! Don't you understand that I have no decency?"

Meg nodded. "Perhaps this will be a chance to redeem yourself."

His expression was sour. "I doubt it. Just tell the woman to come to the castle for food," he said, "and let's be on our way."

"Surely you don't expect them to walk that distance?" Meg exclaimed.

"What do you suggest?" he questioned. "Though I'm a fool

for asking."

"They can ride back with us."

"We've only two mounts," he reminded her.

"I will take the children up with me," Meg explained. "Their mother can ride with you."

"With me?"

"Aye, your stallion can manage the extra weight. Besides, think how jealous your friend Dickson will be when he sees you arriving home with a comely wench." She couldn't resist the urge to smile wickedly. "What with your complaints at the lack of female company and all."

"Don't press your luck, rebel," he warned, as he backed out of the darkened hut, but Meg continued smiling.

She turned to the puzzled threesome watching her and explained their plan in Gaelic. As soon as the woman made certain Ransom was actually out of earshot, she whispered, "Are ye certain we can trust the Englishman?"

Meg grinned at the natural wiliness of the Highlander—the woman had not revealed her ability to speak English until it suited her.

"He is English, that is true," she affirmed, "but he takes no part in the clearances. I don't believe you have anything to fear from him."

The woman looked down at her children, and Meg knew she was weighing their safety against their overwhelming need for nourishment. Taking her slender hand, Meg pressed it reassuringly.

"Come, it will be safe enough. And after you've eaten, I'll find you a dry place to sleep the night. Then tomorrow we'll decide what is to be done with you."

"Who are you?" the woman asked. "Where did you come from?"

"From the islands across the sound. My name is Meg MacLinn—"

"Meg? Young Meg? Revan's daughter?"

Meg nodded, pleased to be remembered. "Who are you?"

"Mairi MacQueen. Do you recall?"

"Of course, the thatcher's daughter!" Meg seized the woman's other hand. "Oh, Mairi, it has been so long!"

"Nearly fifteen years since you and Ailsa used to tease us older girls about the lads." Mairi's pale face lit in a smile. "You'd hide behind the tapestries and eavesdrop."

"Then you'd chase us away with a broom." Meg's laugh was full of delight. "Those days seem so far away now."

"Aye . . . weren't we the young-and-silly things then?" Mairi sighed heavily. "Who could have known all that would befall us?"

"None of us, I'm afraid."

Mairi cast a furtive glance at the doorway, which remained empty. Leaning closer to Meg, she murmured, "What are you doing here, lass? Does this mean your father is coming back to Wolfcrag?"

Even in the dimness of the hovel, Meg could discern the hope that gleamed in the other woman's eyes. She tightened her grip on Mairi's hands. "I . . . I'm not certain, but it very well could. I must get back and speak with him—"

"Meg?" Ransom's voice boomed out, startling them. As his large frame blocked the door, they leaped apart. "What's taking so long?"

"I was just assuring this woman that you mean her and her children no harm. She's afraid to come with us."

"Well, hurry up and convince her," he said gruffly, "or leave them here. The rain's coming down harder, and I'm getting soaked to the skin."

"We'll be right there," Meg promised.

When he had gone from the door, she turned back to Mairi. "Not a word of this to Ransom or anyone else. They all think my father is dead. 'Tis best left that way."

"Aye, so it is."

When they stepped out of the hut, Ransom was waiting none too patiently. The rain had wet his hair until it was almost black in color, and locks tumbled damply onto his forehead. The wide shoulders of his jacket were spattered with raindrops, and the ground beneath his feet was beginning to turn to mud.

"Up you go," he muttered, swinging one of the boys onto

the back of Meg's mare. He frowned as the child shrieked in fear and reached for his mother. Ransom looked at Meg. "What the hell is wrong with him?"

"He's afraid of you," Meg explained. "He wants to ride with his mother."

Mairi spoke in soft Gaelic and patted her son on the leg. The boy immediately grasped her hand and held on.

Ransom shrugged and glanced at Meg. "They can ride together if they wish—but that means you'll have to ride with me."

Before Meg could voice her objection, Ransom turned away. He lifted Mairi into the saddle behind her son, then assisted the older boy up as well.

"Come along," he said to Meg, reaching for the reins of his own horse. He swung himself into the saddle, then stretched out a hand to her.

She hesitated, then took it. Effortlessly, he heaved her onto the saddle in front of him, settling her across his lap. Surprised, Meg started to struggle.

"Stay still," he commanded. "I don't care to be unseated in this mud."

"But I . . . I thought I'd be riding behind you," she protested faintly, sensing he would find amusement in her words. If his rakish smile was any indication, he did.

"I prefer you here," he said. "This way I can keep an eye on you and see that you don't delay us further."

He spurred his horse gently and they lurched forward. Meg clutched his sleeve to keep from toppling from her seat, and he tucked an arm about her waist to steady her. Meg was not pleased to find herself pressed back against his chest, nor was she able to relax when she could feel the ironlike bulges of his muscular thighs beneath her bottom. Apparently, he was back to goading her. It seemed to be his way whenever he was irritated with her, and obviously, his stand in the rain had reminded him of the bad temper he'd been in when they'd left the castle.

Meg glanced back over her shoulder, fully prepared to demand he stop and let her walk. She could do without his petty little revenges. To her dismay, he sensed her movement and bent his head toward her. He was close, so close she could see the fine pores of his tanned skin, see the dark flecks in his sea-green eyes, feel his warm breath upon her cheek. Remembering the kiss he had forced on her earlier, she shrank away, consternated because she wasn't sure whether she dreaded or desired a repetition of that audacity.

Ransom's mouth curled in a bold smile, and his lips found her ear. "Don't think I have given up on that offer I made you this morning," he whispered.

"Have you forgotten Hale Dickson's news, then?" she retorted. "You'll soon be blessed with a wife—what need have you for a mistress?"

"I have a need for you, Meg MacLinn," he said urgently, his voice low, his breath rippling heatedly against her skin. "And, despite the king, I'll not have Clarice."

"Well, you'll not have me, either," she snapped, leaning forward to put some distance between them.

He merely laughed and tightened his hold on her.

The rain had slackened by the time they arrived back at Wolfcrag, but dense fog was rolling in from the ocean. It drifted around them in gray-white tatters.

"I think you'd best put off your leave-taking until tomorrow," Ransom remarked as they crossed the drawbridge.

"Aye, perhaps so," Meg agreed readily enough. It would be a raw and nasty night to sleep on the beach, not to mention that staying at the castle one more night would serve her purposes better.

She accompanied Mairi and her sons to the kitchen, where Fletcher cheerfully seated them before the fire and fed them bowls of stew, tossing one of the meatier bones to the dog who had followed them. When Fletcher had gone back to the preparation of the men's dinner, Meg plied the other woman with questions. Unable to resist the first filling meal she had eaten in days, Mairi answered between mouthfuls, but it didn't take Meg long to piece together the terror and deprivation Mairi and others in the village had experienced. Mairi's own brothers and their families had been in hiding even longer than she had.

"There's no money," Mairi half whispered, ever mindful of the man working at the other end of the kitchen. "And there's no place to go."

"When you return to the village," Meg said, "tell your brothers to bring their children here to the castle. I don't believe Fletcher would refuse them food."

"I can't thank you enough, Meg." Tears stood in Mairi's dark eyes. "You don't know how good it is to see my sons have enough to eat . . ."

The youngest of the boys was already curled against her side, half-asleep. The other was stifling a yawn as he used a chunk of white bread to mop up the remainder of his stew.

Meg patted her friend's shoulder. "I'll just ask Fletcher for some blankets and we'll find you a quiet corner to spend the night."

"But the Englishman?" ventured Mairi.

"Ransom?" Airily, Meg waved a hand. "He'll never need to know."

After seeing Mairi, her children, and the skinny hound settled for the night in one of the empty chambers belowstairs, Meg made her way up to the room where she had seen Rob earlier that morning. She was relieved when she found him alone, both unharmed and unfettered. Until that moment, she hadn't quite believed that Ransom had been telling the truth when he'd said they were free to go.

Rob was staring out the window, although the view was completely obscured by the fog. When she called his name, he whirled about. King barked loudly and ran to greet her, but Rob merely stood, pinning her with a ferocious glare.

"Blast you, Meg!" he exclaimed. "I have been beside myself with worry. What're ye thinkin' of, lass, to go off with the man that way?"

"I wanted to ride along the beach again," she said defending herself. "It was harmless enough. Besides, there's—"

"The last I saw of ye, ye were fleein' from him. Then

Fletcher told me St. Claire had dragged ye down from the chimney, that he was furious." His black eyes snapped with anger. "When I couldn't find ye, I didn't know what the blackguard had done to ye!"

"Rob . . ."

"Let's go home," the man said, his words becoming an earnest plea. "There's naught we can do here except put ourselves in danger. We've been gone long enough—and I miss Ailsa."

Meg laid a hand on his arm. "Oh, Robbie, I'm sure you do, but there's something you don't know."

He raised one thick black eyebrow, but didn't ask. He didn't have to, for Meg rushed ahead with her explanation. "On our ride we met a woman named Mairi MacQueen. Do you recall her?"

He nodded, warily. "Her father and brothers were thatchers. They lived on the hill away to the west."

"Yes, that's right. But they don't anymore." Meg paused for breath. "Rob, they've all been turned out of their homes. Mairi and her brothers are hiding in the burned out village . . ."

"What?"

"It's true. Father's land was given over to a man named Spottiswoode—and he's driving the crofters away so that the land can be used for grazing. He doesn't care if they starve or die from exposure—he only wants the property cleared."

Rob swore softly. "God, can ye imagine what yer father'd say were he here?"

Meg grinned. "He'd not spend long in talking, Rob—and we both know it. I'm anxious to take him the news."

"Then let's go tonight," Rob insisted.

"No, not just yet. I've brought Mairi and her sons to the castle for the night, and I think you should speak to her. You may think of things to ask that I haven't, and I want to be able to give Father a full account." Casually she traced a finger through the mist on the windowpane. "Besides, there's something else I want to attend to before we leave."

Rob groaned. "Dare I ask what that might be?"

"Now, Rob," she warned, "I know you're not going to like the idea . . . and you'll probably end up shouting the roof off . . ."

"Meg MacLinn," he fumed, "what have ye up yer conniving little sleeve this time?"

"It's a plan, Rob. A plan to get the castle back for my family."

Distrust gleamed in his eyes. "How in the devil could ye do that, lass? What kind of a plan is this?"

"The best kind," she replied. "A simple one." She turned her back on the window and leaned against the sill. "You see, Rob, one of Ransom's friends from London arrived this morning with news from court. Ransom is to be married—his bride-to-be is on her way here right now."

"Then we must be certain to congratulate the man before we leave Wolfcrag," he said with sarcasm.

"You don't understand—he doesn't want to marry her. I won't go into his reasoning right now, but I suspect he'd very much like to find a way to avoid matrimony with the woman the king has chosen."

"There's naught we can do about that, Meg."

Her smile was a trifle smug. "Ah, but there is. What you don't know is that Ransom has asked me to become his mistress, and—"

"The filthy son-of-a-whore," bellowed Rob. "I should have cut his throat when I had the chance."

"Shhh, calm down," she begged. "The only reason I told you that was to prove the man doesn't entirely dislike me. That will be helpful to my plan."

"Oh, aye, the plan. I think ye'd better tell me."

"Ransom doesn't want to get married, but the king has ordered it. So . . ." She paused again, her eyes twinkling. "What's the only thing that could prevent him from marrying?"

"If he's dead."

"No, Rob—think!" She waited a few seconds, then blurted out, "If he's already married to someone else."

"But he's not . . ."

"He might be, and very soon. Tonight, after dinner, I intend to propose marriage to him."

Rob's howl of vexation was interrupted by Beale's entrance into the room. "Fletcher says to tell ye yer invited to sup with the captain and his guest, miss."

"Why, how nice," murmured Meg, avoiding Rob's seething gaze. "I'll just go freshen myself."

At the threshold she stopped long enough to toss a final word over her shoulder. "I'll speak with you later, Rob," she said, and his exasperated reply was lost in the noisy closing of the door.

# Chapter Seven

"Marry you?" Ransom's voice echoed throughout the quiet room. "Have you taken leave of your senses?"

"Most likely." Nervously, Meg smoothed the fabric of her skirt. His response had been anything but flattering, but she had expected nothing else. "If you'll give the idea a moment's thought, you'll find it has merit."

Even though Meg had enjoyed the evening meal, she was grateful it had finally ended and that Hale Dickson had chosen to leave her and Ransom alone. She had been aware of his curious gaze during dinner, and his abrupt departure made her suspect he felt his presence was an impediment to whatever intimate evening she and Ransom had planned. It seemed that Dickson, while genuinely fond of Ransom, was not above being entertained by the man's predicament. Bringing him news of Clarice's imminent arrival and then throwing him and Meg together seemed to please him. Crossly, Meg mused that he had probably been the sort of nasty little boy who liked to drop hornets into bottles just to hear them buzz.

She realized Ransom was pinning her with a hard stare.

"In my opinion," he said, "there isn't much good to be said for marriage."

"If you will listen to me long enough, I can point out the obvious reasons for an alliance between the two of us."

"Perhaps you misunderstood our earlier conversation,"

Ransom remarked. "I asked you to become my mistress. I never said a word about marriage."

"Yes, I know. But hear me out . . ."

Ransom dropped into one of the chairs in front of the fire. Almost immediately, Satan padded from the shadows and settled on his lap. Absently, Ransom began scratching the black cat's pointed ears.

"I've been pleased to see Wolfcrag again," Meg softly declared. "But the sight of it as it is only makes me long to see it restored. That's why I'm being so bold as to propose marriage to you."

Ransom laughed. "In the short time I've known you, I haven't noticed any lack of boldness on your part, so I suppose I shouldn't be surprised."

"I'm sorry if this all seems . . . unmaidenly," Meg said tartly, ensconcing herself in the other chair. "But there is no time for niceties."

"I haven't much taste for the niceties anyway," Ransom observed. "So get on with your explanation."

Meg sighed. This wasn't going to be easy.

"I've been perfectly candid with you about my wish to restore Wolfcrag to my father . . . 's people. To his son, who is the rightful heir after all. Just think—Alex has never seen Wolfcrag!"

"I'm amazed that you didn't bring him with you." Ransom's smile was droll.

Meg's head jerked up in a defensive reaction. "I wanted to see it for myself first," she said. "Then, if all went well, I intended to let Alex come with me on the next trip."

"But all did not go well . . . is that it?"

"Obviously I never expected to find the castle inhabited."

"Your father acted against the Crown by supporting the Jacobite rebellion and by ignoring the proscription laws. Surely you expected some retribution?"

"I thought driving what was left of our clan into hiding was retribution enough," she retorted. "I never thought that Wolfcrag might be taken away. I believed it would always be here waiting for us."

"Sad to say, that is no longer the case."

"Ah, but you're mistaken." Meg leaned forward in the chair, her eyes fairly glowing with excitement. "It *is* waiting, and you are the means by which the castle can be given back to the MacLinns."

"Me?"

"You said that your property in Devon will only be returned to you when this place has been successfully renovated. If you marry me in a legal ceremony, I will see to the restoration of Wolfcrag."

"And how in God's name do you propose to do that?"

"The locals will work for me, I know. I'm a Highlander—I speak their language. They'll remember my father and what he stood for—and their loyalty to the MacLinns will induce them to help me."

"And where will you get the money for these restorations?"

"I'm afraid that will have to come from you. But remember, it will be worth it. After all, you stand to get back those things you hold so dear . . . and escape marriage to Clarice Howard."

"I'm to marry a stranger in order to escape marriage to Clarice?" he repeated. "Does that make any sense?"

Meg tossed her head in irritation. "You're not trying to understand! I don't intend to make any demands on you. All I want from this bargain is legal ownership of Wolfcrag. If we marry, you can deed it over to me and no one, not even the king, will need to be the wiser. Once the repairs are completed, you can go back to England and take up your life where it left off."

"And the marriage?"

"Can be dissolved or not, as you please."

"Are you saying that I can divorce you?"

"Yes. Whatever you wish."

"Divorce is a scandalous matter. What if I chose not to seek one?"

Meg shrugged. "It wouldn't matter."

"Why not? Have you no wish for a genuine husband?"

"What would I want with a husband?"

Ransom grinned. "Aside from the obvious, I should think you might want the protection of a man's name. Or the material things he could give you."

"I already have the very adequate protection of my father's name. And the only thing I want from any man is what you alone can give me."

"Oh?"

"Wolfcrag Castle."

"Oh." Ransom appeared to consider this for several seconds before asking, "What about the stalwart Rob? What does he have to say about this?"

"*Fuigh!* I don't need his permission to do as I please."

"Your ire tells me he's against the idea—as well he might be."

"He has no say in the matter."

"All right, let's forget Rob for the moment. Isn't there someone else who might object? Some other young man who wishes to seek your hand in marriage?"

"No, there's no one."

Ransom studied her carefully for a long moment. "You're certain?"

"Of course I'm certain."

"And you don't mind?"

"Why should I mind? Let me assure you, the last thing I want is some lovestruck man trailing my every step! That is why marriage to you would be so advantageous."

Ransom laughed again. "There'd be no love involved, is that it?"

"Thank heaven, yes. We could never love each other. For my part, you're an Englishman, and the English will always be my enemy. And as for you, I suspect I'd be far too unsophisticated and ignorant."

"What about your stepmother? Surely she would raise objections to the match."

"By the time she learned of it, 'twould be too late to prevent it. Besides, once she knew the conditions under which the marriage took place, she'd understand."

"I'm glad someone would," Ransom said.

"Come now! You can't deny that my plan has its virtues, can you?"

"Perchance I should attempt to see if I've grasped them all. You'd take the refurbishing of the castle out of my hands, leaving me free to . . . to do what? Drink and carouse?"

"If you choose. That's entirely up to you. All I ask is that you give me sufficient funds to complete the work, then stay out of my way until it's done."

One dark eyebrow slanted upward. "Am I to be allowed to live within the castle while the work is in progress?"

"Naturally. And I think I can promise that your life will be somewhat improved. I'll engage a few of the village women to give Fletcher some assistance with the cooking and housecleaning. Scotswomen are wonderful cooks, by the way, and I can say with assurance that you'll enjoy their handiwork—fresh-baked bread, griddle cakes, and scones."

"That all sounds very nice, but—"

"Don't forget the most important thing of all," Meg rushed ahead to say. "You were less than enthusiastic about marrying Miss Howard, as I recall. The king cannot command you to marry her if you are already wed to someone else."

"And that is exactly why I must refuse your rather inventive offer." Draping the cat over his shoulder, Ransom rose from the chair and sauntered across the room. He paused in front of a small, framed painting and studied it for a long moment. "No," he said as if finally making up his mind, "I really must refuse."

"Refuse? Why on earth would you refuse?" Meg got to her own feet. "I'll grant you that I, in myself, am no bargain. Oh, I know I run wild and look more like a lad than a lady. I'm noisy and impulsive and . . . and careless, sometimes. But those things would only matter in a real marriage." She moved closer to the astonished man. "They shouldn't matter a whit in a business arrangement, should they?"

"That's not it at all."

"It's not?"

Ransom shook his head. "Don't forget, I've already asked you to become my mistress. You're a very attractive woman, as I imagine you've been told many times. And in spite of your occasional lapses, I find you entertaining."

"Then why do you hesitate?"

"The truth is, I won't allow myself to hide behind your skirts."

"What do you mean? I don't think—"

"If I were to marry you in order to thwart the king's plan, it would be the coward's way out. I have to stand up and make my refusal to him."

"What good would that do? Apparently, both Clarice and your father wish this match, and it seems they have the king's ear. In addition to which, your current status doesn't put you into a position to risk further angering His Royal Misery."

A deep-throated chuckle broke forth as Ransom struggled against reacting to her irreverent remark. "You are a sharp-tongued little minx, aren't you?"

Meg shuddered. "I don't like to think of myself as a minx . . . or a vixen, or any of those silly, simpering things."

"Better a minx than a witch."

"Not in my opinion. A witch seems so much more substantial, somehow."

"I'll defer to your knowledge on the subject," he murmured. "But the fact is, I won't allow a woman—whether she be a witch or a simpering minx—to wage my battles for me. I'll have to find a way out of the marriage on my own."

"What can you do? Steal away and hide in the hills?"

"It's one possibility."

Meg frowned. "Let me tell you, as one who has been forced to do that very thing, it isn't the most satisfying means of solving problems. I should think you'd see how much better it would be to simply marry me."

"I'd be losing my freedom either way."

"You're a fool if you believe that. I've stated honestly that our marriage would be purely business. When we've both accomplished our aims, you can go on your way with no interference from me."

"I'll admit, the offer is very tempting. It's likely to be the only chance I'd ever have of getting back to Devon." Again, Ransom's attention was drawn to the painting.

"Is that your home?" Meg asked, moving to stand beside him.

"Yes . . . my sister-in-law did this watercolor for my last birthday."

"It's very beautiful." Meg stood on tiptoe to examine the picture. Rogue's Run was a two-storied stone farmhouse with a straw-thatched roof and window boxes overflowing with a jumble of multihued flowers. It seemed to perch on a rocky promontory, with the sea stretching out on either side. The water was depicted as an unusual shade of dark aqua, tropical blue underscored by pure, emerald green. Meg realized it was the same elusive color as Ransom St. Claire's eyes.

"How odd," she murmured. "Has anyone ever told you that your eyes are exactly the color of the Devon sea?"

He glanced down at her. "Only my mother, when I was very young. But the Atlantic along the Devon coast is a curious mixture of blue and green. I never thought it possible for a person to have eyes that color."

Meg tilted her head back. "Let me see," she said, and, obediently, he bowed his head, bringing his face to within inches of hers.

Meg ignored the twinkle of amusement in his eyes and concentrated on their color. They were indeed the very shade of deep aquamarine portrayed in the painting. His lashes were darker than his hair, and long enough to curl at the ends. But neither they nor his thick eyebrows looked the least bit feminine. A small scar dissected his right brow, and Meg wondered when and how he had acquired it. Her eyes drifted downward, along the bridge of his nose, past the smooth, lightly tanned skin, to his mouth. His lips tipped upward at each corner, suggesting that he devoted much time to laughing and smiling. Even as she perused the carved contours of his mouth, those lips twitched, then spread into a broad smile.

Jerking herself back to reality, Meg became aware that she had been staring too long. How could she have let herself get so engrossed in his all-too-compelling good looks? Instinctively she knew it would be to her advantage to hide any slight response she might have toward his allure.

Her gaze snapped back to his. "How could your eyes be the very color of the sea?" she half whispered, confused by his nearness.

"Maybe because I've spent so many hours staring into it."

Meg laughed lightly, relieved that the strangely tense moment had passed. Just for a second or two, she had almost envisioned what it might be like to succumb to this man's charm. And that was not a part of her plan. Most definitely not.

"Uh . . ." She cast about in her mind, searching for something to say, and suddenly the most convincing argument she could have made spilled forth from her lips. "Wouldn't it be a shame if you were never to sail the West Country waters again? Or if you were forbidden to ever set foot upon your own property?"

"Worse than a shame," he growled. "It would be hell on earth."

"Then take this opportunity, Ransom—I know it sounds farfetched, maybe even a bit demented, but I believe we can help each other regain what's most important to us."

He stroked the cat's lithe back thoughtfully. "Give me some time to think on it, will you?"

"Of course . . . just don't take too long."

"I promise to come to a decision tonight."

Meg nodded solemnly. "Very well. And while you're contemplating my plan, take an occasional look at that painting." She gave him a grave smile. "It might help convince you we can actually make this scheme work."

"Sounds like a fine idea to me," Fletcher announced firmly.

Ransom stopped his pacing and turned to face his first mate. "But Fletcher, I don't even know the girl."

"What need is there to know her? She's clean and decent; she comes from a good family—"

"Good family?" Ransom nearly shouted. "They're outlaws."

"And you're a smuggler. You should feel lucky that she'd have you."

"Lucky? Oh, I see—you want me married off, don't you? Now that I think about it, you've always preached marriage to me, Fletcher. How is it that a man who has escaped matrimony for forty-odd years wishes it on me?"

"Mayhap it would settle you down, Ran. You've run wild long enough. Get your arse into any more trouble with the law and even your father won't be able to save it."

Ransom ran a hand through his unruly hair and heaved a windy sigh. "You're right about that. But what about Meg? Do you think she really could convince the local workers to help rebuild Wolfcrag?"

Fletcher chuckled. "I think our Miss Meg could convince the Thames to flow backward if she wanted."

"You like her! Fletcher, you scurvy sea dog—you've fallen for the girl yourself, haven't you?"

With a rueful grin, Fletcher scratched his bald head. "I only wish she'd have an old salt like me. If I was fifteen years younger and had my own hair, I'd snatch her up in a minute . . . and then you wouldn't be wasting my time moaning around over whether you should risk your virtue by marrying her or not."

Ransom's expression was wicked. "My virtue isn't at stake. Meg insists this is a marriage in name only—strictly a business arrangement." But his white teeth gleamed in a devilish smile.

"I think it's a good idea," Meg insisted firmly.

"But lass, ye don't even know the man."

"What need is there to know him, Robbie? He's clean and decent enough; he comes from a good family—"

"Good family!" Rob's voice rose in the stillness of the bedchamber. "The man's a criminal—a pirate and worse!"

"And my own father is an outlaw. I'd be fortunate if Ransom would have me."

"Ha! That damned Englishman should be honored that ye'd even consider wedding the likes of him."

"How is it, Rob, that you who have so often tried to interest me in marrying any number of your own friends now think marriage is so wrong for me?"

"Because yer not doin' it for the right reasons." Rob dragged a hand through his black hair, leaving it mussed and untidy. "Meggie, I see what your plan is . . . and I commend ye for wantin' to get back yer family home. But lass, this isn't the way to do it. Ye shouldn't sacrifice yerself."

"Perhaps marriage might be good for me," Meg remarked. "I've run wild too long—I must have been a burden for Cathryn at times." She gave him a sudden, impudent grin. "And besides, there's to be no sacrifice about it. If Ransom St. Claire agrees to marry me, it will be a marriage of convenience only. Purely business and nothing else."

Rob's expression was murderous. "I ken the uselessness of arguin' with ye, Meg MacLinn—but I don't like this at all."

Teeth clamped shut against further words, he stalked out of the room.

Candlelight flickered over Ransom's face, highlighting the strong cheekbones and stubborn jaw. After his conversation with Fletcher, he had sought out Hale Dickson, and the two of them were sitting at a sagging table in Dickson's ill-furnished room, engaged in a somewhat desultory chess game. Ransom found his thoughts returning to Meg and the extraordinary bargain she had proposed.

"You seem awfully gloomy," spoke up Dickson. "Did I miss something after I left Meg's chamber?"

"Dickson," Ransom muttered, as if he hadn't heard his friend's question, "exactly what did you hear about my impending betrothal to Clarice?"

"That the king had agreed to it, and that Clarice would soon be on her way here to inform you of the situation. I heard she was gathering her trousseau even as I rode out of London."

"But it was still only a rumor?" questioned Ransom. "It hadn't been announced publicly?"

"No. As I said, Clarice wanted to tell you herself. No doubt she felt she needed to smooth things over before you'd consent to marry her."

"Did either Father or Clarice know you had heard about the marriage?"

"Not that I'm aware. I spoke to your father only briefly, and not at all to Clarice."

"Good." Ransom settled back in his chair. "In that case, I believe I will accept Meg's proposal of marriage after all."

"What!" exclaimed a shocked Dickson.

"I'd better go tell her now, before she retires for the night."

Dickson leaped to his feet. "I'm going with you. Lord, but you're a closemouthed blackguard."

Ignoring him, Ransom started off down the hallway, and Dickson had to run to catch up. "What proposal?" he queried, but his words were obscured by Ransom's forceful knock on Meg's door.

"Why has that lovely young lady proposed to you?" Dickson insisted. "I thought—"

The door swung open and Meg stood there. "What is it?" she asked when she saw the two men waiting on the threshold.

"I've reached a decision," Ransom said bluntly.

Meg's eyes widened. "And?"

"And . . . I've decided to marry you."

Meg's first reaction was a breathy sigh of relief. Then she asked, "Are you willing to meet all my conditions?"

Dickson looked from one to the other of them, a slow smile breaking across his stunned face.

"Yes," said Ransom.

"You won't interfere with the renovation of the castle?"

"You may have free rein . . . within reason, that is." Ransom shrugged. "Naturally, you must not do anything that would displease our sovereign."

"*Your* sovereign," Meg pointed out. "I will have as little to do with the man as possible."

"Very well."
"What about legal ownership of Wolfcrag?"
"It will be yours as soon as the repairs are finished to George's satisfaction," Ransom replied.
Dickson's smile grew even broader. "Well, well, well."
"And when Rogue's Run has been returned to you?" Meg prompted.
"I'll go back to Devon and leave you alone."
Dickson's smile died abruptly. "What in the thundering hell is going on here?"
"Merely an agreement between the lady and myself," Ransom answered.
"Wait a damned minute, if you please." Dickson clutched the doorframe. "What is this all about?"
"Meg suggested a practical collaboration," Ransom explained. "She'll see to the repair of this castle, and when the work is done and I have my own property back, I'll grant her legal ownership of Wolfcrag and get out of her way."
"Out of her way?" echoed Dickson, unbelievingly. "You don't marry someone and then . . . get out of her way!"
"It's business," Meg put in. "I want this castle for my family's sake, and Ransom wants it repaired so that he might be free to go back to his own home."
"And the marriage?" queried Dickson, his gaze swinging from one to the other of them. "What about that small matter?"
"Meg says I can get a divorce, and that's most likely what I'll do." Ransom grinned. "Come on, Dickson, don't look so disapproving. Think how angry Clarice will be when she arrives and finds me married to someone else."
"So that's what this is really about."
"That's a part of it," affirmed Ransom. "You know the only way I can defy the king is to go into hiding . . . or marry someone besides Clarice before the royal command has been officially handed down."
"It's not fair to Meg," Dickson protested.
"But it is," Meg countered. "I want this castle—at any cost!"

"But haven't you marriage plans of your own?" Dickson shook his head. "Surely a woman like you has had dozens of offers."

"If I'd had an offer I cared to accept, I'd already have done so. Please believe me, Dickson, I'm simply not that interested in being anyone's wife . . . or mother."

"But you'll be Ran's wife!"

"That's different," she said. "This is strictly—"

"Business," finished Ransom.

Dickson rubbed his chin. "It's the damndest thing I ever heard of." He stared down at his feet, but when his gaze returned to the two of them, it was edged with mirth. "Still, you do have a point—Clarice will be furious. I'd like to be here to see it."

"But you'll be well on your way back to England by that time," stated Ransom, "telling everyone how you arrived and found me already married . . . won't you?"

Dickson's smile was broad. "If that's what you want."

"It's what I want."

"Then . . . here's to a successful union between my good friend and his beautiful Scottish lass . . ." Dickson gripped Ransom's hand, grinning lasciviously. "And may there be some delicious surprises along the way, for both of you."

An hour later, just as Meg had begun unbuttoning her dress in preparation for bed, there was another knock at her bedroom door.

"Who is it?" she called, crossing the room to lift the latch.

"Ransom."

"Oh." She opened the door, hastily refastening the last buttons on her gown. "I was hoping you were Robbie."

"I take it he's none too pleased about the wedding?"

"He ranted for an hour," Meg admitted. "But it's what I expected."

"He feels responsible for you."

"Yes, I know." She shrugged. "Perhaps, in time, he'll come to understand what we're trying to do."

"Well, at least he's not overjoyed like Fletcher." Ransom strode into the room, leaving the door ajar behind him. "He's so thrilled by the idea of my becoming a married man that he's looking through recipes right now, trying to figure out how to bake a wedding cake."

"Did you tell him about our . . . arrangement?"

"Certainly, but he chooses to ignore the details. He always was a sentimental old fool."

"But a very nice man."

"Oh, indeed." Ransom glanced around the room, noting the banked fire and the bed with its turned-back covers. "I see that you're getting ready to retire for the night, so I won't stay. I merely came up to tell you that I've sent word to the nearest village, asking the local preacher to conduct our marriage ceremony tomorrow afternoon. Is that too soon?"

"Not for me," she replied honestly, "but what about the banns?"

"An ample offering of gold expedited matters," Ransom told her. "Strange how quickly things can be arranged when the price is adequate."

"Yes, well . . . I suppose that's true. At any rate, I will be prepared."

He started to turn away, then spoke again. "Uh . . . do you have anything to wear for the occasion?"

"Besides this gown, you mean?"

Ransom's face colored. "I mean . . . well, it's a perfectly fine dress. It's just that I wouldn't like to see my bride . . ." His lips twisted slightly. ". . . dressed in black."

Meg laughed softly. "And you said you weren't a superstitious man! No, I have something besides this. It's a gown my stepmother insisted I pack because Ailsa might give a dinner party while I was there. I think it will do."

"Good. So . . . I guess I should say goodnight and . . ." He stopped talking for a moment, studying her carefully. "Meg," he finally said, "have you considered what will happen if you fail? If the people here won't work for you? Are we going to find ourselves trapped by a senseless agreement?"

"No! I know I can do it. Please, just give me the chance!"

"And if the worst happens?"

"You ask Parliament for your divorce a few months earlier." She smiled grimly. "But I don't intend to fail."

Ransom wanted to chuckle at the determined tilt of her chin, but something in her somber gray eyes warned him against it. Perhaps the pretty Highland witch did have a magic power at her disposal.

For some strange reason, he was suddenly content to sit back and see what she was going to do next.

# Chapter Eight

The Reverend Elijah Throckmorton hurried across the courtyard, his prayer book tucked under his arm. His frame was so tall and gaunt that his black vestments flapped around him like a suit of clothes hung on a line in the wind.

Ransom greeted him at the door and ushered him upstairs to the only decently appointed chamber, the bedroom where Meg awaited them.

Both men stopped short when they saw the bride-to-be standing near the windows. Throckmorton's eyes widened at the sight of her wedding finery, but he said nothing. Ransom, on the other hand, couldn't contain the anger that burst within him.

Meg looked every inch the defiant Highland rebel. She was wearing a white woolen dress with long sleeves and a high neck, and draped from shoulder to hip was the blazing red-and-black tartan of the MacLinns. Above her right breast gleamed the clan crest, a silver wolf's head brooch.

"Reverend Throckmorton," Ransom said, "this is my bride, Meg MacLinn." He crossed the room and took Meg by the hand, leaning close to her ear to whisper, "You must be mad! What do you hope to gain by this audacity?"

"You didn't want me to wear black, remember? This is the only other thing I had with me."

"Damn it, you could have left off the plaid! How do you think the king is going to feel about my bride flaunting her kinship to a rebel clan? Not to mention her scorn for all things English . . ."

"London is too far away for him to hear of it," Meg hissed in return.

Recalling the presence of the minister, Ransom spoke in a more normal tone. "Come meet Reverend Throckmorton, Meg. He's from the nearest village."

"How do you do, Reverend? It's so nice of you to agree to officiate on such slight notice." Meg shook the man's bony hand, aware that he was studying her closely.

"MacLinn?" he murmured. "Not kin to . . . to the outlaw MacLinn? I see you wear the wolf's head."

"Yes, my father was Revan MacLinn," Meg said evenly, ignoring Ransom's glare.

"Ah, indeed—a legend in these parts." Throckmorton's skeletal face reorganized itself into a thin smile. "Or so I've heard. The villagers have nothing but the greatest affection for the man."

Meg turned to Ransom, her own smile tinged with an undeniable touch of smugness. He gave her a casual shrug and, in that moment, marveled again at the woman's lack of fear where he was concerned. Was she so certain of his need for her help that she planned to defy him at every turn? He pondered what her reaction might be if he simply walked out of the room and refused to go through with the wedding. No doubt she'd be so furious that she could boil water just by glaring at it!

Unfortunately, he needed Meg as much as she needed him. Marriage to her would prevent him from having to comply with George III's order to marry Clarice, and it was probably the only thing outside of his death that would. The king would be angered that he had not requested his permission to wed the Scotswoman, of course, but he had reason on his side. After all, the English government was anxious to win the Scots over—what better way, he could argue, than by intermarriage?

And even if that argument was patently untrue, it was no more a lie than marriage between him and Clarice would be.

The woman had caused enough grief in his life—he'd never allow her the opportunity to cause more. With Meg MacLinn, at least, he knew where he stood. There would be no wasted emotion, no anguish. Once they had achieved their objectives, they could go their separate ways and that would be the end of it.

Watching Ransom, Meg chewed her lower lip, worried that he was considering not going through with the ceremony. Intuitively, she knew that he was thinking of Clarice Howard, and she silently prayed that he didn't love the woman too much to pledge himself to another.

"Shall we get started with the ceremony?" Throckmorton asked, interrupting her thoughts. "Fletcher has promised me cake and brandy as soon as it's done."

"Just let me fetch the witnesses," Ransom said, "and we'll get on with it."

Meg expelled the breath she had been holding. Apparently, Ransom fully intended to marry her—whether for good or ill.

Hours later, Meg sat in front of the fire in the ruined Banqueting Hall and tried to remember the ceremony that had made her Ransom's wife. It had been so plain and brief that no impression remained in her mind other than the overwhelming conviction that she was committing some terrible act of blasphemy. How had she dared to stand before God and witnesses and promise to love and honor a man she hadn't even known existed a week earlier? Did Heaven hold some special punishment for a wretch who would take a sacred vow knowing she didn't mean a single word of it?

And if her heart had been truly pure, why was it that the only aspect of the entire wedding that remained clear was the final minute? The good reverend had closed his prayer book with a snap and declared she and Ransom legally man and wife. Then, with trembling hands, she had signed the documents he thrust before her and the ceremony had been officially ended. With the exception of one small detail.

"Ahem . . . ," Throckmorton ventured. "It's now your privilege to kiss the bride, Your Lordship."

Ransom's look was unfathomable, causing Meg to wonder again what was in his mind. Did he feel, as she did, that a kiss between them would only enlarge the falsehood they were telling? Or was he still thinking of his former lover? At any rate, they had little choice. It would hardly do to confess to a man of the cloth that the marriage he had just blessed was nothing more than a practical matter.

Meg had glanced at Hale Dickson and Fletcher and saw they were unabashedly enjoying the moment. She herself hadn't known what else to do but stand demurely by and wait to see what action Ransom would decide upon.

As it turned out, Ransom did the only thing he could do under the circumstances. He kissed his bride.

There was a faint devilish glow in his green eyes as he turned to Meg and put a hand on each of her shoulders, gently drawing her close against him. His mouth was set in a firm line, and she wondered if he expected her to put up a struggle. Surely he realized that this marriage was so important to her she would tolerate anything to have it look normal in the reverend's view. Someday the clergyman might be called upon to testify as to the correctness of their union.

The tentative touch of Ransom's mouth upon hers had been startling in its sweetness and warmth. She'd drawn back and looked into his face, swamped by a multitude of emotions she could not name.

Ransom had looked every bit as surprised and intrigued as she, and for a moment he had bent his head imperceptibly closer. Just as she thought he would kiss her again—something that would have given the onlookers pause for thought—he had given himself a small shake and stepped back, letting his hands drop away from her shoulders.

"Let's get to that cake, shall we?" he'd said, and only Meg was close enough to detect the slight strain in his voice. She herself had to acknowledge a certain disappointment, although her usual common sense told her she had no reason to feel that way. Ransom had merely been acting out the part he had chosen to play, and she shouldn't have to be reminded of that.

Now, on her wedding night, she was sitting in the midst of a noisy celebration, feeling the tiniest of regrets that hers could not have been a real marriage, conceived in all the proper emotion.

She glanced about her. None of Ransom's men seemed to question the sanctity of the ceremony they had witnessed that afternoon. As far as she knew, not a single one of them had found it odd that Ransom would marry a woman he had only known a matter of days. Of course, the wedding had provided an excuse for merrymaking, something they had thrown themselves into with great abandon.

As soon as the reverend had finished his cake and brandy and made his departure, Ransom's crew had begun their own particular brand of celebration. They had sacrificed a cask of Madeira and one of the pigs they had brought with them from England, and the castle was soon filled with the smell of roasting pork and the clink of glasses raised in toast.

Meg had been amazed to see the difference Fletcher and the others had made in the Banqueting Hall. Though it had been swept in a haphazard way, at least the floor was cleared of broken glass. Blankets had been draped across the windows, shutting out the worst of the chilling wind, and a fire roared in the huge fireplace, fed continually from a pile of smashed furniture. Two long banqueting tables and an assortment of benches and chairs had been patched and repaired and set up at the end of the room nearest the fire. Dozens of wax candles flickered and glowed, the soft light disguising the scarred wood and plaster, and, for the most part, the room looked much as it had in Meg's childhood.

Most of Ransom's crew had gotten half-drunk waiting for the meat to cook, and by the middle of the evening, many of them were reeling, singing, and shouting in boisterous voices, congratulating the bride and groom, and making up bawdy poems on their behalf. Ransom himself had started the evening in a dour mood, downing glass after glass of the amber wine and looking more glum by the moment. He hadn't even brightened when an ebullient Fletcher served their supper. He'd eaten swiftly, without conversation, and once finished, sat back to watch the others with apparent disinterest.

Meg feared that he was already regretting their agreement, and she knew that if he was going to behave in such a manner, she would soon regret it as well.

"Will you always be this gloomy?" she finally asked, taking a sip of her own wine.

Startled, Ransom looked up. "What? Oh . . . sorry. I suppose I don't seem to be in a proper mood for a bridegroom, do I?" He nodded at the wine. "I believe I'm very drunk."

"An astute observation." Meg set her glass down carefully on the warped surface of the table. "Is it because you're already ruing the bargain we struck?"

He dipped one shoulder in a negligent motion. "It has occurred to me that perhaps I should have taken a while longer to contemplate it."

"For what reason?"

"We talked about petitioning Parliament for a divorce," he stated, "but somehow we neglected to discuss the possibility that you might be widowed."

"Widowed? What are you talking about?"

He leaned closer and fastened his stern attention on her. "Who's to say that your clansmen aren't waiting outside this very moment to steal into Wolfcrag and slash my throat? Look at my men—they wouldn't be much protection, now would they?"

"No, they wouldn't," Meg responded with asperity. "But the notion that my people would kill you is absurd."

"How do I know that?" he queried. "Maybe that was the real plan all along. As my widow, you'd gain both the castle and my money without effort on your part."

Meg slapped the table with one hand. "What a ridiculous idea! Do you think your king would recognize my claim? Not likely. It seems to me that the sensible thing to do is to keep our bargain. Once you've satisfied his requirements, he'll have no further interest in this place. You could deed it over to the Devil himself and no one in England would care."

She drew a deep breath. "And you needn't worry about being killed. If that was the plan, you'd already have a dirk in your back."

She glanced toward the corner where Rob MacLinn sat, glowering. When she'd failed to listen to his pleas for reason, he'd shut his mouth tightly and spent the evening glaring at her in disapproval. At the moment, she'd have given a great deal to see at least one friendly face. Home and family seemed a long way away, and unexpected melancholy rose within her.

"There has to be more to your strategy than you've told me," Ransom insisted. "How do I know you're sincere?"

"You'll have to take my word. And if the solemn vow of a Highlander isn't enough for you, then blast you to Hades!"

Pushing her chair back, Meg stood.

"Where are you going?" demanded Ransom.

"To talk to someone who doesn't shout at me. I've grown extremely tired of your sulking."

"Sulking?" he bellowed. "I am not sulk—Meg, come back here!" He get to his feet. "You'd best obey me! Don't forget, you're my wife now—thanks to your dratted scheme!"

"If you didn't like the idea, you shouldn't have agreed to it," she flung over her shoulder as she walked away. "And if I'm so unwanted, don't expect me to stay here and be reminded of it."

Ransom watched her go, his eyes drawn to the curling ends of her ebony hair swirling seductively around her hips. She was obstinate, disobedient, willful—what kind of wife had he bargained for? And how dare she disregard a direct order?

"Damn it," he muttered, sinking back into his chair. "Damn it all anyway." With a snarl, he seized his empty glass and flung it against the fireplace, then immediately signaled Fletcher for another.

Through lowered lids, he observed Meg as she sought out Rob and began a quiet conversation with him. No doubt she was still trying to justify her marriage, because she spoke earnestly, using her hands in animated fashion, while the thin Scotsman kept shooting dangerous glances his way. Ransom sighed. Obviously, the bridegroom wasn't the only man who had difficulty dealing with Meg MacLinn. Living in a nest of outlaws, she had probably grown up with little or no discipline, had probably been allowed to run wild and do as she pleased. Well, those days would no longer exist. As his wife, she'd be expected to maintain a certain decorum, and like it or not, she'd have to answer to him now.

"I don't relish that look in your eye," grumbled Fletcher, setting a wineglass in front of his captain. " 'Tis a look I've seen many a time—just before you give orders to broadside an enemy ship."

Ransom chuckled sourly. "Full sail ahead," he murmured, raising the glass in a mock salute.

Fletcher followed Ransom's gaze to Meg. With a shake of his head, he said, "Storm's a-brewin', sure as hell."

Ransom drained the glass and slammed it down on the table. "I'll have another," he ordered in a tone that brooked no opposition.

A moment later one of the sailors brought out a hornpipe and began playing a tune. With a whoop, Beale started to jig awkwardly in time to the music, and soon he was joined by several others. The youngest man in the room, a slender, dark-haired seaman named Samuel, advanced to the corner where Meg was deep in conversation with Rob.

"Will you do me the honor of dancing with me?" he asked shyly, smiling. Meg suspected he'd never have had the courage to approach her had it not been for the Madeira he had drunk. Unable to think of a way to refuse his request without embarrassing him, she cast a quick look at Rob. With a stubborn frown, he crossed his arms over his chest, wordlessly declining to help her.

Stung, Meg turned her back on him. He was as unreasonable as Ransom. Was she to be forever surrounded by petty, pouting males whose feathers were so easily ruffled?

*Then be damned to the both of them,* she silently stormed, and favored young Samuel with a brilliant smile.

"I'd be honored," she said.

"This is a Devon country dance," he explained. "Shall I teach you the steps?"

"Please do."

Samuel beamed down at her, taking both her hands. As the music was renewed, Meg paid careful attention to the young man's nimble feet and, in a few moments, attempted to duplicate his steps. Laughing, she stumbled, and he caught her about the waist, steadying her. The other men, who had gathered around to watch, cheered noisily.

Across the room, Ransom's mouth had thinned into a straight line. What game was the wench playing now? Did she think to shame him in front of his crew by acting like a loose woman?

He hauled himself to his feet and lurched across the room.

Meg saw Ransom's menacing advance and ceased dancing as suddenly as if she had turned to stone. Startled, Samuel whirled about and blanched as he saw his captain towering over him. The music stopped abruptly and the room grew as silent as a tomb.

Ransom doubled his fists and rested them on his lean hips, leaning slightly forward to glare at Meg. "By God, woman," he muttered, "you're making a spectacle of yourself."

"I'm only dancing . . ."

"But you're my wife," he stated loudly, "and this is our wedding night. If you're of a mind to dance, it will be with me."

Meg's shoulders squared as she drew herself up to her full height. "Is that so? Well, I dislike being ordered about, and I refuse to—"

"Start the damned music!" Ransom roared.

With a nervous squeak, the hornpipe resumed its merry tune, and the onlookers fell back, clearing a circle around Ransom and Meg. His fingers grasped her forearm and he yanked her into his embrace, his arm curling tightly about her waist. He took two huge, galloping steps, dragging her with him, then stopped to give his fascinated crew members his full attention.

"What in the name of St. Elmo are you starin' at?" he bellowed. "Get partners and start dancing—or clear the floor!"

The hornpipe faltered, then bravely continued as the sheepish sailors paired off and began dancing. Had Meg not been so incensed with Ransom, she would have laughed aloud. Plainly, these men wanted a firsthand view, and wanted it badly enough to overlook the embarrassment of dancing with their shipmates. A hysterical giggle threatened as she watched the brawny Beale dance past with a protesting Yates in tow. This travesty of a dance was a far cry from the *céilidhs* Wolfcrag Castle had witnessed in the old days . . .

Ransom whirled her about and, deliberately, she dragged her feet. She did not intend to make this easy for him in any way. As if aware of her reluctance but determined to disregard it, Ransom simply tightened his hold, lifting her up so that her toes no longer touched the floor. Meg gasped and clutched his shoulders.

"Curse you," she breathed. "Put me down—I don't want to dance with you."

"Oh?" He leered at her, or so it seemed to Meg. "Does that mean you're ready to commence the wedding night?"

She met his steady gaze. "Wh-what do you mean . . . wedding night?"

Clasped against his chest, Meg could feel his rumble of laughter as he replied. "You don't know?"

"Of course I do . . . I mean, I know what a wedding night is. But we're not—"

"Oh, yes, we are."

"What are you saying?"

"I shall be happy to explain," Ransom responded, dancing purposefully toward the deeply recessed window.

Meg renewed her struggles, but her efforts were wasted against his greater strength. He brushed aside the blanket that had been hung to keep out the cold air, and entered the shadowy embrasure. He set Meg on her feet, but retained his hold on her arm. She swept the small area with a glance, and when she realized the total privacy it afforded, her expression grew decidedly fearful.

"I've made a decision." Ransom's smile was unpleasant.

"Not all the advantages of this union are going to be yours."

"Of course they're not," she snapped. "The bargain we made will make it possible for you to get your home back."

"So you say. But it will be a long time before we know that for certain. When we made this agreement, I should have insisted on some sort of guarantee from you . . . just in case your original plan never reaches fruition."

"But it will," Meg declared hotly. "How can it fail?"

"There are a number of ways, I'm sure. I might be set upon by your kinsmen . . ."

"That's nonsense!"

"Or the king might be so angered over this marriage that he'll change his mind and hang me."

"That's not likely."

"There's no way we can know that," Ransom stated. "And in the meantime, you have the benefit of my name, my money—shelter in my residence. If anything should go wrong, what assurance do I have that you won't just simply disappear?"

"I've already given you my word."

He took a step closer to her. "That's no longer enough, Meg. There must be some compensation now . . . in the event you don't uphold your part of our understanding."

She could smell the wine on his breath, see its effect in the hazy warmth of his eyes. She inhaled deeply, trying to calm herself. "What else do you want?"

"I think you know," he half whispered, his gaze dropping to her mouth.

Nervously, Meg moistened her lips. "Do you mean what I think you do . . . ?"

His free hand slipped to her waist and he pulled her against him. Even through the thickness of her gown and petticoats, she could feel the obvious answer.

"This marriage was a matter of business," she protested, "and you agreed to that."

"I've changed my mind."

"You can't. It's not honorable."

His laugh, deep and mellow, filled the dark recess. "How often must I point out that pirates have no honor?"

Meg wrenched free of his hold. "You're intoxicated," she accused. "And . . . and you're a hopeless lunatic if you think I'd ever agree to what you're suggesting."

"Then we no longer have a bargain."

"You can't do this," she flared. "We made a pact."

"And I'm only asking for this one small change. If you can't see your way clear to granting me my husbandly rights, why, we'll just have to declare the marriage annulled."

"Annulled? But it's too late for that. We spoke the vows before Reverend Throckmorton . . ."

"By law, my dear Meg, a marriage that remains unconsummated can be annulled with ease."

"I'll swear it was consummated," she vowed.

"I'll swear it wasn't," he countered. "Whose word do you think the king will take?" His chuckle was nasty. "Besides, a simple examination by the royal physician would settle the issue once and for all."

Meg's throat constricted as she imagined the humiliation of such an ordeal. "You wouldn't dare," she ventured, without much conviction.

"Yes, I would."

His quiet assurance forced Meg to realize the hopelessness of her situation. If she didn't give him his own way, he'd never deed Wolfcrag over to her. Why hadn't she foreseen this? Lord, he was right—she should have known better than to trust such an unprincipled rogue. "You are the most unscrupulous, the most conniving, evil-minded villain I've ever met!"

"Does this mean you've accepted my terms?"

"I . . . oh, I just don't know! I'll have to think on it."

"Don't take too long, Meg," he warned softly.

"I'd like to hear . . ." She made herself look up at him. "What made you go back on your word like this?"

He took a step toward her and she shied away, feeling her shoulders touch the stone wall behind her. She shivered at the chill contact.

"It was what you said, Meg—just a few moments ago." His hands dropped onto her shoulders, holding her when she would have moved away again. "About being an unwanted wife . . ."

Saints protect her, she remembered tossing those very words at him in a fit of pique. "It meant nothing," she assured him. "I was upset. It was only something to say."

"But it disturbed me nonetheless. You see, Meg, I didn't want a wife necessarily . . . but there has never been a question of my wanting *you.*" He smiled, his white teeth gleaming in the gloom. "I did ask you to be my mistress, if you'll recall."

His hands slid along the ridge of her shoulders and up the side of her neck to cup her face. Gently, his thumbs began to caress the curve of her cheekbones, stirring her complexion to a delicate rose color. "That," he continued, "means I want you very much."

Meg thought she would strangle as his mouth closed over hers in soft command. She tried to twist away from his light grasp, but he merely shifted positions, using his body to pin her to the wall, letting his hands drift downward to rest at her waist.

"And I didn't especially care for the way you turned your back and walked away from me," he went on, easing his lips from hers, but letting them hover only inches away. "I don't like being ignored while you flaunt yourself with every other man in the room. You're my wife, after all."

Meg was so outraged she could barely speak. "You're not my master," she spat.

"Perhaps not," he said mildly, "though that is an issue yet to be settled between us. The fact remains, love, that you wanted to marry me and you have. That gives me the legal right to do whatever I please with you . . . and it pleases me to do this . . ."

He moved his large hands upward along her rib cage, letting his thumbs and fingers brush the underside of her bosom. Meg's feeble complaint was lost in a shocked inrush of breath as he dared to cover her breasts, his fingers splayed and radiating heat—a heat she had never imagined could be so enervating. Her knees quivered beneath her, and she knew she would have fallen had it not been for Ransom's body pressed so firmly against her own.

"And this pleases me . . . ," he murmured, sliding the palms of his hands across the soft wool that covered her. Darts of unexpected delight pierced through her, and she felt her nipples bunch and harden. Obviously, Ransom felt it, too, for he smiled, whispering, "And now I know it pleases you as well."

Meg wanted to deny the sensations racing through her, but he was brushing his mouth ever so gently over hers, stroking her lips with his own, his breath moist and warm. He groaned into her mouth, which had shamelessly opened of its own accord, and Meg felt his hips move suggestively against hers.

Whatever emotion she had expected, it hadn't been the sudden thrill of pleasure that soared within her—and Meg was horrified. How could she possibly respond to this man's crudity? Why on earth was she having thoughts of what it might be like to be alone with him in the curtained bed in the upper chamber? She'd only had one objective in marrying him, and that was to regain her father's castle. She neither needed nor wanted a husband, and God forbid, certainly not on the terms he was offering.

Swiftly, she turned her head, causing Ransom's lips to slide across her cheek in a devastating trail of fire. "Stop it," she panted, her chest heaving madly. "I won't have this . . ."

"Meg," he said, his voice deadly calm, "if you refuse this summons to my bed, our marriage bargain has ended."

He let his hands slide insolently down her sides and away from her body as he stepped back and eyed her with a mocking half smile. "I'm going upstairs now . . . to my . . . to *our* chamber. Join me when you are ready."

With that final, self-assured word, he pushed the hanging blanket aside and stepped out into the main room. Meg, so distraught she wasn't even aware of the avidly curious glances they received, followed more slowly. She saw Ransom stop at one of the tables to seize a pitcher of wine and a glass, and all the while, he was talking to Fletcher, who kept casting furtive glances her way. Meg's face burned as she imagined exactly what he was saying to the first mate.

Ransom left the room in long, swaggering strides, his shoulders set in an attitude of arrogance. It infuriated Meg that he was so certain he would get his own way. The trouble was, at this point she wasn't sure that she had any choice but to submit to his wishes.

"Excuse me, Meg," Fletcher said, coming to stand beside her, "but are you all right?"

The expression on his weather-beaten face was sympathetic, and Meg realized that she did have a friend at Wolfcrag—for whatever good it would do her.

"Yes, Fletcher, I'm fine." She tore her gaze from the stairway up which Ransom had disappeared, and met the man's round brown eyes. "I'm just afraid I made a serious error in judgment."

"And what might that be, miss?"

"I overlooked the fact that a marriage isn't legally valid until . . . until it has been consummated."

He shook his head dispiritedly. "The captain has no business expecting you to—"

"No, we made a deal. And now it seems that unless I comply with his wishes, he will refuse to meet mine." Meg frowned. "I should have thought of that. Unless we are truly husband and wife, Ransom could toss me out the minute the repairs are complete and never have to keep a single one of his promises."

"And to think I was in favor of this match," Fletcher commented glumly.

Meg looked surprised. "You were?"

"Aye, when I thought it was to be a real marriage. I didn't exactly figure it to be a love match, what with it all happenin' so suddenly. But I thought Ransom had finally come to his senses, that wedding a decent lass like yourself would tame him down."

"Didn't he explain that the wedding was really only for our mutual benefit?"

"That he did . . . and I'll admit, I was disappointed at first. But you never can tell what might happen, and so, eventually, I accepted it." He frowned fiercely. "Until now. Until the cursed rogue . . ."

"Issued this ultimatum?"

"Yes. It's just not right."

"Well, right or wrong, he's made his intentions clear. And since I have no way of predicting what turn of mind Ransom St. Claire will have next, I can't leave this to chance." She laid a hand on the man's arm. "Fletcher, could you fetch my things and take them into one of the other bedchambers? I'd prefer to disrobe in private." Her next words were issued through clenched teeth. "And while you're there, please inform your captain that I will present myself in his chamber in approximately a quarter of an hour."

"Oh, miss . . . are you sure you want to do this?"

"No, but I have no choice."

Fletcher scratched his head. "Damn Ransom—I believed him when he said this was supposed to be a marriage of convenience."

"Oh, it is, Fletcher," Meg assured him. "And it has suddenly become 'convenient' to begin the marriage with a suitably legal wedding night."

# Chapter Nine

Once she had determined her course of action, Meg knew she had to get on with it before she lost her resolve.

She followed Fletcher upstairs, where he showed her to the room in which Ransom had slept since she had begun occupying his original bedchamber. The furnishings were sparse, but the floor had been cleared and the windows still retained most of their paned glass. The bed listed to one side and its mattress sagged, but it appeared reasonably comfortable. She noticed one of Ransom's shirts carelessly draped over the single, straight-backed chair, and the sight brought to mind the audacious man who was even now waiting for her. Made nervous by the thought, Meg averted her eyes and saw Fletcher coming back into the chamber, carrying her white nightgown.

"Where are the rest of my things?" she inquired, taking the garment from him.

"The damned villain wouldn't let me have anything but this," he grumbled. "Said 'twas all you'd be needin'." His lips pursed in patent disapproval.

"That's all right, Fletcher. Thank you anyway. I can get my other belongings in the morning."

"Aye, I suppose so."

"And, if it's convenient, I think I'll simply exchange rooms with Ransom after tonight," she stated.

Fletcher's eyes widened. "You mean . . . stay here?"

"Yes. With a bit of sweeping and dusting, this will be fine."

"But what about the captain? He'll never agree to such a thing!"

"He'll have to," Meg declared.

"But the marriage . . . ?"

"Surely it won't take the man more than one night to consummate it."

Fletcher uttered a short laugh. "No . . . not likely."

"Well, then, once the matter is settled legally," Meg informed him, "I shall want quarters of my own."

The first mate's eyes rolled upward toward the cobwebbed ceiling. "Blimey, but there'll be a stir over that!"

"I'm sure it won't be the last."

"I'm sure of that myself," Fletcher agreed. At the sound of heavy footsteps outside the door, the Englishman turned. "Ah, here's Beale with a pitcher of hot water for you."

"You'd better get back to the kitchen, Fletcher," the other man said without preamble. "There's some fellows down there lookin' for food. They said their sister told 'em to come here." He cast a wary glance in Meg's direction. "They're Scots," he added.

"Their sister?" Fletcher repeated. He turned back to Meg. "Would that be the young woman you brought to me for a meal yesterday?"

"Aye, it must be." Meg took the pitcher of water from Beale and set it on the chair. "Do you suppose you might have anything extra to give them? They have hungry children, too, just like Mairi."

"I expect we can spare something," Fletcher said with a smile. "There's more than enough to go around tonight. Come along, Beale."

As the two started for the door, Meg had a thought. "Take Rob with you to talk to Mairi's brothers, will you? He'll know them, and perhaps he might learn something more of their circumstances."

"And he can interpret," Fletcher added. "I'm fair certain they'll speak Gaelic."

Meg nodded. "No doubt." She accompanied Beale and Fletcher to the threshold, reluctant to see them go. Once she was alone, she'd have nothing to do but prepare herself for the night ahead. At the thought, she put a hand on Fletcher's sleeve. "By the way, would you please tell Rob not to worry . . . that I'll be all right?"

"I'll tell him," Fletcher agreed, "though I may get my head taken off for it. Your friend is in none too sweet a mood tonight."

"Yes, I know. But he's worried about me."

"So am I, lass."

"Don't be. Even though I deplore Ransom's high-handed ways, it's probably wisest to take this step and eliminate the possibility of anyone claiming the marriage a false union."

"You're a brave one, Meg MacLinn."

When the men had gone, Meg pondered his surprising words and wondered if they were right. She felt more desperate than brave, if the truth were known. She was about to sacrifice herself for an ideal, but what if something went wrong? What if she was being unforgivably selfish in her wish to regain Wolfcrag for her family? Had she embarked on a scheme that would only bring unhappiness and regret to all of them? To her family? To Ransom?

*Ransom.* For the first time since she had made her decision to consummate the marriage, Meg allowed herself to think about Ransom, to ponder what her action might mean to him.

Hadn't he stated without hesitation that he would never marry Clarice? So if living his life without her brought him anguish, surely it was due to his own pride . . . and not to Meg's efforts. She hadn't forced him to marry her, that much was true. There were certain very real advantages to be gained from their union, not the least of which was his freedom to return to England. And anyway, it wasn't as if she was proposing they conduct themselves as ordinary married people. They would lie together this night, and then never again.

Lie together? Meg's mouth went dry as she realized exactly what that innocent-sounding phrase actually meant. At this very moment, the big, red-haired pirate was waiting for her in his bedchamber. She tried to imagine herself knocking at the door to his room, entering it dressed only in her nightgown . . . putting herself into his hands. But her harried thoughts skittered away from such visions, refusing to accept the possibility such a thing could ever happen.

She was not so innocent that she didn't understand perfectly well what went on between men and women. It was simply that she had never pictured herself engaged in such activity. Oh, someday in the far distant future, perhaps. Someday when she was much older, when she could no longer resist her father's efforts to wed her to some appropriate fellow. Someday when she wanted children. But not now, not tonight . . .

Unbidden, a clear image of Ransom St. Claire burned its way into her brain, and she uttered a low moan of despair. Suddenly she could see him waiting for her, an arm resting on the mantel, an arrogant smile on his face. His shirt would be open, displaying that muscular chest furred with copper hair—his eyes would be bold as they surveyed her. And what, she wondered, would he see?

Meg crossed the floor to peer into a cracked and cloudy mirror that hung crookedly on the wall. She was amazed at her appearance—she looked frightened half to death! Her eyes seemed twice their normal size, their grayness nearly obliterated by the black of the pupils. Her mouth was drawn into a tight line, her cheeks were pale. One hand crept upward to clutch the high collar of her white dress—her wedding gown. Her reflection plainly displayed her inner distress. She had never felt such trepidation, and it upset her to recognize that Ransom would see it, too. She turned away from the mirror.

*What am I going to do?* she thought. *How can I talk him out of this?*

She wondered if it would be possible to reason with him, explain her reluctance to legalize the marriage in such a way. But would he agree? Of course, he could agree to anything now, then do as he pleased once the renovations were completed. Then he might publicly denounce their marriage, and as long as she could be proven a virgin, no court would uphold her claim on Wolfcrag. She had known of men who would not hesitate to do such a thing, and not one of *them* was a professed pirate and smuggler. No, she couldn't let her fears cloud her judgment. He was not to be trusted. She had taken daring steps to see that Wolfcrag would be returned to her family free and unfettered, and she couldn't permit her entire plan to be thwarted by this one obstacle. The castle had been out of the hands of the MacLinns for too long as it was; she couldn't let it slip through their fingers yet another time.

She crossed the room to a tall, narrow window. Outside, the night was uncompromisingly black, cold and starless, yet she felt secure within the stone walls of her ancestral home. It was the same sensation she'd had since the moment she'd set foot in Wolfcrag again. It was a feeling she would never willingly relinquish now.

She put out a hand to touch the rough stone wall with fierce possessiveness. She was a MacLinn . . . and she belonged here. Her gaze swept the room, drawn to a spot of bright color—her tartan shawl thrown across the foot of the bed. Its bold red-and-black plaid heartened her, gave her courage.

She would not let Ransom see her looking like a terrified innocent! She had knowingly set forth on this path, and nothing was going to deter her—certainly not an insolent rogue whose very smile bespoke his maddening self-assurance when it came to mere females.

She would don her nightgown and, head held high, march briskly into his room and get the business at hand over with, quickly and efficiently. After all, how difficult could it be? She had only to present herself in the man's bedchamber, then give nature free rein. If Ransom was anything like most men, he would relish the opportunity to demonstrate his manliness, and the act itself would mean nothing to either of them. He'd see it as another meaningless adventure in lust; she'd regard it as one more step in the process of regaining the thing she wanted most in the world.

She smiled softly as she reached for her nightdress. She could always use the time to make plans for restoring the castle. A muffled laugh pushed its way into her throat as she imagined what Ransom would think if he knew she was planning draperies and linen storage while he spent himself in passion.

Meg removed the white woolen gown and draped it over the foot of the bed. Then, using the water Beale had brought, she washed quickly and slipped into her cotton nightgown, buttoning it all the way up to her throat. She had no brush or comb, but using her fingers, she managed to work out the worst snarls in her long hair. She then subdued its natural curliness by plaiting it into a thick braid, which she tied with a strip of cloth torn from the ruffled hem of one of her petticoats. She would not appear before Ransom looking like a wanton.

Her anxiety lessened, Meg left her own chamber behind and walked the short distance to the room where she had first encountered the man from Devon.

*This,* she reminded herself, *will only be another encounter . . . not pleasant, perhaps, but necessary.*

Moistening her lips, she lifted her chin, then reached out to knock on the door. But she was not at all reassured to see how badly her hand was trembling.

Ransom lay in bed, propped against a mound of pillows, studying the gold wedding ring that rested in his palm. It had belonged to his mother, and he had worn it since her death, even though it fit only the smallest finger of his hand.

Neither he nor Meg had foreseen the need for a ring, so during the marriage ceremony that afternoon, when Reverend Throckmorton had called for one, he was grateful that he was wearing his mother's. He'd slipped it off his own hand and placed it on Meg's. He could still recall the coldness of her fingers and the startled look in her eyes. He knew she must have been thinking that it was a stroke of luck he had come prepared, for she obviously had not.

After the ceremony, when the reverend had finished his cake and made his departure, Meg had removed the ring and returned it to Ransom.

" 'Tis fortunate you had this," she had said. "I'd not thought of a ring."

He had taken it, because it was his mother's . . . and because Meg seemed to have no inclination to wear it. But now, in light of the event about to take place, he wondered if he shouldn't have insisted she keep it. It would appear she was determined to treat their marriage most seriously.

He placed the ring on the bed table and his lips lifted in a smile. So the little wench was going to give him his wedding night, was she? To make the ceremony legally binding, Fletcher had maintained. Of course, that could only mean one thing—she didn't trust him to keep his end of their bargain otherwise. He might have been insulted had he not known he hadn't done much to endear himself to her. He'd made his demands, leaving her no option but to comply. Thus, he had to give Meg her due—obviously, she wasn't intimidated by him or his intentions. Smiling, he reached for his wineglass and drained it yet another time.

A knock sounded on his door, but before he could call out, Meg stepped into the room. At the sight of her, Ransom's heart began to hammer. Whatever he'd expected, it hadn't been this.

She closed the door behind her, but her actions were hesitant, as if she didn't know precisely how to proceed. She was wearing the long white nightgown, a garment never meant to be seductive. And yet, somehow, it was. The soft fabric clung to her slender arms and draped enticingly around shapely hips and legs. And even though her bare toes showed below the hem, and her bosom was entirely hidden by the shawl she clutched, the general effect was provocative.

Looking at her, Ransom was instantly reminded of exactly how long it had been since he'd been alone like this with a woman. That dearth of female companionship must be responsible for the involuntary reaction he was having toward Meg—the same reaction he'd had ever since the first day he'd seen her. Distracted, he knew he should summon his good sense and refuse the invitation she was reluctantly offering. But if he'd had any good sense, he'd never have married her, would never have demanded her presence in his bedchamber. Damn him for a drunken lecher, but he fully intended to take whatever this appealing little Highland rebel would allow.

Intending to stride across the room and lead her back to his bed, Ransom made an effort to rise from the pillows. Meg's eyes widened at the sight of his bare torso, and her sharp, strangled gasp sounded on the still air, causing him to swiftly grasp the bedsheet and pull it with him as he stood. Clumsily, he wrapped the sheet about his lean waist and, armed with a scowl, staggered toward her.

Watching the copper-haired giant of a man advancing upon her, clad only in a loose sheet, Meg shrank back against the door. In her wildest imaginings, she had never pictured him thus. Arrogant and insolent, certainly . . . but not dangerous. Not menacing in some vague, primitive way she didn't understand. The fleeting glimpse of nudity she'd had sent her mind reeling—no, she hadn't ever envisioned him *unclothed.* And as fascinated as she was by his tanned and muscular body with its intriguing sworls of curling hair, she was suddenly aware that he would expect her to remove her own clothes and be naked as well. Briefly, she entertained the thought of fleeing. She inched further away from him until her back was against the door.

"So." Ransom came closer to her. "Fletcher tells me you are of a mind to consummate our marriage."

Meg forced herself to look up at him, but her gaze fastened on the gold fishhook in his ear and refused to move higher. She swallowed deeply. "You didn't leave me much choice."

Meg jumped as she felt his hand against her cheek. His fingers gripped a curling tendril of hair and tugged gently until her eyes unwillingly locked with his. "I didn't intend to . . ."

Slowly, he let his hand slide downward, the back of his knuckles grazing her cheek, then her jaw, and then, to her acute discomfort, her shoulder and breast, stopping only inches from one tingling nipple. His touch and the bold look in his sea-green eyes were so blatantly sensual that she could not control a shudder.

"Cold, Meg?" he murmured, letting his hand abandon her breast for her shoulder. The strong fingers slipped beneath her hair to cup the back of her neck. "Mayhap you'd better dispose of your shawl and come to bed now."

The plaid dropped from her nerveless fingers, drifting to the floor at her feet with a soft whispery sound. Meg's eyes grew wider as he bent his head toward hers and she realized he meant to kiss her. Her heart nearly stopped in panic—he was going too fast! She wasn't ready . . .

His mouth settled over hers and her thoughts scattered like frightened sheep. His palm at the nape of her neck was as uncompromising as were his lips. He held her prisoner while his mouth ravished hers, warmly and thoroughly, promising no quarter.

Ransom St. Claire kissed her as though he expected her to submit to him without even a token protest. And the heated mastery of his mouth made that an altogether too real possibility. She had come to his bedchamber resolved to consummate their marriage on her own terms, promising herself it would be a quick and emotionless formality. A mere two steps inside the door and she had already lost control of the moment!

Ransom seemed an implacable barrier. The bones of his face were hard, and his marauding lips were only scarcely less firm. But as he turned his head, opening and slanting his lips across hers, she could feel the heat and softness of his inner mouth, the slight scrape of his even teeth against her lower lip. And she could taste him—taste the wine he'd drunk throughout the evening, feel the burning essence of it on her own tongue.

Ransom raised his head and looked directly into her dazed eyes. "Why have you braided your hair?" he asked. "I like it loose."

With one hand, he grasped the plait of hair and pulled it over her shoulder, then untied the strip of cloth that held it.

Using both hands, he gently separated the entwined tresses and shook them free, letting them cascade over her shoulders.

"Now don't you think it's time you took this off?" he half whispered, as his slightly unsteady fingers moved to the ribbons at the neck of her nightgown.

"No!" Meg's gasp was faint, but the gray of her eyes darkened to near-storminess.

Ransom's eyebrows rose. "No?" he repeated softly. "No?"

"What I meant was . . .well . . ."

"Am I to understand that you wish to conduct our lovemaking within the voluminous folds of this garment?"

Meg couldn't tell if he was truly angry or not. She thought she could detect a glimmer of amusement in his expression, but the candlelight was too inconstant for her to be certain.

"Is that possible?" she asked, her voice sounding insignificant even to her own ears.

" 'Tis the wish of an inexperienced maiden," he scoffed, dropping his hand. "I should have expected such." He turned away.

"Wait," Meg whispered frantically. "Wh-where are you going?"

"To get some more wine," he replied, hitching up his sheet and starting back across the room.

Meg bit her lip. This was not going well at all. She had to compose herself or the opportunity would be lost. This hadn't been her idea, but now that Ransom had initiated it, she didn't want to lose the chance to legitimatize her marriage. If not done now, it would only have to be done later . . . otherwise, the risk was too great. Vowing to delay no further, she unfastened the ribbon at the neck of her nightgown and followed him.

He stood with his back turned, draining another glass of wine.

Meg took a fortifying breath, then seized the hem of her gown and pulled it over her head, letting it drop to the floor. "Ransom . . ."

Something in the tone of her voice made him pause, lower his glass, then turn to face her.

His startled gaze fell to the gown, crumpled at her feet. It traveled slowly, disbelievingly, up the slender contours of her legs, past the lovely curve of hips and waist. He saw that Meg's hands fluttered slightly at her sides, as if she longed to cross her arms over the rose-and-white perfection of her breasts. That she did not illustrated her rigid self-control, and Ransom reflected that she was probably the most courageous woman he'd ever met. His bemused eyes moved upward and came to rest upon her face. Although her cheeks were scarlet with embarrassment, she raised her chin and met his look defiantly. Only the slight tensing of her lips and the visible pulse at her throat hinted at her vulnerability. Torn between sympathy and raging desire, Ransom's own throat convulsed.

"My God," he growled, letting the wineglass slip from nerveless fingers. "You are so beautiful . . ."

Unexpectedly, he opened the sheet he wore and engulfed her in it, pulling her into the shielding circle of his arms. Wrapped within the cocoon of linen, her smaller body arched away from his, as if threatened by his nakedness. Ransom tightened his embrace, reveling in the feel of her sweet softness.

Meg was too stunned to protest. Her mind had still been spinning in wonder over her own act of brazenness, and now it seemed nearly incapable of forming a single, coherent thought. All she seemed able to do was *feel* . . . and the sensations she was feeling were almost overwhelming.

She was appalled at the delicious warmth generated by their bare limbs pressed together, and she struggled against the urge to actually enjoy the teasing rasp of the hair on his chest as it gently abraded her suddenly sensitive breasts. She was profoundly aware of the touch of his hands where they rested on her back, clutching the sheet around them. In an effort to maintain her balance, her own hands crept about his waist, and her fingers experienced the smooth, heated surfaces of his ribs and back. Her face brushed his throat, and she breathed in the faint rosemary scent of Fletcher's homemade soap.

"Meg," Ransom half whispered, "come to bed now . . ."

He stepped back and sat down on the bed, taking her with him. His mouth sought hers again as he fell backward against the rumpled sheets, and he hauled her atop his chest. Ransom could not be sure if it was the sudden descent onto the feather mattress or the sweet innocence of Meg's kiss that made his head reel, but reel it did. The candles on either side of the bed seemed to whirl about, trailing tails of flame whose light burned its way into his addled brain. Beyond the candles' glow, the entire room began to spin . . . slowly at first, and then more rapidly. He heard his own muted groan and squeezed his eyes shut. Damn! Why had he drunk so much blasted wine?

As Ransom ended the kiss, Meg gradually became more aware of their position. She was horrified to find herself sprawled over him in a most unladylike fashion. Her unbound breasts pressed into his heavily muscled chest, and her legs were even more intimately aligned with the granite-hard evidence of his aroused body. Face flaming, she tried to pull away, but one of Ransom's hands came to rest on her buttock, keeping her next to him.

"Lie still," he rasped, eyes shut. "Please, Meg . . ."

"Are you going to be sick?" she inquired in a hopeful tone.

"No," he moaned. "Not if you'll just lie still for a few minutes. This damned room insists on spinning . . ."

Still tangled in the sheet, they lay quietly. Trying to ignore the possessive pressure of his hands on her, Meg raised her head and saw that Ransom's face had grown chalk white and pasty. A tiny hope blossomed within her—was there going to be a reprieve after all?

Holding her breath, she eased away from him, and reckoned it a measure of his distress that he let her go. The hand that had claimed her such a short time ago now dropped limply to the mattress between them.

Five more minutes passed slowly before Meg sensed a change in his breathing. Cautiously, she leaned closer. A breezy sigh issued from his lips, followed by a soft half snore.

Meg had never experienced such relief. Ransom St. Claire had drunk himself into a stupor! There'd be no wedding night tonight.

Then her pleased smile faded as she realized that as long as she remained a virgin, none of her problems had been solved.

*"Fuigh!"* she muttered, sitting on the edge of the bed. Just because Ransom hadn't been successful on this occasion didn't mean he wouldn't try again. And the worst part was, she'd have to cooperate. How much better it would have been to have simply gotten the whole shameful event over with once and for all.

Meg thought furiously as she absently rebraided her hair—there had to be something she could do. She turned and looked over her shoulder at Ransom. He snored again, groaned and stirred, but didn't awaken. He appeared to be so deeply asleep that it would take nothing less than a cannon shot to disturb him.

The idea leaped into Meg's mind with startling suddenness. What if she simply acted the part of the indignant maiden, let him think he'd actually deflowered her before passing out? In his condition, it was highly unlikely he'd remember enough to know for certain one way or the other. And—her mind churned rapidly—what if there was some other, tangible proof? Then there'd be no possible way he could deny it.

Triumphantly, she sprang up from the bed and sprinted across the room, her eyes fastened on the wardrobe which she knew contained her valise. Without warning, her feet became entangled in her discarded nightgown and she tripped. As she went down, she grabbed at a high-backed wooden chair to break her fall and only succeeded in pulling it over on top of her. It struck her collarbone with a painful *thwack,* sending her to her knees. The chair itself clattered onto the flagstones with a noise that seemed to echo throughout the otherwise silent room.

Meg sat shivering on the cold floor, rubbing her bruised

knees and waiting for Ransom's roar of anger. When, after a few seconds, it didn't come, she raised her head and looked in his direction. Seeing no sign of life from the bed, she rose. He was still sleeping as peacefully as a bairn, unaware of her headlong flight across the bedchamber.

Proceeding with more prudence, Meg bent to retrieve the nightgown and slip it over her head. Then, on feet numbed with cold, she tiptoed over the stone floor to the wardrobe. Quietly, she eased open its heavy doors and pulled out the leather satchel.

Inside, beneath her extra clothing, was the dirk she had brought with her. She had not worn it since the day Ransom had so imperiously taken it from her, but after it had been returned to her, she'd put it away for safekeeping. Every Highlander knew there were a thousand uses for a good, sharp dagger.

Looking back at Ransom, Meg hefted the knife in her hand, feeling the weight of the ridged horn handle on her palm. Yes, this was really the only thing she could do . . .

Slowly, moving with extreme caution, she approached the bed once again and eased herself onto the edge of the mattress. Ransom mumbled in his sleep and obligingly turned his back on her.

Bending her leg, Meg shifted further onto the bed, watching Ransom all the while. She glanced down at the dirk she held and heaved a resigned sigh. She had to do it, there was no other way out.

Before she could lose her nerve, she gripped the knife more securely, yanked up the hem of her nightgown, and applied the blade to her own leg. She felt only a sharp sting of pain as the cold steel sliced through the flesh just behind and below her knee. Blood welled instantly, trickling onto the white linen sheet.

*The final proof,* Meg thought with satisfaction. *The last step toward becoming Ransom's legal wife, and the first step toward getting Wolfcrag back.*

* * *

Ransom didn't awake until midmorning, and when he did, it was with a sense of confusion. He yawned and stretched, acknowledging both a nasty headache and a singularly unpleasant taste in his mouth. It had been years since he'd drunk so much wine . . . he must have lost his capacity for it.

He glanced over at Meg's empty pillow and grinned. She must have been shy about awakening beside him and had slipped away to her own chamber. He half raised himself on one elbow and saw that her shawl and nightgown were no longer lying on the floor across the room.

It was probably just as well she was gone, he reflected, settling back against his pillows. It would give them both a chance to adjust to what had happened last night.

He frowned. What *had* happened last night? Suddenly, he wasn't at all certain. He seemed to have so few lingering memories . . .

He recalled that she had been a winsome combination of innocent reluctance and natural curiosity—just the kind of response one would expect in a virgin. The kind of response that fired the blood, yet elicited a sort of protective gentleness from a man. A tantalizing vision of Meg standing naked before him teased his mind, and, unexpectedly, his sluggish blood began to flow with more vigor. The strength of his reaction to that particular memory surprised him. He should be feeling well satisfied right now, but somehow he didn't. In fact, he felt restless and agitated.

But then, he'd probably exercised the greatest of caution with Meg, not wanting to frighten her. In truth, he was far more accustomed to lusty, rather more experienced women than she. Perhaps their lovemaking had not been as fulfilling as his usual encounters, but he prided himself on his patience. A feeling of contentment stole over him as he realized there could be a great deal of pleasure to be had in furthering the erotic education of someone as unschooled, yet responsive, as Meg.

Despite his headache, he smiled. He wished his new bride would return to him so that they could commence with the lessons. Damned if he could remember a single thing about their actual coupling!

The door to the bedchamber burst open and Meg came into the room. To Ransom's surprise, she was followed by several people: Fletcher, his homely face set in prim disapproval, the woman from the deserted village, and Rob, his expression clearly displaying his black mood.

"I'm sorry to bother you, Ransom," Meg was saying as she led the assemblage to the bed, "but these people have agreed to be my witnesses."

"Witnesses? What in the flaming hell are you talking about?" The loudness of his own voice exploded inside Ransom's head, making him wince.

"They are here to see the proof . . ." Meg's words trailed away as she seized one edge of the sheet and tugged.

Ransom made a grab for it, just in time to preserve his modesty. He tucked the linen around his waist and glared at her.

"Proof?" he repeated ominously.

"Yes . . . that our marriage was truly consummated." Refusing to look at him, Meg made a second effort to grasp the sheet. This time Ransom made no protest as she sedately turned back one corner. "There," she said firmly, pointing to a splotch of bright blood on the bedcovering. "That should be all the proof you need that the marriage between this man and myself is legal and proper."

"Ah, lass," muttered Rob, his face a dull crimson. "Ye had no need to shame yerself like this. We'd have accepted yer word."

"I didn't want to take any chances," she stated. "This way, should the matter ever come before a magistrate—or the king—all of you will be able to reinforce my word."

"Indeed we will, Your Ladyship," declared Fletcher with a dark look at Ransom. "And surely no one could doubt the testimony of such upstanding citizens as we."

"Now that you've seen what you came to see," growled Ransom, "I'd appreciate it if all you upstanding citizens would get the hell out of my room."

Meg peeked at him then, and he met her look steadily, letting her know that he was not well pleased with her. Defiance flared within her expression, and arching her neck imperiously, Meg marched from the room, leaving the others to follow. Fletcher allowed himself a thin smile, but Rob still looked very much as though he would like to draw his dirk and make short work of Ransom St. Claire. The woman was both puzzled and amused, and—or so Ransom imagined—eager to begin spreading the word throughout the castle and village.

When the door had closed and Ransom was left in peace again, he lay back and shut his eyes. Where had his earlier smugness gone? Vanished like a puff of smoke in the wind . . . and all because of Meg MacLinn, the outlaw's daughter. He had been fooled into thinking of her as a sweetly innocent maiden . . . but by the good St. Elmo, the little baggage was as much a cold-minded pirate as he had ever been.

The odd thing was that some bedeviling instinct deep inside made him suspect that in some way he had once again lost the victory to this extraordinary Highland lass.

# Chapter Ten

"Fletcher, I'd appreciate it if you'd stop that blasted smirking," Ransom declared, vehemently slamming down his mug of hot coffee. Satan hissed, arching his back and giving his master a sour look before settling back to the nap he was taking in the middle of the table.

"Aye, Cap'n," Fletcher said cheerfully, still grinning as he dumped beefsteak and eggs onto Ransom's plate. "Uh . . . will your lady wife be joining you?"

"You know damned good and well I haven't seen my . . . wife since that charming scene in our bedchamber."

"*Your* bedchamber, don't you mean?" quipped Fletcher, his eyes alight with amusement. "Meg has already chosen a room of her own."

Ransom scowled at the eggs on his plate. "Are you certain about that?"

"As certain as I can be, seeing as how I was the one who toted several pails of water up there so she could start scrubbing down the walls and floor."

"Well, don't expend any more energy on the housecleaning," cautioned Ransom. "I'll have a word or two with Meg—and I'm sure she'll change her mind."

Fletcher fairly chortled. "Ah, so you do fancy having a wife?"

"I didn't say that." Ransom concentrated on cutting the beef. "I merely think the marriage would look more authentic if we were sharing a chamber when our guests from England arrive."

"Oh, I see." Fletcher's tone was innocent. "I dare say you

have a good argument. But it'll be entertaining to watch you try to get Meg to agree."

Impatiently, Ransom thrust his plate away and hunched his shoulders, shaking his head in chagrin. "Entertaining? Don't you mean impossible?"

Fletcher grinned widely. "Maybe not."

"Lord, what have I gotten myself into?" Ransom wondered aloud. "Have you ever seen a more willful woman? She's as stubborn a female as I've ever met."

"Aye, she's a determined one."

"I just hope I haven't put a noose around my neck this time."

Fletcher clapped a hand on the younger man's shoulder. "Try to look at it this way, lad—at least you're not bored any more."

Ransom fixed him with a threatening stare, but couldn't think of a single thing to say. He had a feeling Fletcher was right: life around Meg MacLinn St. Claire would never involve a single dull moment.

"I couldn't believe that little display she staged this morning," Ransom stated, taking another sip of hot coffee. "Didn't you find it a bit unemotional for a woman?"

"Unemotional?" Fletcher squinted his eyes in thought. "No," he finally replied, "I wouldn't call it unemotional."

"Then what would you call it?"

"I'd say it was more like . . . sweet revenge."

"Revenge?" growled Ransom.

"Aye, for the way you acted last night. And there's one more thing I'd say."

"I'm a fool for asking, but what's that?"

"I'd say you sure as sin deserved it."

Whistling, Fletcher walked out of the room, leaving his disgruntled captain staring after him.

Ransom pounded on the door before him, flinching as the noise reverberated in his still-aching head. There was a muffled call from inside the room and his frown eased. He unlatched the door and shoved it open.

"Meg?"

"I'm over here—is anything wrong?"

"Holy God, what do you think you're doing?" Ransom shouted. "Are you mad?"

Meg was perched atop a ladder braced against the back wall of her newly requisitioned bedchamber. Using a cloth-swathed broom, she was vanquishing cobwebs from the dimly lit corners. As Ransom's angered question rang through the room, she swiveled about on the ladder and glared at him.

"Of course I'm not mad! I'm engaged in housecleaning."

"You're engaged in trying to break your silly neck," he corrected harshly. "Come down from there."

"I'm not finished."

"You are."

"These cobwebs have been here for a decade at least."

"Then another ten minutes won't hurt anything. Come down and I'll have Fletcher do it."

"He's busy elsewhere. Besides—"

Ransom grasped the ladder and put a booted foot on the first rung. "Either you come down or I'll come up after you."

"Don't!"

Ransom started up the ladder, causing Meg to utter a small cry and drop her broom.

"What's wrong with you?" she cried.

"I'm used to being obeyed," he replied. "Even by rebellious upstarts like yourself. Besides, you might as well come down now, since you've dropped your broom. There's no sense in risking both our necks."

"Oh, all right! I'll come down . . . as soon as you're off the ladder."

Carefully, Ransom moved backward until his feet were again on the ground. "I'll hold the ladder for you. Come on."

Meg descended slowly, step by step, and just as she was within feet of the floor, Ransom seized her around the waist and swung her clear of the ladder, setting her directly in front of him.

"Don't ever try anything like that again," he growled. "Always ask one of the men to help."

"There's no need . . ." Meg stepped back and gripped the ladder for support.

"There is a need."

"I'm capable—"

"Of breaking your obstinate neck."

"You've already said that."

"Listen, Meg, I'm simply trying to impress on you that you needn't risk bodily injury for something as trivial as house-cleaning. There are more than enough men in this household to carry out your orders."

"I do not need a man!"

A smile broke over Ransom's face as he leaned forward to look straight into her eyes. "That's not true," he said softly.

Meg blinked in surprise. "What do you mean by that?"

"There are some things any woman needs a man for . . ."

"Oh!" Irritated by his insinuation, she considered stalking away from him, but her fall the night before had left her knees so stiff that it had been all she could do to climb the ladder. And sleeping in the chair by the fire instead of sharing the bed with Ransom hadn't helped, either. By morning, any kind of rapid movement was out of the question.

Ransom altered his own stance, standing upright and putting both hands on his hips. "Now, what's this I hear about you and I having separate chambers?" he said.

"That was the plan from the beginning, wasn't it?"

"Your plan, perhaps," he commented, crossing his arms over his chest and inclining his head slightly, fixing her with an intent gaze. "I've always had the notion that it would be to our advantage to share sleeping quarters."

Meg smiled faintly. "No, it wouldn't. I'd be intruding on your privacy."

"Maybe I wouldn't consider it an intrusion."

"We made a bargain for our convenience," she reminded him. "Sharing a bedchamber would only add unnecessary complications."

One of Ransom's auburn brows quirked upward, giving his features a wry expression. "How so?"

"I shouldn't have to explain. You know as well as I do what could happen." She looked away from the spellbinding hold of his aqua eyes, concentrating on the spill of afternoon sunshine coming through the newly washed windows.

"It has already happened once," he murmured. "What would be the harm in letting it happen again?"

She turned back to face him and found him uncomfortably close. She pressed against the ladder. "The harm might be that one day in a matter of months, I could find myself with a child who would never know his father. Even if I was fortunate enough to escape that probability, fostering any sort of marital relationship would be a mistake. It could cloud our judgment—possibly force us into making decisions that would defeat our original purpose."

She was right and Ransom knew it. He was amazed at his own stupidity in even suggesting such a thing. He supposed he had simply been celibate too long, falling victim to the first pretty woman who came along and made herself available. He had allowed himself to be swayed by smiling lips and innocent eyes, by soft, scented skin—and by what he could remember of a pleasant interlude in a feather bed. He should be eternally grateful to Meg for keeping their common goal uppermost in her mind, for rescuing them both from his selfish lust.

"And last night?" he couldn't resist asking.

"It was necessary," she murmured. "It meant nothing."

"I see."

She could hear Ransom draw a deep breath, and then, with relief, she realized he had moved away from her. She turned back to the room and saw that he had thrown himself into the wooden chair near the fireplace. He was smiling, although there was a certain grimness evident in his face.

"So, the marriage is to be one of expedience only? You'll expect nothing of me . . . and I nothing of you?"

"Yes, that's agreeable."

"What if I tell you that I won't settle for that?" he asked smoothly. "What if I want more from our marriage?"

Meg swiftly dropped her gaze so he wouldn't see the sudden apprehension in her eyes. Frantically, she tried to think of some argument to sway him.

"Meg? Look at me. Don't you have anything to say?"

Reluctantly, she faced him.

"Come here," Ransom urged. "We need to talk about this . . ."

Meg sensed that if she didn't go closer, he would only come after her. Maybe, if they had a calm, sensible discussion, there would be some way to reason with him, to make him understand that she had fulfilled her legal obligation and that she would do no more. Stiffly, she took a few steps in his direction.

Instantly, Ransom was out of the chair, hastening to her side. "What's wrong?" he questioned. "Have you injured yourself?"

She shook her head. "No, it's nothing."

"Here, lean on me," he insisted, taking her arm. He frowned down at her. "I knew you shouldn't be climbing around on that . . . good God, what's this?"

Before she realized what he was going to do, his lean fingers had grasped the scooped neck of the black gown she wore and pulled it away from her collarbone. She knew he was examining the nasty bruise caused by her tumble over the chair. Quickly, she decided to tell him the truth – that she had slipped and fallen getting out of bed. He didn't need to know what she had been going to do when the accident occurred.

"Did I do that to you?"

Startled, she glanced up and saw the fierce expression in his eyes. She shrank away from their wrathful heat, and he cursed softly. "Did I force you last night?" He let his hands drop to his sides, and it was then that she recognized his emotion as self-disgust.

"Ransom . . ."

"Damn my black heart," he swore. "I knew better than to drink so much! How could I . . . oh, hell, no wonder you're afraid of me."

Meg's eyes were wide and gray as she stared at him. She knew she should tell him that he wasn't guilty of mistreating her, and yet, if he believed that such a thing had happened, it would weigh heavily in her favor.

Ransom didn't seem to think it strange that she didn't speak. He appeared to be so immersed in his own remorse that he hadn't even noticed her lack of response. Meg was glad, for it saved her from having to lie.

Ransom turned and walked away, hands on his hips, head down. He stopped a few paces from her and remained motionless for a long moment. Finally, he turned and met her eyes.

"I don't know what to say to you, Meg, except that I regret what I've done . . . I didn't mean to hurt you." He spread his hands in a gesture of defeat. "I'll do my damndest to make it up to you, in whatever way you want."

Meg's face felt flushed, and for a second she was sure he would read her culpability in her gaze. In her mind she could hear her stepmother's voice reciting an oft-repeated adage: *There are more ways than one to tell a lie.*

Meg studied her hands, which were clasped tightly in front of her. What should she do? Would she be a fool to tell him the truth?

"Now I understand your request for your own room," Ransom went on. "And, of course, considering the circumstances, I won't deny you."

His misplaced guilt would be the ideal way to keep Ransom from her bed. No, she couldn't tell him. Let him think what he wanted . . . especially if it was going to make her safe from his unwelcome attentions.

"Thank you," she said quietly.

"Tell me the truth, Meg." Ransom closed the distance between them. "Did I hurt you?" he asked solemnly, taking her twisting hands into his.

Meg felt a jolt of sensation at the touch of his lean fingers. She couldn't help but recall how those hands had caressed her the night before. Thank God, Ransom didn't seem to have any clear memory of what happened.

"No," she replied, "you didn't hurt me." That much, at least, was true.

"I'm glad." With a small squeeze, he dropped her hands. "Have you decided how you will exact your revenge?" he asked, striving to keep his tone light.

"I have no need for revenge," Meg stated hastily. "But there is one thing I do need—money for cleaning supplies. There's a broom maker in the village; we'll need dozens of brooms to get this castle swept out. Also, we'll need pails and brushes . . ."

Ransom nodded. "I should have thought of that already. When you come to my room for the midday meal, I'll give you enough gold for your supplies."

Meg did not like taking money from him, but she had none of her own, and, she reminded herself, that had been a part of their agreement. There was no way the repairs could take place without it. Steeling herself against any feelings of supplication, she said, "Again, thank you. As a Scotswoman, I can assure you I'll stretch your money as far as I can."

At her words, Ransom's thoughts centered on Clarice Howard, who would wager and lose ten times such an amount in an evening of gambling. A man would need a virtual fortune to finance the life-style to which she had grown accustomed. It was another area where he had to consider himself fortunate to be wed to Meg. Even though she would ask him for money, it would be well spent, for it would go toward purchasing his freedom to return to the life he loved.

"At least one bag of the gold Hale brought is earmarked for Inverness," Ransom said. "I've got to make a trip there to buy lumber and materials for the refurbishing."

"When will you go?" Meg asked.

Ransom grimaced. No doubt she would be happy to see him gone for a time. And now, knowing how boorishly he'd behaved, he had a need to put some distance between them, too.

"Soon—tomorrow, perhaps. I thought I'd ask if Hale wanted to accompany me. Inverness is the only town of any size in the Highlands, and if I know Hale, he'd appreciate the opportunity to lift a mug and flirt with the tavern maids."

"Yes," Meg said slowly, "it's bound to be more . . . lively there than here." Afraid that he would mistake her comment for that of a peevish wife, she lightened her tone. "In the meantime, I shall see that the cleaning gets underway so Wolfcrag will be ready for the real work to begin as soon as you return."

"I'll employ some glaziers in Inverness," Ransom offered. "I intend to have every window fitted with glass."

"Yes, that's the way it once was," she affirmed. "What about plasterers? Can you hire them as well?"

"That shouldn't present any difficulty."

"Good. By the end of the summer, Wolfcrag should be as splendid as ever."

"Yes, and I should be back at Rogue's Run by the onset of winter."

For some reason, Ransom's casual remark created a strained silence. After a few moments, he finally said, "I suspect I should go find Dickson. He's waiting downstairs . . ."

Ransom turned to leave, but stopped in mid-stride. "Oh, yes, I almost forgot. There's one other thing." He dug into his pocket and pulled forth his mother's wedding ring. He held it out to Meg.

Her eyes grew wary. "What do you want me to do with this?"

"Wear it. If we intend to portray this marriage as real, I think we should at least keep up outward appearances."

"Very well." Meg slipped the ring onto her finger, albeit reluctantly. "But it means nothing . . . is that understood?"

"Yes—understood."

Ransom stood at the top of the castle with the cold, wet wind tousling his hair and tugging at the hem of the heavy cloak he wore. As he gazed out across the wildly churning ocean, he could see something of the rugged beauty of the land, and for the first time since his arrival, he understood the Scots' loyalty. He supposed it was simple, really. Any man had high regard for that place where he felt most secure, most loved, and most accepted. For the hardy people of the north, this sea-riddled land was home. For him, it was the milder climate of the south—Devon, with its peaceful green meadows and its winding country lanes.

With a heavy sigh, he dragged the flapping ends of his cloak more closely about him. Instead of traveling to Inverness, how he'd like to set off for home. He'd be leaving behind the things that plagued him most: Meg, who moved about the castle with enforced cheerfulness, and his own overwhelming sense of guilt for the way he had treated her on their wedding night.

Even being blind drunk was no excuse. He'd never before used force on a woman—never had to. And the fact that he had done so with Meg could only stem from his intense feelings of loneliness and isolation. God, why had he been sent to this desolate piece of earth? So far he'd only encountered soul-wringing solitude and hellish boredom. Why else would he have gone against every principle he held dear? Why else would he have thrust his unwanted attentions on Meg when every instinct told him that, with a little patience, he could have rendered her most willing?

Now he had done his worst, and deep inside, he knew he'd never fully forgive himself. How, then, could she ever grant him pardon?

Oh, he'd made certain he left her alone these past two days. And he'd honored even her slightest requests, from allowing her to settle in her own bedchamber to ordering his men about with mops and pails. But every time he turned around, there was Meg scurrying away from him—and Rob MacLinn glaring, murder in his eye.

Ransom leaned against the stones of the parapet, resting his chin on his crossed arms. Staring moodily at the curving beach below, he mused that the best thing he could do now was to put some physical distance between himself and the woman he had wronged. If he proceeded with the buying trip to Inverness, perhaps Meg could involve herself with the hiring of local men to work at Wolfcrag, and surely that activity would push his misdeed to the back of her mind. Unless something was done to lessen the strain between them, they'd never be able to convince anyone, least of all Clarice Howard, that their marriage was genuine.

So—he'd leave tomorrow. He and Hale could enjoy a week or so of pleasure and relaxation before Hale went back to London and he returned to the castle. They could take in the sights every day, and drink themselves into a stupor every night without fearing the consequences. He'd wager that Inverness had its share of warm, willing lassies—and if he was very lucky, there wouldn't be a single virgin among them!

* * *

"By heaven, Ransom," Hale Dickson exclaimed, "for someone who protests that his marriage is in name only, you certainly are acting a great deal like a married man."

Ransom came to an abrupt halt and whirled to face his friend. The two men were halfway along the narrow stairs that spiraled upward to the second-floor bedchambers. "I'm leaving the castle for a fortnight or so – it's merely a courtesy that I seek out Meg to tell her goodbye. She'll be in charge while I'm away."

Dickson nodded sagely. "Tell me, old man, was it courtesy as well that brought your lovely bride to your bedchamber the night of your wedding?"

Ransom's mouth thinned into a straight line, and he struggled to keep his temper in check. He saw that Dickson's eyes fairly danced with glee, and he didn't care to be a subject for his friend's entertainment.

"I might've known you'd have heard about that. The men in this castle are worse gossipmongers than a gaggle of old women."

"My, but we're testy this morning," Dickson commented slyly. "Not getting enough sleep, friend?"

"I'm getting plenty of sleep," Ransom snapped. He turned and continued on up the staircase.

"Uh . . . nothing keeping you up late these past few nights?" Dickson asked with intense innocence.

"If you're trying to be clever enough to find out whether Meg and I are sleeping in the same chamber," Ransom muttered, "just ask outright. I don't like innuendoes . . . or lewd implications."

Dickson laughed heartily. "Very well. Are you and Meg sharing a bed?"

"No, not that it's any of your business." They had reached the upper hallway and now Ransom strode rapidly along its echoing length, causing Dickson to double his step in an attempt at keeping up. "We've been frank about the nature of our marriage from the beginning, but some of you refuse to accept reality."

"If you're saying that a randy old stallion like yourself can be legally married to a beauty like Meg and not . . . take advantage of the situation, then I must count myself among the number of disbelievers," Dickson panted. "And you have sheep-dip for brains if you think anyone else is going to believe it."

"Ask Meg for yourself, then." Ransom came to a stop before a closed door and raised a fist to pound on the scarred wood. "Surely you'd believe *her.*"

"What? A Highlander? Haven't you always decreed them untrustworthy?"

"You're trying my patience, Dickson." Ransom frowned and pounded again.

The door opened and Meg stood there, a bedraggled broom in her hands. Ransom wondered if she realized how dusty and disheveled she was—and if she knew how unexpectedly appealing he found her. Her skirts were encased in an enveloping apron, and her black hair was covered by a kerchief, now draped with cobwebs. There was a smear of dirt along one cheekbone. He put out a hand to brush a scurrying spider from her kerchief and onto the floor.

"Egad, a spider!" cried Dickson. "I hate the cursed things . . ."

"No!" Meg exclaimed. "Don't step on it."

She dropped to her hands and knees and coaxed the spider into her palm. Gently closing her fingers over it, she gave the two astonished men a fierce look. "No Scotsman would ever kill a spider."

"Why not?" Dickson questioned. "They can be dangerous, you know."

"Nonsense." Meg got to her feet and walked to the open window, where she set the spider on the sill and shooed it outside. "They bring good luck to a household."

"Luck?" considered Ransom. "Why good luck?"

"Haven't you ever heard the story of Robert the Bruce? While escaping from his enemies, he sat in a cave and watched a spider weave her web over and over, never getting discouraged. Then, when the searchers came past the cave where he was hiding, they decided he couldn't be within because of the unbroken web that stretched over the entrance, and his life was saved. We Scots have revered the spider since that day."

"Robert the Bruce?" murmured Dickson.

"Yes, one of Scotland's most beloved kings," Meg informed him. She gave Ransom an arch look. "The one who defeated the English at Bannockburn . . ."

Ransom shook his head. So, they were back to that. Scottish and English . . . enemies. Why did he tend to keep forgetting her hostility toward his nationality? Lord knew, she brought it up at every opportunity.

"We've wasted enough time, Dickson," he said brusquely. "We'd best say our farewells and be on our way."

"You're leaving for Inverness now?" Meg questioned, surprised.

"Yes, I'll be gone for two weeks, mayhap longer. I intend to show Dickson something of the Scottish high life."

Meg could not be certain whether his tone was meant to be sneering, so she merely inclined her head. "Very well. I shall organize the workers while you are gone."

"Is there anything you need from the city?" Dickson inquired.

"No, nothing beyond what is necessary to rebuild this castle."

"I'm leaving Fletcher behind, Meg," Ransom said. "Should you have any needs, speak to him."

"Gadzooks, man," Dickson exclaimed, "if you're going to be so careless with your new wife, I'd like to request that you take Fletcher with you and leave me behind! I'd be more than happy to address her needs."

Ransom glowered. "As usual, friend, you crow like a cockerel. Just beware that you don't end up on a roasting spit."

Hale Dickson chortled. "Threatening talk for such a . . . casual husband."

Meg colored slightly. "I don't pretend to understand all this silly banter," she stated, "but may I wish you a safe and productive journey?"

"You may," replied Ransom. "Take care while we're away . . . and remember to stay off ladders."

"I shall," she said so readily that he suspected she was only placating him. "Farewell."

* * *

Less than thirty minutes later, Meg and Rob stood at her bedchamber window and surveyed Ransom's departure from the courtyard below. Meg recalled other times she and Cathryn had stood thusly and watched her father depart Wolfcrag. Those expeditions had never been as quiet and orderly as the Englishman's—the air had been filled with excited shouts, the barking of dogs, and the clash of hoofs against the cobblestones. The brilliant colors of the MacLinn tartan had brightened the day, filling her young heart with envy that she had to remain at the castle with the women.

Seeing men ride away to unknown adventure was not, she decided, one of her favorite things. And indeed, had there not been so much to do, she'd have asked that Ransom take her along. She couldn't remember the last time she'd seen Inverness.

She rested her cheek against the rough stone wall and observed as Ransom crossed the courtyard one last time and flung himself into the saddle. He rode well for a seafaring man, she conceded, her eyes drawn to the width of his shoulders beneath the light shirt he wore. The springtime wind was raw coming down off the Highlands, and she knew that long before nightfall he'd have need of the heavy cloak rolled and strapped to his saddle.

She sighed. No matter how much she might want to feel that cold wind against her face, or smell the damp earthiness of the bracken, she knew it was just as well she was not accompanying Ransom on his journey. She needed to be away from him, needed to be alone for a time so that she could remember who she was and what her purpose in coming to Wolfcrag had been. Nearly ending up spending the night in Ransom St. Claire's bed had been one of the most serious situations she'd ever found herself in . . . and now, somehow, she had to banish the memory of that encounter from her mind. She couldn't help but notice Ransom's obvious self-reproach, and there had been too many times during the past few days when she had come dangerously close to confessing to him that he'd done nothing wrong.

When the last of the riders had left the courtyard, Rob and Meg turned away from the window and faced each other.

"Well," Rob commented dryly, "now that the Englishman has gone, I think I should return home."

"You needn't have waited for Ransom's departure," Meg pointed out.

"I'll feel better knowing I'm not leaving you here alone with him."

"I've married the man, Robbie. Sooner or later, I will have to spend some time with him. I wish you could believe that I'll be fine."

He refused to meet her eyes, and Meg knew he was not convinced. She hurried on to a new topic of conversation.

"Before you go, Rob, will you ride to the fishing village with a message for Mairi and her brothers? I'd like for Mairi to move into Wolfcrag and begin working in the kitchens, and I thought perhaps the MacQueen men could help with the rebuilding of the cottages around the courtyard."

"Aye, I'll get word to them."

"Tell them to engage any stonemasons they know, as well. Once those cottages are habitable again, the workmen and their families can live in them."

"It will be good to see the work underway before I go," Rob commented.

"There is one more favor I'd ask," Meg said. "When you get home, will you speak to my family?" she asked.

He shook his head. "Of course. But what should I tell them?"

"The truth, I suppose."

"Lord, but your father is going to be furious."

"Father will understand that it wasn't your fault." Meg smiled faintly. "He knows all too well how stubborn I am."

"I'm counting on that to save my life." Rob grinned in return, but she could see more than a touch of doubt in his eyes.

"I'll write a letter to send with you. Perhaps that will help."

"Aye, it might. Well, I suppose I ought to be off to the village. I'll see you when I return . . ."

When he had gone, Meg looked about her, studying her new

chamber. She had made a great deal of improvement, but there was still much to be done. After writing the letter to her father and Cathryn, she'd go belowstairs and see how the cleaning of the kitchens was progressing. Then she'd return to finish scrubbing the floor in her own room.

Bounding recklessly down the stairs, two steps at a time, she was suddenly filled with memories of her childhood at Wolfcrag. How many times had she skimmed along these time-worn stairs, shouting and laughing? Unexpectedly, she realized how very much she missed her father and Cathryn. How nice it would be to see them, to tell them all that had happened to her since she'd left them.

*And why not?* she thought. *I'll just go back with Rob. What harm could there be in a short visit?*

After all, Ransom was away and would be for some time. She could see that work on the castle had begun and then leave further orders with Fletcher. Should there be any difficulties, he could send a messenger for her. What could possibly go amiss?

Her spirits soared. She might not be able to share Ransom's adventure, but she could certainly have one of her own. And she could relieve Rob of the task of telling her father that she had married an Englishman. Even the thought of having to make such a confession could not dampen her sudden enthusiasm.

In another day, she would be on the open water, happily sailing toward the Isle of Carraig.

# Chapter Eleven

The next day, Rob and Meg found their boat where they had left it, down the beach from Wolfcrag. Fortunately, the weather had cleared, and they made the trip across the Inner Sound with the seas no rougher than usual.

Once they reached the south end of Carraig, Meg grew more and more anxious to travel on to her parents' home. When they stopped to collect Rob's bride, Meg agreed to spend the night in the village, because Ailsa, having been deprived of her husband's company, put forth every argument she could against striking out so soon. But even so, Meg was adamant about traveling on the following day. If Rob couldn't be spared to escort her home, surely there was someone else. If not, she'd borrow a horse and go alone.

Finally, after much debate, it was decided that they would spend the night and leave at dawn. That way Ailsa could say a proper hello to her husband, and a proper goodbye to her mother. With that thought in mind, Meg tried to be tolerant of her friends' tender reunion, but nevertheless, she was awake early and urging Rob to get the horses saddled and ready to go.

" 'Tis lucky for ye that I've convinced Ailsa the sooner we get home, the sooner we'll be rid of ye," Rob grumbled.

Even his perpetual moodiness could not dampen Meg's spirits. "*Fuigh,* but you're becoming a gloomy old man! Surely you can understand that I'm eager to see Cathryn and Father—I've so much to tell them!"

"None of which they'll be wantin' to hear," he vowed. "I swear to God, Meg, ye've done it this time."

"Done what? Don't you think Father will be pleased to hear that I've become mistress of Wolfcrag?"

"Aye, and mistress to the damned Englishman who owns it." Rob paused in the act of putting a bridle on one of the fat island ponies. "Lass, yer father is goin' to be furious with ye. And with me, 'tis certain. He'll have my heart for not stopping such a wedding."

"Once he hears the truth of it, he won't be angry, I promise you." Meg stroked the pony's nose and smiled at her friend.

"The truth of it? That ye've sold yer innocence for a broken down heap of stones?" Rob groaned. "I'm daft for facin' the man at all."

Meg's smile grew wider. "Rob, there's something I should tell you."

He cocked an eyebrow at her, looking completely unswayed.

"My marriage was never . . . consummated. Ransom passed out before . . . well, before."

"Are ye sayin' . . . ? But the blood . . ."

"I cut my leg while he slept and smeared the blood on the sheets." Meg's grin was extremely self-satisfied. "Ransom was too befuddled by wine to know what did or did not happen—and so, he believes what his silly male pride urges him to believe."

"Aye," Rob said slowly, "for now. But won't he soon figure it out? What about the next time he . . . ?"

"There won't be a next time. I've fulfilled my obligation—at least as far as Ransom knows—and that's all I intend to do. Trust me, he won't use force. Even he isn't that dishonorable."

"I'm relieved to hear it, lass. It may be the difference between yer father shootin' me or not—after he's done flaying my hide."

"He isn't going to be angry with you, Rob. And besides, we can't tell him everything. I just wanted you to know."

"But—"

"If I tell Cathryn and my father the marriage isn't real, they'll refuse to let me return to Wolfcrag. So I must let them think I'm legally bound . . . that I want to live with Ransom."

"Good Lord, woman," Rob muttered. "Ye're weavin' a verra tangled web."

"I know, but it seems the deeper into this I get, the more important it is to me." Meg laid her head against the pony's short, thick neck. "All my life, I've been hoping for some way to give my father's castle back to him. Now that I've finally gotten an opportunity, I can't take the risk of anything spoiling it. It means everything to me, Rob—everything!"

Early-morning fog drifted around them as they began the journey across the island from Ailsa's mother's village to their own on the northern coast.

The rocky soil made for slow traveling, and Meg's impatience grew with every plodding step of the pony she rode. At times, she walked, thinking she was surely making as much progress as the animal. King, the hound, ran on ahead, his bony tail wagging madly as he splashed through watery bogs, scaring up birds from their nests amid the grass.

Meg loved the islands with their rugged hills, stony beaches and breathtaking views, but now that she had seen Wolfcrag again, she realized that Carraig could never be her real home. How good it was going to be to have her family together again within the sheltering walls of their ancestral castle. She could hardly wait to experience the joy of it.

They arrived at their village by late evening, just as the sun was sinking into the sea. Overhead, the sky was pale gold, and the heaving water beneath reflected back its glorious color. The lonely cry of a gull was lost in Meg's glad shout of greeting.

"Father! Cathryn! I'm home!"

The trio of riders stopped amid a cluster of small, stone cottages built just back from the shore. Curls of smoke issued from nearly every chimney, and the scent of burning peat was strong on the damp air. But there were also the homey odors of supper to welcome them.

A few of the villagers appeared at their doors to greet the travelers, and King began to bark excitedly. A dark head was thrust out the open window of the cottage directly in front of the riders and a loud whoop rang out.

"Hurrah! Meg's home!"

The head was withdrawn, and within seconds a young boy burst out of the dwelling and charged across the yard toward them.

"You've been gone forever," he complained, as Meg slid off her mount and gave him an exuberant hug.

"Not so long, Alex," she said, laughing. "Besides, wait until you hear my news."

"And what news is that?"

The different voice came from the doorway, and both Meg and Alex turned to see the woman who spoke.

"Hello, Cathryn." Meg crossed the grass to hug her stepmother. "Where's Father?"

"I'm here." Revan MacLinn was so tall and broad-shouldered that he had to stoop to get through the door. Once outside, he straightened and gave his daughter an appraising look. "You took your time getting home, lass. Did you wear Ailsa's mother out with your lengthy visit?"

Meg cast a guilty glance at Ailsa, who tossed her light brown curls and smiled nastily. Obviously, she didn't intend to reinforce Meg's alibi.

"Oh, well . . . no, Ailsa's mother is fine, I assure you. But we did do something that you might think was odd . . ." She forced a small, unconvincing laugh.

As the moment of confession drew nearer, Meg's self-assurance was beginning to desert her. She realized they were looking at her, waiting for her to go on. She hadn't ever gone anywhere without the rest of her family before, and she knew they were curious to hear about her adventure.

She gazed at her parents' politely interested faces and wondered how they were going to take her news. For the first time, she admitted that persuading them she had acted with forethought and intelligence was going to be a monumental task.

"I have something to tell you," Meg began. "But I think we should go inside."

"Meg," her father said sternly, "is something wrong?" He shifted his gaze to Rob. "Rob?"

Quickly, Meg formed an answer. "Nothing is wrong . . . I've just done something you should know about." She turned to look up at Rob. "But there's no need for you to stay. I imagine you and Ailsa want to get settled into your cottage before dark."

"Are ye sure, Meg?" Rob looked troubled, but Ailsa laid a hand on his arm as if to warn him against further involvement.

"Yes, I'm sure. Go on, now, and I'll talk to you tomorrow." Meg reached for the valise tied to her saddle. Her father moved to her side, taking the leather case from her hands.

"Alex, unsaddle Meg's pony and give him some grain, will you? Make haste—supper is ready."

He slipped an arm around Meg's shoulders and steered her toward the cottage. "Now, lass, this sounds serious. What trouble have you gotten yourself into this time?"

Trouble, indeed. Meg swallowed hard.

Once inside the small house, her eyes gave the main room an appreciative perusal. "Cathryn," she declared, "you don't know how nice it is to be back here. I've missed you all. And something smells wonderful!"

"It's just stew," Cathryn said mildly.

Meg was aware of the restrained amusement in her stepmother's expression. Her stomach plummeted. Lord, they were expecting her to confess to some silly prank, the sort of thing she had often been mixed up in as a child. A taunting inner voice told her they couldn't possibly be prepared for the enormity of this latest escapade.

Meg drew a deep breath, firmly reminding herself that it

was not merely an escapade. She had taken a very decisive step toward accomplishing something she'd dreamed of doing since the day they'd been forced to leave Wolfcrag. She wasn't a child anymore, and this hadn't been the action of an innocent little girl.

While Cathryn set an extra place, Meg poured water into a basin and washed her face and hands for the evening meal. She could feel her father's eyes upon her, and as she took her seat at the table, she sensed he was puzzled by her evasiveness.

When Alex came into the house, he washed his hands and dropped into his chair. "I'm starving! Meg, you'll have to tell your story while we eat." He took a bowl of stew from his mother with a broad, anticipatory smile.

Meg ducked her head and took a bite of her dinner. Then, pretending to be engrossed in buttering a hot bannock, she gained a few more minutes. But she knew everyone was staring at her and that the time to make her explanations had arrived. Just as she opened her mouth to speak, Cathryn's sharp gasp filled the room.

Meg's eyes flew up to meet the shocked silvery green ones of her stepmother. To her dismay, Cathryn's eyes were fastened on the simple gold ring Meg was wearing.

"Meg, what have you done?"

Meg didn't know any better way to start than by simply plunging in. "Cathryn . . . Father, I went back to Wolfcrag—"

"What!" they cried in unison. Even Alex's spoon stilled.

"I . . . well, instead of spending time with Ailsa and her mother, I asked Rob to take me across the sound to see Wolfcrag."

"I'll have his hide," Revan MacLinn declared.

"No, it's not his fault. I badgered him into it," Meg admitted. "I was curious . . . it had been so long since I'd seen it." She appealed to Cathryn. "You know I've always wanted to go back."

"But the very fact that you didn't mention your plan to

your father or me is proof enough that you anticipated our disapproval."

"Yes, I knew you'd try to stop me. That you'd think it was too dangerous." Her appetite having abandoned her, Meg pushed her plate and bowl aside. "But it wasn't dangerous at all. The only thing . . . well, Wolfcrag is inhabited now."

"Inhabited?" MacLinn's surprise was mirrored in his face.

"Yes, by a group of men the king has sent to rebuild the castle"

"Wolfcrag is being rebuilt?" Cathryn looked from her husband to Meg. "But why?"

"For one thing," Meg responded, "George is trying to make some kind of peace with the locals. Renovating the castle will give them employment and a place to live. He has enough trouble with his unruly North American colonies—he's anxious to avoid problems closer to home."

Meg cleared her throat, then continued. "When we got to Wolfcrag, Rob and I were . . . greeted by Ransom St. Claire. He's the man King George gave the castle to."

"He *gave* my castle to someone else?" MacLinn's fist struck the wooden table, making his plate rattle. Quietly, Cathryn got to her feet and started moving dishes out of his reach. "Damn that English fop! He had no right—that castle has been in MacLinn hands for hundreds of years!"

"Yes, I know, Father. And that's why I made the bargain with Ransom."

"Bargain?" Suspicion replaced the anger in his voice. "What sort of bargain?"

Cathryn moved to stand behind her husband, one hand resting on his shoulder. She straightened her own shoulders, as if bracing herself for the blow she knew was coming.

"First of all, you have to consider the benefits," Meg hedged. "I can help with the restoration of the castle, and in the end it will belong to our family again . . ."

"What sort of bargain?" her father repeated, more loudly.

"Ransom and I were married," Meg murmured.

Eyes blazing, Revan MacLinn rose to his feet. "What did you just say?"

"I said, Ransom and I—"

"I heard what you said!" he thundered.

"Now, Revan," soothed Cathryn, patting his arm, "calm yourself. I'm certain Meg has a reasonable explanation for all this." She turned beseeching eyes on her stepdaughter. "You do, don't you?"

Meg leaned back in her chair and wearily rubbed her eyes. It had been a long journey and she was tired. With perfect hindsight, she knew it would have been better to keep her news until the light of a new day. At least that way she might have had time to come up with a more palatable method of telling them.

"I have an explanation, yes."

"By damn, it had better be good," warned MacLinn. "I'm having a hard time believing that you just told us you've actually married a stranger."

"It isn't really a marriage, Father. It's more like a . . . like a business venture. You see, since Ransom is foreign to the area, none of the local people will work for him. And he hasn't enough men with him to make the necessary repairs. But he has the gold . . ." She rested her elbows on the table and forced herself to meet MacLinn's glower. "Think of it—the castle that should be ours by right will be rebuilt, using English money! And when it is finished, Ransom will deed it over to me . . . and we can take our clan home."

"And your . . . husband?" Cathryn asked. "What of him?"

"He wants nothing more than to return to England."

"England?" shouted MacLinn, dropping into his chair again. "By the great, flaming fires of Hell, don't tell me you've wed an *Englishman?*"

"Father, you're not paying attention! Didn't I just say the castle was being rebuilt with English money?"

"But I thought you meant the king's money. Why would your . . . this Ransom spend his own gold?"

"He didn't have a choice in the matter," Meg said. "George

confiscated Ransom's ship and his home in
won't get them back until Wolfcrag has been re
king's satisfaction."

"But why?" queried MacLinn. "What hold c
have over the man?"

"I don't suppose you'll like hearing this part . . ."

"Do you think I've liked hearing any of the rest of it? No, lass, I think you'd better tell me everything."

"Ransom is accused of being a smuggler," Meg said.

"Oh, Meggie, no," groaned Cathryn.

"And a pirate," Meg went on.

Her father's fervent curse echoed in her ears. "What in the name of God possessed you, Margaret MacLinn?" He stood again, a new expression dawning in his eyes. "Did this damned Englishman . . . force you in any way?"

Meg became aware of Alexander's renewed interest in the matter. Up to that point, he had continued to eat, his eyes moving avidly from one speaker to another. Now he focused his entire attention upon his sister.

Apparently, Meg was not the only one to notice his sudden interest. Cathryn said, "Alexander, if you've finished your supper, why don't you run along to Grandmother MacLinn's cottage and see if there's anything you can do for her."

"But I want to hear this," Alex argued, a dimple dancing back and forth in his cheek.

"It's of no concern to you," Meg stated firmly.

"It is if Father plans to run the rogue through. It'd be my duty to accompany him to Wolfcrag and help dispatch the fellow."

"Go to your grandmother's," Cathryn reiterated dryly.

"But Father . . ."

"Go on, Alex," MacLinn said with a half smile. "Should I deem it necessary to defend your sister's honor, I'll make sure you're at my side."

"Revan," protested Cathryn.

"I'm jesting, love," MacLinn offered. "Something tells me it's a bit late for defending Meg's honor."

not." Flustered, Meg paused. "What I mean is . . . ., under the circumstances, there's no need for defending me."

Alex raised thick, black eyebrows at his sister. "Are you saying that you haven't . . . that he hasn't . . . ?"

"Alexander MacLinn, get yourself to your grandmother's," Cathryn commanded, her snapping green eyes revealing that she would brook no more disobedience on his part.

With a rueful grin, the lanky youth shoved back from the table and, whistling for King, left the cottage.

"Now," said Meg's father, "set us straight. Have you lived with the man as his wife?"

Meg made herself meet his hard stare unblinkingly. "Yes, I have."

"Meg," Cathryn said, "how could you have done something so rash? You're not even out of our sight for a fortnight and—"

"Cathryn, I'm not exactly a baby. For the past two years, you and Father have been reminding me that I'm well past marrying age."

"Aye, but we intended that you marry someone we at least knew," MacLinn argued. "And we sure as hell didn't expect you to marry an Englishman."

"I know, that part is unfortunate," Meg agreed. "But it just so happened that he is the one who owns Wolfcrag now."

"And was that the only reason you sacrificed yourself?" Cathryn questioned.

"Not the only reason," Meg replied. "He's a wealthy man . . . and very handsome."

"Oh, Meg, you don't sound like yourself," wailed Cathryn. "I believe this Ransom must have forced you in some way and now you're trying to smooth matters over, to prevent your father from seeking revenge."

"No, that's not it at all. He didn't force me . . . I wish you'd believe me."

"Then your marriage is genuine?" asked MacLinn.

"Of course."

"Well, if it's so genuine, where is this husband of yours? Why didn't he come to meet your family?"

"He had to travel to Inverness, Father, to purchase supplies so we can get started with the rebuilding." Meg gave him a wary glance. "But you'll meet him in good time. I thought perhaps you and Cathryn might consider going back to Wolfcrag one day . . ."

"To live?" Cathryn inquired, surprised.

"Yes. Think how long it has been since you've seen the castle. And Alex has never seen it."

"Alex's home is here on Carraig," Cathryn stated. "He knows nothing of Wolfcrag."

"Then it's time he did," Meg insisted. "It's his heritage, after all."

"No, Meg—those days are over. We don't belong at Wolfcrag anymore . . ."

Shocked by her stepmother's words, Meg turned to her father. "Surely you don't feel that way, too? You want to go back home, don't you, Father?"

Revan MacLinn shook his head slowly. "I don't know, lass." The room had grown dark, with the only light that cast by the flickering fire. The flames threw leaping shadows against the wall, and the elusive gold highlighted the rugged angularity of the man's face. "I'll have to think on what you've done, on what this means to us."

"But Father . . ."

"Leave it, Meg," he said harshly. "Just go on to bed and let me think in peace."

"Yes, sir." Feeling much more like a chastened child than a mature married woman, Meg slipped out of her chair and hurried from the room.

Each time the clan moved from their winter houses down to the cottages on the beach, the first thing Meg did was to seek out her favorite spot: a smooth slab of stone tucked beneath an overhanging lip of rock. From this vantage point, she could spend hours thinking or reading, or just staring out across the open water.

When she awakened the next morning, she thought immediately of the refuge, and stole away before anyone else was stirring. The air was damp and chill, but she huddled within her woolen plaid and kept warm.

Reflecting on the events of the night before, Meg realized she couldn't have expected her family to react in any way other than the way they had. To them, she probably had done a bizarre thing by marrying the strange Englishman. Perhaps none of her kin had ever known about her obsession with retrieving the clan castle for her father. Maybe they had never understood her guilt, her shame that it had been her mother responsible for its loss in the beginning.

"Meg?"

She turned at the sound of her name and saw her father climbing over the rocks toward her. She hadn't known he was aware of her hiding place.

"Mind if I join you?" he asked, settling himself beside her.

Meg smiled. She really didn't mind; she understood that there was more they needed to talk about.

"Cathryn sent me to tell you that breakfast will be ready soon. You didn't eat much supper last night, so she thought you might be in need of a hot meal."

"Yes, that does sound good." Meg's attention drifted back to the ocean, to the gulls that dipped into the waves, searching for their own breakfasts. "Father," she ventured, "I'm sorry if I disappointed you, marrying Ransom the way I did. I suppose I knew you'd try to stop me if I came to you first."

"We never wanted to regain Wolfcrag at such a cost," he agreed.

"But I don't mind, really. Being Ransom's wife is going to allow me to live at Wolfcrag again . . . and to have a hand in its restoration."

"And you don't mind being tied to a man you barely know? One with whom you've little in common?" Revan MacLinn tilted his dark head and looked into her face. "Meg, I had hoped my marriage to Cathryn would have served as some sort of example for my children—"

"It has," Meg assured him. "I grew up watching the two of you together. I know how happy you've been."

"But don't you want the same thing for yourself?" he asked.

"Of course. But if it's not possible, then why shouldn't I settle for the kind of union that will be mutually beneficial?"

"What about love? Respect?"

"Don't you see? Your love for Cathryn is truly rare." She gave him a soft smile. "You knew you loved her from the first moment. You risked everything to steal her away from her people and take her to Wolfcrag. That was terribly exciting and romantic. Especially when Cathryn discovered she loved you the same way. But Father, that sort of thing doesn't happen to everyone."

"Why not? God knows there have been a dozen or so young men who've shown an interest in you. How can you be so sure that you wouldn't feel that way about one of them?"

"I just know it. The men of this clan are more like brothers to me than sweethearts. I could never hope to fall in love with any of them—any more than I could have fallen in love with Rob."

"Then you have feelings for this Englishman?"

"Ransom? Not likely!" Meg looked astonished. "He's too arrogant, too accustomed to having his own way."

Meg's father turned his head to look out over the water, but not before she caught the hint of laughter in his face.

"You find that amusing?" she queried.

"No, lass. I was just thinking that this Ransom St. Claire sounded very familiar . . . mayhap a bit like someone I know well."

Meg had to chuckle. "All right, I'll admit that Ransom and I are somewhat alike. That's the very reason we'd never get on well together. However, that suits me fine, because I don't really want a husband. I'll be just as glad when he obtains his divorce and goes back to Devon."

"Divorce? Damn, Meg, I won't pretend to understand you."

"Father, please don't tell Cathryn this, but my marriage to Ransom is actually a business concern. We simply consummated the marriage to make it legal . . . but we have no plans to maintain any sort of real relationship. I know Cathryn wouldn't understand that, but I'm hoping you will. It was the only way I knew to get Wolfcrag back."

"I've never known why you feel so strongly about the castle, Meg. You were only a child when we left there."

"I will never forget that it was my mother's fault the castle was invaded by the enemy—"

"That has nothing to do with you!"

"But it does," Meg insisted. "I feel such shame, such responsibility. This is my way of making amends to you, to our clansmen."

MacLinn pulled at a tuft of striped grass growing up between two rocks. "But at what a price, Meg."

"It may seem that way to you, but I knew it would be worth it the instant I saw Mairi MacQueen. Her sons were nearly starving, Father—and their home had been burned."

"What in the devil are you talking about? Mairi MacQueen? Is she kin to the thatcher?"

"His daughter. But she and her brothers aren't the only ones who've lost their homes. Most of your property was given to a man named Spottiswoode, and he's clearing the land to raise livestock. Mairi says that if the tenants don't leave peacefully, he evicts them, then burns their cottages."

Revan MacLinn's face darkened in anger. "The bastard! He's burning them out, you say? For the sake of sheep and cattle?"

"Yes."

"And your bridegroom has done nothing to stop this?"

"He didn't know it was happening at first. And, Father, it's really not his argument."

"No, by God, but it's mine." He swore softly in Gaelic. "The day the MacLinns sit back and allow their kinfolk to be persecuted is the day there will be icicles in Hell. Why didn't you tell me this in the beginning, Meg? Your whole plan makes a great deal more sense now."

"Then . . . you'll go back to Wolfcrag?"

"Aye, I'll go back, lass. And when I do, a number of stout-hearted clansmen will march beside me. We're going to put a stop to this Spottiswoode blackguard and his enforced clearances."

Caught in the rough embrace of the sea wind, father and daughter shared a happy smile.

"I'm cold," Meg suddenly announced, scrambling to her feet. "And hungry."

"Come along then. Cathryn will have a kettle of porridge for us, 'tis certain."

Ransom St. Claire stared into the untouched mug of ale he held, barely aware of the noise and confusion around him. He was tired of the nightly excursions to the little pub tucked away on a back street in Inverness, tired of the smoke and clamor and cheap women.

Next to him, Hale Dickson gently pushed the bosomy barmaid off his lap, saying, "Run along and fetch us something more to drink, will you, love? I need to talk to my friend here."

Ransom raised his head and favored his companion with a blank stare.

Dickson frowned. "Good lord, Ran, what's gotten into you? You're about as lively as a widow at a wake."

"I don't know, Dickson. I just don't feel like spending any more time in this blasted pub. My lungs are begging for a bit of fresh air."

"Are you sure it's your lungs talking to you?"

Ransom scowled. "What do you mean?"

"Are you sure it isn't some other area of your anatomy longing for your pretty young wife?"

"Damn your eyes, Dickson. I've told you a hundred times that Meg isn't really my wife."

"So you're saying that you don't miss her?"

"I'm wondering how she's getting on with the work back at Wolfcrag. There's a huge amount to be done."

"So you do miss her?"

"I didn't say that, Dickson. Curse your rattling tongue!" Ransom flung himself out of the chair in which he sat. "I'm going back to the inn. Stay here and amuse yourself if you wish."

"Wait . . . I'll come with you." Dickson tossed a few coins onto the table. "It's more entertaining to question you about Meg and see you bristle up like a hedgehog."

Ransom stalked out the door and started down the deserted city street. Dickson had to hurry to catch up with his friend.

"What do you think Meg is doing back at your gloomy castle?" Dickson asked, his mouth stretched into a pleased grin. "Do you suppose she's missing you, too?"

"For the last time, Hale—I do not miss that little Scottish thistle."

"But perhaps she misses you?" the other man prompted.

Ransom snorted. "I sincerely doubt that."

"Oh? Do I sense some hidden meaning in those words?"

"Not hidden at all," Ransom remarked. "I said exactly what I meant. There's no reason Meg should miss me."

"What? After you initiated her in the wondrous ways of love?"

They were crossing a small bridge that arched over the River Ness. At his companion's mocking words, Ransom stopped short and turned to face Dickson. "What do you know?" he demanded.

For once, Dickson was taken aback. "What do you mean, what do I know?"

"Did Meg say something about me? About . . . our wedding night?"

"Good Lord, no. Why would she?"

Ransom gripped the bridge's stone railing and lowered his head to look into the water that shimmered below them. "I'm probably an idiot for admitting such a thing to you, Dickson . . . but I made a fool of myself the night of the wedding."

Dickson's smile was broad. "You've always made a fool of yourself where the ladies were concerned, old friend."

Ransom looked up. "You don't understand. I was drunk . . ."

"Indeed you were. I couldn't help but wonder if you were having regrets about not waiting for Clarice."

"God, no."

"Then what? Unhappy about agreeing to wed the Highland lassie . . . or cold feet about shackling yourself to any wife at all?"

"Who knows, Hale? I think I was simply rebelling against being told what to do. I've had a craw full of that lately." He tapped the stone lightly with a clenched fist. "Fletcher hit upon the truth when he called me a spoiled little boy. I didn't see it at the time, but it's true."

"Look, worse things have happened than a groom getting roaring drunk on his wedding day."

"Hale, it was more than that. I fear I—"

"Couldn't perform?" Hale helpfully interrupted.

Ransom snorted again. "No, unfortunately I performed all too well."

Dickson's eyebrows shot skyward.

"I may have been a bit . . . aggressive. Impulsive, if you like. Hell, what am I saying?" Ransom heaved a disgusted sigh. "I forced myself on Meg."

"Forced yourself? Do you mean . . . ?"

"Exactly."

"Rape?"

"It may as well have been. Damn it all, Hale, I'm certain I hurt her."

"Maybe not."

"I saw her bruises myself." Ransom closed his eyes for a long moment. "I should be horsewhipped! Were her father alive, I'm sure the man would geld me . . . and I'm just as sure I'd deserve it."

"Ransom, don't take on so. You couldn't help what you did! You had a belly full of wine."

"And whose fault is that? I tell you, friend, Meg didn't merit that kind of treatment."

"Is this why your new wife has moved into a chamber of her own?"

"Precisely. Under the circumstances, I could hardly refuse her that, could I?"

"Hardly." Hale Dickson scratched his chin thoughtfully. "I suppose this trip to Inverness was an excuse to put some distance between you as well?"

"In a manner of speaking. We do have to buy supplies for repairing the castle, but I thought it might be a good notion to get myself out of Meg's sight for a while."

"Ah, but you've hardly enjoyed your time away from the castle, have you?"

Ransom cast him a curious look. "Why do you say that?"

"Lad, I'm not completely addled. In the last few days, you've turned away more pretty women than most men see in a lifetime. And you've certainly made few inroads on the Inverness wine."

"I learned my lesson, believe me."

"So what do you intend to do next?"

"Finish my business here in the city and go home. A bit of time has passed—maybe Meg will be more amenable toward me. And maybe I can find some way of making up to her for my abominable behavior." He began strolling slowly along the walkway again.

Hale Dickson stared after his friend, a bemused smile hovering about his lips. "Ransom, old chap, you're starting to sound very much like a married man."

"Hmm?" Ransom paused and looked back. "What was that?"

"Oh, nothing. I was just . . . talking to myself. Nasty habit, that."

"Hmmm . . ."

# Chapter Twelve

"So, lass, do you miss your new husband?" The white-haired lady who spoke rested sharp blue-gray eyes on Meg.

"I've barely been here two weeks, Grandmother," Meg protested, pretending great interest in the skein of thread she was untangling. The women were sitting on a bench outside Margaret MacLinn's freshly whitewashed cottage, enjoying the late-morning sunshine.

"Two weeks?" Margaret chuckled. "That should seem a lifetime to a bride."

"Well . . . Oh, *fuigh,* this thread is hopeless!" Meg exclaimed, tossing it aside.

"You never did have the patience for needlework." The older woman smiled sweetly. "Or much of anything else. So, will you please explain to me why you seem to have infinite forbearance where your marriage is concerned?"

"Forbearance?"

"Yes. How is it that you found this . . . this Ransom fellow so appealing that you couldn't wait to marry him, and yet, once the deed is done, you seem perfectly content to idle here while he is off across the water somewhere?"

"He had business to attend to, Grandmother—I've told you that. He'd gone to Inverness, so it seemed a good time for me to come home for a visit."

"And he didn't mind being separated from his new wife?"

Meg sighed. Unlike Revan, Grandmother MacLinn

refused to believe there wasn't some emotional basis for Meg's marriage. And she wasn't above prying if that was what it took to find out all she wanted to know.

"Granny, this marriage isn't quite like yours to Grandfather was . . . or like Father's to Cathryn. It's different . . . I don't know how to explain it."

"You'd like for us to assume it's a marriage of convenience," Margaret said, turning her attention back to the embroidery that lay on her lap. "But Meggie, I know you better than that. Ransom St. Claire must possess some redeeming quality or you'd not have had the stomach to sacrifice yourself." She favored her granddaughter with a piercing stare.

Meg was startled. Sometimes she was amazed by her grandmother's keen perception, and had long since decided that the reason the older woman understood her so well was that the two of them were very much alike. Despite her reunion with her family, Meg's thoughts had turned to Ransom more than a few times during the past week. And it had occurred to her that her decision to wed the Englishman had been made easier by the fact he was neither ugly nor infirm. She'd like to believe that moral character and a pleasing disposition were more important to her than physical beauty, but Ransom was a smuggler with a wild, uncertain temperament. Shamefully, her thoughts were drawn to a memory of his thickly curling auburn hair, his provocative aquamarine eyes, the lean angularity of his face. Undoubtedly, the new master of Wolfcrag Castle was a strikingly handsome man, and some persistent imp within her mind had seized upon that truth. So much for lofty ideals . . .

Lost in her musing, Meg realized her grandmother, puzzled by her long silence, was again scrutinizing her. Unable to recall what had just been said, she attempted to change the subject.

"When do you think the men will return?"

Margaret smiled as if well aware of Meg's ploy. However, her reply was mild enough. "Soon, I suppose. It shouldn't take much longer."

"Meg!" The excited cry rang through the previously still air.

"I'm here, Alex," Meg called back. She smiled at her grandmother. "I think Alex actually missed me while I was gone. Since I've been back, he's hardly—"

Alex rounded the cottage, nearly stumbling over the bench where the two women sat. His breath whistled sharply as he panted, "Meg, there's someone to see you. I think it's your . . ."

His words died away as a large figure stepped around the corner and stood, blocking the sun.

Meg stared upward, unable to distinguish anything but the massive size of the man standing there. But even though his facial features were obscured by the blinding light behind him, she could easily envision the angry frown etched upon them. A barely restrained wrath seemed to emanate from him in waves.

"Ransom?" she ventured. "What are you doing here?"

"I might ask you the same question," came the now familiar voice of her husband. "Is this the way you honor the bargains you make?"

Slowly, Meg got to her feet, her thread falling unheeded to the grass. "What do you mean by that?"

"Aren't you supposed to be seeing to the restoration of Wolfcrag Castle?"

"Yes, of course. But I . . . when I left for Carraig, work was already underway. Has something gone wrong?"

"Don't you think it was your duty to remain at hand to ensure that it didn't?"

"I needed to see my family, let them know what had happened to me."

Margaret MacLinn cleared her throat, gently reminding Meg of her presence. With an air of distraction, Meg said, "Uh . . . Ransom, this is my grandmother, Margaret MacLinn. Grandmother, this is Ransom St. Claire, my . . . my husband."

Ransom moved closer to the older woman, and as he altered his stance, the sun was no longer behind him. Instead, its bright rays fell upon his face, highlighting every bold feature. Margaret smiled and offered her hand.

"I'm delighted to meet you," she said. "Meggie was just telling me about you."

"Oh?" Ransom's answering smile was wicked. "I'm sorry to have missed that. I'm certain her description was . . . enlightening."

"Oh, indeed. Fascinating in the extreme." Margaret tilted her head to one side. "I cannot tell you how happy I am for the opportunity to see you for myself. I didn't expect you to appear on Carraig."

"Neither did I," declared Meg. "How did you find this place?"

Ransom's face lost some of its charming affability. "Fletcher told me how to get here."

"He . . . he *told* you? But he promised . . ." Meg threw up her hands in disgust. "He was sworn to secrecy! He vowed to reveal my whereabouts only in the direst of circumstances."

"Rest assured, when I returned to Wolfcrag and found you gone, the situation was very dire." Ransom gave her a closer look. "But don't worry—I haven't revealed the location of your clan to the authorities. I doubt they'd find anything to interest them, anyway." He gave the handful of cottages huddled on the shore his brief attention. "It doesn't look as if much of a subversive nature goes on here."

Meg and her grandmother exchanged a quick glance. "Did you come alone?" Meg queried. "Where's Hale?"

"You'll be disappointed if you thought he'd be here to champion you. He left for London directly from Inverness—to start spreading the news of our marriage." He scowled at her. "But I'm not alone. Beale and Yates are with me. They're securing the boat."

"There's no need," Meg said hastily. "I mean . . . well, I've seen my family now, so if you'd like, we can start back to the castle."

"So soon?" he murmured.

"I've been here two weeks," she explained. "There's no need to linger—now that . . . uh, Cathryn and the others know where I'll be." She patted her grandmother's shoulder. "Granny, why don't you chat with Ransom while I fetch my things and tell Cathryn goodbye."

"But Meg," broke in Alex. "What about Fath—"

"Oh, good heavens," Meg exclaimed. "I forgot to introduce my brother. Ransom, this is Alexander. Alex, Ransom."

"The lad greeted us when we landed, Meg," Ransom reminded her. "We've already met."

"Of course." She seized Alexander's hand. "Well, come along, Alex, and help me gather my belongings."

"Wait a moment," spoke Ransom. "We don't need to leave now. Morning will be soon enough."

"But what if there's a storm tomorrow? Those clouds building in the west are a bad sign."

"If it's stormy," Ransom said calmly, "we'll just wait until the weather clears. Why hurry now? You've obviously been willing to while away the days until I appeared."

His tone reminded Meg of his anger. "But you were right when you said I shouldn't have been away from the castle so long."

"I didn't say that," he corrected her. "I didn't think you should have left at all. We had an agreement."

"I needed to explain matters to my family."

"You could have sent a messenger."

Meg shrugged. "It didn't occur to me. I wanted—"

"Here they come, Meg," Alex breathed in a low voice.

Meg felt her heart sink as she caught sight of the small flotilla of boats moving into the sheltered bay. Already she could hear men shouting and the first, frantic bellowing of cattle.

"What the hell is that?" muttered Ransom, taking in the incredible scene.

"Nothing," Meg stated firmly. "The men are just moving some cattle onto the island for the summer pasturing."

Ransom's look was skeptical. "Moving them from where?"

"Uh . . . well, from the Isle of Skye," Meg replied. "It's not so far from here, you know."

"But why . . . ?" Ransom fell silent as he turned away to study the activity taking place in the choppy waters.

"The grass on Carraig is very thick and nice," Meg offered, somewhat lamely.

"No," Ransom said. "I meant . . . if they're your cattle, why not keep them on the island all the time?"

Alex turned away to hide his smile and Meg glared at him. "Well, because—"

A loud Gaelic curse rang out, and Meg swung her gaze back to the water. The bobbing heads of cattle could clearly be seen, and here and there among them were small, roughly built fishing boats. Filled with shouting, laughing men, the boats were being used to herd the animals toward the beach. As the boats drew closer, it was possible to see that young calves, legs bound, were lying on the bottom of every boat.

"I've never seen anything like that," Ransom uttered. "I'm going to take a closer look." He strode off across the narrow lawn and onto the sandy beach, heading purposefully toward the water's edge.

"Oh, my God," Meg gasped. "I can't believe this!"

"Your Ransom is quite a striking man," Margaret commented. "Although I can't imagine why he wears that awful earring."

Meg whirled to face her grandmother. "That doesn't matter right now, Granny. Don't you see? We've got to get him away from here quickly." She shook her head in despair. "I told him Father was dead, and if he talks to anyone, he'll find out that's not true. Besides, the cattle! Oh, Lord!"

"Calm yourself, Meg. The man's your husband. He'll be loyal to you and your family."

Meg moaned. "You don't understand. His loyalty must be to his king. Once he finds out these cattle are stolen, he'll send word to the English government. And now he'll be able to tell them where we are!"

"There's only one thing to do," Alex stated boldly. "We'll

have to kill him, Meg. We can't let him leave here."

"But if he and his men fail to return to Wolfcrag, his first mate will know precisely where to look for them. Oh, damnation, what have I done?"

"Dinna fash yerself," mumbled Alex, giving her an awkward pat on the back. "Father will know what to do."

Meg ground her teeth together. "I've got to try and get Ransom away before he sees Father."

With that, she started off to the spot where Ransom, transfixed by the spectacle unfolding before him, stood in the sand.

Cattle thrashed in the water, heads up, nostrils flaring. Men yelled and whooped, deftly maneuvering their boats about, careful to avoid the flailing hoofs. The noise grew deafening as the first of the cattle struggled up onto dry land and the herdsmen and the watching villagers alike began to cheer.

A giant of a man with curling red hair launched his boat and leaped onto the sand. Throwing back his head, he roared, "Remember the MacLinn!" The onlookers answered the cry lustily, until it fairly echoed around the bay.

"What in the name of God was that?" asked Ransom.

"The clan war cry," Meg absently replied. "Look, Ransom, we really should be on our way. It's growing late."

"What is it you don't want me to see, Meg?"

"I . . . I don't know what you mean," she protested. "I'm only trying to make amends for staying away from the castle so long. I didn't realize you'd think I planned to renege on our bargain."

Ransom shook his head. "Now I'm growing truly suspicious. You're altogether too meek . . . and that bespeaks trouble of some sort."

Before she could think of a plausible response, the huge redheaded man caught sight of her and waved, his teeth gleaming in a broad smile. "Look at these animals! Aren't they beauties, Meg?" He released a calf from his boat and watched with delight as it staggered across the sand.

Meg nodded, her voice caught in her throat, nearly suffocating her. "Aye."

"Who's this?" the big man asked, gesturing toward Ransom with a hamlike hand.

"He's my husband, Owen," Meg said. "Ransom, this is Owen MacIvor, an old family friend."

"Old?" boomed Owen. "Lord, today I feel like a young pup. Nothing like a little reiving to stir a man's blood."

"Reiving?" repeated Ransom, a question in his voice.

Owen nodded. "I forgot you were English. Reckon you wouldn't know about such things." He grinned. "Stay on Carraig long enough and you can go on our next raid."

Meg felt Ransom's distrustful eyes upon her, and her mouth went dry. Thankfully, distraction appeared in the form of a shaggy red cow, who, bawling unhappily, trotted through the sand toward them to reclaim her calf. Owen gave a shout of laughter and, waving his arms madly, advanced on both animals, turning them toward the pasture beyond the cottages. At the same time, Meg spun away, determined to make an equally hasty escape. Unexpectedly, she found her arm imprisoned in a firm grip.

"What's going on here, Meg?" Ransom said, pulling her around to face him. "These cattle . . . they're stolen, aren't they?"

She stared up at him, wishing she had a choice other than telling the truth. But something told her Ransom already knew her well enough to detect a blatant falsehood, and if she declared the cattle anything but contraband, it would be the boldest of lies.

Mutely, she shook her head in affirmation.

"God damn it," Ransom swore softly. "What kind of wife have I saddled myself with?"

Stung, she couldn't resist retorting, "*I* didn't steal them!"

"No, but your family did. You're guilty by association." He tightened his hold on her arm. "And because I'm married to you, I'm guilty as well."

"Being a thief shouldn't be anything new to you," Meg stormed.

"Why, you little . . ." His fierce words trailed away as if he couldn't think of an insult sufficient to express his ire. He seized her by the shoulders, looking very much as though he'd like to give her a good shaking. "I'd advise you to keep a civil tongue. Knowing what I do, I'm now in a position to do you and your people a great deal of harm."

Meg's chin shot skyward. "More likely, you're in a position to get yourself killed. Do you think the men of this clan will simply stand by and let you accuse them?"

"So now I know the kind of marriage bargain you made," he rasped. "It's just as I suspected—you lured me here to have me murdered."

"I didn't lure you! You came because you didn't trust me." Meg tried in vain to free herself from his hands. "And I'll wager you had to beat Fletcher to get the directions to Carraig."

"And if I did, whose fault is that?" He glared at her, his blue-green eyes sparking angrily.

"Mine, I suppose!"

"Oh, indeed. And if I have to beat you as well—"

"I hope this rather noisy encounter is nothing more than a lovers' quarrel."

At the sound of the deep voice, both Ransom and Meg whirled about. Revan MacLinn stood observing them, a frown on his chiseled features.

"Who the hell are you?" Ransom demanded.

"A man who dislikes hearing his only daughter threatened," came the succinct reply.

"Daughter?" Ransom turned his head and looked at Meg. *"Daughter?"*

Meg moistened her suddenly dry lips. "Now, Ransom, give me a moment to explain . . ."

But Ransom ignored her, turning back to the tall, black-haired man glowering at him. "You're—?"

"Revan MacLinn."

"The outlaw?"

"I've been called that."

Ransom looked at Meg, one dark eyebrow raised in imperious question. "I thought your father was dead, Meg."

"I realize I implied that, but—"

"Is there no end to the lies you tell?"

"I was trying to protect him."

"I've no need to look to my children for protection," railed MacLinn. "And certainly not from any weak-livered Englishman."

Ransom's affront was obvious in the set of his shoulders, the tilt of his jaw. "Provoke me further," he warned, "and there'll be no protection from any source."

"Why, you miserable English whelp," growled MacLinn, stepping closer. "I ought to carve up your carcass for the gulls." His hand closed over the dirk he wore at his waist.

"Try it . . . if you've a taste for blood," returned Ransom, his own hand cradling the hilt of his sword.

The two men stood nearly chest to chest, staring into each other's eyes with defiance. Of equal height and breadth, the only difference between them was their coloring—Revan MacLinn, black-haired and bearded, Ransom with hair like tarnished copper—and their age. MacLinn's deeply golden eyes met the aqua-green ones of the younger man and displayed no fear. At forty-one, he was as strong and athletic as ever—he recognized no danger in the Englishman. Likewise, Ransom was prepared to meet any challenge presented by the Highland outlaw.

Alarmed, Meg moved between the two men, a hand on each brawny chest. "Stop it!" She felt the tension in the muscles beneath her hands and realized their animosity was real. "You're both grown men—why don't you act like it?"

"I am," MacLinn grated. "No grown man stands by and watches someone abuse his daughter."

"I wasn't abusing her," Ransom shouted. His face darkened. "Though, God knows, the witch would deserve it."

"Witch?" MacLinn pushed against Meg's hand, closing the distance between himself and Ransom. "You, sir, dare much.

A whistle from me would have my men rushing to my aid. They could slice you into fish bait before you saw the shine of their blades."

"I have men of my own," countered Ransom.

"You brought two men, Ransom," Meg stated. "Be reasonable."

"I am. Three Englishmen could best a whole damned clan of Scots any day."

A fierce growl emanated from between MacLinn's firmly clenched teeth. "Blast your eyes, man! Are ye tired of living?"

"Stop it!" Meg cried a second time. She shoved harder against the two straining bodies. "Calm yourselves!"

"I'll not stand here and be insulted by some sea-slimed sailor," vowed MacLinn.

Ransom bristled. "Nor will I cower before a common cattle thief—"

"Oh . . . *fuigh!*" Meg shrieked. "I give up! Go ahead and kill each other—just don't expect me to stand here and watch!"

She spun about in the loose sand and stalked away, leaving the two combatants staring at her retreating back.

"Well," MacLinn said after a few seconds, "aren't you going after her?"

"Why should I?" asked Ransom.

"Because she's your wife."

"She's your daughter."

"Aye, but when she cast her lot with you, she took the responsibility for her well-being and heaped it upon your shoulders." MacLinn's lean jaw twitched, and his mouth curved into a distinct smirk.

"Are you saying that it's my right to exercise control over the woman?" Ransom demanded, folding his arms over his chest and giving Meg's surprisingly alive and healthy father an intense look.

"It's your right to try," the older man said, a chuckle barely concealed by his stern tone.

"Good, because I'm of a mind to trounce her lying little arse."

"Ye'll not lay a hand on the lass."

Ransom's brows arched in question. "Then how can I control her?"

" 'Tis your problem."

"No, it's yours again. I've just decided to leave her here on this island."

"You entered into marriage with her," argued the Scotsman. "You've made a legal agreement."

"I no longer choose to honor it."

"You're exactly like all the other English blackguards I've ever known—the minute it becomes inconvenient, your honor evaporates like dew on a hot summer morning."

"Don't speak to me of honor," raved Ransom. "Not after the way your daughter has dealt with me. If she's told the truth about anything, I've yet to discover it."

"Meg had her reasons. Mayhap if you gave her a chance, she'd explain them to you."

"Oh, I'm sure of it." Ransom's sarcasm distorted his usually mellow Devon drawl. "Why don't I simply follow her now and allow her that opportunity?" He waved his hand, indicating the scene of turmoil still occurring around them. "Maybe she can make sense of all this."

"You do that, Englishman. But don't lay one finger on her."

"I'm not in the habit of beating women," Ransom snapped. "Although I must confess, in Meg's case, I'm sorely tempted. She's a maddening female who tries my patience nearly beyond endurance."

Revan MacLinn gazed at him a long moment. "All right, now I've changed my mind," he finally said. "Perhaps it's best if you take your men and go. Leave Meg here with us and dissolve your marriage as you please."

"I'm not leaving without her," Ransom said, amazed at his displeasure with MacLinn's offer. "I married the wench in good faith, and I fully expect her to carry out her part of our bargain."

"Nay. Getting Wolfcrag back wouldn't be worth it." MacLinn narrowed his keen eyes. "Make your farewells and go."

"I don't take orders from you, Scotsman. I'm staying."

"Oh?"

"Until your daughter is prepared to return to Wolfcrag and carry out her duties."

"She might have something to say about that."

"Yes, I know."

"Then why don't you go after her and see how she feels?"

Ransom frowned. "I intend to." He took a few steps, then looked back. "But not because you suggested it."

MacLinn shrugged and, after a long silence, turned back to help with the herding. Beneath his breath, he muttered, "Mayhap you'll have a marriage after all."

Meg had just reached her parents' cottage when someone grabbed her shoulder and jerked her to a halt. Temper flaring, she turned and struck out, barely missing Ransom's head.

"What do you want?" she hissed.

"I want some explanations from you," he barked. "And I'd prefer them now."

She stood her ground, eyes gray and furious. She was standing just beneath the thatched eave of the whitewashed hut; he towered over her, far too tall for the small dwelling. Meg felt as if she were facing a vengeful giant.

"Why did you tell me your father was dead?" he charged.

"To protect him, naturally."

"Is that the same reason you failed to inform me your clan still engages in stealing cattle?"

She nodded.

"What else are they involved in?" he asked.

"Nothing worse than brewing illegal whisky up in the hills."

Ransom dragged a hand through his curling hair. "Good God, what have I gotten myself into? Do you know what kind of clemency I can expect from the king if he ever finds out I've married into a family of outlaws? Or that my father-in-law has a price on his head that would feed the orphans of Edinburgh for a year?"

"He won't find out."

"What other lies have you told me, Meg?" he softly queried, bending his head to look into her eyes.

She felt the color rise in her cheeks. He had yet to discover the worst falsehood of all.

"You know everything about me now," she said.

"Damn it, Meg. I came home from Inverness determined to make it up to you for . . . well, for what happened on the night we were married. I'd acted like a brute and I was sorry." He grasped the rough edge of the thatch, stirring to life the fresh scent of dusty straw. "But when I found you gone, I was furious. I thought you'd broken our agreement . . ."

"Didn't Fletcher tell you I had only gone home to set matters right with my family?"

"He told me, but I didn't believe him. I think that's why he eventually gave me the directions to Carriag. He thought I should come here and see for myself."

"But your arrival on the island couldn't have come at a worse time," Meg admitted.

"I'll allow it was something of a surprise to be greeted by a herd of swimming cattle . . . and the reputedly long-since-deceased outlaw MacLinn." For an instant, a faint smile hovered about Ransom's mouth. Then he sobered. "Are you going back to Wolfcrag with me?"

"I mean to keep my part of our arrangement."

"And what of your parents?" he queried. "Your father says he'll not let you go. That it isn't worth it just to get Wolfcrag back."

Meg smiled. "He only said that because you were so nasty to me. If you could find a way to be somewhat more . . . civil, I think he'd relent. Besides, he knows I'm too old to be told what to do."

Ransom pulled a loose reed from the roof. "And too obstinate," he added.

"I'll ignore that observation," she remarked, making a wry face. "The important thing is that we convince everyone we're capable of carrying off the marriage deal we've made. Tonight they'll hold a *céilidh* to mark the safe arrival of the stolen cattle. That will be a perfect time for us to demonstrate how well we can get along with each other."

"What's a *céilidh?*"

"A celebration with food and music." She gave him an arch glance. "And, of course, a great deal of whisky."

Ransom opened his mouth to protest the obvious jab, but thought better of it. Instead of a mere vocal denial, he'd wait and prove his sobriety to her in the best way, by refraining from touching so much as a drop of the dangerous brew. When he took Meg to bed this time—and from the smallness of the cottage, he happily deduced he'd *have* to share a bed with her—he intended to be in full command of himself.

"So, you see," Meg continued, "if we are cordial to each other tonight, it will influence my family to let us honor our agreement."

"Maybe this would be a good time for us to begin reassuring *them,*" Ransom murmured, inclining his head to indicate two women walking along the lane that led to the cottage. "Is one of them your stepmother?"

"Yes, the red-haired one. The other is Della MacSween, the doctor's wife."

"Then let's show them how well we get along," he suggested, an impish gleam in his eyes.

His hands went to her waist, and he pulled her from the shelter of the thatched eaves and into his arms. With a smothered gasp, Meg seized his shoulders to keep from falling.

Ransom bent his head and laid his mouth deliberately over hers. He felt her momentary resistance, recognized her urge to struggle against him . . . and rejoiced in her ultimate decision to surrender, even if only this once.

Every day that he had been away from her, even the busiest days in Inverness, his mind had been tormented by her image. She had distracted and irritated him from the first moment he'd met her, and she still did. But somehow that irritation had turned into a rather pleasant sort of anguish. He hadn't known it until he'd set foot in Wolfcrag again and found it disturbingly empty without her. He'd pretended anger, simply because he wasn't willing to accept the fact that the emotion he'd felt was fear—fear he'd never see her again. Fear that he'd never know where his relationship with her might have taken them. Meg had forced her way into his life, and he had no intention of letting her depart it so easily.

His left hand moved to curl possessively around her neck, the skin of his wrist teased by the heavy fall of her silky hair. His other arm slid more closely about her, his palm resting on the small of her back, holding her to him. He raised his head and looked into the depths of her eyes, oddly pleased with the stunned acquiescence he saw there. Perhaps Meg wasn't finding it so difficult to accept his touch as she had in the past. Encouraged by the thought, he slanted his lips over hers again, renewing their intimate contact. Meg stirred within his embrace, but didn't break away. Taking that as a good sign, he deepened the kiss and was elated to hear a faint sound issuing from her throat.

Meg didn't necessarily want the interlude to end, but she sensed that Cathryn and Della had halted on the pathway and were staring at them. Sooner or later, she would have to face them, and something told her it would be easier to do it now while she still had some presence of mind left. She laid a hand upon Ransom's chest and was instantly distracted by his overwhelming warmth and the rapid tattoo of his heartbeat. She could almost believe he was as much affected by their playacting as she herself was . . .

Taking his cue from her, Ransom raised his head and smiled. "It seems we're no longer alone, my love." He gave the two startled onlookers a broad smile.

Meg blushed deeply as she met Cathryn's bemused gaze. It was apparent that her stepmother had credited the scene with all the passion they'd been pretending, and the deceit of it made Meg feel guilty indeed.

"Oh, Cathryn . . . Della," she stammered, despising the color she knew flamed in her cheeks. "I . . . I . . . may I present my . . . er, this is Ransom St. Claire."

"How do you do?" murmured Della MacSween, with undisguised interest.

Cathryn's lovely face fairly glowed. "Meg—your husband! Why didn't you tell us he was on his way to Carraig?"

"Because she didn't know," Ransom said smoothly. "I decided to surprise her." He gave Meg a wink and an affectionate hug. "As you can see, I did."

"You've managed to surprise us all," Cathryn declared. "As did Meg with the news she had married so suddenly."

"Aye, I can only imagine what a revelation that must have been."

"Well, now that I've seen the two of you together," Cathryn said, "I think I understand the situation a bit better. I'm delighted to meet you, Ransom . . . and very grateful that you've found your way into Meggie's life." She tilted her head to consider Meg. "She has run wild for far too long. A strong husband is exactly what she needs."

Silently, Meg groaned, firmly avoiding the knowing and very amused look Ransom turned upon her.

"Aye," he said in his butter-smooth West Country accent, "I couldn't agree with you more."

# Chapter Thirteen

The night was lighted by a huge bonfire that had been built on the beach by the jubilant villagers. Fifty head of stolen cattle now grazed in the meadow behind their cottages, and men and women alike were in the mood to celebrate. Even Ransom's companions, Yates and Beale, had overcome their original trepidation and were enjoying both the feast and the illicit whisky.

Meg sat on a blanket in the sand, eating a roasted potato dripping with butter and listening as her clansmen recounted tales of the reiving.

"Where did the cattle come from?" Ransom had asked, curious in spite of his chagrin at discovering his new in-laws still engaged in illegal activities.

"From the mainland, lad," Owen MacIvor shouted, with a laugh. "They belonged to the stingiest old fool to ever set foot to sod."

"Aye," broke in another man. "He was evicting the crofters from his land so he could raise cattle—"

"And now he has no cattle!" Alex's wicked glee delighted the others, and a roar of laughter went up.

"How do you know this fellow won't find his animals?" queried Ransom, reaching for another boiled crab from a platter heaped with them. "What if he tracks them here?"

"We're no amateurs, lad," MacIvor protested. "We drove the cattle into the water at the Kyle of Localsh and swam them across to Skye. Then we separated the herd and drove some one direction, some another. A few days later we met up again along the northeast coast and swam them back to Carraig. Anyone followin' us would have the Devil's own time figuring out what was takin' place."

"And even if he'd show up on Carraig," Rob MacLinn put in, "we'd simply herd the cattle into the hills. There're a dozen places to hide them."

"But it's a safe enough wager that the old man won't venture this far from home," MacIvor crowed.

Meg had to laugh at Owen MacIvor's comic arrogance, causing Ransom to give her a swift, accusing look. She knew he was still displeased with her for the lies she had told, but, to his credit, he was doing his best to create an aura of civility between them. When they had joined the others on the beach in the gathering dusk, he'd spread a blanket on the sand for them to share, and he'd refrained from making a single comment when most of the male population of the village had arrived at the *céilidh* dressed in the forbidden kilt. He'd even been guardedly cordial to her father.

Meg began to relax somewhat. Perhaps everything was going to work out after all.

A burst of feminine laughter caught her attention, drawing her gaze to the people on the other side of the fire. Her stepmother was leaning forward, stirring the contents of one of the huge kettles sitting at the edge of the embers. As Meg watched, she saw her father step up beside Cathryn to encircle her waist with a muscular arm and whisper into her ear. Cathryn's clear, slightly flustered laughter had a happy, contented sound—a sound that was abruptly stifled as Revan MacLinn stole a quick kiss.

Meg experienced a tiny stab of envy. From the time she was a child, she had been aware of the deep love and affection shared by her parents—but not until that moment had she realized how very much she wanted something like it for herself.

Meg stole a secret glance at Ransom. Even if their marriage had not been one contrived for their mutual profit, it was doubtful they could ever achieve a harmonious relationship like that of Revan and Cathryn. They were both too stubborn, they argued too much. Ransom didn't trust her, and she couldn't always afford to tell him the truth. They had dissimilar backgrounds and opposing ambitions. By the time their marriage had dragged on a year, they'd be at each other's throats . . .

Meg's eyes were drawn back to her father and stepmother. Cathryn had abandoned the cooking pot and was giving her husband her full attention, cheeks flaming prettily as he made his laughing, lurid suggestions. To Meg, the couple didn't look much different than they had fifteen years ago. At thirty-two, Cathryn was as beautiful as ever. Slender and graceful, with no sign of gray in her copper hair, she could easily be mistaken for a young girl. It was only the faint lines at the corners of her eyes that gave her away. That, and the fact that she now had a son taller than she.

Revan MacLinn had a tinge of silver at his temples and in the cropped beard he wore, but he, too, appeared far younger than his years. Life on the island among his clansmen had kept him fit, for the men worked long, hard hours at fishing, hunting, and farming, and then played with equal fervor. Mock battles kept all the males of the clan in splendid physical condition, as did the athletic games and horseraces in which they loved to indulge. As if to demonstrate his superb strength, MacLinn swept his charmingly protesting wife into his arms and imperiously called for the fiddler, so they might dance.

Meg smiled contentedly. The happiest times of her life had revolved around the music and merrymaking of the clan. Old Seamus, the fiddler, needed no coaxing to provide a lively tune for dancing. Soon the night was filled with the melody of an ancient reel and the *shushing* sound made by the sand scattered by dancing feet.

Owen MacIvor seized his plump wife Elsa and whirled her around, causing her to shriek with laughter. Looking on with delight, their seven children clapped and shouted encouragement to their incorrigible father. Meg noticed Dr. MacSween fall into step with his wife, Della, and was amazed that the short, bald man could manage to maintain his dignity even cavorting about on the beach by firelight. Della's full skirts swirled high, her white petticoats gleaming in the darkness, and her lovely face was filled with pleasure as she executed the intricate dance steps.

Meg had known these people all her life, and her affection for them was boundless. Suddenly, she found herself imagining them all at Wolfcrag, free to sing and dance as they pleased. It was a dream she'd cherished for a long, long time. And now, barring some unforseen disaster, it could soon become a reality.

Ransom stared at the woman beside him, fascinated by the play of light over her rapt features. Lost in contemplation of her clansmen, he was certain Meg had no idea how beautiful she looked. A glow from the surging flames bathed her flawless skin with pale color; it shone in her eyes and gleamed on her slightly parted lips. The warm wash of gold beckoned, silently begging for the touch of his hand.

Almost against his will, Ransom reached out and caught hold of a lock of Meg's hair that had curled around the collar of her gown. Startled, Meg met his eyes.

"Would you care to dance?" he asked, surprising even himself.

Meg lowered her eyes, unable to prevent herself from recalling the last time they had danced. Ransom had been drunk and angry, pulling her behind the draperies at the castle to command her presence in his bed. The thought of his impetuous behavior and all that had followed brought a tinge of rose to her cheeks.

She heard his low chuckle and knew Ransom had read her mind. "I'm not drunk tonight," he murmured. "I won't shame you in front of your people."

"It's not that," she protested. "I'd rather watch, that's all."

"Is it because you don't think I can do this dance?" he asked.

Meg grinned. "No . . ."

"Then what is it?"

"You've not been invited to join in," she explained.

" 'Twould be rude to do so without an invitation from our chieftain."

"And since your father wanted to carve me into fish bait, I assume that an invitation won't be forthcoming anytime soon?" A thin smile curled one corner of Ransom's mouth.

"I've told you," Meg reminded him, "you've got to prove yourself to him . . . and to the others. You're one of the enemy, remember."

"Ah, yes, so I am." Ransom tugged gently at the strand of hair he still held. "And so I'm likely to remain." He released the ringlet and let his hand fall.

"It's just as well, really," Meg observed. "If you were to join the dancing, they'd expect you to wear a kilt."

"Me?" he choked. "Wear a skirt?"

"It's not a skirt," she corrected, unsuccessfully trying to hide her amusement. "In fact, only the bravest and brawniest of men dare to don the kilt."

"Not bloody likely." Ransom's attention returned to the dancers, however, and he found himself thinking that not one of the men before him looked the least bit feminine. Especially not Meg's stalwart father, or his friend, Owen MacIvor. With arms and legs like oak trees, Owen stood in massive splendor while his pretty little wife danced all around him. Though Ransom himself would never risk being seen in woman's garb, he had to admit that the costume did nothing to lessen the masculine image of the men of Clan MacLinn.

"Since we can't dance, shall we take a stroll along the shore?" Ransom asked. "It's not my wish to sit here and watch the others grow increasingly drunk."

"Then have some whisky yourself," Meg suggested. "I don't mind."

"Maybe not, but I do. I vowed to abstain from drink tonight. And from the looks of Yates and Beale, it would be wise if I, at least, kept my senses about me."

"Afraid my family is just waiting for the chance to fall upon you and do murder?" Meg gently mocked.

"No, I'm just in the mood to see the moonlight on the sea." Ransom got to his feet and, putting out a hand, pulled Meg to hers. "Come along—'tis a wife's duty to obey her husband."

Meg stopped short, digging her slippered feet into the sand. Ransom grinned and tugged on her hand. "I was only jesting, Meg. Don't be so touchy."

Relenting, Meg let him pull her along behind him, out of the circle of firelight and into the night beyond. They walked a while through the sand, and then Ransom led her closer to the rocky edge of the water. Strewn along the curve of the bay, the rocks were worn smooth by the wash of the waves, which even now swirled over them with a soft, sibilant sound.

Ransom paused to look upward. "There isn't much moonlight after all," he commented. The pale ivory moon was shaped like a scythe and hung high in an ebony sky.

"Reivers always go out in the dark of the moon," Meg told him.

Ransom glanced down at her. "So do pirates," he said, after a few seconds. Then he grinned, and there was just enough light for her to see the white gleam of his teeth. That same illumination touched the gold hook in his ear with colorless fire.

"Why do you wear that earring?" Meg asked. "I've never seen one like it."

"There was only one other. My grandfather wore it."

"Your grandfather?"

"Yes, on my mother's side. No one seems to know why he wore it—he always claimed that he was the catch the day the Devil went fishing." Ransom chuckled quietly. "Actually, he probably just wore it to arouse curiosity. He was like that."

"You remember him, then?"

"Vaguely," Ransom replied. "I was very young when he died, but I do have a memory or two of him. He was a gigantic man, or so it seemed to me. Big and loud and bellowing." Ransom smiled at the recollection. "He had a head of wild red hair and a flowing beard to match. When he was twenty years old, he lost an eye in a duel and ever afterward wore a patch. I can still remember how frightening he was, and how much I loved being terrified by the old pirate."

"He was a pirate?"

"Aye, it seems to run in the family."

"But if your mother was the daughter of a pirate, how did she come to marry into the aristocracy?"

"Money, of course. Isn't it always that way? My father had a parcel of heavily indebted land, a manor house and, most importantly, a respectable name. Old Selwyn Channing—my grandfather—adored my mother, who was his only child, and he wanted nothing more than to see her well established in society."

"And he arranged a marriage between her and your father?" Meg questioned.

"Yes, to her sad misfortune." Ransom started walking slowly down the beach, and Meg followed.

"Why do you say that?" she asked.

"Because my father is the dullest, most unimaginative stick of a man he could possibly be. Mother was accustomed to a lively, exciting life—sailing with Grandfather, or living in their seaside home at Rogue's Run. She had no wish to be shut up in a musty manor house on the outskirts of London. She missed the sea, her family."

"But why did your grandfather arrange such a union?"

"In his defense, I suppose he couldn't foresee what a priggish bore my father would turn out to be. He knew him only as a decent but impoverished young man who was willing to share his title and his place in society for a great deal of Grandfather's ill-gotten gold. What he couldn't know was how the acquisition of that gold would change him, turn him into a selfish, grasping man with no generosity of spirit or soul."

"Your mother was unhappy, then?"

"Exceedingly. But by the time the marriage had grown intolerable, my grandfather was a very ill man. Mother kept her unhappiness from him, determined to ease his last months. She took my brother and me to Rogue's Run to visit as often as she dared . . . and we continued to go there, even after Grandfather had died and left the estate to my grandmother. Mother was always grateful that he never knew how much she hated being a St. Claire."

Meg glanced up at him, just able to make out the somber expression on his face. "What became of your mother, Ransom?"

"Oh, there was a scandal . . . as usually happens in these matters. She was a beautiful woman, and once the local gentry had surmised how unhappy she was, there were any number of gallant gentlemen willing to offer her consolation. One was more persistent than the others, but when she repeatedly refused him, he grew angry and shot her to death."

"Oh, my God!" gasped Meg. "How old were you? What did you do?"

"I was sixteen. And I set out to kill the bastard with my bare hands."

"Did you?" Meg whispered, alarmed by the fierce burn of his eyes. "Kill him, I mean."

"No." He spat out the denial as if it was distasteful. "Somehow he got word I was coming after him. He barricaded himself inside his country house and committed suicide—cheating me out of the satisfaction of killing him myself."

"Could you have done it?"

"God in heaven, yes, I could have done it!"

"But you were only a boy . . ."

"A boy who'd just discovered his mother's body, remember. The blackguard followed her into her garden and left her there to die. By the time I found her, it was too late. She bled to death in my arms, with only enough strength left to tell me her killer's name . . . and that she loved me."

"The man who . . . killed her was obviously deranged."

"That was no defense." Ransom's gaze moved back to the restless ocean. "What you don't understand, Meg, is that my mother was all I had. You grew up in a family where you were loved and wanted. The only one who ever cared anything for me was my mother. Whatever his logic, her murderer brought about the loss of everything good in my mother's life . . . and in mine."

"But surely . . . your father . . ."

"My father couldn't stand the sight of me. I was too much

like old Selwyn, and therefore a constant reminder that it was his charity we lived on. When my mother died, everything of importance was gone. And the final injustice was that I couldn't even avenge her death." He shook his head slowly. "That was the most frustrating thing of all."

"What did your father do?"

"Ah, yes . . . my father. He was properly mortified by the whole disgraceful matter, so he buried my mother and forgot her. As did everyone else in time. Everyone but me, that is."

"I'm sorry for you, Ransom. You loved your mother very much, and it must have been awful to lose her that way."

"As a lad, I couldn't imagine anything worse. With her dead, I was left completely alone. My father and brother are a great deal alike, and they had each other. There was no room for me, and I wouldn't have wanted to fit in even if I could have."

"So you became the rebellious son?" Meg mused. "Wearing that earring was just to goad your father, I take it. To remind him of all he chose to forget."

"Yes, exactly. And it worked. He despises me more every day."

"And your brother?"

"Thinks what Father tells him to think. He's merely an obedient St. Claire puppet."

Meg regarded him soberly. "Your family must have been a sad disappointment to you."

Ransom smiled. "They tell me it's the other way 'round."

"*Fuigh!* What do they know?"

Ransom's deep laughter sounded on the night air. "Can you actually be defending me, Meg?" He leaned closer. "What a wifely thing to do."

Tossing her head, Meg looked away. "It would seem the celebration is ending," she said, indicating the figures drifting away from the bonfire. Ransom's smile grew and he reached out to take Meg's hand. "Does that mean it's time to seek our bed?"

"Our . . . bed?" Meg repeated uncertainly. His devilish

expression warned her that he had some sort of mischief in mind.

"That little cottage does contain an extra one, doesn't it?" he asked, a dark eyebrow winging upward in amusement. "Or must we sleep on the beach tonight?"

"I hadn't really thought of it," Meg confessed, irritated with herself that she hadn't foreseen this dilemma. "If we were staying at the big house, there'd be plenty of extra beds."

"The big house?" Ransom asked, steering her back toward the bonfire.

"Yes, the one where we live most of the year. It's inland a few miles . . ."

"You mean that you don't always live here along the sea?"

"Heavens, no! These cottages don't offer much protection during the autumn and winter. We only come down here for the summer . . . to fish and pasture cattle."

"So what is your usual home like?" he questioned.

"There's a village with cottages that are bigger and more snug than these. And more sheltered from the winds. As chieftain, my father lives in the largest house, which has two stories and is built of stone." Meg glanced up at him. "It's quite nice, really."

"Well, it's a relief to know your clan is still able to live comfortably," Ransom remarked wryly. He felt like a fool for assuming the exiled clansmen were abiding in virtual poverty. With their talent for appropriating other people's property, he supposed there was no reason for them not to live graciously.

As they neared the fire, they encountered several couples making their way back toward the cottages.

"Here, laddie, lend us a hand," boomed Owen MacIvor when he saw them. He had two sleeping youngsters in his arms, as did his wife. Three more drowsy children trailed them.

"Oh, you poor things," crooned Meg, kneeling in front of the children. The smallest of the three, a little girl with sunny curls and a myriad of freckles, rubbed her eyes with her fists and yawned mightily. Meg laughed and scooped her up.

"Here," she said, turning to Ransom, "you take Molly and I'll see to the others."

"Me?" Ransom's eyebrows drew together in a frown as Meg gently shoved the child into his reluctant arms.

Held high against his chest, the little girl smiled sweetly. "Pretty," she said, touching his gold earring with one finger. Then she laid her head on his chest and snuggled more deeply into his arms. Ransom's gaze slewed sideways to encounter a highly amused Meg.

"I'm glad you find this so funny," he grumbled, awkwardly patting the child's back.

Meg merely grinned and, taking the other children by their hands, followed Owen and Elsa down the pathway that wound among the cottages. She had forgotten how touching it was to see a big, ferocious man so completely intimidated by the tender innocence of a child. She kept her eyes on the ground beneath her feet, hoping to hide her silly sentimentality from Ransom. If he even suspected how close she had come to admiring him in the last few moments, she knew she'd regret it. He'd find some way to mock her, or to turn the situation to her disadvantage.

At the MacIvor's cottage, the children's mother and father took charge of them again, thanking Meg and Ransom.

Young Molly stood in the doorway, a stubborn look on her round face.

"What is it, darlin'?" her father queried.

"Wanna say goodbye to the pretty man," the child announced, pointing at Ransom.

Ransom stood on the path, an expression of mild horror on his face. Meg realized that he had no idea what was expected of him.

"Kneel down and talk to her," she whispered, earning an even more horrified glance from him. Meg squared her shoulders; she had no intention of letting Molly MacIvor be disappointed.

As though he recognized the intent in Meg's demeanor, Ransom sighed and dropped to his knees. Almost immediately, the child ran to him, throwing chubby arms around his neck. "I like you," she said. "Will you come see me again?"

After a few seconds, Ransom gave a nod. "Yes," he said solemnly, "I'll come see you again."

"Promise?" Molly insisted.

"Promise."

The child hugged him again, then skipped into the cottage, looking back to wave one last farewell.

"You haven't been around children much, have you?" Meg asked idly, as she and Ransom turned down the lane toward her parents' house.

"Lord, no. I suppose it was rather apparent?"

"It was." Meg grinned. "You acted like a man with no idea of how to hold a bairn . . ."

"Perhaps I simply need practice," he suggested, and before she sensed his movement, he had slipped an arm around her waist and swung her up into his arms. Meg cried out and clutched at his shoulders.

"Put me down," she ordered, laughing in spite of herself. "What do you think you are doing?"

Without relinquishing his hold, Ransom strode along the sandy path. "Trying to improve my skills when it comes to handling children," he taunted.

"Shall I seize a handful of your fine red hair?" threatened Meg, trying to wriggle out of his firm grasp. Ransom chuckled as he shifted her weight and gained a better purchase on her knees in their casing of skirts and petticoats.

"Try it if you dare," he said softly, his green eyes aglow with wicked glee.

"I say, has Meg injured herself?" called Alex, trotting alongside them.

"No," they snapped in unison, startled by the boy's sudden approach.

"Then why can't she walk?" he asked.

"I'm perfectly capable of walking," Meg stated, giving Ransom a meaningful glare. "Ransom was just . . . just . . ."

A broad, beaming smile broke over Alex's handsome young face as he watched the Englishman set Meg on her feet. "Oh," he chortled, "I understand!"

Meg fought to control the blush she felt rising beneath her skin, but it bloomed to life anyway, coloring her cheeks with telltale rosiness. "You don't know half of what you think you do, Alexander Christian MacLinn," she snorted, brushing past him to enter her father's cottage.

"I know enough," Alex argued. "I know what people do on their honeymoon—oh, hello, Father, Mother." Alex's vehement stream of words came to an abrupt end as he stood facing the couple sitting in the candlelit kitchen.

Meg had only just begun to fathom the awkwardness of the situation. She was going to have to spend the night here in this cramped cottage in Ransom's company. With two tiny bedrooms and a kitchen, there wasn't much extra space . . . and even if she dared suggest Ransom sleep in the loft with Alex, she knew her father and stepmother would have further cause to wonder about the validity of her marriage.

Her heart trembled in her throat as she watched Ransom enter, to dwarf the room. She was trapped. She couldn't send him away; neither could she escape to quarters of her own. At least for tonight, they were going to have to share the same bed. And it would be up to her to make certain he understood that she was only allowing it in order to keep up appearances.

Aware that her father and Cathryn—not to mention the avid Alex—were staring at them, Meg cleared her throat and said, "Ransom and I are going to retire now. We'll see you tomorrow morning." She lifted one of the candles from the mantelpiece.

Cathryn smiled. "Rest well, then."

Revan MacLinn glared at them, not deigning to speak.

With remarkable aplomb, Ransom returned Cathryn's smile and, bidding everyone goodnight, crossed the room behind Meg and ducked past the bedroom doorway.

"My room is through here," she said, leading the way across the one shared by her father and stepmother and into the chamber beyond.

The room was small and square, its whitewashed walls bare except for two curtained windows, open to the cool night air. Other than a plain oak chest of drawers, the only furniture in the room was a bed covered with a bright quilt. Ransom's eyes were drawn first to the bed, then to Meg's face. Color still flared along her cheekbones, and her eyes were bright with embarrassment.

"Listen, Meg, I know that this is—"

"Shh," she quickly interrupted, speaking in a whisper. Moving closer to him, she murmured, "Unfortunately, my people can hear every word we say, so guard your tongue. The situation is humiliating enough."

Ransom regarded her somberly. "Are you saying that we have to—" he began in a normal tone.

"Whisper!" Testily, she finished the sentence for him. "Please, Ransom, let's not stand here discussing this."

He shrugged. "Fine. I'm ready to go to bed."

As he said the word *bed,* his gaze fastened on Meg's face, but she quickly turned away. She was already too aware of the offending piece of furniture and all it represented without him having to say the word aloud. She busied herself placing the candle on the dresser and shielding its flame from the breeze coming through the window.

"Go on," she whispered to Ransom. "You get into bed first."

"Very well."

She heard the rustle of cloth and peered about in time to see his lean fingers grasp the hem of his shirt and pull it over his head.

"You're undressing!"

Ransom's low laugh rumbled quietly through the room. "I don't usually sleep in my clothes, Meg."

"But . . . couldn't you . . . ?" She saw his hands drop to the waistband of his trousers. "I mean, perhaps tonight . . ."

As his pants started sliding downward, Meg whirled away and blew out the candle. The room fell into semidarkness, making her feel somewhat more comfortable. She stood still, staring at the wall in front of her.

All at once, she felt Ransom's hands on her shoulders and his voice in her ear. "Don't be afraid of me, Meg. I know you are, and I understand why." His hands slid away. "But I promise not to ever hurt you again."

Meg wondered if she could trust him. When several moments passed and she hadn't spoken, Ransom moved away, and, in a moment, she heard the creaking of the bed's rope frame.

Meg drew a deep breath and began unbuttoning her gown with unsteady fingers. She would have liked to wear her petticoats to bed, but realized how that would look should anyone come into their room. And with the lack of privacy in the little fishing cottage, that was altogether too great a possibility. Meg opened one of the drawers in the chest and took out her nightgown. She slipped it over her head and undressed beneath its ample folds. Stepping out of her gown and undergarments, she folded them and placed them neatly on the chest. Barefoot, she tiptoed toward the bed. In the dim light, Ransom's eyes appeared to be closed, but she had an odd feeling that he had been watching her only seconds before. Gingerly, she lifted the bedcovers and slipped under them, careful to keep to her side of the narrow bed.

Meg lay quietly for a while, hardly daring to breathe. After a time, the seductive softness of the feather ticking lulled her, and bit by bit, she began to relax. With as slight a movement as she could manage, she settled more deeply into the mattress, stretching out her legs. She could hear Ransom's even breathing and, from the next room, the sounds of her parents getting ready for bed.

Eventually, Meg's eyelids grew heavy and she turned her head to burrow into the pillow. There, only inches away was Ransom's face, his twinkling eyes staring directly into hers. Meg's breath caught in her throat—the only thing that prevented her from crying out. Knowing he had alarmed her, Ransom smiled and slid closer, until his head was nearly on her pillow. Meg's eyes widened as the bed's rope frame creaked faintly.

"I didn't mean to startle you," he said in a solicitous whisper.

"You didn't," she whispered back.

"Good."

His smile gentled and, with unerring accuracy, he moved to place his mouth upon hers. His lips barely touched hers, softly caressing in what she feared was a prelude to something more ardent. The kiss was warmly pleasant, however, luring Meg's thoughts away from prudence. It wasn't until Ransom put a hand on her shoulder that she drew back, causing the bed to squeak again.

Meg squeezed her eyes shut and murmured, "Don't move—it makes too much noise."

"I didn't move, Meg. You did."

She opened her eyes and saw the deviltry glinting in his. "Just go to sleep," she responded through clenched teeth.

"But I'm not sleepy." He leaned closer, so that his mouth was only a fraction of an inch from her ear. His breath, moist and heated, brushed against her skin and stirred her hair.

"You were the one who wanted to go to bed," she reminded him, putting her own mouth next to his ear.

"But I didn't say anything about going to sleep."

Exasperated, Meg lowered her head to her pillow once more, and Ransom began grazing her jawbone with his mouth, teasing the flesh with slow, nibbling kisses.

Meg fought for composure, breathing deeply. He was making it difficult for her to concentrate on her wish to be left alone. If only he didn't have a way of doing things she'd never before experienced—things that slightly shocked yet somehow tempted her.

"Ransom, please," she objected.

"Meg, listen to me," he commanded in a whisper. His deep, rasping voice was channeled into her ear, sending shivers coursing through her. "I know I hurt you before . . . but let me show you what it can be like."

"No!" Her answering whisper exploded in the silent room, horrifying her with the sudden rush of quiet noise. She prayed that neither her father or Cathryn had heard the protest.

"Don't be afraid . . ."

Ransom kissed her again, and this time his tongue nudged

at the seam of her lips. To Meg's disgust, her resistance faded easily, and she found herself parting her lips in some kind of instinctive invitation. Ransom lost no time in accepting her compliance and urged the kiss deeper.

Realizing she would have to put a stop to his outrageous onslaught immediately or be lost, Meg insinuated her hands between them and shoved at his chest with all her strength. Ransom's head came up and he gripped her shoulders, a look of determination on his face.

"We can't do this," Meg hissed. "Someone will hear."

"No one will hear," he assured her in a barely audible tone. "I can be very, very quiet when necessary."

"Ransom . . ."

Meg gasped as he shifted closer to her, one lean, naked leg sliding along hers to rest on her hips. Her nightgown had been pulled upward with the movement of his leg, and now she could feel his warm, furred flesh against her bare thighs. The heat of his body beckoned and enticed her, and Meg fought the desire to snuggle closer to him. She was torn between her newly kindled curiosity about the man and her need to assert her authority and make him behave honorably.

"You can't ravish me in my own parents' house," she frantically pointed out. "I could scream . . ."

"I'm not going to ravish you," he whispered against her mouth. "And even if I were, you're lying about screaming." His lips brushed hers with brazen intent. "You cringe each time the bed creaks," he observed. "Why do you think I'd believe your threat to scream?"

"You're hateful," Meg mumbled, but her words were cut short as his hand moved downward to cup a breast. Gently, he spread his fingers over the rounded flesh, laying claim to it. That audacity had barely registered with her when his thumb began kneading her instantly taut nipple.

"Ransom," she moaned. "Ran . . . oh! Oh, Lord . . . stop that!"

With a faint chuckle, he continued tormenting her, letting his fingers wander to the buttons at the neck of her nightgown. Muttering, she struggled, ineffectually batting at his hand as he deftly slipped the buttons from their fasteners. As the thin cotton fell away, she could feel the intriguing roughness of his arm against her chest. She opened her mouth to make a feeble complaint, but he stilled her words with another kiss.

Meg closed her eyes again, seduced by the firmness of his lips, by their undeniable mastery. He had so easily taken control of the situation; she had so quickly granted him that power over her. She could tell herself that she didn't want to create a scene by calling out to her father, but even in her current confused state, she was well aware that it was fascination with what Ransom was doing that kept her silent. Bemused, she felt his mouth leave hers to scatter tiny, random kisses along her temple, down the side of her face, and into the hollow of her throat. She wondered if he could hear the pounding of her heart . . .

"Meg," he murmured, raising his head to look into her eyes.

"Mmmm?"

"You're so lovely. Your skin is like silk . . ."

It dawned on her that he was staring down at her breasts, bared by the opened nightgown. Belatedly shamed by her acquiescence, Meg seized the edges of the garment in an attempt to cover herself. Calmly, Ransom gathered both her hands into one of his and held them.

"You're not afraid of me, are you?" he queried softly. "You're just being difficult now."

"I am not!"

Meg tried to flounce away from his hold, and the bed creaked ominously. Ransom grinned and bent close to her ear. "Behave yourself, Meg, or your parents will think something untoward is happening in here."

She glared at him, but stopped struggling. "Will you please release me?" she whispered.

"Not just yet," he replied, and Meg was dismayed by the dark look of intent that came into his sea-colored eyes. Slowly, deliberately, he raised her arms above her head and, with a sudden swift motion, shifted his body until it was half covering hers. Then, with a look that licked over her skin like flame, he lowered his head and placed a burning kiss on first one breast, then the other. When his lips parted and he took one nipple into his mouth, Meg's body arched upward, causing the ropes to emit a short, sharp protest. But Meg never heard it, for the sweet, tugging pressure of his mouth against her breast brought such a rush of blood to her head that her ears roared with it. Her heart thundered in her chest, threatening to burst forth from her body.

Her outraged denouncement of him died in her throat as she collapsed weakly against the pillow and surrendered to the strange magic he was working. Never had she felt pleasure that was so intense it was almost pain; never had she known that she could be so sensitive to a man's touch.

Without her realizing it, Ransom had released her hands, and now they crept downward to grasp his head, her fingers lacing through his thick, auburn hair. Her dilemma was such that she meant to push him away, but she ended up merely drawing him closer.

Ransom's hand drifted beneath the bedcovers to grip the hem of Meg's gown. Slipping past the thin cotton barrier, he stroked one bare leg, from the slender length of thigh to the rounded hip. His palm caressed the delicate curvature of her ribs, then the flatness of her stomach, moving ever lower until his fingers tangled in the curls below. When his hand encompassed the very heart of her being, Meg moaned and moved against him, her hands clutching his shoulders. Satisfied that she was finished with fighting him, Ransom nuzzled her mouth with a tender kiss, then put his lips to her ear once more.

"You'll like this, Meg . . . I promise." And his fingers began a tentative exploration that, bit by bit, became a rhythmic motion that brought new fire to her body.

Meg bit her lip, completely helpless against the sweet agony he wrought. All shame and trepidation was lost in the maelstrom of surging desire he was bringing to life within her.

"I didn't know," she gasped, her breath coming in quick,

hard pants. "I didn't expect . . . oh, God! Ransom, what are you doing to me?"

"I want you to know what it means to feel desire—to be burned alive by passion. 'Tis a wondrous feeling, Meg . . ."

Sudden, sweet explosions began to jolt her body and she clung to him, helpless against the strength of the climax that shook her. Sobs of bewildered joy were wrenched from her throat, and Ransom held her tightly, smothering her cries against his chest. He pressed a kiss to her forehead, where her hair curled damply, then tipped her chin upward to bestow a long, slow kiss.

"See? Wasn't that nice?" he asked teasingly.

Meg glanced up at him with a shy smile. "Aye—it was very nice," she affirmed.

Ransom smiled in return. "And there's so much more that I intend to show you."

Meg's gaze faltered as she digested his words. She was suddenly unable to face his triumphant expression, the slumberous look in his eyes. Her wanton response to his daring touch baffled and frightened her . . . and she had only just begun to wonder how the night's events were going to change their situation. How on earth, after the way she had acted, could she ever again expect him to treat their marriage as a matter of simple business?

# Chapter Fourteen

Ransom awoke the next morning with the conviction that he couldn't spend another night like the one he had just endured. He vowed to do whatever was necessary to get himself and Meg away from Carraig without further delay. He couldn't tolerate sleeping under the MacLinn roof one more time, with a nervous Meg half-afraid to speak or move. No, he wanted the privacy that his own quarters at Wolfcrag would offer. He wanted to be alone with his wife to continue the lesson in passion he had begun the night before.

Ransom had held Meg until she'd fallen asleep, even though he'd been tormented by her nearness. Determined not to overstep the boundaries he'd set for himself, he had lain awake, hands and teeth clenched against the frustrations building within him. He'd hurt and frightened her once before; he wouldn't do it again. When, in the early morning hours, he'd finally drifted off to sleep, it had been to dream of waking to a drowsily tousled Meg, her skin warmly flushed, her arms shyly welcoming. Instead, the next morning he had awakened to find her gone and himself the sole occupant of the feather bed. Her sweet, heathery scent clung to the pillows . . . and to his own flesh. For a few moments he was content to lie quietly, recalling Meg's unexpected abandon the night before. But soon the memories of slow, drugging kisses, and the feel of her increasingly willing body next to his, became too arousing. While lodged in the bosom of her family, there was no way he could do the things he wanted to do, and so it was necessary to divert his mind. He must keep busy, must think of other things—until they were once more alone.

The smell of food and the rattle of crockery told him the family had already gathered for breakfast, and, experiencing a strong urge to see Meg again, Ransom got out of bed and pulled on his clothes. The sooner they left the village, the sooner they would be back at Wolfcrag.

"Good morning, Ransom," Cathryn MacLinn said when he entered the cottage's main room. "Did you sleep well?"

Ransom's eyes sought Meg, but she turned away, busily stirring something in a kettle slung over the slow-burning fire. "Yes, I slept well enough," he replied, adding a belated, "Thank you."

"Sit down and have something to eat," the woman invited. "We've ham and bannocks . . . and porridge."

As Ransom seated himself in one of the wooden chairs, Meg's younger brother vacated his. "Mother," he said, "I'm finished. Do you mind if I go now?"

"Go where?" Cathryn queried, as she sliced ham.

"To the meadow behind the village." Alex tilted his head and gave his mother a winning smile. "We're practicing our swordplay this morning."

"Swordplay?" Cathryn's accusing gaze swiveled toward the fireplace, where her husband sat mending a fishing net. "What sort of nonsense is this?"

"It's not nonsense," Alex protested. "If I don't improve my skill, how am I going to take on the cursed English?" He frowned. "Oh . . . pardon, Ransom. I didn't mean you."

Ransom nodded and accepted his breakfast from Cathryn. He was too concerned over Meg's refusal to acknowledge his presence to take offense at the boy's declaration.

"And just exactly whom did you mean?" Cathryn asked, her hands going to her aproned waist.

"I meant those bas . . . uh, those blackguards back in Scotland. The ones who are driving our people from their homes." Alex cast an anxious glance at his father.

"What business do you have worrying about such matters?" Cathryn asked. "Revan, do you care to explain what is going on?"

Revan MacLinn raised amber eyes to his wife's face. " 'Tis nothing, love. Just boys' play."

"Do you think I'm daft?" she blazed. "Boys don't play with swords. Yesterday they practiced their riding, the day before that it was archery. You're making plans to do battle, aren't you?"

"Now, Cathryn," soothed her husband. "It won't come to that."

"No," she agreed, "it won't. Not with my son. I won't allow it!"

Ransom ate slowly, his gaze bouncing back and forth between the red-haired woman whose anger burned like a flame and the giant, black-bearded man whose quiet answers fell like stones into a bottomless pool. Meg was washing dishes, her back still firmly turned upon him. The pleasant mood of the *céilidh* was well and truly gone.

"Can I go, Mother?" Alex persisted, impatiently stepping from foot to foot. "The fellows are waiting . . ."

"No," Cathryn said.

"Go ahead, son," Revan MacLinn interrupted, "but be careful to see that no one gets hurt in your skirmishes."

"Yes, sir!"

When the boy had gone, Ransom dared a quick look at Cathryn. The stunned expression on her face was enough to tell him that her wrath was about to burn out of control. He wondered how MacLinn could sit there so calmly.

"How dare you ignore my wishes like that," stormed Cathryn, untying her apron and flinging it in her husband's face. "Alexander is my son, Revan, and you have no business letting him court danger for such a silly cause!"

"Silly?" roared MacLinn, slowly rising to his feet. The top of his head nearly brushed the ceiling, but Cathryn didn't back away. She stood her ground, head held high.

"Listen to me, woman," MacLinn continued. "Alex is my son, too, and I won't have him mollycoddled any longer. Do ye want him to grow up a milksop, hanging on his mother's skirts?"

"Yes, if it keeps him from getting himself killed."

"When I was his age, I'd already fought in battles, Cathryn. Hellfire, I wasn't much older than Alex when I took over as chieftain of my clan."

"Those were the old days," Cathryn snapped. "Things are different now."

"How different do ye think they are when landlords can still turn families out of their homes for the sake of a few pounds sterling? When one man's cattle are deemed more valuable than another man's children?"

"This is not my son's fight."

"Is he a MacLinn?"

"Surely you cannot doubt that?"

"Then it is his fight, Cathryn, whether you like it or not." His tone softened. "This may come to nothing, love. But if there is trouble, mayhap knowing something about weaponry will keep Alex from getting killed."

Cathryn's face was chalk white, her eyes burning with indignation. "You do what you want about your damned landlords and their cursed cattle, Revan, and your silly playing at war. But leave my son out of it. If you dare disregard my wishes in this matter, I swear I'll do everything in my power to stop you."

"And just what is it you think you can do?" he countered, the beginning of a smile tugging at his mouth.

Cathryn glared at him. "You'll find out in good time, I assure you." With that darkly intoned statement, she brushed past him and stepped through the front door. "I'm going to see Della," she said, the words tossed over her shoulder.

Revan MacLinn's smile died abruptly, and, dashing to the floor the fishnet he held, he whirled and stomped out of the cottage, heading in the opposite direction from his wife. Ransom, fork arrested halfway to his mouth, stared after the man. The kitchen seemed to ring with the echo of the couple's angry quarrel.

Suddenly, he realized Meg was staring at him, a stricken look on her face.

"Are you all right?" he asked, rising from the table.

"I've never heard the two of them argue before," she murmured, disbelief etched on her features.

"Husbands and wives do it all the time, so I've heard."

Ransom's attempt at humor only earned him a fleeting glance and a slight frown.

"Father won't call off the battle play," she said, as if talking to herself. "After what I told him about the situation at Wolfcrag, he'll be more determined than ever that the lads know how to defend themselves."

"Meg," Ransom began. "Maybe you should—"

"Maybe I should try talking to Cathryn," she muttered in a half-audible tone. She started for the doorway, but Ransom stepped in front of her.

Meg stopped, looking at him in surprise, as if startled to find him still there. "It's really all my fault," she said distractedly, slipping past him and disappearing through the door.

"I'll be damned," Ransom swore softly. "It was bad enough when she wouldn't look at me. But to look and not even see me is a worse insult yet."

Ransom St. Claire found himself quite displeased by his new wife's conspicuous neglect. Wrathfully, he kicked his chair across the room and went in search of his men without finishing his meal.

Meg made no objection to Ransom's plan to leave for the mainland, although she was still upset over the quarrel she had witnessed between her father and stepmother. She worried over it, even as she packed a trunk with her belongings.

"It's hopeless—neither of them will listen to me," she said. "They've always gotten on so well together that I can't remember ever hearing them speak harsh words to each other. I thought Cathryn's only regret was that she never had other children after Alex . . ."

"Perhaps that's why she's so protective of the lad," Ransom

commented. "But whatever the reason, she'll forget about it once she sees your father doesn't really intend to go to war."

Meg slammed the trunk lid and began fastening the hasps, uncertain how to respond to her husband's blithe statement. In her opinion, it was altogether likely that her father did intend to do battle on behalf of his beleaguered clansmen at Wolfcrag.

"I just hate to leave them while they're so angry with each other," she finally said.

"I shouldn't think their anger would last long," Ransom ventured. "It must be a natural state between married people."

Meg glanced up. "What do you mean?"

"Well, consider us." He put both hands on his hips and gave her a long, studying look. "Only last night we were getting along so well, and then this morning you'd barely look at me. Or speak."

Meg turned away to take her cloak from the chest of drawers. "I . . . I, uh, don't know what you mean."

"Come now, Meg. Of course you do."

"No . . ."

"Is this how it's always going to be?" he asked. "Each time we make progress in getting to know each other, you draw back."

"Getting to know each other?" Her incredulous words burst forth before she could contain them. "Is that what you call it?"

"Meg, listen to me. There was nothing wrong with what happened last night." Ransom reached for her, but she quickly retreated from his touch.

"I think you should ask Yates and Beale to load my trunk into the boat now," she said. "I'll just go say goodbye to my grandmother."

With that, she darted past him and out of the room, leaving Ransom with the impression that abruptly departing in the middle of conversations with him was getting to be an intolerable habit with his wife.

* * *

Meg said farewell separately to her father and Cathryn, with neither of them agreeing on any sort of compromise. Cathryn remained the stubborn mother hen, and Revan MacLinn wouldn't discuss the matter at all, asking only that Meg keep him informed of events at Wolfcrag. Stomping her feet in angry frustration, Meg was about to start a tirade of her own when, unexpectedly, Ransom swept her into his arms, strode across the sand, and unceremoniously deposited her in the waiting boat.

"What are you doing?" she cried. "What ails you, Englishman?"

"You," was his terse reply. "We don't have time to stand about chatting."

"I wasn't chatting. I was attempting to reconcile my parents."

"They got together without you in the beginning—they can do it again. Besides, it might behoove you to see to your own marriage."

"What do you mean by that?"

"I've decided not to tolerate your evasion any longer. Last night proved that you don't really despise or fear me any more."

"Last night proved nothing," she insisted. "Only that you can overpower me with your . . . your boorishness."

Ransom grinned, resting both hands on the gunwale and leaning toward her. "I may have overpowered you," he said intimately, "but it was not with boorishness. And I will confirm that this evening when we are alone."

Meg fumed. "You'll not touch me!"

"You're my wife," he growled. "I'll touch you whenever I please."

A low burst of embarrassed laughter caught their attention and they turned to see Yates and Beale standing by. Ignoring them, Ransom looked back at Meg. "Now, call your hound," he ordered, "and let's set sail."

Irritated by the vapid grins on the faces of Ransom's men, Meg gave them a glare and uttered, *"Ciod e tha cur ort?"*

She chuckled as Yates and Beale nearly fell over each other in their rush to back away from her. It was apparent they still weren't certain that she wasn't a witch.

Her amusement faded and she sighed. If only she were a witch—the first thing she'd do would be to turn Ransom St. Claire into the rutting swine he so obviously was!

Hours later, Meg was still taking refuge in her righteous indignation. Ransom's thinly veiled threat on the beach brought to mind the scene that had taken place in her bedroom the night before. And each time she remembered her unrestrained reaction to his amorous advances, she found her self-pride smarting. How could she have been so . . . so immodest? So wanton?

Meg huddled deeper into her cloak, fearing Ransom would detect the bloom of color in her face and accurately discern the direction her thoughts were taking. It seemed he'd hardly taken his eyes off her since their journey back to Wolfcrag had begun. Avoiding his probing gaze, she bent to pet King, who lay sleeping at her feet.

Unlike Meg and Rob, the Englishmen had come directly to Carraig by crossing the Inner Sound, eliminating the need for traveling overland; they followed the same route for the return trip. Although it had been chilly on the open water, the winds were mild, barely stirring the ocean. And now, in the late afternoon, as they neared the Scottish shore, the island-studded water ahead of them looked peaceful and welcoming.

Meg stole a covert glance at Ransom, who was positioned in the helm of the boat. He seemed so at home there, surrounded by the sea. The careless breeze tumbled his auburn hair low across his forehead and stirred the flared tails of the jacket he wore. Meg's eyes dropped to his sturdy boots, planted firmly against the bottom of the boat, then traveled upward, along leanly muscled legs and narrow hips. Her gaze lingered on his hands as they gripped the tiller. Strong and brown, they were undoubtedly capable of guiding the small boat through the seemingly endless miles of water. Just as they had been unerringly capable of leading her to an almost frightening ecstasy the night before.

Meg's throat went dry with humiliation at the recollection of her moans and soft, mindless cries of passion. How could she have allowed herself to behave like that? Writhing against Ransom, all but begging him to take her? She had kissed him with an abandon she'd never dreamed existed within her.

She shook her head in despair over her actions and mentally reproached herself. She couldn't ever permit such a thing to happen again. Common sense told her that if she and Ransom continued to engage in such seductive pleasures, she could lose sight of her original purpose. It would be too tempting to immerse herself completely in the bold Englishman, too easy to actually begin caring for him. And that would never do. They had a bargain, and in order to see that it was not compromised, it must be the only thing they shared. There was no room for emotion or passion or tender feelings in a business arrangement, and the instant they set foot on the mainland shore, she intended to call a halt to any idea Ransom had of making love to her.

It would be difficult, she acknowledged, as her eyes drifted upward, past his square, broad shoulders and sinewy throat to his face, where her gaze lingered along his rugged jaw. Despite her anger at him, he was a man who inspired exciting and highly decadent thoughts—she would have to be careful.

When the focus of her attention shifted to include his entire face, Meg became aware that Ransom was returning her stare, his green eyes amused. Stunned by her lack of sophistication in dealing with him, she turned her back and pretended interest in the colony of gray seals sunning themselves on one of the rockier islands they were passing.

*Good Lord,* she fumed silently, *how can I ever hope to control Ransom when I can't even seem to manage myself?*

"I see the wagonloads of goods have arrived from Inverness," Ransom said as Fletcher led him and Meg into the courtyard. Absentmindedly, he scratched the ears of the black cat he carried.

"And the cottages are nearly all thatched!" Meg exclaimed.

"And inhabited," Fletcher proudly added.

"Inhabited?" queried Ransom. "By whom?"

"The workmen and their families—the thatchers themselves. And, of course, young Mairi and her sons are living in one." Fletcher looked somewhat defensive. "A lass with small children needs some privacy, you know."

"I won't argue that," Ransom drawled, "but what I don't know is, who the hell is Mairi?"

"The kitchen girl," Fletcher explained. "I'm certain I mentioned her to you."

"Surely you remember," Meg prompted. "She's the woman we found in the deserted village."

"Ah." Ransom swiveled about to give her a hard stare. "One of your 'witnesses,' as I recall. But I thought we brought her here to have a meal. I didn't know we were going to provide employment for her."

"It isn't charity, you know," Meg argued. "Mairi is a good cook and a hard worker. And Fletcher can use the help—he has far too much to do."

"Granted. But what about the others? Why must we house the thatchers? Their work is done."

"Not necessarily, lad," broke in the first mate. "They are carpenters, as well . . . and they can lend the stonemasons a hand. Besides, they have no place else to go. Since you've been gone, the evictions have increased."

"Ransom," Meg cried, "you've got to do something to stop that horrible man before someone gets killed. You promised you'd talk to him."

"I've hardly had time these last weeks, have I?"

"Perhaps not. But you'll have time now."

Fletcher interceded. "Not to worry, lass. I think Ran will have his audience with Jonathan Spottiswoode one way or the other."

"What's that supposed to mean?" asked Ransom.

"He was here the other day lookin' for you. Seems he had some sort of trouble he wanted to discuss."

"And?"

"And he left a man here to send word the minute you arrived back at Wolfcrag. It's my guess that our disgruntled neighbor will be appearing soon."

"Damnation," swore Ransom. "What I really want is a hot meal and my bed . . ." He cast a swift look at Meg. " 'Twill be just my luck to have to deal with Spottiswoode tonight. God, I wonder what kind of trouble he's had . . . and why he thinks I can do anything about it."

"I . . . uh, believe I'll have Yates and Beale carry my trunk on upstairs," Meg said. "I'd enjoy a bath before the evening meal."

"Fine. I'm going to have a word or two with some of the workers you and Fletcher saw fit to hire."

"You can't unhire them," she protested.

Ransom looked impatient. "No, I suppose not. But promise me you'll not employ anyone else without my approval. There's a limit to the gold we can spend, you know."

"I understand." Turning away, Meg addressed Fletcher. "Could I speak with you for a moment? There's something I'd like to ask about."

"Ah, yes," Fletcher responded. "That little matter we discussed before you left, if I'm correct."

"You are."

"I'm pleased to tell you that everything is in order, Your Ladyship."

They exchanged a knowing smile.

"The two of them are enough to make a man's blood run cold," Ransom, walking away, muttered to his cat.

Jonathan Spottiswoode made a timely appearance just as Fletcher and Mairi were setting dinner on the table. Feeling obliged to do so, Ransom invited him to stay and share the meal.

"Why, I'd be delighted, Your Lordship," announced Spottiswoode, spreading his coattails and seating himself before the fire. "We have much to discuss."

"So I understand."

Spottiswoode took the glass of wine Ransom offered and raised it. "But first, shall we drink to the success of your recent marriage?"

"Very well."

When both men had sampled the wine, Spottiswoode remarked, "I must say, I was astonished to learn you had taken the outlaw's daughter as your wife."

"It came as something of a surprise to me," Ransom admitted, turning to stare into the fire. "We had not known each other long."

"I shouldn't think so. The MacLinns haven't been seen in the area for a number of years. It struck me as rather odd that the lass should make an appearance now."

"A matter of coincidence," Ransom assured him. "Nothing more."

Idly, Ransom kicked at a log that had rolled onto the hearth. He was contemplating the best way to bring up the subject of Spottiswoode's mistreatment of his tenants. No doubt the man would not take kindly to interference, and it seemed imprudent to make an enemy of his closest neighbor from the outset. Tact was his best weapon.

He heard Spottiswoode's sharp gasp behind him and pivoted about to find his guest transfixed, gaping at Meg as she came down the stairway.

"My God," Spottiswoode quietly exclaimed, "she's beautiful. Now I understand your reasoning, St. Claire."

Irritated by the arrogant statement, Ransom studied his wife as she made her way toward them. She was, he had to agree, looking incredibly lovely. A tiny smile tugged at his mouth as he reflected she'd probably had no intention of making such a dramatic entrance. It was obvious to him that she'd chosen the plainest gown in her wardrobe, and that her hair had been dressed in the simplest of styles. But simplicity suited her. The gown, high-necked and unadorned, was a perfect color for Meg. It was the exact rose-violet shade of the heather that grew in hidden, misty glens. Her eyes, too, reminded him of the mist, silver and mysterious . . . with a hint of danger. Having seen the stranger, she had surmised his identity and was prepared to do battle.

Meg's hair had been drawn back severely, fastened at the nape of her neck with a large gold clip, but wayward tendrils had already worked their way loose, to curl about her face and neck with winsome irreverence. The instant she set foot on the main floor, Meg came to a halt and drew herself up to her fullest height. As Spottiswoode approached her, she angled her head slightly, but did not offer him her hand.

"Meg," Ransom spoke up. "This is our neighbor, Jonathan Spottiswoode. Sir, may I present my wife, Meg St. Claire?"

"I'm so pleased to make your acquaintance, Your Ladyship," Spottiswoode stated. "You're a charming sight for this provincial setting."

Meg's smile was cool. "I understand, Mr. Spottiswoode," she returned, "that you are inclined to evict your tenants from their homes."

*So much for tact,* thought Ransom. *I should have known Meg wouldn't mince words.*

He saw an immediate need for a distraction of some sort. "Uh . . . dearest," he crooned through clenched teeth, "Mairi is waiting to serve our dinner. Let's be seated, shall we?"

With a firm grip on her arm, he steered her toward the table, relieved that she allowed him to do so without a struggle.

Though he looked somewhat disconcerted, Spottiswoode continued his blatant scrutiny of Meg, making no effort to hide the fact that he was pleased with what he observed. Thinking the fellow presumptuous, Ransom was half tempted to sit back and let her verbally chop him to bits.

There was no subtlety about Spottiswoode—not in looks or actions. He was tall, rawboned and rather awkward, with a shock of coarse black hair, a long, equine face, and large features. He could not be termed handsome, and yet there was a certain intriguing quality about his appearance. His eyes were dark and unabashedly bold; his full lips suggested a frankly sensual nature. He was, Ransom suspected, the type of wealthy, powerful man women often found attractive, especially those who could overlook his moral shortcomings.

Mairi was silently efficient as she moved about the table, serving baked grouse. As soon as she was gone, Ransom tried to turn the conversation away from the evictions, but Meg would have no part of it.

"I'm truly interested in your reason for ousting those people from their homes," she persisted.

Spottiswoode smiled faintly, dabbing at his mouth with a napkin. "Madam, I assure you, the loss of those cottages could not be a burden to anyone. Most of them are in a sad state of disrepair, some on the verge of falling down."

"As the landowner, is it not your duty to repair those homes and make them livable?"

"Nay, not when there is no profit to be gained by doing so. I'm a progressive man, Lady St. Claire—I look to the future. And the future of Scotland is in cattle and sheep."

"And its people?" Meg questioned. "What about them?"

"The day is coming when there will only be room for productive citizens. As I see it, it will be good for some of these ne'er-do-wells to be forced out into the world to earn their keep."

"The local people work hard," objected Meg. "How can you insinuate otherwise?"

"As a landlord, I may be in a somewhat better position than you to judge the worthiness of my tenants, wouldn't you say?"

"No, I don't—" Meg began, only to be interrupted by Ransom, who spared her a warning glance.

"Meg, I'm sure that Mr. Spottiswoode has taken note of your . . . uh, our . . . objections to his policy of eviction. Perhaps we can arrange a time when we might all sit down and discuss the matter in a reasonable fashion. However, this evening, I believe he has come here to discuss another matter."

Meg frowned at him, but did not speak, taking up her fork again instead. She speared the grouse as violently as if it were Spottiswoode's heart.

"Aye," confirmed Spottiswoode, "a serious matter indeed."

Relieved that Meg offered no further obstacle to the conversation, Ransom leaned back in his chair. "How serious?" he asked, lifting his wineglass to his lips.

Spottiswoode bared his long teeth in a cold smile. "To my way of reckoning, very serious. Just this past week I had over fifty head of cows and calves stolen from my property. I thought you might know something of it."

Ransom choked on his wine and fumbled clumsily for his napkin. Above the square of linen, his accusing eyes met Meg's infinitely innocent ones.

"Cattle? Stolen?" he sputtered. "Why would I know anything of it?"

"No reason, other than you're my nearest neighbor," Spottiswoode rejoined. "Unfortunately, it seems there is little information to be had. My herdsmen tell me the animals were driven off by a ragged band of men, none of whom they recognized. Scotsmen, to be sure . . . possibly from the islands."

"From the islands?" echoed Ransom. "What makes you say that?"

"The sheriff tracked the stolen herd to the Kyle of Localsh, where it appears the cattle were driven into the water. It seems logical the only reason for an action of that sort is if the thieves were from Skye or one of the other islands."

"But perhaps it was a trick," Ransom halfheartedly suggested. "A ploy to throw the law off the track."

Spottiswoode skillfully severed a leg from the grouse on the plate in front of him. "With all deference to your lovely wife, I must admit that my first thought was of the MacLinns. Rumor has it that ill-fated clan now resides among the islands across the sound. And naturally, when I learned that MacLinn's daughter had returned to marry the new laird of the castle, well . . . you can imagine my suspicions."

"I don't believe I care for your insinuation, Spottiswoode," Ransom spoke up. "You are speaking of my wife, after all."

Spottiswoode seized the grouse leg and waved it airily. "Ah, but you didn't permit me to finish. I was about to mention that all that took place before I discovered that your new bride was such a . . . proper and, may I say, engaging lady."

"Well," Ransom affirmed, "neither Meg nor I know anything about the matter."

"I really can't imagine why you'd ever suppose my clansmen would have nothing better to do than travel such a distance to steal your cattle," Meg mused aloud.

"Other than the fact the animals are of valuable lineage?" asked Spottiswoode. "Well, I inferred that it was a means of harassing me."

"Why would anyone wish to harass you, Mr. Spottiswoode?" Meg sweetly inquired.

"Of course, you're right," he declared. "What reason could there possibly be for anyone to wish harm to a man who is simply minding his own affairs? I must have been misguided in my thinking. Well, perchance the culprits will be found out soon enough."

"I'm sure of it," Ransom said testily. "Now, sir, can I interest you in a slice of Fletcher's fruitcake? There's none to compare . . ."

The evening dragged on for an eternity before Spottiswoode finally made his departure.

"I shall look forward to your company again soon," he murmured, unexpectedly seizing Meg's hand and drawing it to his mouth. As his fleshy lips touched her skin, Ransom found himself wanting to boot his neighbor out the door and all the way across the drawbridge. It gave him only minor satisfaction that Meg, as soon as her hand was released, made no effort to hide her distaste, hastily wiping the back of it against her skirts.

"That man is a rodent," Ransom snarled, once the door had closed after their retreating guest.

Meg shuddered. "I won't entertain him in this castle again."

"Nor would I ask you to. He seemed altogether too smitten by your charms." Ransom stepped closer to her, letting his hand slide caressingly from her shoulder to her elbow. "Understandable as that might be."

Meg drew back. "I'm going up to prepare for bed now," she announced.

"We have had an exceedingly long day."

Ransom watched as she climbed the first steps.

"Meg," he said suddenly, "why didn't you tell me the cattle your father stole came from Wolfcrag?"

"Perhaps I didn't know."

"And perhaps you did—but you thought I might appear more innocent if I didn't."

"Perhaps." Meg tilted her dark head and favored him with a bland look. "Good night, Ransom."

Ransom forced himself to sit by the fire and drink a glass of brandy before following his wife to bed. It took every ounce of patience he had to linger there, all the while vividly imagining her undressing and brushing out her hair. Finally, unable to restrain himself a moment longer, he set the brandy snifter aside and ran up the stairs, taking them two at a time. He had waited a long time for this night.

His bedchamber was in darkness except for a small fire on the hearth. Too eager to bother with lighting a candle, Ransom stripped off his shirt and strode toward the bed.

"Meg?" he whispered. "You're not asleep, are you?"

As his eyes grew accustomed to the darkness, he could see that although the bed was neatly turned back, it was empty. He whirled about to search the dim corners of the room. Meg was nowhere to be seen.

An angry growl erupted from Ransom's throat as he flung himself from the room and down the corridor. Pausing outside the chamber where Meg had slept before the journey to Carraig, he tried the door and found it locked. Fighting the anger that boiled up within him, he shouted her name.

"Meg, are you in there?" He pounded on the door with a hard fist. "By God, you'd better answer if you are!"

King barked twice, and then Meg's voice reached Ransom's ears, sounding calm and assured. "I've retired for the night, Ransom. What is it you want?"

"You know damned good and well what I want," he roared. "Now, open this door."

"I'm sorry, but I can't do that."

"You *can't?*"

"All right, I won't. I prefer to sleep here, if you don't mind," she said. "Alone."

"I do mind!" He heaved a gusty sigh. "I thought we had settled all this."

"We did." There was a long pause. "We settled it the day we got married. This union is for our mutual benefit, nothing else."

"And don't you think sharing a bed could be for our mutual benefit?"

"Ransom! Keep your voice down. Do you want everyone in the castle to hear you?"

"I don't give a damn if they do. Now, Meg, listen to me. I'm tired and I want to go to bed."

"That's a good idea . . ."

"Then open the door."

"No."

"Why are you being so obstinate, Meg? Do you want me to beg? Do you want me on my knees? Is that it?"

"No, I just want to be left alone."

"And I want to see your face when you say that."

"Go away, Ransom. Please."

"Meg, I swear, if you don't open this door right now, I'll kick it in."

"You can't—Fletcher has fitted it with a bolt lock."

"Oh, so that was the little secret the two of you shared? I should have known he'd aid you in badgering me . . ."

"I'm not trying to badger you."

"Then open this door!"

"Ransom, be reasonable. There's nothing to be gained by this."

"I beg to differ. Now, either open the door or stand back, because I intend to come in, one way or the other."

"Go away!"

Backing across the hallway, Ransom got a running start, hurling his entire body against the heavy door. The door shuddered and groaned, Meg uttered a small cry of alarm, and her hound began barking excitedly. Jaws clenched in determination, Ransom retreated and made a second effort. Beneath his shoulder, the wood cracked and splintered.

"Stop this foolishness before you get hurt," Meg implored. "Can't you just adhere to my wishes and leave me alone?"

"I've considered your wishes since the night we were married, Meg," he panted, resting against the doorframe. "I've done everything I knew to make amends for my behavior—but you never intend to let me forget that mistake, do you? No, it would best serve your purposes to keep me paying for that night the rest of my life."

"That's not true."

"Splendid, because I don't mean to go on paying anymore. Will you open this door?"

"No!"

"Have it your way."

With that, he backed off once more and struck the door with the full force of his body. The ancient wood splintered and tore apart.

As Ransom reached through the fissure in the door and slid the bolt lock free, he could hear Meg's sharp intake of breath. He lifted the latch and slowly swung the door open. Meg took a step backward. King snapped and growled, careful to stay within the shelter of Meg's skirts.

Ransom stood there, his naked chest heaving from his exertions. A dark bruise already discolored the flesh of his shoulder.

He began walking toward Meg, his eyes glinting in challenge, his mouth set in a grim line. Meg swallowed deeply, as if trying desperately to maintain her courage. He knew she hadn't believed he'd bully his way past the stout wooden door, and now that he had, she probably didn't know what to expect.

"Don't come any closer," she warned.

"I'm through playing games, Meg."

She lifted her chin. "So am I."

He advanced another pace or two, then came to a sudden stop as he saw her raise the hand that had been hidden in the folds of her nightgown. She was clutching a brass flintlock pistol, whose barrel was pointed with unfaltering accuracy at his bare chest.

"I suppose Fletcher gave you that little toy, too?"

"He did . . . and showed me how to use it, I might add."

"I'm not afraid of you, Meg. I don't think you'd kill me."

"No," she agreed, "I probably wouldn't." She lowered the barrel of the flintlock until it was aimed at his groin. "But that doesn't mean I won't shoot you."

Ransom stopped moving. "Damnation, woman! What is it you want from me?"

"I want you to abide by our original agreement. Your name and protection until this castle is restored, and then a deed to Wolfcrag and a discreet divorce. There is nothing more I want from you, Ransom—nothing at all."

Ransom's disgusted gaze skimmed over her. The light from the candles in the wall sconces gleamed along the ornamental stock of the gun she held. For a moment he contemplated taking it from her, but knew it wasn't worth the risk. He didn't doubt for a second that she would fire it as promised . . . but when the time came for him to be unmanned by Meg St. Claire, he didn't want it to be with a pistol. He deemed it wiser to retreat—for the moment—and not have to experience life as a eunuch.

"Very well, Meg, if that's what you want, you shall have it. But heed my words, the day will arrive when you'll change your mind . . . and then you may have to use that weapon to get me *into* your bed!"

Meg's smile of relief was a bit wobbly. "Thank you for doing the sensible thing." She turned her head slightly. "You can come out now, Fletcher. Everything's all right."

The door of the massive wardrobe opened and out stepped the seaman, a sword in one hand and a dirk in the other. He nodded at Ransom. "Evenin', Cap'n."

"Fletcher?" Ransom breathed. "By God, you dare much."

"Aye." The man's grin was unrepentant. "Shall I throw myself into the dungeon?"

"I . . . oh, damn the both of you!" Ransom exclaimed. He

turned, shoved the ruined door out of his way, and stalked from the chamber. King, braver now that Ransom was retreating, ventured forth to take a few daring nips at his heels. Sharply, Meg called the dog back, but even though Ransom slowed his pace, she didn't call out for his return.

Halfway to his own room, he stopped, still stunned by the betrayal. His wife and his first mate had conspired against him and, by the looks of it, hadn't planned on taking any chances with his behavior. Suddenly, Ransom didn't know whether to laugh or start ripping stones from the walls with his bare hands.

He had only one clear thought: since he'd married Meg MacLinn, he couldn't remember the last time he'd been bored.

# Chapter Fifteen

For the next week, Ransom moved about the castle with a glower and a sharp word for anyone who crossed his path. He spent long hours shut in his room with only Satan for company, and his disposition grew more unpredictable as each day passed.

One afternoon, feeling restless, he climbed the steep stairway to the roof of the castle. It had become a favorite place to go when he needed to meditate, and he readily acknowledged that the welter of thoughts within his head badly needed untangling.

He strolled along the slippery slate walkway that ran around the edge of the roof, stopping to lean against the huge stones of the parapet. His troubled gaze sought the calming sight of the ocean spreading away from Wolfcrag to the faint, nebulous horizon. He saw the white sails of a ship in the distance, and his heart lurched. That's where he should be—*wanted* to be! Standing on the deck of his own brigantine, sails set for some exotic location. And, he promised himself, that's where he would be, as soon as the renovation was done and his bargain with Meg completed.

Meg. The woman was beginning to haunt him. She had altered his life in several significant ways, and he wasn't at all pleased with that reality. As if ordered by some prankish Fate, her voice drifted upward on the wind. Leaning farther out, he looked straight down into the courtyard and saw his wife surrounded by a group of men who appeared to be listening intently as she talked. Highlanders, by the look of them, and in need of work, if he was any judge. He'd given Meg orders not to employ any more people, but if she obeyed his wishes, it would be the first time.

Anger rose in his chest, and he struggled against the feeling. Actually, he wasn't so much angry with Meg as he was annoyed—her rejection of him was a punishing blow to his vanity. No man liked being turned away from his wife's bedchamber, and Meg should consider it her good fortune that he'd decided to be agreeable about it.

The worst of it was, as she had pointed out, they'd made a bargain—and she was keeping her end of it. Every time he wandered about the castle, or even looked out the window of his room, he could see the frenzy of activity, could tell how rapidly the repairs were being made. Why, then, was he so reluctant to do his part?

It should be a simple matter to play the role of indolent lord, to laze around the place, enjoying a leisurely existence, keeping both his eyes and his hands off his make-believe wife. But inactivity was starting to pall, and ignoring Meg was like trying to overlook a tempest at sea. Each time he thought he'd been successful at forgetting her, he'd hear her laughter or someone would call her name . . . or some unbidden memory would implant itself firmly before his mind's eye . . . and he'd be lost; the deck would tilt beneath his feet, and the furious wind would pluck away his hard-won indifference.

Too many sleepless nights had shown him the truth. He was beginning to succumb to Meg's subtle spell. No matter what he'd tried to convey to Yates and Beale, the woman really was a witch. She had to be, to affect him so strongly. How had he allowed her to completely take over his life? He'd been bored and lonely and eager for a bit of feminine companionship, but he'd never asked to be saddled with a chaste wife and her miscreant family. Damn it all, a mistress was what he'd wanted! If he had any sense, he'd go back to that notion and forget his imitation marriage.

The object of his ire was speaking again, talking loudly

enough to be heard over the pounding of hammers, and, unashamedly, Ransom eavesdropped.

"We've got plenty of carpenters and masons, and the plasterers arrived yesterday," she was saying. "But those of you without particular skills can cart away debris and burn it. You can scrub and clean, and your wives can help feed the workers."

Ransom's lips tightened. Meg had never intended to follow his orders, that was evident. He fumed silently for a few seconds, easily reaching the decision to go down and teach her some respect. His first action would be to shake her until her teeth rattled.

Ransom all but ran down the flights of narrow, spiraling stairs. By the time he arrived at the courtyard level, he was nearly panting. Unobtrusively, he leaned against a shadowed wall to gain control of his breathing.

"Are we to be paid for our labor?" he heard one of the men ask.

"Of course," Meg replied. "At the end of each week, I'll see that you're paid your wages in gold."

"Gold?" commented another. "Who in this country has gold?"

"Lord St. Claire," Meg answered. "He has agreed to make funds available for the rebuilding."

"But hauling trash and scrubbing walls . . . is that not woman's work?"

"*Fuigh!* For the promise of regular wages," a young fellow with a freckled face exclaimed, "I'd do any kind of work."

"Pluck the hens, Dougall?" challenged one of the others. "Wash the plates and bowls?"

"Aye," the youth responded. "Why, I'd even be willing to sew the laird's undergarments."

His bold statement was met with a round of raucous laughter, which Ransom was perturbed to see Meg join. Had such a cheeky remark been made to a proper English lady, no doubt the speaker would have suffered the sharp edge of her tongue.

"Now that would be quite a task," Meg declared merrily,

"for I suspect Ransom St. Claire's drawers must be made of iron!"

The renewed roar of laughter brought a grimace to Ransom's face. He didn't like overhearing the impudent wench making sport of him.

"Why do ye say such a thing, lassie?" asked one of the Highlanders, a shocked expression on his lined face.

"From what his first mate tells me, it seems Ransom's backside is frequently in trouble. Fletcher says the laird's father has gnawed on him so often he needs 'arse armor'!"

When Ransom stepped out of the shadows, the men's chuckles died abruptly, but because he was standing behind Meg, she was not yet aware of his presence. Innocent of the danger, she dared another statement.

"Do you suppose he wears his iron drawers into battle? Or to bed?"

"Come now, Lady St. Claire," Ransom drawled, "we're married. You know very well what I wear—or do not wear—to bed."

Meg spun about, one hand covering her mouth, which had dropped open in stunned surprise. The stricken look in her eyes told him she recognized her situation was unfavorable at best.

"Ransom, I . . ." It seemed Meg was contemplating biting off her tongue before it could get her into further trouble.

"What's this?" he sneered. "The glib Highland rebel having difficulty speaking? How astonishing! Especially after the way words were tumbling out only moments ago."

"I was merely getting acquainted with some of the men who are coming to work for us," she stammered. "I was making a jest, that's all."

"Forgive me if I fail to find humor in jests at my expense. Somehow I expected a bit more loyalty from my . . . wife."

Ransom's words brought a look of shame to Meg's face, and she shifted uncomfortably, aware that the onlookers were hanging on every syllable uttered.

"Could we please continue this discussion in private?" she asked.

"As you wish," Ransom readily agreed. "Discharge these men to their duties and join me in my bedchamber."

He started to walk away, but turned for a last, parting volley. "By the way, Meg—with your habit of landing your own backside in peril, maybe you might find a pair of iron drawers useful, too."

Blushing, Meg ignored the muffled laughter around her and began issuing orders in a curt voice. "Those of you interested in employment in this castle can fetch your wives and meet me in the Great Hall in an hour. I will assign your duties then."

When the men had gone on their way, Meg smoothed her hair and, taking a steadying breath, marched up the stairs to Ransom's chambers. She would have preferred their interview take place in a more public area, but she had the feeling he was going to vent his anger, and, in truth, fewer people would hear his tirade if it occurred behind a closed door.

Once inside his room, she shut the door and leaned upon it, unwilling to get too close to the man who lounged against one of the bedposts.

"I want to apologize for making unsuitable comments about you in front of the workers," she ventured. "I was only trying to put them at ease."

"It's not them you should be worrying about. Didn't I tell you not to hire anyone else?" he queried.

"Well . . . perhaps you did mention that," she hedged. "But I can explain."

He looked doubtful. "Then, by all means, do so."

Meg took a cautious step forward. "I've been thinking, Ransom—"

"Always a dangerous proposition."

"Don't be hateful," she snapped. "I'm concerned for your welfare as much as my own."

"Now that is comforting. Go on."

"As I said, I've been thinking matters over. If Hale Dickson was right, Clarice and her entourage should be arriving at Wolfcrag before too much longer."

"And?"

"And I thought it would be to our benefit to have as much of the work done as possible. That way, when she returns to London to inform the king of our marriage, she will also be able to confirm how well the restoration is proceeding."

Ransom looked thoughtful. "Yes, that's true enough. But can we afford the extra work force?"

"Those men are desperate for a means of feeding their families," she argued. "Besides, would you quibble over a few shillings?"

Ransom sighed heavily. "The money I have isn't going to last forever, Meg. Do you know how costly it is to purchase lumber? Damask for draperies? Furnishings? I've nearly depleted the sack of gold I took to Inverness—and by the time you've finished paying wages from the other, it will be gone as well."

"I'm not a spendthrift—I'm being as frugal as possible. But Ransom, these people . . . they need our help."

"We can't save the entire population of the Highlands, woman! Every time I turn around, I see a dozen new and different people living within the castle walls. I'm telling you, Meg, enough is enough."

She bowed her head. "All right."

"And don't think I'll be fooled by your show of submission," he warned. "I've seen it before and know how little it means."

Meg's head jerked up and she met his speculative gaze.

"Meg," he continued, his tone signaling a change of topic, "there's something else I want to tell you."

"What's that?"

"About the other night . . . when I broke into your bedchamber?"

She nodded uncertainly. "Yes . . ."

"I want you to know that it won't happen again." He gave her a wry smile. "I've realized that you're upholding your end of our agreement and I'm not. But all that is going to change."

"It is?"

"Absolutely." He altered his position, drawing her eyes to the stretch of fabric across his broad shoulders. "When we made our pact, you were the first and only woman to set foot in Wolfcrag since my arrival here. I suppose that fact accounts for my pursuit of you. But now, thanks to your ingenuity, there are any number of young women here."

"Most of them are married," Meg said faintly.

"Most, but not all. There's your friend Mairi, for instance. She's a pretty-enough lass. No doubt she'd be grateful for a little protection for those two sons of hers."

"Protection?"

"The point is, Meg, don't you worry about the matter any further. I've decided to honor your wishes and leave you to your housekeeping chores. I just thought you'd want to know."

"Why . . . yes," she murmured. "That's . . . well, it's certainly a relief. I didn't enjoy the other night, and I'm sure Fletcher isn't comfortable jeopardizing his relationship with you."

"Have the workmen repair the door to your chamber, but be assured, you won't find it necessary to lock me out again."

Meg lowered her eyes. "Thank you."

"Now go on about your duties. I think your idea of having at least the main rooms finished before Clarice arrives is an admirable one, but there's much to be accomplished."

"Yes, I'd best get the workers started." Meg put her hand on the door latch.

"Oh, Meg, one more thing."

She turned back to face him.

"Send Mairi up, will you? I'd like to speak with her."

Meg's eyes darkened to the color of a stormy summer sky, but she spoke calmly. "Very well."

However, as she left the room, she couldn't resist shutting the door behind her with a force that surprised even her.

*Well,* Meg asked herself, *what did you expect?*

*I expected him to be angry,* she answered. *To shout and threaten.*

*He didn't shout once,* she mused. *And he didn't seem all that angry. He offered assurances, not threats. Isn't that a nice change?*

*I don't know — it just didn't seem like him, somehow.*

*You're upset because he told you he'd fix his attention on other women,* she accused herself. *You don't like that much, do you?*

*Why wouldn't I? I don't want him making his lecherous advances to me! I'm not some simpleminded, love-starved female who wants to be overpowered . . . am I?*

Meg flicked the reins and urged the horse she was riding forward along the beach path that wound south from the castle. She had chosen to take a solitary ride rather than join the others for dinner in the noisy Banqueting Hall, where Fletcher had started serving the meals. She had been dismayed by her reaction to Ransom's words earlier in the day and had subjected herself to what was meant to be a stern lecture. Instead, it had turned into a somber soliloquy that had stunned her. She was alarmed to detect a touch of disappointment in her response to Ransom's vow not to bother her again. Disappointment and . . . yes, jealousy. For some reason, she didn't at all like the idea of him making Mairi his mistress . . . and she didn't dare examine her reasoning too closely.

The cool evening air was refreshing as it stirred the hair at her temples and swirled the shawl about her shoulders. She loved the salt tang of the ocean, the sunbaked smell of the kelp that had dried on the rocks during the afternoon. A turnstone, its black and white feathers ruffled by the breeze, picked among the pebbles on the beach, searching for crustaceans.

The sun slipped lower in the sky, but even though it was still early summer, Meg knew it wouldn't be dark for quite some time yet. She decided to take advantage of the lingering light to ride to one of the settlements she had not yet visited since her return to Wolfcrag.

The cluster of houses was less than a mile from the castle, strung along a grassy road. Just as Meg's horse reached the summit of a long, low-lying hill, she began to smell smoke, and suddenly the tranquil gloaming was shattered by a woman's shrill screams.

With a muttered curse, Meg spurred her mount and galloped recklessly toward the cottages. She was appalled by the scene that met her eyes.

The straw roof of one of the dwellings was ablaze, sending sparks shooting skyward, threatening the roofs of the adjacent buildings. A woman surrounded by crying children was pleading with two men who were using pitchforks to toss the contents of a wooden farm cart into the flames. As she drew nearer, Meg could see that the cart was filled with clothing and household goods. One of the men drew back a hand and struck the woman, sending her sprawling into the dust. The children immediately swarmed upon the man and he swatted at them as though they were flies, tumbling them roughly to the ground at his feet. Meg jumped from her horse and ran headlong into the fray.

"Stop it!" she cried, seizing the man's arm.

"Well, we're to have a bit of fun, is that it?" exclaimed his companion, tossing aside the pitchfork he held to grasp Meg around the waist and swing her about.

"Let me go, you bastard," she shouted and, with a well-aimed kick, gained her freedom.

The other woman sat dazed and disbelieving. "Who are you?" she asked in a half whisper. "Why do you risk your life to help us?"

"That doesn't matter," Meg returned, gasping for breath. "Who are these men and what are they doing?"

"We work for Jonathan Spottiswoode," the first man stated, edging closer to Meg. "And we're evicting these worthless crofters."

"But you can't just burn their home and their belongings . . ."

"They were told to go," he snarled. "Stubborn fools."

At that moment, the fire arced against the sky, and a fiery tongue of flame leaped easily onto the next cottage. Meg flinched as the woman began screaming again.

"My God, Brodie's in there with Grandfather!" The slight, dark-haired woman struggled to her feet, only to be encircled by the children, their terror evident in their faces. "Someone help them!"

Meg turned toward the cottage, which was instantly engulfed in fire, but one of Spottiswoode's men grabbed her arm. Frantically, she wrenched herself free, heedless of the sound of tearing cloth or the feel of bruising fingers on her wrist.

"Not so fast, lassie," the man said, laughing. "You're too pretty to be burned alive."

"But there are men in that cottage," Meg cried. "Aren't you going to help them?"

"Let the damned Highlanders roast like the pigs they are," he declared.

Blinded by fury, Meg slapped him with all her strength, and, taken by surprise, he tottered backward. She slipped out of his grasp and dashed toward the smoke-filled cottage. Behind her, she heard him yell, "Get the others! We're going to teach this witch a lesson!"

Just as she reached the doorway, a figure emerged, staggering beneath the burden it bore. Meg could see that it was a young man carrying a body over his shoulder. Coughing and gasping for air, he sank to his knees, and she helped him lay the older man on the grass. As she leaned forward to listen for the sound of breathing, she found herself caught up in a rough embrace. Spottiswoode's man dragged her backward, his hands locked cruelly about her upper arms. Still choking, the young Highlander lurched to his feet to come to her aid, but the second man snatched up his pitchfork and, using the handle as a weapon, hit him squarely in the head. Without a sound, the Highlander crumpled to the ground and lay still. Sobbing, the panic-stricken woman and children hovered over him.

"And now for you . . ." Spottiswoode's agent tossed down the fork and turned on Meg, followed closely by his comrade. "We'll teach you to interfere when we're following the landlord's instructions."

The flames created eerie shadows on their grinning, bewhiskered faces, and Meg backed away, chilled by the look of intent in their eyes.

"Don't touch me," she warned. "You don't know who I am . . ."

"We'll have time for introductions later," one promised, chuckling. "But we're going to get better acquainted first."

A second too late, Meg sensed his action and tried to twist away, but he threw his arms about her and began trying to wrest her to the ground. His partner attempted to grab her flailing feet and trip her, but he was hampered by Meg's petticoats and her frenzied kicking.

Meg fought her captors with the last remnants of her strength, realizing there was little chance she could gain her freedom. What a fool she had been to ride out alone, without even her dirk to defend herself. She would have given ten years of her life to feel its worn handle against her palm at that moment!

"You may as well stop fighting us," one of the fellows muttered, leering at her. "A wee lass like yourself doesn't stand a chance against us."

"And here come our companions," the other announced. "No doubt they'll want to join in the fun."

Meg was dimly aware of the sound of hoofbeats. Her heart sank, for she knew she could never fight off all of them. Desperately, she made one last attempt to escape her attackers. With as much force as she could manage, she drew up her knees and kicked out. The toe of her shoe caught one of the men in the throat and he fell, wheezing and strangling for air.

"What the . . . ?" swore the man still crouching above her. Before he could discern her advantage, Meg turned her body, bringing up an elbow to strike him in the nose. He howled as the blood spurted, and sat back on his heels. To Meg's amazement, the young Scotswoman stepped up to him and, using one of the abandoned pitchforks, poked it at his chest. He cried out in alarm and remained crouched there in the dirt.

Sensing the approach of riders, Meg crawled toward the other pitchfork, coming to her knees with it clenched in her hands. Her hair had worked loose from its knot and hung in her eyes, but it didn't entirely obscure her view of the horsemen positioned in a semicircle about her. Slowly she got to her feet and brushed back her hair.

White-faced and shaking, the younger woman moved to stand beside Meg, and the two of them faced the enemy. At their feet, the injured men began to rouse themselves.

Meg brandished her pitchfork threateningly. "Don't move," she cautioned, "or I'll run this right through your cowardly heart."

"And you don't think my companions will overpower you?" he sneered, wiping his bloody nose with the back of one hand.

"It won't matter to you, because you'll be dead." Meg swept the circle of riders with a haughty look. "Besides, once they find out who I am, they'll see the advisability of leaving me alone."

"And just who are you?" A big man with a pockmarked face leaned forward in his saddle and studied her insolently. "The lady of the manor?"

A spattering of faint laughter sounded, and Meg's begrimed chin rose high. "I am," she said. "I'm Lady Margaret St. Claire. My husband is the laird of Wolfcrag."

The woman beside her drew in a sharp breath, and Meg could sense her surprised look. The horsemen grew silent, as though considering her revelation. Those few who had drawn their pistols now lowered them, as if waiting to hear more of what she had to say.

"Need I tell you how displeased Lord St. Claire is going to be when he learns of my treatment at your hands?" she went on, hoping her imperiousness would convince them. It was all she could do to hold the pitchfork steady and keep her voice from trembling.

"The Englishman?" another of the riders murmured.

Meg nodded. "Aye. He's a personal friend of the king's, you know."

The pockmarked man smirked. "Why would Lady St. Claire be out here at this time of the evening?"

"I was taking a ride," Meg replied, astonished at her own

cool tone, "when I came upon this scene. You can be certain I will go straight to Mr. Spottiswoode to make my complaints."

The man with the scarred face, obviously the leader of the group, shrugged. "Then mayhap we should leave him to deal with you."

"I believe that would be to your advantage," Meg declared.

"Very well. As for you . . ." He pointed at the Scotswoman. "Take your brats and go. You have until sundown to be off Spottiswoode's land."

The woman burst into tears as the horsemen began slowly riding away. Meg watched until she was certain even the two men who had attacked her were going before she turned to offer comfort. When she did, she saw that the crofter himself was struggling to his feet.

"Are ye truly the Lady St. Claire?" he asked groggily.

"Yes, I am," Meg answered.

White teeth gleamed in the Highlander's dirty face. "The outlaw's daughter?"

"Yes . . . who are you?"

"Brodie MacLinn," he replied, holding out a grimy hand. "A distant cousin of yours, I suspect. And a man who's waited for the return of the outlaw MacLinn since I was a wee lad."

Meg shook his hand. "I only wish my father could have been here tonight. He'd have scattered those blackguards like sheep."

"Aye, we need a man like him," spoke up the woman. "Hello . . . I'm Lorna, Brodie's sister." She went to kneel beside the old man, who was awake and watching them warily. "This is our grandfather, Hamish MacLinn, and these are our brothers and sisters." The children, who all appeared to be less than ten years of age, huddled close to their sister and nodded solemnly.

"I'm pleased to meet you," Meg said. "But what happened here tonight? Why did those men burn your home?"

"We'd been told to leave," Brodie said, stooping to help his grandfather to his feet. "But Grandfather has been ill, and we had no place to go. We didn't think they'd come back so soon."

"But where are the other people?" Meg indicated the row of cottages, all burning now that the fire had spread unchecked. "Why didn't they help you?"

"They're all gone," Lorna said. "They left more than a month ago. They had kin in the south—we have no one."

"Our parents died in an epidemic last year," Brodie explained. "We've just barely managed to survive since then. There's been no work . . ."

"I know," Meg agreed. "Times have been hard." Wearily, she straightened her shoulders. "But they're going to get better now, I promise. Do you have horses?"

Her abrupt question caught them off guard, but after a few seconds, Lorna said, "Two—in the meadow over there." Her face twisted bitterly. "The meadow that's to be used for grazing our landlord's sheep, ye ken."

"Brodie, if you'll get the horses," Meg went on, "I'll help Lorna get your grandfather and the children into the cart. Then I want you to go to the castle—ask for Fletcher and explain what has happened. Tell him I said to feed you and find you beds for the night."

"But where will you be?" queried Lorna.

"I'm going to pay a visit to Spottiswoode," Meg stated. "I have a number of complaints to take up with the villain."

Spottiswoode's home, a square manor house of gray stone, had not yet been built when Meg lived at Wolfcrag. She found its spare, classic lines as unappealing as the man himself—and as much an intrusion on a way of life that had existed for centuries. She left her horse in the hands of an astonished groom and stormed her way into the house.

"Madam!" exclaimed Spottiswoode's shocked housekeeper as Meg pushed past her in the entryway. "Who are you? What do you think you're—you can't go in there! The master is at dinner!"

Spottiswoode looked up from his meal, an annoyed frown

visible on his bony face. Annoyance gave way to surprise as he watched Meg approach. "Lady St. Claire?" he murmured, looking stunned by her disheveled appearance. "What has happened to you?"

Meg was aware that she looked frightful. Her gown was torn, her face dirty, and her hair straggling over her shoulders. At the moment, she was far too incensed to care.

"I've just come from Brodie MacLinn's cottage," she all but shouted. "The one you ordered burned."

Spottiswoode, who had begun to rise from his chair, sat back down and, resting his elbows on the table, steepled his long, large-knuckled fingers and gave a wry chuckle. "I take it this is not a social call."

"Your men did this to me," Meg continued. "But I suffered nothing by comparison to the crofters. Do you realize that an elderly man was nearly burned alive?"

Spottiswoode sighed heavily. "Your Ladyship, those people had adequate warning. They were told two days ago to move out."

"But Lorna and Brodie's grandfather was too ill to move—and they had no place to go."

"I can't be concerned with the petty details of their miserable lives, madam. I have my own livelihood to consider."

"Why should your livelihood, as you call it, be more important than the safety of others? Don't you care anything about those children? That old man?"

"Nay. Why should I? And why should you, for that matter? You've married well, raised yourself above your lowbred beginnings. Why don't you stay in that castle of yours and mind your own affairs?"

Meg clenched her hands at her sides, making an effort to keep from flying at the man and clawing his face. "How can you—a Scot yourself—betray your own people?"

"They're not my people," he avowed. "I'm a Lowlander, not a heathen from the north."

"That shouldn't matter—"

"But it does."

"Well, I won't just sit back and ignore what you're doing.

Those are my clansmen, and this was once my father's land."
"It's mine now, however, and I shall do as I please with it." Spottiswoode rested his hands on the edge of the table. "I don't want you to interfere again, do you hear me?" Slowly, he got to his feet, his chair scraping against the stone floor. "You can rescue all the pitiful crofters you wish—take them into your husband's home, bankrupt him by feeding and clothing them. I don't care! But stay away from me and my property . . . and keep that pretty nose out of my concerns, or it will be too bad for you."
"Are you threatening me?" Meg demanded.
"Call it that if you like. I prefer to think of it as a neighborly warning." He started toward her, a cold smile barely altering the sober lines of his face. "And, my dear, I know of several ways to handle obstinate women like yourself." He stopped directly in front of her, putting out a hand to touch the torn shoulder of her dress. "But I might not be so gentle as my men were . . ."
Meg backed away, her distaste clearly written on her features.
"Don't touch me," she protested, slapping at his hand.
"Why not?" he questioned, keeping pace with her retreat. "If you behave like a strumpet, you must expect men to treat you as such."
"My behavior is of no concern of yours."
"It is when you trespass onto my property and try to countermand my orders—or when you burst uninvited into my home. When you act in that manner, you place yourself at my mercy. And it becomes my duty to discipline you in whatever way I see fit."
"Might I suggest that you see fit to simply hand my wife over into my safekeeping?" came a deep voice from the doorway. Both Spottiswoode and Meg whirled about, startled.
"Ransom!" Meg breathed, flooded with relief.
"What in hell did you think you were doing?" he growled, an edge of steel to his usually mellow drawl. He stood there glowering at her, filling the doorway with his impressive size.
"I . . . I came to make a protest to Mr. Spottiswoode," she

answered, her voice sounding small and insubstantial in the large room. "He's continued with the evictions . . . people were nearly killed tonight, Ransom."

"So Lorna and her brother told me. But you shouldn't have taken it upon yourself to come here."

"Exactly what I've been telling the lady," spoke up Spottiswoode. "What I do within the confines of my own property has nothing to do with either of you."

"I might have agreed with you if you hadn't threatened my wife," Ransom replied. "I didn't like what I heard you saying to her, and I sure as hell didn't like you putting your hands on her. The next time you or any of your men touch her, it will be my pleasure to kill you."

"Now, see here," Spottiswoode croaked, his face growing crimson. "I don't have to listen to this . . ."

"I don't care whether or not you *listen,*" Ransom informed him. "I only care that you *believe* it."

He bent a dark look on Meg. "As for you, let's go. I'm taking you home." He gripped her arm and steered her toward the door.

Meg looked back over her shoulder at the enraged Jonathan Spottiswoode. "If you don't stop evicting the crofters, you'll be sorry! I'll find some way to stop you!"

Ransom gave her a hearty shove, his rough hold on her arm all that kept her from stumbling. He pushed her past the gaping housekeeper in the foyer, out the door, and down the front steps.

Once they were out of earshot of those in the house, he stopped and yanked her around to face him.

"Don't you ever do anything like that again," he rasped. "My God, do you realize what could have happened to you if Brodie and his sister hadn't nearly killed themselves getting to the castle? Damn it, Meg, you're too intelligent to go careening about the countryside, landing yourself in one scrape after another! What if I hadn't been able to get here in time? Do you think Spottiswoode intended to pat you on the head and send you home?"

"Ransom, I can take care of myself. . . ."

The expletive he uttered was short, harsh, and disbelieving in the extreme. His eyes glittered furiously in the dark as he raked them over her. With all her soul, Meg wanted to cringe before him, and it took every bit of discipline she could muster to remain upright, head high. Steadily, she met his look.

"Thank you for coming to my aid," she said stiffly. "At least now we know what kind of man Spottiswoode is . . . and we know that it's important for us to find some way of stopping him."

"We?" Ransom thundered. *"We?* Look, Meg, I only came after you tonight because you're my wife and I owed it to you."

"Owed it . . . ?"

"Besides, what do you think would become of the restoration of Wolfcrag if something happened to you?"

Meg swallowed deeply as his sharp words cut through her. "So that's why you came . . ."

Ransom stared at her, battling the urge to take her into his arms and assure her that no, that had not been it at all. He'd come because he was filled with terror at the thought of what someone like Spottiswoode or his hirelings might be capable of. He'd risked his life and that of his stallion to get to her in time because he'd suspected her danger at the hands of the profligate landlord. And he'd nearly lost all sense of reason when he'd seen the man lay his lecherous hands on Meg.

He closed his eyes tightly, but he couldn't shut out the sight of her—her face pale and drawn beneath the streaks of soot, her eyes blinded by tears she was too proud to shed, her mouth softly vulnerable. He'd never wanted anything more than he wanted to pull her into his sheltering embrace and kiss away her misery. But it had only been a matter of hours since he'd told her he wouldn't regard her as his wife anymore, that he'd focus his unwanted attentions on someone else. If he wasn't good enough to share her bed, her life, then he didn't want to be involved with her on any level at all.

He opened his eyes and drew a deep, fortifying breath. "How many times," he said, "do I have to remind you that this is not my fight. As you so often point out, I'm a despicable

Englishman, and these petty squabbles among you Scots is of no interest to me."

"Petty squabbles?" she echoed disbelievingly.

"All I care about is seeing Wolfcrag made presentable again."

"People are losing their homes," Meg cried. "Someone is going to get hurt or killed. Doesn't that matter to you?"

"Not in the least."

"Then you're as bad as Spottiswoode. No—worse! You're worse than him because you should know better. You've had enough sorrow in your life that you shouldn't want to wish it on anyone else."

Ransom heaved a weary sigh. "Let's go home, Meg. You'll have to be up early if you intend to start preparing for Clarice's arrival."

For a long moment, Meg considered a dozen different scathing remarks she might make. She even contemplated slapping that superior expression from his wickedly handsome face. But finally, too dispirited to summon the energy, she gave him a disdainful look and swept past him to seize the reins of her horse.

"You can go to hell, Englishman," she mumbled.

"What did you say?" he asked quietly.

"Me?" Meg swung into the saddle and faced him with feigned innocence. "I was only expressing my gratitude for your intervention. But you can be certain it's for the last time. I'll never trouble you with my problems again."

# Chapter Sixteen

During the following week, Meg steadfastly kept her distance from Ransom, only speaking directly to him on one occasion.

She had managed to secure the last vacant cottage within the castle grounds for Brodie MacLinn and his family, but even with decent meals and regular care, his grandfather, old Hamish, failed to get better. In Meg's opinion, his age and illness combined with the shock of losing his home had sent him into a malaise from which she began to fear he would not recover. In desperation, she finally went to Ransom and asked his permission to send to Carraig for Dr. MacSween and his wife, Della.

Ransom had given his consent readily enough, without even scolding her for taking in seven new mouths to feed. In fact, his manner had been somewhat distant, which could only mean he was preoccupied with Mairi or one of the other available women about the castle. She had seen him talking and flirting with various ones, and had told herself she was relieved. Without his unwanted attentions to deal with, she was free to concentrate on the renovation.

And, in truth, if anything in her life was going well, it was the restoration of Wolfcrag Castle. The carpenters had already replaced much of the ruined moldings and woodwork on the lower floors and were making admirable progress on the main stairway. The stonemasons and plasterers had repaired a good number of the fireplaces and even now were putting the finishing touches on the Great Hall.

Nearly every female dwelling within Wolfcrag's walls was busy day and night sewing draperies and bed hangings, and wagons of furniture, dishes, and linens had been unloaded.

The Banqueting Hall had regained its old magnificence. The walls were freshly plastered and whitewashed, the MacLinn arms repaired and painted. The flagstones had been scrubbed and scoured, and new carpets put down. There was glass in the windows again, and brocaded draperies. Long oaken tables and chairs lined the walls, and it was here those living within the castle gathered for meals.

Now, almost every evening, the English sailors and the Scottish workers sat together in the Banqueting Hall to eat their dinner and share a night of singing and storytelling. Meg found it a poignant experience to hear the old stones ring with boisterous sound again, and was so moved that when she sent the message to Dr. MacSween, she included one to her father, urging his return to Wolfcrag.

But the accomplishment of which she was most proud was the suite of rooms that had been prepared for Clarice Howard and her entourage. The refurbishing of those chambers had even taken precedence over the work yet to be done in the kitchens, much to Fletcher's chagrin. Only a few more days and they would be in complete readiness for Ransom's erstwhile fiancée.

However, as luck would have it, Meg was on her hands and knees scrubbing out the last of the garderobes when Mairi came scuttling into the room, frantic in her anxiety.

"They've arrived," she panted. "Just now . . ."

"Who?" inquired Meg, glad for the opportunity to rest a moment. She had knelt on the stone floor of the cramped privy so long that her knees felt bruised and aching. Stiffly, she got to her feet and poured the bucket of dirty scrub water down the *lang drap,* or toilet hole.

"The English woman," Mairi explained. "Her and a bevy of others."

"My God," gasped Meg, one reddened hand going to the mobcap on her head. "They're here already?"

"Aye."

"Then I don't have much time to bathe—"

"Oh, there's no time to bathe, Meg. They're here now—in the courtyard, I mean."

"But how can that be? Didn't the sentries give warning of their arrival?"

"They didn't see them until they were demanding the drawbridge be lowered." Mairi smiled timorously. "Don't you remember? You asked the men on sentry duty to help in the kitchen gardens today."

Meg groaned. "So I did."

"Lord St. Claire sent me to bring you downstairs. He wants you there to greet the guests."

"But I can't go down looking like this." Meg dropped the scrub brush into the empty wooden pail and thrust it at Mairi. "Here, take this and go tell Ransom to offer them some refreshment. I'll be down as soon as I can."

Mairi clutched the pail. "Uh, His Lordship . . . well, he told me to bring you immediately. And not to let you out of my sight because you'd find some way to . . . to shirk your duty."

"Shirk my duty?" Meg exclaimed. "You can tell His Lordship . . . oh, never mind, I'll tell him myself! Once he sees how I look, he'll be glad to allow me time to get presentable."

Meg hastened from the room and down the hallway, all the while trying to decide which of her better gowns she should wear. No doubt they'd all be rustic by comparison to Clarice's newly acquired wardrobe, but she had to make the effort to look as proper as possible. Ransom was waiting impatiently at the foot of the stairs, Satan brushing back and forth against his leather boots.

"Come on," Ransom entreated, "Fletcher has already admitted the visitors to the Great Hall."

"But I can't go in there looking like this," Meg protested. "I need time to bathe and change clothing. You go on in—"

"You're the lady of the castle," he pointed out, taking her arm and pulling her to the doorway of the hall. "You should be with me. After all, aren't we supposed to be making a show of unity?"

Seeing the crowd of people in the room beyond, Meg pulled

free of his hold. "We can do that as soon as I'm appropriately dressed. Ransom look at me—I can't greet strangers this way!"

He gave her a swift, assessing glance. "You'd look fine if you'd just take off that silly cap."

"But I—"

"Ransom!" A tall blond woman appeared in the doorway. "Aren't you ever going to come say hello to me?"

"Clarice." The carefully uttered word gave no clue as to Ransom's state of mind. Satan, on the other hand, was not so reluctant to express his sentiments. After a quick sniff at the hem of Clarice's cloak, he arched his back and emitted a loud hiss, scampering away down the corridor.

Clarice Howard made a wry face. "I've always hated that cat!" Then she tilted her head and smiled coquettishly, holding out her hands to Ransom. "I see I've taken you by surprise," she continued. "But the least you can do is make me feel welcome. Oh, I didn't realize you were occupied with a servant. Well, send her away and give me a proper greeting."

Meg watched in stunned surprise as Clarice took Ransom's hands and tugged him toward her, out of sight of those in the room behind them. She ran slender, bejeweled fingers up his arms to his shoulders, then grasped his head and drew it down to her level. With a brilliant smile, she leaned forward to kiss his lips. Meg felt anger twist within herself, and she considered seizing handfuls of the woman's elaborately curled hair and pulling with all her strength. The somewhat wild look Ransom was giving her told her he suspected her impulse, but she couldn't discern if he approved or not.

"My God," Clarice sighed, "it has been far too long since we were together. You don't know . . ." She began punctuating her words with the small kisses she placed upon Ransom's throat. ". . . how much . . . I've . . . missed you."

"Clarice," Ransom said, a tide of crimson rising along his neck, "stop this . . ." Gently, but firmly, he gripped her elbows and set her away from him.

"Darling, you're not still angry with me, are you?" Clarice was a beautiful woman, and her pretended pout only emphasized that fact. Her perfectly shaped eyebrows drew together in a charming frown, her hazel eyes twinkled mischievously, and her lush, scarlet mouth pursed into a tempting moue. "I can explain everything, if you'll only give me the chance. Edmund—"

"This has nothing to do with my brother," Ransom curtly replied. "It's another matter entirely."

"Oh?" Clarice laid one hand upon his chest. "Don't look so serious, Ransom. When you hear my news, you'll see that nothing can be so bad."

"Clarice, there's something you don't know."

The Englishwoman's clear, silvery laugh rang out, drawing the attention of those waiting in the room beyond. "Then perhaps you should stop looking so gloomy and tell me." She flicked an impatient glance at Meg. "You—go away. Don't you know better than to stand gaping at your betters?"

Meg wished the slab of stone beneath her feet would open and drop her directly into the dungeons below.

"Clarice," Ransom said, "this is . . . may I present my wife, Meg?"

The blonde's already fair skin whitened to the color of a linen sheet. "Your . . . wife? Ransom, is this some sort of . . . jest?"

"No," he said, reaching for Meg's hand and placing it in the crook of his arm. "We've been married some weeks now. Didn't Hale Dickson tell you?"

"Hale?" Clarice murmured distractedly. "No, I haven't seen him. Ransom, you can't be married! And especially not to this . . ." Her voice trailed away as if she'd suddenly realized the impropriety of saying more. But her eyes dwelled pointedly on the rough, reddened hand resting on his arm before moving slowly up and down the length of Meg's faded gray gown, to the dusty white cap that topped her tangled curls. "No," she said slowly, "I don't . . . I *won't* believe it!" She stomped her foot, her lovely eyes filled with tears. "Ransom, how could you?"

"Clarice, I—"

"Ohhhh!" Clarice's cry started as a moan of angry frustration and trilled upward into a shrill scream. With a last, baleful look at Ransom, she crumpled gracefully to the floor.

"God damn it," he swore, looking helplessly at Meg.

Meg would have liked to suggest they leave the woman there, but already several of Clarice's ladies-in-waiting had heard the scream and were rushing to her assistance. "Pick her up, Ransom," she prompted. "We need to take her upstairs."

Grimacing, he scooped Clarice into his arms and started up the stairs. "Come along," he said brusquely to Clarice's companions. "I'll take your mistress to her chamber and you can tend to her there."

As Meg followed them up the steps, she heard Clarice moan and saw her drape an arm about Ransom's neck. The sight of her white hand with its jewels and painted nails lightly stroking the back of Ransom's auburn hair made Meg's temper raise dangerously.

*Clarice Howard is no more in a swoon than I am myself,* she thought.

On the second floor, Meg darted ahead down the hallway to throw open the door to the suite of rooms assigned to the guests from England. With the ladies-in-waiting gathered around, Ransom lay Clarice in the center of the curtained bed and hastily stepped back. In a matter of seconds, Clarice stirred and opened her eyes.

"I . . . I'm sorry to be such a bother," she half whispered, pausing dramatically to allow a single tear to trickle down one flawless cheek. "But Ransom, what have you done? Why didn't you wait for me to arrive?"

"For one thing, I didn't know you were coming," he reminded her. "In fact, Scotland is the last place on earth I'd expect to see you."

"I told you I wouldn't forget you," she cried. "Surely you must have known I wouldn't leave things as they were."

"Uh . . . this isn't the time to discuss all that," Ransom said. "We can talk about it later. For now, I need to get out of the way and let your women make you comfortable."

Clarice quickly sat up, placing slippered feet on the carpet and reaching for Ransom's arm. "Yes, I suppose I should get out of these dreadful clothes. Will you help me up, please?" She clung to him for a long moment. "I'm terribly embarrassed to be seen looking so travel worn." Her meaningfully disdainful gaze flashed to Meg's attire once again, while Meg stoically took stock of Clarice's finely woven cloak and the matching satin gown beneath it.

"Shall I have some bathwater brought up?" Meg sweetly inquired, earning a haughty glare.

"I would appreciate it," Clarice said, her tone cool. She turned back to Ransom, and her words warmed noticeably. "Darling, there must be something that can be done. Just give me a minute to think."

"What do you mean," queried Ransom warily.

"I'm talking about this . . . this ridiculous marriage of yours. There has to be a way to dissolve it."

"I have no wish to dissolve it."

"Come now," Clarice chided. "Surely you can't claim it's a love match?" She laughed again, a brittle edge to the silvered sound. "I mean, for God's sake, look at her!"

Meg bit her tongue and tried to keep her anger from showing in her eyes. As lovely as her outward appearance might be, inwardly Clarice Howard was a mean-tempered viper.

"We weren't prepared for guests," Ransom explained. "Perhaps you don't realize that Meg has been working day and night to get the castle in order."

"No, I didn't realize." Clarice swept the room with another of her acid looks. "Probably because there's still so much to be done."

Meg let her own gaze move over the freshly whitewashed walls hung with exquisite tapestries, the new glass windows and drapes, and the huge tester bed with its velvet hangings and bedcovers. No expense had been spared in these rooms, and it disturbed her that Clarice could dismiss it all with a demeaning shrug.

"I'll go now," Meg said quietly, "and arrange for your bath. Shall I send your mother and the others up?"

Clarice sighed. "I suppose so." She placed an indolent hand on Ransom's chest, causing him to step back as though he'd been burned. "Even if things are far different from what I expected, we still need a place to stay. You won't turn me away, will you, Ran?"

He shot a quick look at Meg, cleared his throat. "Of course not. Uh . . . I'll just go help Meg."

"Must you?" Clarice demurred. "We have so much to talk about . . ."

Meg had no wish to stay and witness the renewal of their acquaintance, so she started out of the room. As she disappeared into the antechamber, she heard Clarice say, "What was it, darling? Is our little country mouse with child? Did some irate father with a musket force you into wedlock?"

Unexpectedly, Meg heard Ransom's deep laughter.

Slamming the door behind her, Meg stalked down the hallway, muttering Gaelic curses all the way. She wasn't even aware of Ransom's approach until he seized her arm and dragged her to a halt at the top of the stairs.

"Meg, wait—"

"Leave me alone," she snapped, wrenching her arm from his grasp.

He looked surprised. "What's wrong? You're not upset by Clarice, are you?"

No, she hadn't expected the Englishwoman to be particularly pleasant. Oddly, it was Ransom's own betrayal that stung.

"Of course not. Now get out of my way, I have work to do."

"Why are you so angry, Meg?" he insisted.

Her gray eyes signaled the storm brewing within. "It's just the nature of we 'country mice,' I suppose."

Ransom laughed again, a sound mellifluous with delight.

Meg bristled indignantly. "I hate it when you laugh at me!" she cried, whirling away and starting on down the stairs. Ransom came after her, taking her by the wrist and bringing her to a stop.

"Meg, I wasn't laughing at you," he declared. "I was laughing at Clarice's notion you were anything like a mouse. Lord, that's like calling a fire-breathing dragon a . . . a chameleon!"

"You think I'm a dragon?"

Instantly, Ransom sobered. "You choose to misunderstand, Meg. And I won't waste time playing games with you."

"No," she said sarcastically, "why should you, when your old playmate is waiting so impatiently?"

"Look, I'm not interested in taking this discussion any further. I simply came after you to warn you to guard your tongue."

*"My* tongue!"

"Yes. If you'll recall, you asked Clarice if you should send her mother upstairs. You need to remember that we weren't supposed to know about Clarice coming here. If she thinks about it, she'll realize you shouldn't have had any idea her mother was traveling with her."

"Then I guess you'll just have to keep her so occupied she won't have time to think, won't you?" Meg knew she was being nasty, but she was beyond caring. She had only just begun to visualize how awkward their situation was going to be while Clarice Howard was a guest at Wolfcrag.

Ransom's face darkened. "Aye—maybe that's exactly what I'll have to do."

"I'm certain you've had a great deal of experience along those lines."

"Oh, indeed. And Clarice is a woman to appreciate that experience. She's no timid virgin!"

Meg's snort was loud and inelegant. "That much is obvious!"

"You sound jealous, Meg."

"Jealous of that . . . that jaded bawd? You're welcome to her, and moreover, she's welcome to you!"

"How kind of you to give us your blessing," he drawled.

"The two of you are well suited. At least she'll divert your lustful attentions from Mairi."

"Mairi?" For an instant, Ransom seemed truly puzzled, but then his face cleared and he smiled wickedly. "It seems I have so many women I can't keep them sorted out, doesn't it?"

Meg grimaced. "Yes, it seems that way. But at least it prevents you from pestering me."

"And that bothers you, doesn't it?"

"Ha! It suits me perfectly, because it leaves me free to pursue the renovation."

"Well then, we'll just continue that way, shall we? I won't interfere with your . . . housecleaning, and you don't interfere with my whoring!"

"Excellent."

They glared at each other a moment longer, and then Meg turned her back and went on down the stairs.

Hours later, Meg sat impatiently in front of the broken mirror she had propped up on a wooden chest in her bedchamber. With a glum expression, she watched as her hair was brushed and curled and pinned by Mairi.

"I've almost finished, Meg," the other woman assured her. "Sit still a bit longer and you'll look beautiful."

That was just the problem. Meg wasn't at all certain she wanted to look beautiful. Somehow, it seemed a capitulation. Clarice Howard had made such an issue of Meg's unkempt appearance that afternoon that to go to the effort to improve it almost seemed she was rising to the bait. She didn't really want to give Clarice the satisfaction of knowing her words had hurt.

Still, she recalled her own horror when she'd first faced her reflection after leaving Clarice's chamber. She *had* looked awful! Her face had been streaked with dust, her hair a rat's nest shoved beneath the disreputable mobcap. Her gown was old, faded, and had been splotched with dampness from the scrub water. Her hands had been red, the nails dirty, and her feet had been encased in ugly work shoes. The mere fact that she'd had to meet Clarice while looking her worst galled her, and if for no other reason, she had decided to look her best before going down to the evening meal.

"Don't fuss any longer," she said to Mairi. "It looks fine."

"Be patient, now," Mairi chided.

"It seems I've spent hours getting ready for dinner," Meg sighed.

"It'll all be worth it when you see Clarice's face." Mairi chuckled. "She'll be so envious it'll turn her eyes green."

"They're already green," Meg stated. "Well, brownish green

. . . and beautiful. Oh, why am I doing this, Mairi? No matter what, I'm still going to look like an unrefined country miss."

"Only in your own mind. Clarice will be furious, and Ransom . . . well, he'll definitely be pleased."

"You don't sound as if that bothers you very much," Meg ventured carefully.

"Why should it? The two of you are married. There are those of us in this castle who'd like to see you take some notice of each other."

"But I thought . . . you and Ransom . . ."

The brush in Mairi's hand stilled in midair. "What in the name of all that's holy are you suggesting?"

"I . . . well, I've seen the two of you together," Meg stammered. "I just thought—"

"Well, you thought wrong." Mairi tipped her nose into the air. "I'm a respectable woman. What makes you think I'd have aught to do with a married man?"

"Oh, I don't know, Mairi." Meg rubbed her forehead with the tips of her fingers. "I'm so confused . . ."

"Aye, that's plain enough to see. I expect it's because you're in love with the laddie. That'll muddle your thinking for sure."

"In love?" Meg nearly choked. "Me? In love with Ransom? You must be mad."

Mairi simply smiled and gave Meg's hair a final pat. "You'll admit it in good time. You're too afraid right now."

"Afraid of what?"

"Of caring for a man you think too wild and reckless to make a suitable husband. A man who isn't one of us." Mairi met Meg's astonished eyes in the mirror. "Ransom St. Claire is as handsome a man as I've ever seen, Meggie . . . brash and bold, full of the Devil himself. Because of that, he's a perfect mate for you."

"Perfect?" Meg murmured faintly.

"Aye. Now me . . . why, he'd scare me witless. I wouldn't even begin to know how to deal with him. No, give me some quiet, tranquil man who likes hearth and family." Her smile became a little dreamy. "A man like Fletcher, perhaps."

"Fletcher?" Meg was having difficulty dealing with Mairi uttering one surprising statement after another. "Are you saying you're . . . that you'd like for Fletcher to . . . ?"

"I am, and I would. The only problem is, he thinks he's far too old for me. Oh, but Meg, I do think he cares something for me. He's been like a bear with a sore paw all week, grumbling because Ransom has sought out my company so often. He won't believe me when I tell him Ransom is simply trying to make you jealous."

"*Me* jealous?" Meg slapped both hands on the chest in front of her, making the mirror shudder dangerously. "I think you've completely lost your senses, Mairi."

"Then don't waste time sitting here listening to me babble on. It's time for you to join your guests for dinner anyway."

Meg took one last, quick glance into the looking glass and silently admitted she wasn't unhappy with the results of her primping and preening. At least she wouldn't shame Ransom this evening as she had no doubt done earlier in the day.

But, she mused, the fact that she was concerned about it didn't mean she was in love with him; it only meant she was being unerringly scrupulous about upholding her end of the bargain. She had to make the marriage look authentic, didn't she? And someone as worldly and sophisticated as Clarice would never believe a man like Ransom would willingly marry a backcountry scrubwoman. She had to make some show of being a lady—one with qualities Ransom St. Claire would find attractive.

Ransom let his eyes roam slowly around the room, amazed at his unexpected feeling of proprietorship. He was actually enjoying the sight of the Banqueting Hall filled with his men, the Scottish workers, and the guests from England. Dinner had not been the harrowing experience he'd feared. Fletcher and Mairi had cooked and served a meal of which they could be proud, and now that it was finished, some of the locals were entertaining with song and dance, and the newly arrived visitors seemed enthralled by it all.

All but Clarice, that is—and there was very little that could please her in her current petulant mood. Ransom dared a rapid glance in her direction and almost laughed at the bored set of her features. She'd made it clear that she was interested only in a quick meal and a rendezvous in whatever private corner he chose, and it amused him that Fletcher had seen fit to arrange the entertainment. Perhaps, if she grew bored enough, Clarice would acknowledge the uselessness of her mission and cut her visit short. The sooner she accepted Meg as his wife, the sooner she could go back to England and inform the king of his marriage.

Ransom was seated at the head of the table, with Meg and Clarice on either side, directly across from each other. With scant effort, he could study both of them and found himself making an idle comparison.

Clarice, patrician nose in the air, seemed more intent on scrutinizing Meg than she was in listening to the haunting Highland air being sung by Lorna MacLinn. Her blond hair had been rolled into elaborate curls held by jeweled pins that sparkled and flashed each time she turned her head. Other jewels adorned her ears, her fingers, and the sweep of breast bared by the nearly indecent cut of her green satin gown. There was no doubt whatsoever that Clarice was one of the loveliest women Ransom had ever seen, but it was a beauty that somehow left him feeling cold . . . and a little melancholy. There had been a time when he'd assumed that feeling had stemmed from the discovery of Clarice's infidelity, but now he knew he no longer cared whether she loved him or his brother, probably because he'd realized she was incapable of truly caring for anyone but herself.

Meg, on the other hand, might not be especially enamored of him, but she had proven over and over again how much she loved her family, her friends, and those people she so eagerly took under her wing. She was a strong woman, but there was also something soft and giving about her. Something nurturing, he supposed, although he had no idea where that word had come from.

Meg sat, intent on the music, her hand idly stroking Satan's back as he lay contentedly sleeping in her lap. She'd gathered the animal into her arms when Clarice had shrilly objected to his presence on the dining table. The cat had favored Clarice with an extraordinarily human scowl and given himself quite happily into his new mistress's care.

Ransom almost chuckled aloud as he catalogued the differences between Meg's appearance that afternoon and the picture of perfection she now presented. Being at such a disadvantage must have stung her pride, for it was obvious she had taken great pains with her toilette. He had detected the delicious scent of lilies when he'd seated her for dinner, and knew she must have spent some time in a scented bath. That thought, combined with the faint, heady aroma of flowers, was enough to heat his blood. Standing behind her, he'd been tempted to stroke her bare shoulders, to lean down and place a small kiss just below her ear. But even he had recognized the impulse was triggered by a possessiveness Meg would not appreciate, and he had resisted, though it cost him dearly to do so.

Meg's hair, as glossy and black as a raven's wing, had been piled atop her head in a simple style that suited her. There were no fat rolls of curls or jeweled pins, just one or two soft tendrils of hair that curled invitingly against her slender neck. Ransom's lips tightened into a firm line as he imagined entwining those strands of hair around his fingers, envisioned using their silken strength to draw her face close to his . . .

Her mouth intrigued him, he realized. It lacked the scarlet perfection of Clarice's, but it was neither hard nor practiced looking. Meg's lips were soft and mobile, an enticing rose pink that glimmered in the light of a hundred candles. He watched, fascinated, as she bit her lower lip in concentration, lost in the music that soared through the hall. He'd seen that mouth curved into charming smiles, thinned in anger, softly welcoming in moments of innocent passion.

*Damn,* Ransom thought, squirming uncomfortably in his chair, *it's too blasted hot in this room. Why in hell did Fletcher order such a big fire built?*

But the fire that threatened to consume him had nothing to

do with the one that burned on the hearth; it came from within and was fueled by the fresh, unsullied presence of the lovely, exasperating lass he had taken to wife.

"Is something wrong?"

The whispered words brought him out of his reverie, and he found himself gazing into eyes that were the same misty blue-gray hue as the gown Meg wore. Even though her eyes were shadowed by thick black lashes, Ransom could detect actual concern within them.

"No, nothing," he hastily replied. He leaned forward and placed a hand on her arm. From the corner of his eye, he could see Clarice stiffen to attention as she observed the contact. "I was just thinking how beautiful you look tonight."

Meg's first, swift smile showed her pleasure at the compliment, but she quickly controlled her mouth, forcing it into a wry grimace. "I took off that silly cap," she said.

Ransom laughed, delighted by her impish sense of humor. There was something decidedly pleasant about the husbandly pride he was feeling. Even the memory of the harsh words they'd spoken to each other only hours ago wasn't enough to dim his enjoyment of the moment. Most of the time, he knew, he and Meg used indignant anger and barbed remarks to keep some distance between themselves.

The singing had ended and circles were being formed for a country reel. On impulse, Ransom seized Meg's hand. "Come," he demanded with a smile, "let's dance."

Meg cast her eyes in Clarice's direction. "Perhaps you should—"

He gave her no time to finish. "Don't deny me," he teased, then leaned forward to whisper in her ear. "You wouldn't let me join in the dancing on Carraig because I wasn't wearing a kilt. But surely, here in my own castle, I can do as I please."

"Very well," she conceded. She rose, placing Satan in the seat of her chair, and the movement caused the tendrils of hair to swing softly over her shoulder. "But I would have thought you'd prefer to dance with Mairi or Clarice or one of your other . . . women."

With those lightly mocking words, she walked away, leaving

him to follow. He caught up with her just as the music started and, locking an arm around her waist, swung her easily about. She looked up at him, her expression pensive, but before he could question her thoughts, she was claimed by the next man in the circle and Ransom had to watch her being whirled out of his reach. Each time they came back together, she merely smiled demurely, and by the end of the dance, he was completely fascinated by her strange mood.

Badly wanting to go somewhere private with Meg, Ransom was irritated to find Clarice at his elbow, her openly inviting smile thoroughly unappealing to him. He fought an urge to shake free of her, and realized he barely felt civil toward her.

"Ran, are you going to ignore me all night?" Clarice pouted. "Here I've come all this way to see you, and you've hardly paid me a moment's attention."

"I don't mean to neglect you, Clarice," he said, hating himself for the lie. "Would you like for me to introduce you to one or two of our eligible young men so that you can join in the dancing?"

Clarice's eyes narrowed. "I'd prefer to dance with you, Ransom." She lifted her chin, refusing to acknowledge Meg's presence by his side. "After all, you're the one I came to see. And our friendship goes back a long, long way."

Ransom cleared his throat. "Clarice, I—"

A sudden commotion near the doorway caught their attention, and the three of them turned to see Fletcher motioning frantically. The other people in the room stepped aside to let them through, and there was a low murmur of concern and dismay.

A man, his head swathed in a bloodied rag, sagged against the wall. Huddled next to him was a sobbing woman who clutched a baby to her thin breast.

"Oh . . . beggars," Clarice muttered with disinterest. She took Ransom's arm. "You should get rid of them—they're likely to be carrying vermin."

Impatiently, Ransom shook off her hand. "What happened?" he inquired of Fletcher.

"Spottiswoode again," the first mate answered. "Turned

them out of their home—killed their livestock and broke up all their household goods."

"Damn him!" Meg moved forward to put an arm around the woman's shoulders. "Don't worry," she said, "you can stay here." Her declaration earned a grateful nod from the injured man.

"Ransom, are you going to allow these people to stay in your home?" Clarice asked. "How can you be certain they aren't thieves or murderers?"

With a scornful look at the Englishwoman, Meg called for Mairi and Lorna and gave them instructions about caring for the family. When the three of them had been led away, she faced her husband. "You've got to do something to stop that man, Ransom. You can't just let this sort of thing keep happening!"

"What sort of thing?" Clarice queried.

"Meg. . ." Ransom's tone carried an unspoken warning that Meg chose to overlook.

"Someone is going to get killed. Don't you even care?"

"Naturally I care," Ransom ground out. He glanced at the circle of people watching them and heaved a huge sigh. Grasping Meg by the arm, he said, "If you'll excuse us for a moment, I'd like a word with my wife." He dragged her into the hallway beyond.

"Meg, what is wrong with you?"

Eyes blazing, Meg put her hands on her hips. "With me?" she challenged. "What is wrong with you? Can't you see what a bastard Spottiswoode is?"

"Yes, of course—"

"Don't you see any need to stop him?"

"Have you forgotten that he is only acting on orders from the king?"

"That doesn't make it right!"

"No, it doesn't. But what you have to realize is that I can't interfere. Even harboring these refugees in my home is an act of treason."

"I can't believe it," she cried. "You're more concerned about your reputation than you are about those poor people's lives."

"For God's sake, be reasonable. We have a castle full of visitors from England, Meg—do you want them informing George that we're turning Wolfcrag into a haven for rebels?"

"You would refuse them help?"

"No, but we don't have to be quite so public about it. Do what you can for those crofters, but be discreet."

There was a bright spot of color in each of Meg's cheeks. "You know, for a few minutes tonight, I was almost able to forget that you're a damned Englishman."

"And I'd almost lost sight of the fact that you're a rebellious, troublemaking little shrew."

"Well, perhaps it's a good thing we came to our senses and recalled reality."

"Perhaps it is."

They glared fiercely at each other.

"Ransom, darling, what's taking you so long?" scolded Clarice, appearing in the doorway. "I'm still dying to dance with you."

"Then I won't keep you waiting any longer," Ransom declared, with a nasty smirk in Meg's direction. She tightened her lips and continued to glare.

"I do hope you won't mind if I . . . borrow your husband for a while, Meg," Clarice purred, leaning forward to afford Ransom an unrestricted view down the front of her gown.

*"Fuigh,* no," Meg said fervently. "I'll gladly deliver him straight into your hands. Do with him what you will."

And at that moment, given her current state of temper, she believed with all her heart that she truly meant every word.

## Chapter Seventeen

Worry etched itself across Meg's features as she walked through the courtyard and into the castle. Absentmindedly, she greeted the plasterers working atop scaffolding erected in the entryway, and started up the stairs.

She had just come from Brodie MacLinn's cottage, and old Hamish was no better. She had helped Lorna feed him herbal tea and bathe his fevered brow, but secretly she believed that if Dr. MacSween didn't arrive soon, it would be too late to save the elderly man.

Wearily, she climbed the stairs. More than ten days had passed since she'd dispatched the message to the doctor. He'd sent back word that he couldn't leave Carraig until one of his patients there had been delivered of her first child. The pregnancy had been difficult, and there was considerable reason to assume the birth—which was expected any day—would be the same. In the meantime, he'd sent detailed instructions telling them how to care for Hamish until his arrival.

So Lorna and Meg had followed Dr. MacSween's written directives, and even though the tisanes and poultices had alleviated the worst of his fever and coughing, Hamish was still far from well. He seemed lost in a world that existed only in his memory; he spent hours each day rambling on about people he had known and events that had taken place in the past. Oftentimes, Meg would sit enthralled while Hamish told her tales of the grandfather and uncles she'd never known. He'd talk happily for a time, and then, without warning, he'd become confused, unable to even remember who she was. He had no recollection of recent events, no idea of where he was or how he came to be there.

Hamish was such a sweet, endearing old soul that Meg prayed daily there was something to be done for him, fastening her hope on the timely appearance of Dr. MacSween.

Now, in the privacy of her bedchamber, Meg began stripping off the gown she wore. It had become her habit to dress in old garb each morning in order to help with the myriad tasks left to do about the castle, but before the midday meal, she bathed and donned more suitable clothing for mingling with the visitors from England. To her surprise, she had found Clarice's mother a most charming and amiable lady, and she had come to enjoy afternoons spent chatting not only with her but with all the women in Clarice's entourage. She had learned a great deal of life at court, and though she was certain she'd never care to experience it firsthand, she did find it pleasant to hear about.

Clarice herself never attended these informal gatherings; she was always busy elsewhere. Meg knew that she and Ransom often went riding or spent time gaming with those few of his men who hadn't volunteered their services to the renovation. Clarice had even joined Ransom and a half-dozen others on their most recent buying trip to Inverness. Sensing that Ransom would expect her to object, she'd voiced no opposition to the journey. But once they were gone, she'd had to labor diligently to keep her mind free of conjecture about what the two of them were doing while out of sight of Wolfcrag.

Fiercely insisting to herself that it really didn't matter, Meg kept a surreptitious watch over Ransom and Clarice. She did not believe he had bedded the Englishwoman, for there was a slightly dissatisfied air about Clarice, a somewhat petulant set to her perfect features. Meg was well aware that Clarice took advantage of every opportunity to put herself in Ransom's way. With artful gracelessness, she managed to brush against him a dozen times a day. During meals, she touched his hand repeatedly or leaned close to gaze seductively into his eyes.

Meg didn't like Clarice's coyness, but she realized that it would have provoked her temper far more had she not sensed Ransom's subtle withdrawal from his persistent houseguest. Sometimes the expression on his face hinted at distaste, and Meg perceived that, as a man who enjoyed a certain success with the ladies, he preferred to do the pursuing. It would seem he was not entirely comfortable being the one stalked.

Barefoot, dressed only in her shift and petticoats, Meg was pouring water into a porcelain bowl when she heard the click of the door latch behind her. She turned, expecting to see Mairi. Instead, Clarice Howard stepped into the room, her curious eyes making a slow, deliberate survey of her surroundings. At last, her avid gaze came to rest on Meg herself, and her scarlet lips twisted with smugness.

"So," she murmured, "this is where you disappear to. I wondered—"

"Is there something I can do for you?" Meg inquired with forced civility.

"Oh, indeed there is. You can answer a number of questions for me."

Carefully, Meg set down the pitcher. "What questions?"

"Why don't you and Ransom live as man and wife?"

"I, uh . . . I don't know what you mean," Meg stalled.

"I think you do." Clarice strolled casually across the room to the tall windows. She glanced outside without interest, drumming tapered nails upon the stone sill. "I've been watching the two of you, and I'm fairly certain that every night Ransom retires to his chamber alone. Now, by following you, I know you must come here to sleep."

"What is so unusual about that? Many married couples have separate rooms."

"Newlyweds?" Clarice smirked. "I know Ran well enough to know that if he truly cared anything about you, he wouldn't tolerate separate beds for even one night."

"Perhaps you don't know Ransom as well as you think," Meg said. "Or perhaps he has changed."

"Or perhaps," put in Clarice, "your marriage is something of a sham."

"A sham?"

"Don't look so shocked," the other woman said. "You wouldn't be the first peasant lass to marry a man for his money and title." Clarice closed the distance between them, making a thorough perusal of Meg's scantily clad figure. "What perplexes me is, what reason could he have had for marrying you? You don't know the first thing about beautifying yourself; you're hardly a credit to him socially." She looked thoughtful. "Rumor has it that your father is a notorious outlaw, but for the life of me, I cannot imagine Ransom St. Claire taking you to wife just to protect himself. And he swears you are not with child." Clarice walked slowly around Meg, studying her from all sides. "I'd like to know exactly how you came to ensnare him."

Meg fought to control the bitter temper rising within her. She would not stoop to a cat fight with this woman.

"Why don't you ask Ransom?"

"Because," Clarice admitted, "when it comes to you, he is as closemouthed as it's possible to be. There are times when I think he is merely using me for some strange purpose of his own—perhaps to make you jealous. And then there are times when I believe he might be persuaded to renew our affair." She frowned. "He loved me once, you know."

"Yes, I know."

"He told you that?"

"He said he loved you until he discovered you were only using him to remain close to his brother Edmund."

Clarice sighed. "That was the truth of it in the beginning. I'd cared for Edmund for a long time, so it came as something of a shock when he announced his intention of marrying a Devonshire heiress. It was even more distressing to learn that, within months of their marriage, Edmund found he actually had feelings for his wife. He wanted nothing more to do with me—"

"And so you turned to Ransom?" Meg was amazed at the strength of her disgust with Clarice. Even considering her own resentment against him, Meg recognized the fact that he had deserved better treatment at Clarice's hands.

"Yes. Stupidly, I thought Edmund would be plagued by

envy seeing the two of us together. Of course, he was too enamored to pay me the slightest attention." Clarice looked about for a chair, then settled into the only one in the room, spreading her skirts about her. "And then it ceased to matter. I had begun to really understand Ransom's worth. He's twice the man his brother is, and I must have been blind not to have seen it from the first.

"But, of course," she went on, "Ransom was too proud to continue our affair once he learned the truth. So he buried himself on that estate in Devon and refused to see me."

"Then why did you follow him here?" Meg inquired.

"Because I knew him well enough to realize he'd be bored to death in this wilderness. And because I'd heard rumors there were no women at Wolfcrag, that Ransom was alone and homesick." She pulled at a thread on her gown, a slightly mocking smile curving her mouth. "The king was quite pleased with my idea of marriage to Ran. I think he believed it would be the final step in transforming him. And so, I left London with high hopes and endured the nightmarish journey up here . . . Only to find him already married. I have to tell you, Meg, it was a bitter defeat for me."

Meg nodded, not speaking. She had the uneasy feeling that Clarice had a great deal more to say.

"A defeat I'm not entirely ready to accept." Clarice's smile grew wider. "That's why I'm so pleased to find your marriage isn't a love match. Tell me, what would you take to give him up?"

"What?"

"Tell me why you really married Ransom and I'll see that you get whatever it is you want. All you have to do is disappear from his life and never contact him again."

"But I—"

"Was it money?" Clarice asked. "Because if it was, I can reward you handsomely for divorcing him."

"I didn't marry Ransom St. Claire for his money," Meg snapped. "Or his title."

"Then why?"

"I refuse to discuss this any further. If you want information, you'll have to go to Ransom."

"You're going to be difficult, I see."

Meg's unease grew. "What do you mean?"

Clarice leaned forward. "I'm not as silly as that gaggle of geese I brought with me. Don't you think I'm aware of what's going on? I'm certain our good king would be interested to learn that you and Ransom are giving shelter to a number of Scottish rebels. That you've opposed Jonathan Spottiswoode, a good and loyal subject, at every turn. Ransom's situation is tenuous at best. Do you think George is going to be lenient with him another time?"

"Are you threatening to go to him with this ridiculous tale?"

"I am—and it's not ridiculous. I'm in a position to do considerable damage to your husband, Meg . . . and there's only one way to stop me."

"And that is?"

"Step aside. Give me the opportunity to try and win Ransom back. I don't think he loves you . . . and you certainly don't seem overly fond of him. Just tell me what it is he promised you, and I'll see that it's yours . . . as soon as you remove yourself as an obstacle in my path."

"If Ransom loves you, nothing would stand in his way."

"He does love me," Clarice declared fiercely. "He just hasn't allowed himself to get over his anger at me. With a little help from you, I can make him see that."

"What can I do?"

"Give me free rein. Make yourself as scarce as you can and let me have an evening alone with him."

Meg's head had begun to ache, and she rubbed her forehead wearily. "Do whatever you want," she finally said. "If Ransom wants a divorce, I'll give him one."

They were, she reminded herself, going to divorce at some point anyway. What difference could it make whether it was now or later, as long as he deeded the castle over to her? With the work progressing so well, it probably wouldn't have been long before Ransom would have made the same suggestion. And if the thought of Clarice and Ransom together was more painful than she'd expected, it was a pain she'd have to cope with. She hadn't planned on a future with him—she'd always known they'd go their separate ways. How much better it would be for that to happen before they grew any closer.

"I'm glad you're going to be reasonable, Meg. Now, what is it you want?"

"I don't want anything from you, Clarice. But if Ransom wishes to resume your affair, I promise I won't stand in the way."

There was a long silence, during which Clarice watched her closely, as if trying to determine her sincerity. At length, she rose from the chair and said, "I appreciate your good sense. Thank you." She started for the door. "I intend to commence my campaign immediately with a quiet dinner for two this evening. Will you make the arrangements?"

Meg swallowed her pride with some difficulty. "Yes, I'll speak to Fletcher."

"I'd like for it to be served in the small parlor in my suite of rooms. My women will be dining belowstairs so we can be alone. After the meal, if all goes as I hope, we will go back to Ransom's bedchamber."

Meg inclined her head. "As you wish."

When Clarice had gone, Meg sat down on the side of her bed and contemplated what she had agreed to do. It was necessary if she was going to protect Ransom, herself, and the inhabitants of Wolfcrag . . . wasn't it?

Within the hour, Mairi arrived at her door, breathless in her haste. "Fletcher says to come quickly, Meg—your father and Dr. MacSween have arrived!"

Meg paused at the top of the stairs, a sudden lump in her throat at the sight of her father standing in the hallway below. After so many years, he was back at Wolfcrag and obviously thunderstruck at its return to glory.

Meg flew down the stairs and into his arms, laughing and talking at the same time. Her father held her tightly, but didn't utter a word. After a moment, Meg drew back to study him. He looked tired, far more so than the day's journey from Carraig should have warranted. Chilly fingers closed around her heart.

"Father, what's wrong?" She gave Dr. MacSween a trembly smile. "Where are the others? Didn't they come with you?"

Dr. MacSween patted Revan MacLinn's shoulder. "I'll just have your man show me to the sick man's cottage, and you and Meg can have some privacy."

Meg gripped her father's hand and led him into the Great Hall. Removing his cloak, he slumped tiredly in a high-backed chair, thrusting his booted feet toward the small fire that burned on the hearth. A light summer rain had turned the day chilly. Meg lighted several candles and sent Mairi for food and wine.

"You'd better tell me what's wrong." Meg took the chair next to MacLinn. "Something has happened, hasn't it?"

MacLinn nodded, his amber eyes shadowed. "It's Cathryn," he said. "She has left me—and taken Alexander."

"Left?" Meg cried. "Why? Where did she go?"

"She was upset over the military training we were giving the lads . . ."

"I remember."

"When I refused to discontinue it, she took Alex and ran away. She waited until I'd ridden out to check the herds and would be gone all day, so I had no way of stopping her."

"I can't believe Alex would go with her."

"It wasn't his choice, but Meg, your brother is growing into a fine man. Unbeknownst to Cathryn, he left a note explaining that he considered it his duty to go with his mother and take care of her. He thought she planned to take refuge with her relatives in the border country." MacLinn rubbed a hand over his bearded chin. "Two weeks ago I got a smuggled message from him. They're in Briarthorn Castle near Edinburgh."

"Are you going after them?"

"Aye, when the time comes." Revan glanced up as Mairi entered the room, accepting the glass of wine she offered. "But I'll be in no hurry, for I hope Cathryn will come to her senses and return of her own will."

"What if she doesn't?"

"Then I'll go for her. If she wants to stay there, that's fine, but I'll bring my son home no matter what."

"I don't understand how she could do this," Meg stormed. "I thought she was more loyal to the MacLinns than that."

"Don't be too hard on her, Meggie." MacLinn leaned his head against the back of the chair and closed his eyes. "You probably don't know how badly Catriona feels about never having other children after Alexander. She has allowed herself to love him too fiercely, to become too protective of him. She's frightened of losing him, that's all."

Meg hadn't heard her father use the Gaelic form of Cathryn's name in a long time and knew it meant he was remembering the days when their fiery love was new. It was clear that even though he felt betrayed by her abandonment, he loved her dearly and missed her bitterly. Exhaustion was evident on his features and in the fatigued droop of his wide shoulders.

"Let me show you to a room where you can rest, Father. We can talk more later."

"Aye, that sounds fine. 'Twould seem I haven't slept well in a fortnight."

Halfway up the stairs, he paused. "There's something else, Meg. The men of the clan are ready to come to Wolfcrag and begin their campaign against Spottiswoode . . . but they've a need for money to buy food and supplies. Did you say your husband had given you gold?"

"Yes," she replied slowly, "some. I have to pay wages this afternoon . . . but I suppose I could spare enough to outfit your men."

"Good." MacLinn looked sheepish. "I'd do it myself, but Cathryn took every cent she could lay hands on. She thought it would thwart my plan if I couldn't buy the necessary supplies."

Meg couldn't suppress a momentary flash of admiration for her stepmother. The woman had been courageous indeed, if she had dared such an action against her husband.

"I'll get you the money now—but I'm afraid we can't breathe a word of it to Ransom."

"Of course not," MacLinn agreed. "The bloody English dog

wouldn't care to know he was paying for the liberation of the enemy."

Meg experienced a twinge of guilt, and an unexpected loyalty toward Ransom. But she knew the uselessness of defending his honor to her father. "What shall I do with the gold?"

"Find the doctor and give it to him. Some of the men who came with us can take it back to the island."

"Very well. Come, I'll show you to an empty bedchamber."

Revan MacLinn put an arm around his daughter's shoulders and gave her an affectionate hug. "I haven't told ye, Meggie, what a wonderful job you've done resurrecting this old castle. It looks magnificent."

"Thank you," Meg murmured, almost too proud to speak.

"I only wish Cathryn could see . . ." His brows drew together and his voice trailed away. "Show me to my bed, lass. I feel like I could sleep for a century."

"Damnation, girl, have you lost your mind?" railed Fletcher. "What in the name of St. Elmo do you hope to gain by throwing Ransom to that she-wolf? Dinner for two in her chambers? Pshaw, that sets my teeth on edge!"

"You don't understand," Meg began.

"No, I don't! He's your husband, isn't he?"

"Yes, but—"

"Then why do you want him to end up in that strumpet's bed? I thought you'd gotten over your anger at him for . . . well, for what he did."

"Fletcher, please—you don't know all the circumstances."

Fletcher flounced across the kitchen to check the contents of a steaming cook pot. After stirring wildly, he clanged the metal lid and all but threw the wooden spoon back onto the work table. Meg followed him, her voice taking on a pleading note.

"If you'd just calm down, I might be able to explain," she said.

"I doubt it. I've lost a lot of faith in you, lass. You're acting like some weak-kneed English *lady* who doesn't have the innards to fight for her man."

"He's not my—"

"I thought you Highland women were strong . . . but I guess I was mistaken. You don't even have the gumption to keep Ransom occupied so that he doesn't have time to chase every pretty gal in sight." He rolled his eyes toward the corner of the room where Mairi sat peeling vegetables. "And now you intend to hand him to that whey-faced vixen on a silver platter. You're a disappointment, Meg St. Claire. Damned if you aren't."

Meg drew herself up, glaring at him. "Well," she retorted, "I'm very sorry to have met with your disapproval. But I'd appreciate it if you would do as you're told and . . . and keep your opinions to yourself!"

Halfway up the stairs, Meg paused, one hand clutching the newly smooth banister. Fletcher was right, and she knew it. His disappointment in her hurt, but it was nothing to the bitter disillusionment she felt with herself.

"Oh, God," she whispered, staring blindly ahead, "what have I done?"

Ransom was furious with Meg. All through the intimate little dinner with Clarice, which the Englishwoman had made certain he understood his wife had sanctioned, he'd thought of nothing but what he would do the instant he could get his hands on her. God alone knew what he'd been through in the past two weeks trying to encourage Clarice within Meg's presence . . . and then avoid her when Meg was out of sight. It had been a foolish and dangerous game, and in the end it hadn't worked. It had only led to increasing obsession on Clarice's part and, apparently, left Meg unaffected. Had she cared anything at all for him—had she felt one iota of jealousy—she'd never have thrown them together in a situation that made it almost impossible for him to escape Clarice's covetous grasp.

Of course, Clarice had led him to believe the other members of her entourage had chosen to dine *en suite* that evening, or he'd never have gone to her room. He'd fully expected to share a meal with Lady Howard and the ladies-in-waiting. The cozy setting that had met his eyes had been something of a shock, but nothing compared to the announcement that not only had Meg known of the tryst, she'd helped arrange it.

Clarice had been alternately charming and provocative, but her wiles had failed to move Ransom. He was already out of sorts because the Scottish outlaw had shown up at Wolfcrag earlier in the day. He was concerned with keeping the man's presence a secret from the guests, because he felt fairly certain the king wouldn't understand his familiarity with such an infamous traitor. And the knowledge of Meg's treachery was the final blow. All he wanted to do was get away from Clarice and go to bed—alone.

Clarice pouted, then fumed, then resorted to tears, but Ransom remained adamant. "I'm a married man, Clarice . . . and a dalliance with anyone other than my wife is of no interest to me. I'm sorry if . . . if I led you to believe otherwise."

When he left, Clarice followed him down the hallway, ignoring the fact that she was clad only in a sheer negligee. Even as he threw open the door of his chamber, she clutched his arm and made one last appeal.

"Ran, please give me a chance. I know you're still hurt and angry about Edmund, but darling, I swear I can make it all up to you."

"I'm not in the mood, Clarice." Ransom shook off her hand. "I suggest that you just go quietly back to your room . . ."

The blood drained from the woman's face, leaving her looking surprisingly haggard. Her hazel eyes widened in disbelief, then narrowed in anger. Her savage glare was fastened on something in the chamber beyond Ransom. Puzzled, he turned to seek the cause of her sudden agitation.

The first thing he saw was a white cotton nightgown neatly draped over the foot of his bed. The second thing he saw was his wife, propped against the pillows, the sheet clasped to her breasts. The light of a single candle glimmered on her bare shoulders and caught the shine of her ebony hair, which tumbled wildly about her. Whether nervously or with intended seductiveness, Meg moistened her lips as she gazed at him with enormous, shining eyes. Ransom felt as if his heart had begun beating in triple time.

Meg tilted her head and smiled. "Come to bed, Ransom," she said, patting the coverlet enticingly. "I've been waiting for you."

# Chapter Eighteen

"Why, you lying, conniving little . . ."

Clarice's wrathful voice died into silence as Ransom looked back at her. He knew something was going on between the two women, but his astonished pleasure at finding Meg in his bed was too great for him to ask questions.

"I'm sorry, Clarice," he said in low tones, "but I can hardly invite you in. We'll talk in the morning, shall we?"

Gently, but firmly, he began closing the door. Clarice balked for a moment, her face distorted with anger, but after a few seconds she shrugged and managed a small, stiff smile. As though summoning the remnants of her pride, she turned and walked away.

Meg's breathing eased as Ransom shut the door and bolted it; her breathing became erratic again as, with an odd expression on his face, he crossed the room to stand at the foot of the bed.

"What are you doing?" he rasped.

Meg offered a timid smile. "Trying to seduce you," she admitted in a whisper.

"Well, there's something new," he said, a crooked grin pulling at his mouth. "But do you believe it's possible for a woman to seduce a man?"

"I really wouldn't know," she replied archly. *"Highland men* don't have to be seduced."

"Damnation," he growled. "Must I always have to suffer comparison to Highland men?" He walked around the end of the bed, coming to sit on the side next to Meg. "It's an insult to my manhood."

"Then let me make amends," Meg murmured, raising her arms to encircle his neck. Softly, she pressed against him and gave him a slow, deliberate kiss. She could feel his surprise, could sense the instant it gave way to eager response.

"Is it?" Meg asked. "Possible for me to seduce you, I mean."

"Lord, yes," he muttered. His words were lost as she kissed him again. "Meg . . . wait . . ."

She continued kissing him, using every iota of experience she'd ever had in the matter. When she hesitantly touched the tip of her tongue to the corner of his mouth, he gasped and reacted with such ardency that she repeated the action, daring to trace the fuller line of his bottom lip. She immediately found herself dragged away from the pillows and onto his lap. There seemed to be every evidence that not only was it possible for her to seduce him, but that he was ready and willing.

Meg was aware of a pleasurable thrill at the thought. She had been more than a little apprehensive that he might rebuff her advances. She'd realized that she might have waited too long, that he might already be so deeply involved with Clarice that he'd lost interest in her.

Meg had been forced to admit the truth to herself. As improbable as it might be, she was utterly fascinated by Ransom St. Claire. No, she was in love with him—and how that could have happened was beyond her. She had never wanted to love him; he was an English patriot who scorned her heritage, her way of life. He hated her country, couldn't wait to be gone from it. And still, her silly, rebellious heart had completely surrendered itself to him, even cognizant of the pain that action might bring. With brutal honesty, Meg amended that thought. The pain was definite, inevitable. There was no way she could ever have any sort of future with this man; they were destined to go their separate ways. Their lives were too different to ever come together with any kind of permanence.

Why then had she chosen to acknowledge her passion for

him? Why had she decided to court Clarice's vengeance and risk her own pride for the sake of this night with him?

Nestling her face against the firm, warm flesh of Ransom's throat, Meg reflected on the reason. It had a great deal to do with the fact that she loved him, of course. But she could have nurtured that emotion in secret, never confessing it to anyone, least of all Ransom. Something, at some point, had persuaded her not to do that. Mairi's silent disapproval and Fletcher's irate scolding had had a bearing on it, certainly. But somehow she thought her decision had even more to do with the sadness on her father's face, the wariness that hinted at his fear of having lost everything that was dear to him.

More and more lately, Meg had found herself believing that her marriage to Ransom was the only one she would ever have. Even after he obtained his divorce and went back to England, she knew she would still consider him her lawful husband. For whatever reason, she couldn't see herself with any other man. The truth was, she didn't want any other man . . . and if it wasn't possible to have the one she did want, then she'd have what time she could with him and make that suffice for the rest of her life.

And while she had nervously waited in Ransom's bed, she had come to realize something else. If they did live together as man and wife, and the result was a child, might that not be a blessing of some kind? They were legally married, so their bairn would never have to suffer the stigma of illegitimacy . . . and when Ransom had gone, the child could be her comfort. It could be the focus for the remainder of her life. Suddenly, what had once seemed a genuine dilemma now seemed a wonderful opportunity.

At any rate, she knew that whatever occurred between them tonight was going to change her life forever, but she no longer shrank from that reality.

"Meg, listen to me," Ransom said, breathing raggedly. "There's no need for this . . ."

"But it's what I want," she said simply. "Don't you . . . don't you want it, too?"

She caught the sound of a moan deep within his throat and

had to listen carefully to distinguish his words. "God help me," he murmured, "yes. Yes! But remember what happened before. I don't want to hurt you, Meg . . . I don't want that ever again."

Guiltily, Meg closed her eyes. Would he find out the real truth about the supposed consummation of their marriage? And if he somehow comprehended her virginity was intact, would he be angry about it? She sighed against his neck. It really didn't matter. She would have this time with him regardless of the consequences.

"Don't worry about that," she replied. "You won't hurt me."

He turned his face to hers, nuzzling her temple with a kiss. "I don't understand. What made you change your mind?"

"Seeing you with Clarice, perhaps."

At his sudden, swift smile, she gave his shoulder a playful nip. "That pleases you, does it?" she said, her chin making a defiant lift.

Ransom took advantage of her tilted face to kiss her. "It does." He chuckled. "I worked damned hard to let you see the two of us together all the time. And I worked even harder staying out of Clarice's clutches." He shook his head. "I didn't think my plan had been very effective when I walked into that dinner for two tonight. I couldn't believe you'd agree to something like that."

"I wouldn't have, except that Clarice made a number of threats. I didn't know what else to do." For a long moment, Meg stared down at the sheet tangled between them. Finally, she looked back into Ransom's eyes. "She said she'd go to the king and tell him you're harboring Scottish rebels at Wolfcrag, that you have associations with an outlawed clan. I thought I should tell you what you're risking if you go through with . . . with this night."

His eyes, the color of a lazy southern ocean, softened. "Meg, don't you know that I'd hazard anything to be with you like this? Besides, Clarice's petty vengeance doesn't bother me. George wanted me to win the rebels over, remember—and what better way to do it than take them in and befriend them? I think I can prove to him that I've made more converts for him by my actions than Spottiswoode has by his."

"Clarice wasn't the only reason," Meg confessed. "My father arrived today with the news that Cathryn has left him."

"So Fletcher told me."

"Ransom, as much as those two have always loved each other . . . well, for something like that to happen only proves how fleeting any happiness we may have in this lifetime is. I . . ." Shyly, her eyes fell again. "I've decided that it would make me happy to live as your wife for the rest of the summer, or however long we might have before you go back to England."

"I never expected to hear you say anything like that," Ransom stated. "And I only hope you aren't letting your anxiety over your parents' unhappiness cloud your judgment."

"There's one other reason for my decision," she whispered, head bowed.

"Oh?"

"Yes. Promise you won't laugh at me." She did look up then, her gaze stern. "I think I might be in love with you."

Ransom's smile faded. "But Meg, I—"

Meg laid the tips of her fingers against his lips. "Don't say it, Ransom. I know you don't love me . . . I'm not asking you to. I know that wasn't a part of our bargain." She removed her fingertips, replacing them with her mouth. She kissed him slowly, softly, thoroughly, finally drawing away to whisper, "All I want you to do is make me your wife . . . for however long you choose."

From that moment, Ransom took charge. He lifted her, sheet and all, and placed her back against the pillows. Then he braced himself above her, leaning over to return her kiss, making the touch gentle, a mere brush of his mouth across hers. His lips moved to her ear, and his breath stirred tendrils of hair as he whispered, "Are you certain, Meg?"

She gazed up at him, her eyes tracing the strong lines of his face, marveling again at the fathomless depths of his aqua eyes. Slowly, she nodded.

Ransom felt his chest constrict, but couldn't be sure of the reason. It probably had something to do with the way Meg lay looking up at him, so innocently trusting after the way he had treated her before. Her eyes were huge in her heart-shaped face, not frightened precisely, but wary. Her attitude of watchful waiting told him that she was, in spite of her brave words about Highland men, little more than an untried virgin. And her first experience had been at his clumsy hands.

He knew that was only one of the reasons he should leave her alone, get off the bed and depart on a run. He sensed that this act would bind them together for the rest of their lives, as surely as if theirs had been a genuine marriage. But they had so little chance of ever having any sort of life together that he needed to call a halt, let matters proceed no further.

Unfortunately, she had managed his seduction well. All he could think of was how sweet and smooth her skin was, how good she smelled—how much her hair resembled fine black silk as it cascaded over the pillows. The urge to press his lips to the pulsing heartbeat in her throat was too much to be denied; he was certain he could not survive much longer without feeling her breasts beneath his hands.

He eased himself away from her, struggling to control his raspy breathing. He had to give her one last chance to change her mind, and he concluded the best way to do that was to demonstrate his intentions in the most explicit way he could think of. He stood at the side of the bed and, his eyes on hers, purposefully began removing his clothing.

Meg snuggled back into the pillows, unable to keep a smile from her lips as she watched Ransom unlace his shirt and pull it over his head. He tossed it aside and bent to take off his boots. Each move he made was so calculated that she couldn't help but be amused. Intuition told her he was trying to scare her off, giving her a last opportunity to flee his chamber in maidenly terror.

What he failed to understand was that she had seen him unclothed before and her reaction had never been one of fright. Rather, his body intrigued and enticed her, fired her natural interest and curiosity. No, if Ransom hoped to scare her away, he had chosen exactly the wrong approach!

She admired his broad, hair-hazed chest, then let her glance drop to the flat stomach and lean hips slowly being revealed as he shoved his trousers downward. Even the flagrant proof of his excited readiness didn't daunt her, although its unabashed impudence brought a show of color to her face.

Somehow, she tore her gaze away, moving it upward again. She saw that Ransom was watching her carefully, looking as if he fully expected her to scream and swoon. Her smile grew and, with studied invitation, she held out a hand to him.

"Are you having any doubts?" he queried, taking her hand and allowing her to draw him down beside her.

"No, of course not. Let's just . . . proceed, shall we?"

He was not a man to refuse such an offer. Not after waiting so long for her to make it. Carefully, he raised himself over her, sliding one bare leg along hers. He pushed aside the folds of linen crumpled between them, letting his gaze drop to her bosom and linger there, delighting in the soft perfection of her body.

Of its own volition, his hand moved to shape itself to one of the gently rounded breasts, and a shaft of desire pierced him as the nipple beaded and thrust against his palm. Absorbed, he stroked the curve of her flesh and let his thumb circle, then press, its rose-hued center. Meg stirred and cried out softly, her eyes growing wider and darker. Ransom lowered his head and brushed a kiss where his thumb had been. She clasped him convulsively, as if the touch had pained her, and he soothed her with a kiss on her shoulder.

"Just relax and everything will be fine," he promised. "I won't hurt you this time."

Ransom could tell she was making an effort to calm her suddenly nervous self, and he feared she was recalling that other, awkward lovemaking.

He shifted his weight, bringing his lower body into intimate contact with hers. She made an almost inaudible sound, but he surmised that it was a sign of pleasure. The thought was substantiated when he felt her arms slide around him, drawing him closer with a hint of impatience. But then the caressing stroke of her small hands against his back drove all thoughts of any kind from his head. Blindly, he sought her mouth and gloried in her sweet response. He kissed her without restraint, urging her lips apart with deep, softly hot kisses that seemed to melt her trepidation.

When she feverishly began to return his kisses, Ransom began slowly easing his body into hers, careful to lessen any pain she might feel. The muscles of his back and shoulders quivered as he exercised rigid control; his face was carved into a strained mask.

And then the harsh lines of his face rearranged themselves into stunned surprise as his gentle thrusting encountered an unyielding barrier. His mind reeled—something was terribly wrong! It was as if she were a virgin again . . . or, harsh reality dawned on him, a virgin *still.* The implication had only just begun to sink in when Meg, sensing his hesitation, arched her back and drove herself against him, accomplishing what he had balked at doing. Her short, sharp gasp alerted him to the pain she must have felt.

Unable to hold onto the flash of anger he'd experienced, Ransom covered her mouth with quick, tender touches of his own, and Meg did not cry out again. The only sign of her distress was the knotting of her hands into fists against his back. He grew still, waiting, and finally her hands began to relax, resuming their restless exploration.

Ransom's further movements were cautious at first, and then, when she did not protest, gradually increasing in vigor. He was captivated by the woman beneath him, thrilled by the satiny brush of her hair against his face, the gentle kneading of her fingers along his shoulders and arms. He derived great pleasure from the sound of her rapid breathing in his ear—the tiny, mindless gasps that indicated she was beyond the pain and encountering at least a part of the ecstasy that lured him.

Relentlessly, he was driven onward, away from all thoughts of anything but the delightful sensations that were coursing through him. They stimulated and provoked and eventually compelled him to a shattering fulfillment that crashed over him in wondrous waves of satisfying euphoria. He clenched his teeth against the shout of joy that would have broken forth, but he could not control a shuddering moan that was wrenched from his throat against his will.

In his arms, Meg began a breathless chant. "Ransom, oh, Ran . . . Oh, Ransom!" Her movements became frenzied, tortured, and they inspired his spent body to move again. Within moments, he had guided her to the edge of sanity, and with soft, biting kisses and the swift, powerful thrusts of his hips, he pushed her over. Ransom couldn't recall another experience that thrilled him half as much as clasping Meg to him while her body shook with cataclysmic tremors and she whimpered in heedless delight.

For long moments they lay together, breathing harshly and unable to speak, and then Meg turned in his arms and kissed him just below the ear. "I love you," she whispered softly, and succumbed to sleep with the suddenness of a child.

The morning light spilling through the windows awakened Meg. Sleepily, she tried to burrow deeper into the bed, but it seemed hard and unyielding. Surprised, she opened her eyes to find Ransom sitting up against the pillows and herself sprawled across him, her head on his sheet-covered lap. As she sat up, his hand fell away from her hair, which she realized he'd been stroking.

"Good morning," she murmured with a drowsy smile.

"Did you sleep well?" he inquired, with a slight lift to one corner of his mouth.

Meg stared at the movement, thinking how much she'd like to kiss him there. But suddenly something in his expression made her uneasy.

"Yes . . . and you?"

"How do you think I slept, Meg?"

Her contentment vanished. He was angry—but, of course, she could have expected nothing else. She looked at him, but couldn't seem to summon an answer.

"Will you ever stop lying to me?" he queried softly.

"Ransom, I'm sorry . . ."

"Why did you let me think I had attacked you in a drunken frenzy?" he asked, his tone deceptively lazy. "Didn't you know how that would make me feel? Didn't you realize the self-contempt I would have?"

"You don't understand . . ." Meg clutched the sheet to her breasts, desperately trying to sort out her muddled thoughts. "I didn't plan it that way, but when you . . . well, passed out . . . it seemed the perfect way to make you believe our marriage had been legalized."

"No matter how you try to justify it, the entire thing was a monumental lie. You went to a great deal of trouble to set the stage. Tell me, where did the blood come from?"

"I cut my leg." Meg looked down, unable to meet his accusatory gaze.

"And the bruises?"

Quickly, her eyes flew back to his face. "I fell. And if you'll recall, you were the one who first mentioned the bruises. I never intended to try and make you believe you'd forced me."

"You didn't correct me."

"No, I didn't," she agreed. "It seemed a bit of luck, really. It kept you away from me, and at the time, that was what I wanted."

"And now?"

Her smile was slightly mocking. "Obviously, I seem to have overcome my objection to your attentions."

"Momentarily, perhaps. But how can I trust you, Meg, when you've done nothing but lie to me from the minute we first met?"

"I'm not a liar . . ."

"Oh, indeed?" He rubbed his square chin thoughtfully with a forefinger. "Let me think. Exactly how many falsehoods have you told me? Well, there was that little matter of your father being dead. And your promise to oversee the initial work on the castle when you ran off to Carraig instead. You lied about the stolen cattle; you lied when you promised not to employ any more workmen. And then last night I discovered the worst lie of all."

"It wasn't that bad."

"It wasn't? For weeks you let me think I was some kind of monster. You may not think that's so terrible, but I do. And, Meg, I'm not fond of being made a fool of."

Guilt made Meg defensive. "Maybe you're not the fool," she snapped, edging away from him. "Maybe I am. I should have known it would be a stupid mistake to . . . to take a chance on you learning the truth. Damn it, if I had just left well enough alone, you'd have awakened with your precious Clarice this morning . . . and no one would ever have known the difference!"

She pulled the sheet around her and slid off the opposite side of the bed, reaching for her nightgown.

"What do you think you're doing?" Ransom demanded.

"I'm going to put on my nightgown and leave."

"Oh, no you don't," Ransom cried. "You aren't leaving until we get this settled."

"What is there to settle?" she asked, her chin jutting stubbornly.

"You'll find out," he promised grimly, sliding out of bed on his own side and starting after her.

The sight of the boldly naked man coming toward her was enough to send Meg into headlong flight, even though she quickly discovered there wasn't much opportunity for escape. She darted toward the garderobe, but he caught her in midstep and whirled her back to face him. A wolfish smile had bared his white teeth, and the golden earring—the only thing he wore—sparkled in the morning sunlight.

"For once, tell me the truth," he growled. "Do you intend to start acting like a real wife?"

Meg struggled within his grasp and suddenly felt herself pulled flush against him. The warmth of the contact, and the swift, unexpected reaction of his body, made her gasp with startled delight. She gave a small laugh and threw her arms around his neck. The twinkle in his green eyes told her that his anger was abating very quickly.

"Do you want me to act like a wife?" she whispered, and raised her mouth to his. Ransom took the kiss she offered and was well on his way to making his desire for more known, when the door to the chamber nearly buckled under an onslaught of blows.

"Ransom, you bloated cow's udder, are you in there?"

"Damnation," Ransom muttered. "It's Hale Dickson. What in the name of all that's sacred is he doing here again?"

"I say, Ran, dear fellow—are you busy?" Dickson's suggestive laugh reached their ears. "Open this cursed door and greet an old friend."

"A friend who may not live to get any older if he isn't careful," Ransom called out. "What do you want?"

Reluctantly, Ransom released Meg, who scrambled into her nightgown and made a dash for the bed. He waited until she was adequately concealed by the bedcovers before wrapping about his own waist the sheet she had dropped and striding to the door. Sliding the bolt free, he yanked the door open to reveal Hale Dickson. A wide grin on his face, Dickson looked past Ransom to Meg.

"Good morning, Lady St. Claire. So nice to see you again." He dragged his gaze back to Ransom, letting it linger on the sheet. "Hmm, interesting choice of apparel, Ran."

"How is it we're to be favored with your presence a second time?" Ransom barked.

"Simple. It has become my fate to wander endlessly up and down the breadth of the British Isles at the whim of my sovereign. When I got to London and reported to George that you had married a Scotswoman, he commanded me to return to Wolfcrag to escort Clarice back to England. He thought the poor minx would be heartbroken." He rubbed his gloved hands together. "And is she?"

"Go find out for yourself," Ransom replied. "And if she is, mayhap you can help assuage her grief."

Hale looked horror-stricken. "God forbid. I'd rather snuggle up to a viper."

"That could be arranged," Ransom said dryly. "Now, if you'll give me a moment to get dressed, I'll join you downstairs and we can talk."

Both men turned in surprise as a clatter of footsteps

sounded on the flagstones of the hallway. Lorna MacLinn, still in her night clothes, a shawl clasped about her, ran into the room.

"Meg," she cried, "oh, Meg! Something terrible has happened."

No longer worried about modesty, Meg left the bed and hurried across the room to put her arms around Lorna. "What is it?"

Lorna's eyes filled with huge tears that spilled over and ran down her pale face. "It's Grandfather—he's gone. He must have wandered away from the cottage sometime during the night."

"Oh, no!" Meg's eyes sought Ransom's. "We've got to do something. We've got to find him."

"I'll get dressed and organize a search party," Ransom said. "It won't take us long to find him. He's in no condition to go far."

Meg hated the waiting; she would've preferred being out with the men searching for old Hamish to staying at the castle and trying to calm Lorna and her brothers and sisters. When the first hour of the manhunt had turned up nothing, she'd asked Mairi and Fletcher to prepare a hot meal for the searchers, but now there was nothing for them to do but mill about the courtyard, waiting.

Even Clarice seemed to be biding her time, willingly delaying the discussion Meg knew the two of them must have sooner or later. Hamish's disappearance had destroyed any chance of keeping Revan MacLinn's presence secret, so Meg suspected the other woman was busily gathering further information with which to incriminate them.

It was midafternoon by the time one of the sentries on the castle walls shouted that a group of horsemen was approaching.

Clutching Lorna's small, cold hand, Meg watched as the riders entered the main gates. Her father and Ransom were in the lead, and their grim faces filled her with foreboding.

Meg felt Lorna's grip tighten painfully as she saw the woman's brother come into the courtyard. Brodie was riding slowly, cradling his grandfather in his arms.

Revan MacLinn dismounted and went to take Hamish from the younger man. Brodie slid from his horse, his features drawn with sorrow as he sought his sister's eyes. With a cry, she ran to him, and he spoke a few, quiet words before taking his grandfather's body from MacLinn. Then, surrounded by Lorna and her brothers and sisters, and followed by Dr. MacSween, Brodie crossed the courtyard and disappeared inside his cottage.

Meg, fearing the worst, went to Ransom. "What happened?" she asked. "Is Hamish still alive?"

"Just barely. But I don't see how he can make it, Meg. Spottiswoode's men beat him badly . . ."

"They beat him!" she gasped. "But why?"

"He must have been delirious, because he wandered away from the castle and went back to his burned-out cottage. Some drovers were there, running sheep, and they claim he attacked them."

"Even if he did, he was sick," Meg protested. "He wouldn't have known what he was doing!"

"I'm sure that's true. But Spottiswoode's men took advantage of the situation. Seems they were bored and in need of a little sport."

"But to beat a harmless old man like that . . ." Meg shuddered, suddenly cold even in the summer sunshine. "We can't let them get away with it, Ransom."

He nodded solemnly. "No, we can't. But now isn't the time to think of revenge. First we have to see what can be done for Hamish."

"Aye, Lorna and Brodie will need us."

They started across the courtyard, and, to Meg, it seemed the most natural thing in the world when Ransom took her hand, enclosing it protectively in his larger one. They had just reached the threshold of the cottage when a low, keening cry reached their ears.

"Oh, my God—that's Lorna," Meg whispered.

And then Dr. MacSween came out of the dwelling, shaking his head. "We were too late," he muttered. "There wasn't a damned thing I could do for him."

A harsh Gaelic curse shattered the sudden silence. "This time Spottiswoode has gone too far," declared Revan MacLinn. "He'll have to pay."

"Aye," muttered another, "that he will."

"Let's not do anything rash," counseled Ransom. "We have a need to be coolheaded about this."

"Oh, we'll be coolheaded enough even for ye, laddie boy," promised MacLinn. "I'm sending for my men, but it will take them a few days to get here. By that time, we'll have a plan laid out." He turned his amber eyes back toward the cottage from which the unmistakable sounds of mourning had begun to issue. "But first," he said, "we have a burying to attend to."

On the following day, the people of Clan MacLinn laid old Hamish to rest on a sweep of moorland that faced the sea. Defiantly, they chose a plot of ground that belonged to Jonathan Spottiswoode, and Ransom would have wagered all he owned that they were disappointed the landlord did not try to interfere with the ceremony.

Even though the chapel at Wolfcrag had yet to be restored, the residents of the castle crowded into it to hear the Reverend Throckmorton read a service for Hamish. And then, his hastily constructed coffin resting on the shoulders of four strong men, the deceased was borne away to his final resting place. The mourners kept pace slowly, the women keening and the children sobbing piteously.

Meg, her face anguished, walked beside Ransom, her fingers clutching his arm for support. He hadn't been able to ascertain her mood, which seemed to waver somewhere between outrage and grief. She'd spent the night sitting up with Brodie and his sister, trying to soothe the younger children, and now her exhaustion was evident in the dark circles around her eyes and the weary slant of her shoulders. As soon as the funeral was over and they had returned to Wolfcrag, Ransom was determined to see that Meg was put to bed for some much-needed rest. He himself was going to lie beside her, to hold her in his arms and shield her from the outside world. Oddly enough, his earlier anger with her had faded, and now he was concerned only with her welfare.

The pallbearers lowered the coffin into the ragged hole that had been hewn in the rocky soil, and Hamish's grandchildren stepped forward to scatter the first handfuls of earth over it. The skirts and shawls of the mourners whipped in the fierce wind that blew straight off the ocean, making enough noise to disguise the thud of the clotted soil thrown against the wood.

And then the most unearthly din Ransom had ever heard came sweeping down the glen, making the hair on the back of his neck stand up. Squinting into the sun, he could see a kilted piper standing on an outcropping of rock, his arms encircling the strange instrument Meg called the bagpipes. This was the first time the pipes had been played in his presence, and he was startled by the nearly discordant sound of it. High and somewhat shrill, the music reverberated across the hillside, unnatural in the serene setting, and yet somehow soothing.

"He's playing a lament," Meg explained, sidling closer to him. "Hamish would have loved that. Poor, dear old soul."

Ransom glanced down at his wife, surprised at the fervor in her tone. Her smoky gray eyes, which had earlier brimmed with tears of sorrow, now glowed with an extraordinary inner light. He could almost believe the piper's tune had lessened her sadness, was filling her with peace. He looked about him and saw that everyone, even the most grief-stricken, seemed to draw strength from the lament. No wonder, he reflected, that the Scots marched into battle to the sound of the pipes. Clearly the weirdly beautiful music spoke to some wellspring of courage and dignity deep within every one of them.

Meg had never looked as beautiful to him as she did now, her face raised to the sea wind, her eyes fixed upon the piper.

Her lips were slightly parted in rapt wonder, and her hair had escaped its covering to swirl madly about her face. Seeing her against the wild backdrop of hills and heather and restless ocean, Ransom knew he was seeing the true Meg. And the realization destroyed a hope he hadn't really even known he'd harbored. Meg belonged here, in a land that was more savage and untamed than the one he had come from. She'd never be happy in an English drawing room; she'd never find peace in a dusty Devon lane.

Long after the skirling of the pipes had ended and the mourners had made their way back to the castle, Ransom could hear the melancholy music echoing in his ears.

# Chapter Nineteen

Meg gripped the reins tightly in one gloved hand, raising her free one to adjust the mask she wore. She looked about at the other six horsemen who, like her, had halted their mounts on the ridge overlooking the house where Jonathan Spottiswoode lived. One by one, each of them nodded, and then, letting the horses pick their way in the semidarkness, the riders started down the hillside.

Meg was excited, the need for revenge strong within her, but her anticipation of the event ahead was shadowed by her feelings of guilt. If Ransom knew where she was at that moment, he'd be furious. When she'd slipped out of Wolfcrag, she'd left him and several others deep in discussion about how best to handle the matter of Hamish MacLinn's death. It was a discussion from which she'd been barred . . . and for that, she harbored genuine resentment.

Still, the meeting—which Ransom had insisted was to be for men only—would work to her advantage. It would provide alibis for Ransom, her father, Fletcher, and Brodie MacLinn, all of whom were closeted with the Reverend Throckmorton, Hale Dickson, and the district sheriff. Later, if Spottiswoode tried to point the finger of guilt at any of the men from Wolfcrag, they'd have credible witnesses to swear they hadn't been near Spottiswoode's property this particular night.

It galled Meg that Ransom hadn't wanted her included in the plotting against the man responsible for Hamish's death.

She knew he was only trying to protect her, but if her own father thought she should be there, Ransom ought to be able to accept it, too. Highland women were no strangers to acts of vengeance—or to violence, if it came to that.

And so Meg had decided not to wait for the men to agree on some way to punish Spottiswoode. Her father wanted swift, absolute justice; Ransom would vote for prudence. The sheriff, never one to oppose Spottiswoode, would want to uphold the law; the reverend would want to pray over the matter. No, avenging the innocent death of a clansman was too important to leave to such uncertainty. Someone had to act quickly and ruthlessly . . . and, in Meg's opinion, that someone was her.

The plan was nearly flawless. Who would suspect a woman? Especially one who'd been publicly humiliated by being summarily ordered to her room by an adamant husband. Dressed as she was, in a pair of dark trousers with a hat pulled low over her face, she'd be mistaken for a lad . . . and the others, also dressed in dark, nondescript clothing, would be as unidentifiable.

Once Meg had conceived the plan, she'd had to act rapidly. She'd taken Mairi into her confidence, and Mairi, in turn, had asked her brothers for help. Both men had agreed to join Meg, and she'd given them permission to discreetly enlist four others. To her amazement, the two most unlikely men in the castle—Yates and Beale—had volunteered their services, as had one of the carpenters and the stable boy. The latter had saddled seven horses and led them as unobtrusively as possible across the drawbridge one at a time, in order to avoid the noise of an ordinary departure.

Meg glanced at the sky. It was probably about as dark as it was going to get, given the lingering twilight of the summer months. By her calculations, they needed to make the raid on Spottiswoode's house and return, undetected, to Wolfcrag in something less than an hour. Ransom and the others couldn't be counted on to continue their conclave much longer than that, and it was her plan to be safely back in her bedchamber when her husband came looking for her.

Behind Spottiswoode's house were a number of low, stone byres. Moving as silently as shadows, four of the riders dismounted and entered each one, driving out the cows and calves that were inside. As soon as the buildings were empty, Meg gave a signal, and Beale, his broad face split into a huge grin beneath the half mask he wore, brandished the tinderbox he held, then set to work. In a matter of seconds, the first thatched roof was alight, with a hissing crackle that filled the night with ominous sound. Astride their horses again, each rider opened the sack of pitch-soaked torches that hung at their saddles and, thrusting them within the flames, lighted them.

After using the torches to spread fire over each of the thatched roofs, the raiders galloped into Spottiswoode's yard and, firebrands held aloft, began circling the house. Through a lighted window, Meg caught sight of Spottiswoode himself sitting at a late supper. Leaning forward, she swung one of her torches against the windowpanes. The glass shattered, and as the burning torch was hurled into the room, she saw Spottiswoode leap to his feet, heard his shout of alarm. Flames scattered across the carpet, reaching greedily for the tablecloth and for the long drapes at the window. With an exultant cry, Meg spurred her horse and rode away.

In a wild conglomeration of shouts and Gaelic curses, the horsemen galloped around and around the house, breaking windows and setting fires. In less time than Meg would have imagined possible, the entire dwelling was in flames, and the members of Spottiswoode's household staff were fleeing from every doorway.

"Let's go!" one of Mairi's brothers shouted, and Meg joined the others in obeying. Spottiswoode himself had just run from the burning building, and as much as she would have liked staying to see his reaction, Meg knew it was too dangerous. In moments, his hirelings would be appearing, and her little band of raiders had no wish to linger and face armed men.

With a last, bloodcurdling cry, she turned her mount to flee . . . and, in that moment, the unthinkable happened.

She saw Spottiswoode lift his hand, and then a shot rang out, causing her horse to whinny in terror and rear up on his hind legs. Taken unaware, Meg felt herself sliding from the saddle. She hit the ground with such force that, for several long seconds, she couldn't catch her breath. Not seeing her fall, all but one of the others had gone on. The last—Yates, by the sound of his voice—halted and came to her aid.

"Are you hurt, lass?"

"No, I'll be all right." Stiffly, she hauled herself off the ground and scrabbled for the reins. "Go on," she cried. "Don't wait!"

"Are ye sure?"

Even though the mask she wore somewhat obscured her vision, from the corner of her eye she could see Spottiswoode moving closer, the pistol in his hand raised to fire again. "I'm sure," she gasped. "For God's sake, go!"

Desperately, she threw herself into the saddle and kicked her heels into the horse's sides. The animal lurched hesitantly, then began to move. As it settled into a long stride, Meg hunkered low, clinging to its neck.

The second shot echoed loudly above the sound of hoofbeats, and with it came the searing touch of fire. Meg's realization that she'd been hit was accompanied by the knowledge that she had to stay in the saddle or all would be lost. Fighting wave after wave of pain, she threaded her fingers into the coarse hair of the horse's mane and hung on with every bit of her waning strength. Such was her determination that she found herself nearly at the gates of Wolfcrag before she became aware that, at some point in the skirmish, her hat had flown from her head, leaving her long hair blowing freely in the night wind.

While the others took care of the horses, Yates half carried Meg to her chamber. There they were met by an anxious Mairi who took one look at Meg's blood-soaked shirt and turned white.

"Don't you dare swoon," Meg warned. "It's nothing—the ball merely creased my side."

"But the blood—"

"Just help me get it cleaned and dressed before Ransom gets here," Meg said. "The more harmless my injury looks, the better it will go for me."

"Jesus in heaven!" gasped Yates. "You ain't goin' to tell the captain, are you?"

"I have to, Yates. Don't you see? Spottiswoode probably recognized me when my hat came off. I'm going to need Ransom to help me think of a way out of this. Besides, I've already lied to him so many times . . ."

"He won't like this one bit."

"No, he won't." Biting her lip, Meg lowered herself into a chair and began unbuttoning the torn shirt. "But we can't worry about that now."

Hastily, Yates turned away. "I'll stand watch outside the door, lass—that way I can tell you if someone's coming."

"That's a good idea." Meg gave him a tired smile and indicated the piece of black cloth hanging from his shirt pocket. "Don't forget to burn that mask. And Yates, thanks for your help. I still don't understand why you and Beale wanted to go along tonight, but I'm grateful you did."

The big man looked pleased. "Guess it was just our way of lettin' you know we're sorry we ever thought you were a witch. Besides, we've got some good friends here at Wolfcrag, and it don't seem right, the way that damned Spottiswoode has been treating 'em."

"Well," Meg said softly, wincing as she pulled the bloody fabric away from her side, "we avenged poor old Hamish tonight, didn't we?"

"We sure did. Lord, miss . . . er, Your Ladyship, but you're a rum one, you are. Never saw another female like you."

When he had gone, Meg slipped out of the shirt and tossed it and her mask onto the fire, where they smoldered lazily. She groaned in pain as she reached for the poker to stir them.

"Here, let me do that," said Mairi, setting down a basin of water.

Meg gladly relinquished the poker and returned to the

chair. As soon as Mairi had completed that chore, she ordered Meg to remove her ruined chemise so they might examine the wound. It was, as Meg had thought, merely a crease in the flesh, but the skin was both torn and burned by the passage of the lead ball. Meg chewed the inside of her cheek to keep from crying out as Mairi used soap and water to cleanse it.

"It will probably heal without any problem," predicted Mairi, "but I think you should let Dr. MacSween look at it."

"Later," Meg said. "Just bandage it for now."

Mairi's expression was disapproving, but she did as she was bid, efficiently wrapping Meg's rib cage with strips of soft, white cloth. "Now," she said, "let me find you a gown to put on."

"Yes, I'd better make myself presentable just in case Mr. Spottiswoode decides to pay us a visit tonight." Meg sighed. "I wish Ransom would come up. I'm in a mood to get this over with."

"Shall I send Yates for him?"

Meg closed her eyes and drew a deep breath. Unable to trust her voice, she nodded, then began a silent lecture that was meant to keep her fear at bay.

*At least,* she reminded herself, *I'm not going to lie to him this time . . .*

As Ransom entered the chamber, it was obvious his mood was buoyant. He strode across the carpet to Meg's side, smiling broadly. "I think we've come up with a plan that even you'll think has merit."

"Ransom, there's—"

"You know, your father has a good brain for a Scotsman. Oh, I'll admit, there are times he could have used it to better advantage, but—Meg, is something wrong?"

Meg had risen slowly, feeling faint and tired now that the rush of excitement from the raid had ebbed. She stepped behind the chair, using its high back to lean upon. Her gray eyes were huge and serious in her pale face, and they sought Ransom's gaze with a silent plea for understanding.

"I have something to tell you," she said abruptly, wishing her voice sounded stronger. "You won't like it, but that can't be helped right now."

"What do you mean?" he demanded warily.

"I'm not going to lie to you about this."

His disquiet was expressed by a low growl. "Meg . . . ?"

"I led a raid against Spottiswoode tonight."

He looked startled, and then he laughed. "That sounds like a lie to me, Meg."

"Well, it's not! Listen to me," she cried in exasperation. "There isn't much time—he could arrive here at any minute. Ransom, some of the men and I rode over there and set fire to his house."

Every trace of humor drained from Ransom's countenance. Suddenly he whirled away and began pacing madly up and down the bedchamber floor, as if struggling for self-control. "You chose a hell of a way to start telling the truth," he finally declared, stopping to glare at her. "Meg, what in the name of God possessed you to do such a stupid thing?"

"Don't tell me you don't think he deserved it!" she flared. "After the evictions and the crofts he burned. After . . . Hamish!"

"Of course he deserved it, and more. But damnation, Meg, it wasn't up to you to exact revenge. Why couldn't you have stayed out of it and just let us men have handled it?"

"Because I wanted to see that it was handled right!"

His mouth curled in contempt. "Then why do I get the feeling that it wasn't? You may think this is a sarcastic observation, but something tells me that if your scheme went so well, you'd never have made this confession. Why is it that I have the overpowering conviction that, in some way, you need my help now—and that that's the only reason in hell you're being so uncharacteristically honest?"

Meg's gaze fell before the scorching green fire of his. He was right, and she knew it. And even admitting it to herself made her feel guilty and ashamed.

"Uh, Ransom . . ." Mairi's tentative words made both of them remember she had been a quiet witness to their quarrel. "I think you should know that—"

"No," interrupted Meg, her tone brooking no argument. "We don't have time for . . . for unimportant details now." She overrode Mairi's would-be protest by turning back to Ransom. "I'm sorry that you're angry with me, but the fact is, Spottiswoode may come storming in here at any moment . . . and I'm asking you to provide me with an alibi."

Ransom, hands on hips, sighed wearily and looked up at the ceiling, as if appealing to some higher power for understanding. "I know I'll regret asking this question, but is there any particular reason Spottiswoode should suspect you had anything to do with the raid?"

"As we rode away, the hat I was wearing blew off." She made herself meet his furious scowl. "I'm certain he saw my hair and that he'll have a fairly good notion it was me."

"Christ Almighty!" Ransom swore with vehemence, then began his pacing again. "I have an overwhelming desire to just chain you up in the goddamned dungeon. That'd be the only way to keep you out of trouble. And even there, you'd probably talk the mice into arming themselves and marching against the rest of the castle."

Meg's smile was wan. "I'm sorry . . ."

"You've already said that," he snapped.

"I know . . . and I mean it. If you'll just think of some excuse to give Spottiswoode, I swear I'll refrain from any more wild escapades. I will become the meekest, most obedient wife you can imagine, if only you'll help me out this one, last time." She shrugged slightly. "It's not myself that I'm worried about. It's the others . . . the men who went with me."

"Ah, yes, the men." Ransom ceased all motion. "And would you care to give me the names of your misbegotten companions?"

"No, not really. I think you'd want to punish them."

"Punish? For indulging your idiocy? For taking the law into their own hands? For risking your neck as well as theirs?" He came close enough to tower over her. "Good God, Meg, why would you think I'd want to punish them? Why, I want them to make a full report to the king, so that he won't have to be content with merely confiscating my property—hell, he can draw and quarter me as well!"

"Oh, *fuigh!* Forget I asked for your help," Meg spat. "I'll talk to Spottiswoode myself."

"Like hell you will," Ransom thundered.

At that instant, Yates tapped on the door, opening it to stick his head inside. "You've got visitors, Cap'n."

"Spottiswoode?"

"Aye. Uh . . . he seems a tad agitated."

"I can just imagine," Ransom muttered. "Go tell him I'll be right down."

"I'll go with you," Meg began.

Ransom pointed his finger at her. "You stay in this room, do you hear me?"

"But—"

"I'll tell him you've retired for the night."

"I—"

"Meg, I'll handle this. Don't you leave this room." He started for the door, then paused. "We'll continue our discussion once I've managed to get rid of our caller."

Meg inclined her head, but promised nothing. When Ransom had gone, she turned to Mairi. "I've got a wonderful idea."

"Saints protect us," Mairi whispered, her face chalky. "Not another one!"

Jonathan Spottiswoode was so enraged that his shouting brought people from all over the castle. For several lengthy minutes they had stood in the Great Hall and listened to his furious tirade against Highlanders in general and MacLinns in particular.

"And you, sir," he declared, looking at Ransom. "I'm shocked that as an English gentleman sent here by his king, you'd have anything to do with such a dastardly crime."

"Indeed, Spottiswoode, I regret that your home was

burned, but I assure you, I had nothing to do with it. Nor did my father-in-law take part in the raid against you. Fortunately, there are reliable witnesses to that fact."

"Aye, myself included," spoke up the Reverend Elijah Throckmorton. "Had Fletcher not detained me with an offer of cake and wine, I'd not have been here to confirm it. But since I am, I must tell you, none of these gentlemen was away from Wolfcrag this night."

"And you'll be pleased to know the sheriff was present for our discussion," Revan MacLinn added. "Surely you wouldn't doubt his word?"

Spottiswoode's eyes narrowed. "Don't forget, I got a good look at one of the raiders. And though I can hardly credit even the likes of you with such a thing, I believe you sent a woman to do your shameful work."

"A woman?" croaked Throckmorton. "Is that some kind of jest?"

"Man, I've just lost my home and all of my possessions," Spottiswoode exclaimed. "I'm in no mood for jesting. One of the riders was thrown from his horse, and I tell you, it was a woman. I saw her long, black hair." He pointed a bony finger in Ransom's direction. "And I believe it was your wife!"

Ransom forced a laugh. "Meg?" His mind was still digesting the fact that Meg had been thrown. Had she been hurt? Was that what Mairi had been about to tell him?

"My daughter?" chimed in MacLinn. "Are ye daft, Spottiswoode?"

"I saw her, I tell you. I don't know of another woman hereabouts with that mass of black hair that reaches to her hips."

"Impossible," Ransom stated firmly. "Meg retired early. She hasn't been out of her chamber all evening."

Spottiswoode snarled, "I wouldn't expect you to admit it. But I've heard enough rumors about the outlaw's daughter to know she's wild enough to be capable of something like this."

"Like what, Mr. Spottiswoode?" Meg's cool voice sounded from the stairway, and every eye in the room trained itself on her as she slowly descended, one hand trailing along the banister. "My maid just told me your home has been burned to the ground," she continued, crossing the room to stand at Ransom's side. "May I offer my condolences?"

Ransom stared down at Meg in amazement. Except for the youthfulness of her face, she could have been a staid matron disturbed from her nap by the fire. She was wearing the silly, ruffled hat he so disliked, and had a shawl clutched about her shoulders. Seeing Mairi hovering anxiously in the background, he had to wonder what little game his willful wife was now playing. Since she'd ignored his direct order to stay in her room, he'd have to play along . . . but by damn, if they extricated themselves from this mess, there were going to be some drastic changes made in the chain of command at Wolfcrag.

Meg's smile was deceptively sweet as she spoke again. "You weren't, by any chance, accusing me of having anything to do with the fire, were you?"

"You were there," Spottiswoode charged. "Don't deny it—I saw you!"

"That's ridiculous. I've been in my quarters all evening. Just ask Mairi."

"I saw your hair!"

Meg's laugh was lightly mocking. "Give me some credit for intelligence. Don't you think I'd have disguised myself if I were going to commit a crime?"

"You were in disguise. But when I shot at you, your horse reared and you fell. Your hat came off and I got a good look at that long hair of yours."

"You shot—?" Ransom choked.

"I'm afraid you're mistaken," Meg hastily interceded. "It couldn't have been me you saw." Quickly, she snatched the mobcap from her head, sending a chorus of stunned gasps around the room.

Ransom's heart tumbled over in his chest. What on earth had she done to herself? Her gloriously beautiful hair was gone—chopped short into a tousled cap of shiny black curls that untidily framed her face. He nearly bit his tongue to keep from bellowing in outrage.

"You see, sir, I no longer have long hair," Meg said calmly.

"I found it too difficult to keep clean while renovating the castle. There are so many cobwebs and—"

"You must have just cut it!" Spottiswoode's thin face had turned dark red in color. "Do you think I'm a fool?"

"Do you think I'm one?" Meg shot back. "Am I so simple that I'd let you see me setting fire to your house, then run home to cut off my hair in the hope of tricking you? The truth is, my hair has been short this past week or so. Ask my husband." She waved a hand about the room. "Or any of these good people."

"Throckmorton?" prompted Spottiswoode.

The preacher smiled nervously. "I'm sorry, but I really couldn't say. Lady St. Claire's head was covered during the service for old Hamish . . . and I don't remember seeing her hair."

Hale Dickson stepped forward from his position among the onlookers. "I can tell you that when I arrived from London yesterday, the lady had already cut her hair. At first I was incensed, thinking she'd ruined her looks, but the more I see of this Meg, the better I like her."

"Aye, that's the way of it," agreed Fletcher. "I tried to talk her out of it, but she wouldn't listen. You could have heard the captain roar for at least ten miles!"

Ransom began to breathe easier. Perhaps they could pull off this hoax. "I've never thought I'd want a wife who looked like a lad," he said, encircling Meg's shoulders and pulling her close to his side. Fortunately, his next words covered her sudden, sharp gasp. "But I'm beginning to grow accustomed to the new Meg . . . and I believe I'll keep her."

"Don't you think I realize that you've all got something to gain by lying?" sneered Spottiswoode. "I haven't heard one so called witness who's not partial."

"Then perhaps you'd like to hear what I have to say," suggested Clarice Howard.

Ransom watched in horror as his former mistress made her way through those gathered. His hand tightened convulsively on Meg's shoulders, and his mind raced, trying to think of ways to undo the damage he was sure Clarice was about to inflict. He could feel Meg's tension and sympathized with her self-disgust at not recalling the presence of the woman who had so much to gain by discrediting her.

"You can be certain I'd never lie to protect Meg St. Claire," Clarice avowed. "I came all the way from England to marry Ransom, only to discover the little Scottish upstart had gotten his ring on her finger first. No, it's safe to say I have no love for her."

Spottiswoode's smile was coldly triumphant. "So, you're willing to make a statement about the lady's hair?"

Clarice favored Meg with an arch look. "If you'd care to bring the sheriff back, I'd be happy to make a declaration in his presence."

Spottiswoode signaled to two of his men, who lounged in the doorway.

"Of course," Clarice went on, "as much as I'd like to incriminate the chit, I'd have to be honest and admit that she cut off her hair more than a week ago. I was hoping Ransom would find it so repugnant that he'd turn to me." She heaved a dramatic sigh. "Obviously, it didn't work in my favor."

Ransom exhaled slowly, aware that Meg was just as relieved. Something told him that without his support, her knees would have given away beneath her. Glancing down at her, his momentary feeling of relief vanished. Something was wrong—her skin was pasty, her upper lip beaded with perspiration.

"So, it seems the lot of you intend to stand against me," Spottiswoode observed. "But there is one other thing . . ." He advanced on Meg. "When I fired my pistol, I believe I may have grazed the woman. An examination of Lady St. Claire's person should prove or disprove my theory that she was involved in the raid."

Ransom stepped in front of Meg, his hands clenched into fists. "Are you mad? Do you think I'd allow you to put your filthy hands on my wife?"

"Aye, and if my daughter was injured," MacLinn put in, "do ye think she'd be standing here before you? You're just desperate for someone to blame."

"Go on home, Spottiswoode," Ransom said. "Send the sheriff, if you wish, but don't come back yourself."

"Go home?" screeched the man. "I have no home, thanks to you and your cursed wife! Where am I to sleep tonight? In a burned-out byre?"

"That's more than you allowed your former tenants," Meg quietly pointed out. "Why don't you do as they had to do?"

"I'll best you yet," Spottiswoode yelled. "I'll find a way to exact my revenge, and when I do—"

"Get out," Ransom instructed, his tone savage. "Yates, Beale—find as many men as necessary to escort Mr. Spottiswoode off my property."

Spottiswoode didn't wait for an escort. Fuming with anger, he summoned his cohorts and stalked from the room, with a muttered admonition that he'd be back.

The moment the man had gone, Yates and Beale on his heels, Ransom turned to Meg. She was swaying on her feet. "Are you all right?" he queried.

The shawl she had been clasping slid from her fingers and fluttered to the floor, revealing the blood-soaked bodice of her gown.

"Meg . . . my God!"

"I . . . I don't feel very well," she murmured, and pitched forward into Ransom's arms.

Shouting for someone to fetch the doctor, Ransom lifted Meg into his arms and started up the stairs.

"MacSween's in the kitchen," Revan MacLinn said. "I'll get him."

Mairi, uttering tiny cries of dismay, ran ahead of Ransom to open the door to Meg's bedchamber. She hovered, hands fluttering helplessly.

"Meg should have told you she was hurt," she fretted.

"Yes, but I know full well how obstinate my wife can be. Pull back the bedcovers, will you?"

When she had done so, he lowered Meg onto the bed. "Bring me a basin of water and some cloths—and a nightdress." He knelt beside the bed and began unbuttoning the gown Meg wore. His fingers shook so that he had only reached the last button when Mairi returned with the items he'd requested.

"Here, sir, let me do that," she offered.

"No, I'll take care of her. You go wait for Dr. MacSween and bring him in the minute he gets here."

"Very well."

Tenderly, Ransom lifted Meg so that he could free the gown from her shoulders. With a faint moan, she leaned against him, turning her face into his chest.

"Here, sweetheart," he murmured, "let me get this damned dress off you . . ."

Meg helped by raising her arms, and in a matter of seconds the bodice of the gown hung about her waist. Deeming it the easiest way to proceed, Ransom laid her back upon the pillows and, grasping the cloth bunched about her, ripped it in half, tossing the ruined garment aside. Swiftly, he untied her petticoats and pulled them free, then removed her slippers and hose.

Meg was tired and dizzy, but she could still appreciate the warmth of his hands on her legs and feet. His touch was gentle, soothing—and as careful as if she were something precious. She smiled sleepily when he pulled the sheet up to her waist, then eased himself onto the edge of the bed to remove the bloodstained chemise she wore.

"Are you still angry with me?" she asked, opening her eyes to look up at him.

He braced his hands on each side of her shoulders and leaned over her, his face unreadable. "I may never get past being angry with you, Meg. Damn, how could you risk so much?"

"You know the answer to that as well as I do," she murmured.

"Yes, I suppose I do." He brushed a kiss on her forehead. "You don't have a prudent bone in your body, do you?"

"If I do," she whispered, "I'm sure it's aching right now."

He chuckled. "Meg, Meg . . . what am I to do with you?"

He rested his forehead against hers for a long moment before sitting back. "You nearly got yourself killed, you little idiot."

She smiled at his affectionate tone. "Spottiswoode couldn't kill me."

"I wasn't talking about him," Ransom dryly informed her.

She made a small face. "Beast," she muttered.

Ransom reached out to brush his hand over her short cap of curls. "So . . . you had to sacrifice your beautiful hair to save your careless neck."

"It'll grow back."

He sifted the soft black tresses through his fingers. "Yes, but not before I—" He broke off abruptly, but Meg knew what he'd been going to say. He'd be gone from Scotland months before her hair was long again. The pain that thought brought her was far worse than the burning in her side. And, she feared, would take much more time to heal.

"The doctor will be here soon," Ransom said. "We'd better take this thing off."

He untied the ribbon on her chemise and helped her sit forward so that he could remove the undergarment. The bandage Mairi had placed over Meg's wound was scarlet with blood, and when he'd unwound it, Ransom tossed it into the fire. There, lying on the hearth, was one perfect black curl, and he grimly realized what Meg had done with the hair she'd cut.

All desire for banter gone, Meg lay on her side, back turned and arms crossed over her breasts, while Ransom used a wet cloth to clean the shallow furrow along her ribs. He had just finished when Dr. MacSween, black leather bag in his pudgy hand, bustled into the room.

"It's a lucky thing for you, Meg, that your stepmother is away visiting her kin," the physician said. "She'd have your young hide for this latest venture. Aye, that she would."

Dr. MacSween cleaned Meg's injury, smeared it with a fragrant salve, and bandaged her ribs again. Then, ordering her to get into her nightgown and have a full night of rest, he went back to his supper.

Ransom, who had been standing at the windows, looking

out into the night, which had finally grown dark, came back to the bed. "Are we sleeping here tonight, then?"

Somewhat surprised that he would stay with her, she said, "This bed is comfortable enough, even though it does lean to one side."

Smiling, Ransom waved Mairi away and, when the door was closed, began stripping off his clothing. Careful not to jostle Meg, he slid into bed beside her, drawing her close within the circle of his arms.

"Don't ever scare me like that again," he softly ordered, resting his face against her heather-scented hair.

"No," she agreed. "From now on, I'll try to behave."

"Promise?"

"Mmm . . . yes, I promise," she said, snuggling sleepily against him.

Ransom's arms tightened. Now that his mind was temporarily free of worry for her safety, he realized just how much he'd like to hear Meg whisper the startling phrase she'd used the night before: *I love you.* And, he silently admitted, he'd like to be able to make the same pledge to her.

But, considering the circumstances, he was a man without that right—and he knew it. He couldn't stay in Scotland, and he couldn't ask her to live in England. Their worlds were too different, and their individual situations made it impossible to bridge the gap. In a matter of weeks, he'd go home . . . and she'd remain at Wolfcrag. They'd made a bargain, and he would see it through to the end, even if the thought of it filled him with soul-wrenching melancholy.

Early-morning sunshine spilled warmly through the tall windows and onto the bed, its touch gently awakening Meg. She turned to see Ransom still sleeping beside her, his arm across her waist, one leg entangled with hers. The heat of his body soothed the ache in her side, and she nestled closer.

With a fingertip, she traced the golden curve of the earring he wore, then let her finger trail lower, to rest against the thrumming pulse in his neck. Ransom was so vital, so strong and alive, that his very presence made her feel safe and protected. She'd always be grateful that, in spite of his anger at her, he'd stood up to Spottiswoode, told lies that might jeopardize his own future, and that, instead of the wrathful tirade she'd expected, he'd quietly and tenderly cared for her as if she really were his beloved wife. Suddenly, without either of them wanting it, their game of pretense had taken on a new and poignant reality. But it was, she knew, a reality that couldn't last.

And yet she was filled with an undeniable desire to make what they could have last as long as possible. This moment, this day, this small slice of time—it was theirs to do with as they pleased, and she wanted nothing more than to recapture the joyous pleasure she'd found in Ransom's arms two nights ago.

Meg inched closer to Ransom and began kissing his chest and shoulder. She knew he had awakened because of the absolute stillness of his body. She kissed the hollow of his throat, the underneath side of his chin, his jaw. Then she brought her mouth to within a fraction of an inch of his and waited, holding her breath. She didn't have to wait long—with a frustrated groan, he clamped his hands over her upper arms and his body surged upward, his mouth catching hers in a bold, proprietary kiss.

"Tease me, will you?" he murmured a moment later, lying back upon the pillow. He raised one hand to cradle her newly-shorn head against his shoulder.

"I thought you were going to sleep all day," she explained, letting her fingers begin a tantalizingly slow exploration of the muscled planes of his chest.

He stilled her hand with one of his own. "That's probably not a bad idea."

"No," she whispered, "it's a very bad idea."

"Meg, you're in no condition to—"

"I'm fine," she insisted. "Or I will be . . ." She struggled into a sitting position and began unbuttoning the nightgown she wore. ". . . just as soon as you stop arguing and help me with this silly thing."

Ransom couldn't deny a pleased grin. "Something tells me your doctor wouldn't condone this."

Meg started pulling the nightgown over her head. "I won't tell him if you won't."

Ransom's avid gaze swept over her, from her rumpled hair to the swath of bandage just below her naked breasts. He seemed powerless to stop his immediate and impassioned response to what she was offering.

He reached for her, carefully pulling her back down beside him. "I'll never breathe a word of it," he promised, his lips against hers.

# Chapter Twenty

Jonathan Spottiswoode was back at Wolfcrag the following afternoon. He demanded an audience with Ransom, away from the presence of either Meg or her father.

"I hope you haven't come to make more unfounded accusations," Ransom said, closing the door to a small, private chamber behind him.

Spottiswoode smiled nastily and seated himself, and even though his clothing was soiled and wrinkled, he spread the split tails of his frock coat with the fussiness of an old maid. "There's nothing unfounded about the charge I'm making today, Your Lordship." He uttered the title with sarcastic courtesy. "Your wife and her clansmen were responsible for destroying my home, and I can prove it."

"How so?" Ransom asked coolly.

Again, the man smiled. He then reached into his vest pocket and pulled forth a tarnished metal object, which he tossed onto the table between them. "We found this in the ashes of my house. I believe it belongs to your wife."

Ransom picked up the piece of metal and discovered it was a wolf's head brooch, fire-blackened and slightly misshapen. Even so, it was easily recognizable as the MacLinn-clan crest. Not only did Meg own such a brooch, but she wore it often—even though its very existence was against the laws of Britain.

Casually, he tossed the brooch down again. "This means nothing," he said evenly. "It could belong to any number of people. Besides, how can you prove you found it in the ashes of your house? For all I know, it could have been recovered from one of the crofts your men burned."

"Yes, that's true. But in a court of law, my word could as easily be believed as yours. Especially considering your recent conviction as a smuggler and thief."

"Don't threaten me, Spottiswoode."

"Was I threatening?" Spottiswoode smirked. "I merely intended to point out the possibilities. You'd have your witnesses, and I'd have mine." He shifted in his chair, steepling his long fingers together, clearly enjoying the moment. "Of course, your witnesses are all named MacLinn or have some connection to the clan. Or they're from your own crew of sailors, from whom one could expect a certain amount of blind loyalty. And then there's poor old Reverend Throckmorton—a more addled attestant I can't imagine."

"What makes your witnesses any better?" Ransom inquired.

"They're not my kinfolk, for one thing. True, some of them are employed by me, but most I've only known the short time I've been in the Highlands. Who could fail to believe them when they testify that your wife tended to interfere in my business affairs? That both you and she made threats against me?"

"All supposition, Spottiswoode."

"But damning nonetheless. And then there are the men who came here with me last night, who took a look about your stables while I talked to you. Those fellows are willing to swear they found several horses that appeared to have just been ridden hard. I'm certain the sheriff could learn a great deal by interrogating your young stable lad."

Ransom tamped down the apprehension that was stealing over him. Spottiswoode had something of a case against them; all it would take to expose Meg's crime would be for one of the men who'd ridden out with her to make a blunder. If her culpability were discovered, the authorities would have little mercy, considering her relationship to a notorious outlaw.

"I can tell by the expression on your face that I've worried you," Spottiswoode commented. "So let me hasten to add that, with some cooperation from you, we can see an end to this matter. One that doesn't involve the courts of law."

Ransom merely glanced at him, one dark eyebrow arched inquisitively. He didn't trust the man, but knew he had no choice but to hear him out.

"Look, St. Claire, your wife and her men did their work well. My home is destroyed and what livestock I had left scattered all over the countryside." He looked down at his clothing and shrugged, spreading his hands wide. "I don't even own any other clothes anymore, and what's worse, the strongbox containing my papers and money was lost in the fire." He leaned forward, bony shoulders hunched. "I need money, you need clemency for your pretty young wife. Let's admit that we're each in a position to help the other out."

"In what way?"

"It's simple—buy my property." Spottiswoode grinned at Ransom's startled response. "It makes sense, I assure you. I'm sick of the Highlands, sick of being treated like a pariah by the locals. Pay me what I ask for my land and I'll leave this godforsaken place and settle elsewhere. I'll also sign a legal document absolving Lady St. Claire and your men of any crime against me. All I ask is safe conduct to London. When I'm gone, you can deed the property to your wife or back to her father, for all I care."

"How much do you want for your land?"

Without hesitation, Spottiswoode named a price Ransom knew was twice over what the property was worth. "Let's bargain," he suggested.

"No, I've already offered you the only deal I'm willing to make. Either accept it now or quit wasting my time."

"If I don't?"

"I'll summon the authorities so quickly you won't even have time to smuggle that wife of yours to the islands. And, by the saints, I'll see you ruined in court."

"If I buy your property and arrange for your escort to London, would you be willing to stand as a witness to the completion of the work on this castle?"

"Gladly, provided all my provisions are met."

Ransom sat quietly for a few seconds, then rose to his feet and stood looking down at the Scotsman. "All right, I'm agreeable to your offer. Can you be ready to leave for the south by morning?"

Spottiswoode's laugh was bitter. "I'm ready to leave now. There's nothing to keep me here, after all."

"But it will take some time to arrange for your escort. My men will be ready to go at dawn tomorrow. I'll advance you half the money then, the rest once you've spoken to the king."

"Fair enough. And of course, I'll need your word that no unfortunate accidents will befall me on the way to London. I've entrusted written accounts of your wife's misdeeds with our local sheriff and one of my most reliable men, so if anything happens to me, they'll go to the king with enough information to make her life extremely miserable."

"You're a coldhearted bastard, Spottiswoode."

The man's long teeth showed in an even wider smile. "I'm glad we see eye to eye, then," he said. "I'll be waiting for your men tomorrow." He paused at the doorway. "Do give your lovely wife my regards, won't you?"

When Spottiswoode had gone, Ransom called together the inhabitants of Wolfcrag and explained the situation. Most of them, Revan MacLinn included, seemed to think the bargain Ransom had struck with Spottiswoode had merit. With the land back in possession of those sympathetic to the MacLinns, life could take on some semblance of normalcy again.

"As soon as the castle is finished," Ransom pointed out, "the crofts can be rebuilt, and some of those people crowded in here can return to their own property." He flashed Meg a quick look. "I, for one, will welcome a bit of privacy."

Meg knew her answering smile was stiff, but she was filled with such foreboding that she couldn't seem to summon genuine pleasure. Ransom fully believed his worries were over, and she could only pray he was right.

"Hale," Ransom continued, "I'd like for you to head up Spottiswoode's escort back to England."

Dickson ran a hand through his gingery hair. "Lord, man, I just got here. Don't I even get to rest my weary bones?"

"You can rest in London." Ransom chuckled. "Come along, now, while I fetch the gold to buy Spottiswoode's land." He held out a hand to Meg, giving her cold fingers a squeeze. "You come, too."

Inside his bedchamber, Ransom knelt to unlock the trunk where what valuables he'd brought to Scotland were kept. He rummaged through the clothing folded on top.

"You know, Hale, buying out Spottiswoode is probably the best way of getting rid of him. Well, other than killing him."

"And our good king does frown on such activities as murder," Dickson remarked, laughing as he flung himself into a chair. "Meg, seat yourself. You look decidedly uncomfortable."

Meg forced the faintest of smiles and clasped her nervous hands at her waist. She had yet another confession to make to her husband, and she knew he was not going to be pleased.

"Meg?" Ransom was now leaning into the depths of the trunk, and his voice was muffled. "I can't find . . . ah, here it is." He rocked back on his heels and held up a hemp bag. His eyes sought Meg's as his face creased in a frown. "Why is it so light?"

He didn't wait for her reply, but opened the bag and turned it upside down. Three gold coins dropped onto the carpet, and though he shook the pouch, nothing more fell out.

"Where the hell is the rest of the gold that was in here?" Ransom asked, his tone deadly calm.

"I . . . didn't have the opportunity to tell you," Meg began, "but . . . well, I . . . it's gone."

"Gone?" It was apparent that his calm was not unshakable. "Gone where?"

"For wages, mostly." Meg moistened her dry lips. "And I made a loan to my father."

"What sort of loan?"

"He needed money," Meg stammered, "because Cathryn took all he had when she left."

Ransom shook his head in disbelief. "You gave him money to outfit his little army, didn't you?"

Meg saw no option other than to affirm his suspicion.

"By God, do you believe it?" Ransom turned to Hale Dickson, who was watching with an expression of alarm. "My wife has spent my money to buy supplies for an army of traitors!"

"They're not traitors," she cried. "And it didn't all go for that."

"No, a goodly amount went to the workers you hired. And kept on hiring, long after I ordered you to stop. I should never have given you free rein with that gold. You've fed and clothed the entire countryside."

"I'm sorry," she retorted. "If you feel it was wasted, I'll find a way to pay you back."

"You don't understand, Meg." Tossing the empty sack aside, Ransom stood and faced her. "Without this money, I have no way to purchase Spottiswoode's land, no way to keep him from charging you with arson."

"But . . . what about the money Hale brought you?"

He kicked at the coins on the floor with the toe of his boot. "That's all that's left of the money Hale brought me."

Meg's eyes widened. "What about . . . ? Well . . . I assumed he'd just brought you more." She glanced over at Hale, her face growing paler. "You didn't bring more money from England?"

"Meg," Ransom said tiredly, "there was no more money in England. That was the sum total of my fortune."

"I distinctly remember Hale telling you that the king was sending you *part* of your money . . ."

"Yes, the only part I'm going to get. It took everything else to pay off the fines the government levied against me. Those two sacks of gold were all that stood between me and bankruptcy." He bent to retrieve the three stray coins. "And now, this is all that's left."

"Ransom . . . what are we going to do?" Meg said in a stricken whisper.

He shrugged. "It's a bit late to worry about it now, isn't it?"

His quiet attitude filled Meg with dismay. For once, she wished he'd shout at her. Perhaps if he filled the room with loud threats and accusations, she could summon her own anger. And perhaps hot, unbridled anger would make her feel better. At that moment, her stomach was churning and her chest felt as if a millstone were resting on it.

"I'd be glad to lend you what money I have," Hale Dickson said into the silence. "It won't be enough, but it might help."

Ransom shook his head. "You have your own expenses, Hale. I can't take money from you."

"If you value my friendship, you scurvy sea scum, you'll take what I offer and be glad for it." Hale eased himself from his chair and crossed the room to put an arm around Meg. "And I'd like to suggest you have a little more understanding for Meg's situation."

"You would, would you?"

"No, Hale," Meg interjected, "he's right to be angry with me. I did spend the gold irresponsibly. For some reason, I thought there'd be an unlimited supply."

"Maybe, when you were making your bride bargain," Ransom said, "you should have chosen a wealthier man."

Meg's eyes stung with unshed tears, but she lifted her chin in her familiar gesture of recalcitrance. "I know you think I deserved that, and you're probably right. But this isn't the time to air our differences—we have to figure out how to deal with Spottiswoode."

Ransom clamped his mouth shut and walked away, a muscle in his jaw twitching. He curled his hands into fists, and Meg had the unsettling feeling it was to prevent himself from throttling her. He paused at the windows, staring unseeingly out into the summer day. Meg dared a swift look at Hale, who winked and smiled encouragingly.

After a moment, Ransom turned away from the window. "All right, Hale—I'll accept your offer. It doesn't seem I have much choice, actually. But in addition to what gold you can spare, there's one other thing I'd ask of you."

"Name it, Ran."

"I've decided to personally escort Spottiswoode to London. I'd like for you to stay here at Wolfcrag . . . see to Meg and the others."

"I'd be glad to, of course," said Dickson. "Setting out on another long journey is the last thing I want to do right now."

"I don't need anyone to look after me," Meg stated.

Ransom looked at a point just beyond her shoulder. "Just this once, I'd like for you to keep quiet and do what is asked of you."

"But I—"

"Meg, your rash behavior created this quandary in the first place. Is it too much to ask that you simply stay out of the way and let me try to resolve the problems?"

"I wish you'd look at me when you speak to me," she murmured, chilled by his unexpectedly distant manner.

"Maybe I'm afraid of what I'll see if I look too closely," he said. "Maybe I don't want to learn the truth about you . . ."

"What truth?"

"That it was just another lie when you said you cared for me. That all along, you've really only wanted and needed the things I could do for you—this castle, the money to rebuild it, food and shelter for your clansmen."

"I did want those things in the beginning . . ."

He stood looking down at her, his eyes darkened to the color of a storm at sea. "Then you should congratulate yourself. It seems you're going to be successful. The castle is so close to being finished that, with Spottiswoode and Clarice to testify, the king is certain to consider it a *fait accompli* and I can deed it over to you. With any luck, I'll be able to buy Spottiswoode's property, and you can have that, too. Hell, I'm even going to approach the king about a pardon for your father."

"Ransom, I've never asked you for—"

"And the best part is, in a few short hours I'll be out of your way forever, and you won't even be bothered with making a token show of affection or obedience."

"Ransom," Dickson interceded, "don't you think you're being a bit hasty?"

"Haste is one of the few choices I have left, Hale. And the way it looks to me, the sooner I act, the better. What purpose would it serve for me to linger here now?"

"But . . . your marriage. Surely something can be worked out."

"That was all worked out in advance, Hale." Ransom slid his cool gaze back to Meg. "I'll petition for a divorce just as soon as it seems feasible to do so without raising too much suspicion. You may have to remain Lady St. Claire for another year, at least. But Devon is a long way from Scotland, so you can rest assured that I won't be an obstacle for you."

"You're not coming back?" Meg whispered.

"No, I'm not coming back." His smile was wry. "That was my end of our agreement, remember?"

He then turned to Dickson and began discussing the details of the departure. After a few moments, Meg, head held high, silently slipped from the room.

"I'll never sign that damned document," roared Revan MacLinn, tossing the sheet of parchment onto the table in the Great Hall. "The day I sign a pledge to obey that two-faced jackanapes you call a king is the day they can slice me to bits and feed me to the sharks!"

Wearily, Ransom sighed. "I give up," he intoned. "You're as stubborn as your daughter. Just forget the whole damned thing!"

Fletcher looked from one irate man to the other. "Calm down, Cap'n. We'll go over this one more time." He turned to MacLinn and, speaking slowly as if to a child, said, "This document states that you regret the crimes you've committed against the English government—"

"Which I don't," broke in the Scotsman.

"And that, if granted a pardon, you'll become a loyal subject—"

"Which I won't."

Fletcher rolled his eyes upward toward the ceiling, but continued. "And it says that you will persuade your kinsmen to give up their lives outside the law and join you in obedience to the Crown."

"Which I can't." MacLinn pounded the paper with a fist. " 'Tis a tissue of lies. I won't sign it."

"What harm can there be in putting your *X* to it?" Fletcher patiently inquired.

"I can probably read and write better than your cursed king," MacLinn blazed. "It's an affront to me that you English prigs think all we Highlanders are illiterate."

"I know you're an educated man," Fletcher affirmed. "But your claim that all Englishmen think the Scots are ignorant is the whole point of this conversation. George and his ministers would expect you to be unable to sign any document—they'd never question a simple *X*, especially if the signature was witnessed by such upstanding subjects as myself and Hale Dickson."

"But the document would be worthless," MacLinn said.

"Exactly," ground out Ransom. "But it would satisfy the king, and leave you free to do what you pleased—within reason, of course. You might have to leave off stealing cattle, but you could come back here to Wolfcrag to live without fear of reprisal. You could have done with hiding out on some isolated island."

MacLinn rubbed his bearded chin thoughtfully. "Are ye sure it would fool the king?"

"Not entirely," Ransom admitted. "I can only try. But as anxious as George is to heal the rift between your country and ours, I'd wager there's every chance he'll accept the document at face value."

MacLinn's white teeth flashed in a broad smile. "Now that I've thought on it, there is some sort of ironic justice in the idea. I like making a bargain with the government that actually means nothing at all."

"Why not?" Ransom sighed tiredly. "It seems to be the only kind of transaction you MacLinns understand."

* * *

It was late when the knock sounded on Meg's door, and she leaped to her feet, filled with relief. She knew Ransom was quietly, coldly furious with her, but she'd never expected him to purposely ignore her on his last night in the castle. There was so much she wanted to say to him, so many things to explain and apologize for . . .

She wrenched the door open . . . and was nearly overwhelmed by her bitter disappointment.

"Are you alone?" Clarice Howard asked, peering over Meg's shoulder into the room beyond.

"Yes."

"I thought you might be. Ransom and Hale are downstairs drinking themselves into a stupor."

"Oh."

"There are some things I'd like to say to you, Meg. May I come in?"

Meg stepped back and held the door wide. Clarice, elegant in a high-necked wine-red gown, swept past her and seated herself in the chamber's only chair. The room was dark, lighted only by the fire and a single candle on the bedside table. Knowing that Clarice would readily surmise her miserable mood, Meg made no effort to hide it. Instead, she dropped onto the hearth and sat, hugging her knees. Her gaze was drawn back to the fascinating depths of the fire.

"I wanted to tell you that I'm leaving Wolfcrag in the morning," Clarice announced. "I'm going to accept Ransom's offer of an escort back to London."

"How nice for you," Meg mumbled with vague sarcasm. Then, with more sincerity, "I must say farewell to your mother and the others."

"Yes, they aren't well pleased to be leaving." There was a brief silence before she continued. "Another thing I wanted to tell you was that . . . well, even though you did default on our agreement the other evening, I don't plan to go to the king with any accusations against you or Ran."

Surprised, Meg turned her head to look at Clarice.

"Thank you . . . though, of course, I don't pretend to understand you."

Clarice laughed gaily. "Sometimes I don't understand myself."

"Tell me," Meg asked, "why did you lie to Spottiswoode for me?"

"I didn't do it for you, Meg. I did it for Ransom." Clarice's smile was self-deprecating. "I'm not ordinarily so generous, but . . . God, I couldn't bear the look of terror on his face. He was so frantic on your behalf that his very expression was enough to give you away."

"That should have pleased you."

"You'd think so, wouldn't you? Instead, seeing Ransom like that . . . well, it brought out some fierce, protective instinct within me. I doubt anyone has ever believed me capable of really loving Ransom unselfishly, but my lies to Spottiswoode would seem to prove I do." Casually, she raised a hand to fluff her blond hair, but her laugh had a harsh edge to it. "I didn't like seeing him so concerned over you, but that didn't change my feelings for him. I guess you'd say that was true love, wouldn't you?"

"I don't know."

"Come, now," Clarice chided. "I believe you love him in the same way."

"What does it matter if I do?" Meg burst out. "He's leaving tomorrow, so what I think or what I feel is unimportant."

"The only reason he's leaving Scotland is that he's running from something that scares him to death."

Meg's eyes widened. "Ransom scared? I don't believe it."

"Well, you might as well, because it's true. You have to remember, Meg, that his experience with loving people hasn't been too gratifying up to this point. His mother, the only one to love him without reservation, died young and tragically—his father rebuffed him—and . . . I betrayed him. He loves you, Meg, but he's afraid to even admit it to himself, let alone you. And so he's running."

"No, you don't know . . ." Meg lowered her head to her knees and closed her eyes. "In a sense, I betrayed him, too. I went against his every command . . . I squandered his gold . . ." Her head came up. "Or, at least, he thinks I wasted it. No, the only thing Ransom feels for me right now is contempt."

"I wish that were true," Clarice sighed. "But if it were, he'd never have agreed to take the money from me to buy Spottiswoode's property for you."

"He's taking money from you?"

"A loan only. He's borrowing a sum from me, another from Dickson. And, knowing Ransom as I do, nothing short of love would prompt him to do something like that."

"I . . . I think you're wrong, Clarice."

The other woman shrugged and rose from the chair. "Have it your way. I just wanted you to know I'll be leaving tomorrow, and that it has been a unique experience staying here."

At the door, Clarice paused to look back. Although her features were indistinct in the gloom, Meg could not doubt the sincerity of her parting words.

"I envy what you have—or could have—with Ransom, Meg, but I want you to know that that's not going to stand in my way should I have an opportunity to resume my affair with your husband." This time her laugh was loudly mocking. "Good Lord, I've never felt the need to warn the other woman before! Either I've come to admire you, Meg St. Claire, or I'm growing addled in my prolonged spinsterhood!"

Meg awoke to the sound of thunder the next morning, and the sight of glowering skies fit her mood perfectly. She had spent the night alone in her own chamber, and even though a glance at the courtyard told her preparations for the departure were underway despite the weather, she'd heard nothing from Ransom. It seemed that he intended to end their months of marriage without so much as a single word. And as badly as she'd wanted to believe Clarice, it was her feeling that if Ransom harbored any affection for her, he'd have come to her last night. His deliberate neglect was as plain an avowal of disinterest as she could ask for.

And yet, there had been those moments recently when she'd felt he truly did care for her. The night she'd waited in his bed had been one of the most memorable of her life, and he'd acted every bit as enthralled as she. She knew he was experienced in such matters, but could he have pretended such passion, such tenderness? Could his kiss have been false, the words he'd whispered so fervently nothing but lies? She couldn't make herself believe it.

She dressed swiftly, not even taking time to brush her short hair. Then, seizing a cloak, she ran from her room and went in search of Ransom.

She found Fletcher in the kitchen, where he was bundling up food to send with the travelers. He himself had elected to stay at Wolfcrag, and it was no secret that Mairi was the reason. Fletcher glanced at Meg's anxious face and began to smile. "Searching for the captain, are you? Well, he's gone up to the parapets for a last look around. The caravan's almost ready to leave, but if you hurry, you can catch him."

Flinging her thanks over her shoulder, Meg ran up the narrow steps that spiraled upward through one of the towers.

Breathless by the time she reached the top, she had to struggle with the small, wooden door that opened onto the roof. The wind caught it and wrenched it backward, and Meg was pelted with a shower of icy raindrops. Ignoring them, she stepped onto the walkway.

Ransom was standing with his back to her, leaning against the huge stones of the parapet and gazing out across the heaving ocean. She approached him slowly, suddenly shy and uncertain.

"Ransom?" she ventured.

Startled, he spun about. "Meg? What are you doing out here in this rain?"

"I came to say goodbye." She pulled her cloak more tightly about her and raised her face to look at him. "You were going to go without seeing me, weren't you?"

"I . . ." He ran a hand through his damp hair. "To tell you the truth, I'm not sure what I would have done. I was just standing here debating with myself." He indicated the wall, then turned back to stand near it, redirecting his gaze to the misted horizon. Meg moved to stand beside him, hugging the square-cut stones to keep from throwing her arms around him and begging him to stay.

"If there's any view in Scotland I'll miss," he commented, "it'll be this one."

"It is beautiful," Meg agreed, her heart sinking like a stone. It was evident he intended to keep their conversation on an impersonal level. That, she rapidly decided, would be a complete waste of time for her. She'd humbled herself by seeking him out, so she might as well learn what she needed to know.

"Clarice told me that she's going with you. That she's loaning you money to buy Spottiswoode's land."

"That's true. It was something of a surprise when she made the offer."

"But then Clarice has been a good friend these last few days." Meg studied her hand lying against the gray stone. Even without the benefit of sunshine, the gold ring she wore shone richly. "Ransom, there's something I have to ask . . ."

She looked up at his profile, which was strikingly etched against the backdrop of rain-washed sky. For an instant his lashes lowered, obscuring his expression, and she sensed that he dreaded her question.

"Will you tell me the truth?" she persisted. "Please."

For a moment she thought he hadn't heard her, but then he turned to rest his back against the stones, his arms crossed over his chest. "I'll try."

The look she had feared seeing in his eyes wasn't there. She'd expected some sort of exhilaration now that he was about to return to his beloved Devon, but instead he looked as unhappy and confused as she felt.

"Do you care anything at all about me?" she asked in a faint voice. "Do you . . . do you love me?"

His eyes burned fiercely green, like emeralds tossed into fire. "I thought I explained to you that I don't believe in love, Meg."

"Because of Clarice?"

"Because of every damned thing in my life," he said harshly.

"I see."

"You knew from the beginning I wasn't interested in love or tender emotions," he reminded her, speaking through clenched teeth.

She nodded. "Yes, I know. I had just thought . . . hoped . . ." Abruptly she turned away to stand with her back to him, head slightly bowed. "Anyway, it really doesn't matter now, does it? Just let me wish you a safe journey . . . and good luck in dealing with the king."

"Thank you."

"Well," she said brightly, "I won't detain you any longer." Grasping her sodden skirts in both hands, Meg hurried toward the door. She had just reached for the iron latch when she heard his voice.

"Meg . . . wait!"

She stood still, without turning. Her heart pounded desperately in her chest and she uttered a silent prayer.

"Meg, I . . ."

She felt his hand on her shoulder as he easily turned her about. Whatever he'd been struggling to say died in his throat and was replaced by a deep, savage groan.

His arms were like bands of steel as he pulled her against him and rested his cheek against the top of her hair. He held her so tightly she could barely breathe, but she didn't care. It was a wonderful feeling to be clasped against his warmth, to be comforted and shielded by his strength once again.

Meg thrust her own arms about his waist and clung to him, fighting back the tears that threatened. She drew a deep, sustaining breath and pressed her face against his damp shirt. His scent was that of wind and rain and the damp leather coat he wore.

Ransom took her chin in one large hand and gently compelled her to look up at him. Then, with both hands cupping her face, he allowed himself a leisurely survey of her features. His anguished gaze moved slowly, almost as if he were memorizing every inch of her countenance. He bent down and lightly kissed away the single tear that had traced its way along her cheek. Then, without lifting his face, he moved his mouth to hers and kissed her as warmly and deeply as if he did, indeed, love her.

After a moment, his hands dropped away from her, and, suddenly, the heated sweetness of his mouth was gone, supplanted by the chilling touch of the rain. Filled with dread, Meg opened her eyes and saw that Ransom had stepped away from her.

"Don't go," she breathed.

"I have to, Meg." There was a look of finality in his gaze. "It's better for both of us if I do."

"No, Ransom." Meg clutched the edges of her cloak so tightly her hands ached. "Stay with me . . . please!"

He crossed the narrow space between them and laid a gently restraining finger against her lips. "Remember your heritage," he murmured. "Didn't you once tell me Highland women don't beg?"

Then, with quick, long strides, he disappeared through the doorway to the stairs, and, helplessly, Meg watched him go.

*"Slàn leat,"* she whispered brokenly in Gaelic. "Fare thee well, my love."

Later, she couldn't recall how long she had simply stood there in the rain—it could have been minutes, it could have been an hour. But she remained motionless until she heard the creak of wagon wheels and the clatter of horses' hoofs that signaled Ransom's departure on his journey home to England.

Then she turned and fled into the shelter of Wolfcrag.

# Chapter Twenty-one

*September 1770*
*Devon, England*

Ransom stood on the balcony of his country manor and looked out over the bay beyond. The beach at Rogue's Run was as magnificently beautiful as always. In the distance, the line of blue horizon was shading to soft, indeterminate gray. Closer, the jagged rocks of Hartland Point were awash in a placid sea, turned aquamarine by the long, golden shafts of sunlight on an early-autumn evening. Just below him, the hedges that bordered the lawn running down to the ocean cast deep shadows, and the asters and Michaelmas daisies growing in their shade glowed like blue and white stars.

Ransom lifted his face to the slight, balmy breeze and felt the salty sting of sea air in his nostrils.

"It's good to be home, isn't it, fellow?" he murmured to the black cat nestled in the crook of his arm. Satan yawned and stretched, kneading his front paws on the sleeve of his master's knitted sweater. Absently, Ransom scratched the animal's head, and the resultant purr droned loudly in the stillness.

Satan seemed content, but Ransom knew the cat was just as lost as he. In the two weeks since they'd come home to Rogue's Run, he'd seen the cat prowling aimlessly through the house, as if looking for something . . . or someone. He knew exactly what secret yearning had prompted the search, for it was the same urge that compelled him from his own lonely bed every night to wander through the silent house, eventually either lighting dozens of candles to dispel the gloom, or else sitting alone in the dark, staring at nothing.

Then there had been those days when, sure inactivity would drive him mad, he'd saddled a horse and ridden recklessly along the beach, sometimes stopping to throw himself into the crystalline waters to swim until he was exhausted. He often reflected that he'd never been able to swim in Scotland, even in the heart of the summer, for the water was simply too bone-chillingly cold. And with that thought would come a vision of misty gray seas, jagged rocks, and stony beaches. And it seemed the sound of a sharp and biting wind still echoed in his ears.

He sighed. Would he ever get the memories out of his head? It was time to forget Wolfcrag, time to fully return to the old life he'd left behind here in Devon. But once he'd been welcomed by his household staff and settled in, a curious restlessness overtook him. He didn't want to be alone, but he couldn't abide other people. He shunned his friends, not so much because he didn't want to see them, but more because he was oddly reluctant to speak of his stay in Scotland, and he knew they'd want to hear every detail.

He'd spent hours walking or riding along the flowered lanes that he'd remembered so fondly while in the north—and they were, indeed, lovely beyond belief. And yet, he'd felt as though he was strolling through a dull and lifeless painting in which the trees and flowers were scentless daubs from an artist's brush.

All the while he'd been in London, he'd been chomping at the bit, eager to get back to the country. His business with the king had taken nearly a month, but once he'd finally accomplished all that he could, he'd set out for home with jubilant haste and a new deed to Rogue's Run in his pocket. But slowly, day by day, the jubilance had died, and now all he felt was a strange, disquieting emptiness that had inexorably drained every ounce of joy from him. He had not experienced such desolation since the day his mother died, and he was at a loss as to how to deal with it.

The faintly dusty scent of the ivy that nearly obscured the stone railings of the balcony on which he stood brought him back to the present.

He knew what the problem was. Lord, he ought to. It was the same one that had plagued him day and night since he'd encountered it early last spring. His problem had hair as black as the Devil's heart and eyes as gray as the rain-washed skies of her homeland. She had a smile that promised Heaven, and a temper that evoked Hell. She was an outlaw's spawn with scarcely more scruples than her scoundrel father. She was willful and wayward . . .

And, damn it, he missed her. Missed her like sin every waking moment, and had lost count of the times he'd turned to her in his sleep. He'd expected to regret the absence of her beguiling presence in his bed—after all, theirs had been a tempestuous relationship that had only recently been consummated. But what he had not expected was that he'd miss her so at mealtimes, or that he'd recall with such poignancy sitting by the fire with her in the evenings.

Somehow, the little Highland witch had carved a place for herself in his heart. But what could he do about it? There was no room for her in his life.

He was back in Devon where he belonged. This was where his family had lived and owned property for centuries. He had a responsibility to the land and to the people . . . and to himself.

He looked out at the bay again, his eyes stealing to the sleek, two-masted ship floating quietly at anchor there. Suddenly, he realized how much he wanted to feel the pitch and roll of the deck beneath his feet. Perhaps, now that the brigantine was his again, what he needed was a long sail. The endless stretch of ocean out there beyond civilization would help him clear his mind and reorganize his life. It had never failed him yet.

For the first time in weeks, Ransom felt like smiling. Even the prospect of one final obligation could not daunt him. He'd pay an obligatory call on his father and brother and then set sail, remaining at sea until his life's direction became clear to him.

Ransom figured he had two choices. Three, actually, if he cared to count the possibility of settling down beneath his father's thumb and learning to be an obedient son.

But since he didn't relish that particular option, he was left with the remaining two. He could square his shoulders and meet his problems head on, or he could become a fugitive from reality and live out his life as a lonely recluse, bereft of his heart's desire and forever impoverished in spirit.

*October 1770*
*Scotland*

Meg tossed aside the quill pen and leaned back in her chair, trying to ease her stiff spine. She had pored over the accounts all afternoon, until her head ached and the columns of figures blurred before her tired eyes.

Wearily, she left the cherrywood desk and crossed the room, settling herself into a cushioned window seat, drawing up her legs, and tucking her skirts around them. Now that work at Wolfcrag was complete, she had chosen a new room for herself—one where she and Ransom had never spent time together.

It was a small chamber on the third floor of the castle, a room with only one window to offer distraction. The walls were whitewashed and nearly bare, the furnishings simple. As plain and peaceful as a convent cell, it had become her retreat . . . and she found she was spending more and more time alone there.

She did so, she told herself, because there was very little to be done at Wolfcrag now. The workmen had finished their task of renovating the castle and had gone about their own lives. Many of the ruined crofts on the lands lying adjacent to Wolfcrag had been rebuilt, and when the weather permitted, work continued on the rest. But autumn had come to the Highlands with a vengeance. For every day of sunshine, there were several that were cold and dreary. Days when rain slashed against the glass panes and the hounds curled up by the fire.

Days that Meg got through by throwing herself into her crusade to repay her debt to Ransom St. Claire. Once the oncoming winter had passed, the people of Wolfcrag were going to plant crops, half of which would be for their own use, the other half to be sold for cash to use in repaying Ransom for his purchase of Spottiswoode's land. It might take a few years, but the debt would be paid.

Meg and her father had come up with the plan following the arrival of an envoy sent by Ransom more than six weeks ago. The man had shown up at the castle quite unexpectedly, bringing with him a sheaf of legal documents. True to his word, Ransom had deeded Wolfcrag to Meg, and all the land that Spottiswoode had once owned was now the legal property of Meg and her father. In addition, Revan MacLinn and the members of his clan had been given a document granting them a full pardon for their crimes against the English government—on the condition that, henceforth, they conduct themselves as law-abiding citizens and avoid any future resistance against the Crown. The document also stated that MacLinn's son-in-law, Ransom St. Claire, had been made responsible for their good behavior and would answer to the king should any MacLinn default. Meg had to smile as she remembered her father's triumphant shout of laughter when he'd read that.

"Serves the English swine right after the way he deserted ye," MacLinn had said. "It fair puts me in the mood to go reiving, ye ken."

But he hadn't. Instead, he'd promptly had the pardon and a copy of the pledge of loyalty he'd signed framed and hung on the wall in the Great Hall. He frequently reminded all and sundry that the former meant nothing because he'd signed the pledge with an *X* instead of his actual signature. Had it not been for his smoldering anger over Cathryn and Alex's continued absence, Meg was certain her father would have been perfectly content to be back within the walls of Wolfcrag. As it was, he seemed as much at odds as did Meg herself.

Thus, the two of them had busied themselves reestablishing their clan in the area. When her father's small army had arrived at Wolfcrag ready to do battle with Jonathan Spottiswoode and his men, they had been bitterly disappointed to find the dilemma already resolved. They were pacified only when Revan MacLinn suggested they return to Carraig to collect their families and bring them back to the mainland. By the time the exiled clansmen returned to Wolfcrag, many of the crofts were ready to receive them.

Meg and her father had called a meeting of the residents of Wolfcrag and the surrounding properties, and it was swiftly decided that Ransom St. Claire should be repaid. If each man was willing to sacrifice a percentage of his yearly income toward the debt, he would, once Ransom had been reimbursed, be allowed to own his own croft or cottage, free and clear. But only, Meg insisted, if the money to pay the debt was earned honestly. And, to a man, they agreed. Their days of being an outlawed clan were behind them.

Meg was jolted back to the present by the sound of King growling in his sleep. The hound, lying on the rug before the hearth fire, was apparently dreaming of chasing rabbits, for his front feet twitched and his tail thumped the floor. Meg watched him for a time, a faint smile on her lips. Had it not been for his company, she was sure there had been times when she would have died of loneliness. It was only here, in the privacy of her room, in the presence of her beloved pet, that she could give in to the sorrow she felt. She refused to add to her father's worries by letting him see how miserable she was, but she doubted she would ever get over blaming herself for Ransom's departure. She missed him more each day, and the prospect of spending the rest of her life without him was overwhelmingly dismal. She had been touched when his man had arrived with the legal documents, but crushed with disappointment that Ransom had sent no message to her. Up till then she had harbored hope he would change his mind and come back to Scotland.

She glanced down at the golden ring on her finger, silently admitting it was one of the reasons she'd felt he might come back. When he'd left, he hadn't asked her to return the ring, even though it had belonged to his mother and even though he said he planned to eventually petition for a divorce. That, and the fact that he'd also left behind the small painting of Rogue's Run, had filled her with hope. But then his messenger had come and there'd been no word for her . . . and little by little, hope had begun to die.

Needing a diversion from her thoughts, Meg got up from the window seat, intending to go back to her desk. Instead, she found herself approaching the picture of Ransom's home in Devon, the only adornment on her stark walls. She stood gazing at it, lost in the sweet, pastoral beauty of the scene.

What must it be like to live in a place where the sea breezes were warm and gentle, where flowers grew in multicolored profusion? A place where life was tranquil and unhurried, and where everyone spoke in slow, mellow accents as rich as country cream?

Rogue's Run *was* beautiful—no wonder Ransom loved it so. Meg traced the doorway of the house in the painting with a forefinger and tried to imagine him standing there. To her sorrow, it was all too easy to do. In her heart she had to acknowledge that there was nothing in Scotland capable of ever luring him away from Devon again.

Abruptly, she turned from the painting and went back to the window. She noticed, with some surprise, that the sun was shining and it was one of those rare, warm autumn days. She leaned forward to unlatch the window and push it open and, along with the sunshine, she admitted the sound of children laughing and calling to each other as they played.

Looking down into the courtyard, she saw Fletcher and Mairi sitting on a bench, watching Mairi's sons at play with Brodie and Lorna MacLinn's brothers and sisters. Meg derived genuine pleasure from seeing Fletcher drape a possessive arm about Mairi's shoulders. Shortly after Ransom's departure, the two of them had been quietly married, despite Fletcher's protestations over the difference in their ages. Now Mairi and her children seemed wonderfully happy, and Fletcher went about the castle whistling cheerfully, with a smile for everyone. Meg could certainly find no fault with the efficient way they ran the kitchens, nor could she begrudge them their newfound happiness simply because her own world lay in shambles.

The glint of the sun on something white took her eye, and she caught sight of a ship far out in the sound, its sails unfurled to the wind. Immediately she thought of Ransom . . . but then, she reminded herself wryly, everything she saw these days reminded her of Ransom.

With a sigh, she left the window and went back to the desk and the columns of figures that symbolized her financial indebtedness. Once she managed to pay back what she owed Ransom, she'd be able to forget him.

It was a lie she'd told herself many times, and she didn't believe it any more now than she had before.

Meg couldn't stand it another moment—if she did not get out of the Banqueting Hall, she was going to embarrass herself by bursting into tears, something no one in her clan had ever witnessed. The castle residents had gathered for their usual evening fete, and even though she'd been congratulating herself on the progress she'd made in erasing Ransom from her mind, the music had put her into a strange, melancholy mood. And now Hale Dickson, who had proven himself a staunch friend, had totally surprised her by suggesting he and Lorna MacLinn sing a duet. In a small flare of self-pity, Meg told herself that Hale could have chosen any song but the one he did—a love ballad from Devon which, he announced, he'd spent the afternoon teaching Lorna.

It seemed to Meg that from the very first words, every eye in the room was on her. Testily, she wondered if they expected her to swoon at the mere mention of the word Devon. Well, she wouldn't swoon, but she had to admit that the pretty song filled her with sadness and longing for things she could never have. And suddenly, she had to get out of the hall. It was stifling—too crowded and too warm. Trying to be as unobtrusive as possible, she was making her way to the door when she encountered Fletcher and his new wife.

"What's wrong, Meg?" Fletcher inquired solicitously. "You don't look too well."

"I . . . it's hot in here. I need some fresh air."

"Ah, a walk along the beach, perhaps?" Mairi suggested, smiling at Fletcher.

"We just came from there," he explained, "and it's invigorating, I can assure you." His grin was conspiratorial. "If you don't want anyone to know where you've gone, slip out the secret passageway as we did. Mairi left a cloak just inside the tunnel."

He patted his wife's hand and they beamed at each other. Inwardly, Meg groaned. All the doting lovers in this castle were enough to turn a person against romance.

"Thank you," she murmured, and hastened across the room to the darkened window embrasure where the entrance to the hidden tunnel was located. With a swift glance to be certain no one was watching her, she touched the turn stone and slipped inside the door that opened.

It took a moment for her eyes to adjust to the darkness, but once they did, she easily found the cloak Mairi had left hanging from a rough place on the rock wall. Slipping it about her, Meg started down the passageway, knowing her way so well she wasn't bothered by the lack of light.

At the far end of the tunnel, she stepped out onto a small, private beach and raised her face to the bracing wind. Almost immediately, she saw the ship, its masts tall and straight. It appeared to be at anchor just beyond the shallow water of the bay behind Wolfcrag. She was filled with a sense of alarm—were they to be invaded? Had the English king tricked them by issuing a false pardon to lure the outlawed clan back to Wolfcrag? Meg didn't know—she only knew she had to warn her father.

She whirled to run back into the castle and was unexpectedly set upon by two men who sprang from the shadows. Before she could scream, one of them clamped a hand over her mouth and began dragging her through the sand toward the water.

All the apathy of the past few weeks disappeared, and Meg discovered her will to survive was as strong as ever. She didn't know who these men were, or what they wanted with her, but she wouldn't go docilely. She kicked out at one of her captors, all the while trying to bite the hand over her mouth.

"Jesus! She bit me!"

"Toss her into the boat," the other one yelled. "Let her scream — no one will hear her."

Meg felt herself being lifted, and then she was dumped unceremoniously onto the damp bottom of a small boat. It lurched beneath her as one of the men climbed aboard, and then the crunch of sand beneath the hull told her the other one was pushing them off. They fully intended to steal her and sail away!

She raised up. *"Ciod a tha ort?"* she hissed. *"Is ann a tha thu air bhoil!"* The man who had carried Meg now seized her again, preventing her from throwing herself overboard.

"What'd she say?" The second fellow leaped into the boat and reached for the oars.

"I said that you must be insane," Meg gasped. "What do you think you're doing?"

"Following orders, is all."

Orders? Meg took a closer look at the men and decided they were common English sailors . . . no doubt the type of men George would hire to do his dirty work. It wouldn't look well for the Royal Navy to be engaged in kidnapping or worse.

She renewed her struggles, but the man holding her simply twisted the ends of her cloak about her, effectively restricting her movements.

"What do you want with me?" she asked.

"Nobody is going to hurt you," the sailor at the oars said. "Just behave . . . and don't bite or kick either one of us again."

Something in his tone calmed Meg. He didn't sound like a bloodthirsty killer bent on massacre. He actually sounded more like a man reluctantly doing as he'd been told, and with that thought came the inclination to believe him. Perhaps the situation wasn't as dire as she'd first thought. Perhaps . . .

No, she wouldn't let herself start thinking of Ransom now.

She fastened her attention on the beauty of the evening. The sun, a ball of chilly fire, was sinking into the water along the horizon, and its fading light gilded the waves. Gulls, their shrill cries echoing on the wind, swooped to pluck unsuspecting fish out of the sea. Behind them, Wolfcrag grew smaller and smaller, and Meg knew they must be drawing close to the waiting ship. She shivered in the sharp wind and clenched her cold hands into fists.

By the time they had reached the ship and were using a rope ladder to climb onboard, Meg experienced a curious emotion. She was no longer frightened. Rather, she was exhilarated, filled with a sense of adventure. No matter what or whom she discovered on this vessel, she would relish the challenge.

The ship's crew had crowded on deck to greet them. "What do we do with her?" the first sailor asked.

A tall, swarthy man with the scarred face of a buccaneer stepped forward. "I'll take her," he said, grasping Meg's arm. "The captain's waitin' below."

"Who are you?" Meg managed to ask as the burly man propelled her across the deck and down a short companionway. "Where are you taking me?"

"I'm the first mate," he replied, his mouth twitching with a smile. "And I'm taking you to the ship's captain. Seems he has business with you."

"What sort of business?" Meg demanded.

The man's smile grew wider. "I really couldn't say, milady." He knocked on a closed door. "I've got the woman, Captain."

"Send her in," commanded a deep, resonant voice.

The sailor opened the door and gently shoved Meg inside, closing it after her.

Meg found herself in a ship's cabin, alone except for the man who stood near a glowing iron stove watching her. Dressed in a white shirt and snug trousers tucked into black knee boots, he lounged casually against a desk. Cradled in one arm was a huge cat who immediately abandoned his stroking fingers to leap to the floor and approach Meg with a piteous meow. Numbly, she knelt and gathered the cat into her arms.

"Satan," she whispered, laying her cheek against his sleek black head. She closed her eyes and breathed deeply, trying to control the riotous beating of her heart. Still kneeling, she raised her eyes to the man who remained standing across the cabin from her.

He was so tall that his head nearly brushed the ceiling. His hair was thick and curling, dark auburn in color, and matched by a pair of heavy brows that were drawn down over eyes she knew would be Devonshire blue if she could see them in the shadows. The only light in the room came from a lantern hanging above the desk, and as the ship pitched slightly, the lantern swayed, casting its glow on the pagan earring in the man's left ear, giving him the appearance of a rogue or a pirate.

"Ransom." Meg's lips moved in the soundless uttering of his name.

He crossed to her then, gently taking the cat from her and placing him on the desk. Satan uttered a disgruntled mew, but curled up on the papers scattered there, as if willing to allow them their moment.

"Hello, Meg," Ransom said quietly.

Slowly, Meg rose to her feet and stood gazing defiantly at him. She was all too aware of his size, of the way he towered over her in the small room. And yet she felt no actual fear even knowing she was at his mercy.

"Why did you come back?" she demanded, startled by the anger in her tone. "What do you want?"

"I believe we have some unfinished business."

"Damn you, Ransom St. Claire," she burst out. "You'd better not have come to make more trouble for my family. I won't let you hurt them!"

She spun about and flung herself at the door, fumbling with the latch. In two giant strides, Ransom was behind her, halting her flight by placing a hand on either side of her shoulders and using his body to pin her against the door.

"Meg," he said, his mouth close to her ear. "I'm not going to hurt anyone. That's not why I came back."

"Then why did you?"

"I needed to talk to you."

"You didn't have to have me kidnapped just to talk," she retorted. "Did your damned king send you to betray us?"

"Good God, no! I came here for my own reasons. But I wasn't sure you'd even see me . . . or give me a chance to explain." His words were low, sincere. "I knew that if I showed up at the castle unannounced, your father might simply run me through or have me shot before I ever got to you."

Meg closed her eyes, fighting against the pleasure she felt at the way his heated breath stirred her hair. She was agonizingly aware of him, from the press of his broad chest upon her back, all the way to her calves, which were sheathed by the muscled leanness of his own. His weight and warmth against her brought back every memory she'd tried so hard to suppress.

"Meg, please listen to me," Ransom whispered, resting his face against her hair. "I'm sorry for this little conspiracy. I couldn't think what else to do."

"Fletcher knew, didn't he?" Meg asked softly. "He knew, and he tricked me. And Mairi and Hale . . . they all knew!"

"Don't be angry with them. When I sent my men to request Fletcher's help, he only agreed because he realized matters between us have to be settled once and for all. The others will explain the situation to your father so he won't worry. Meg, I didn't know any other way for us to have privacy."

Feeling defeated, Meg leaned her cheek against the wooden door. "Then say what you have to say. It seems I have no choice but to hear you out."

Unbelievably, he chuckled. "In the short time we've known each other, you've taught me many lessons. Shall I search your person for weapons?"

"No," she spat. "I have none . . . but had I known you'd be here, I'd certainly have brought my dirk."

He was silent for a long moment. "So you do wish you had killed me?"

"Yes—no! Oh, God, Ransom . . ." She twisted about to face him. "I don't know what I wish . . . except that we'd never met." She lowered her eyes. "No, that's not true, either. Without you, we wouldn't have Wolfcrag back, and my father wouldn't be a free man."

"Meg, look at me."

She did as she was bid, even though it infuriated her that her eyes swam with tears. She didn't want him to see any weakness in her. Although she expected his expression to be accusing or cynical, his green eyes were somber.

"There's something I have to tell you," Ransom said, letting his hands drop from the doorframe to grip her elbows. "Something I should have told you months ago." He laughed shortly. "Only I couldn't have told you, because I didn't even know myself.

"I didn't know until I'd left Scotland behind." His hands were unsteady on her arms. "Meg, I can't remember the last time I slept clear through the night . . . or laughed, or actually experienced pleasure. London was a nightmare, Devon not much better. And even when I was at Rogue's Run, I was in some kind of terrible limbo . . ."

"Ransom, I don't understand what you're trying to say."

"It's so simple, Meg—so simple. And yet it took me so damned long to realize that I loved you."

"You . . . what?"

"I love you—and I missed you so much while I was in England that I thought I might die before I could get back here to you." He bowed his head. "You told me you loved me, asked me to stay with you . . . and cruelly, I threw your words in your face. Can you ever forgive me for that?"

"You weren't cruel. I only thought that you didn't . . . love me," Meg murmured. "You never said you did."

"My only defense is that I didn't know . . . I truly didn't recognize what love meant." His smile was slightly lopsided. "I admit I wanted you in my bed, but I thought that was just ordinary lust. I enjoyed your company because you made me laugh, but that was nothing more than friendly affection. And when Spottiswoode hurt and threatened you, I was outraged. But it didn't seem enough somehow—until I was away from you. Then it began to dawn on me what I have done. It's as if I'd studied the individual threads so closely I'd missed the true design of the tapestry. Lust and affection and protective feelings are all a part of love, Meg, and I didn't know. But now I do, and that's what I've come back to tell you." He brushed her mouth with his. "I love you. More than anything in my life."

"Ransom, I—I don't know what to say . . ."

"Tell me you still love me."

"I do . . ."

He cradled her face in his hands, tenderly sealing her lips

with a thumb. Meg saw the pain that flickered in the back of his eyes, and knew it cost him dearly to speak his next words aloud.

"Don't say it unless you mean it, Meg. Don't tell me you love me if there's even the slightest chance you'll ever stop. I've been disappointed before and . . . well, I never wanted to care for anybody else. Now that I do, I'm scared as hell of losing you."

"You won't be disappointed this time," she declared. "I won't leave you, and I swear, I'll never let you leave me again."

"Then you do love me?" he queried.

"Yes! And I've missed you so!"

As if relieved, Ransom leaned his forehead against hers for a few seconds. Then he kissed her quickly and set her away from him. "Now, let me take your cloak so we can sit down and talk. Would you like some hot coffee?"

Meg tilted her head, giving him a quizzical look. "We've been apart for more than six weeks and you ask if I want coffee?"

He looked surprised, then somewhat sheepish. "It's a cold night . . ."

Meg unfastened her cloak and tossed it carelessly aside. "Aye, it is that. But there are better ways to warm ourselves."

"But we've much to catch up on," Ransom hedged. "I assume the documents I sent were in order? Uh . . . has the work been completed on the castle . . . ?"

His words died into silence as he stood gazing at the woman before him. He discerned a new maturity about her. She was thinner, and there were vague shadows around her smoke-colored eyes. Her hair, still short and tumbled, now reached the collar of her blue gown, where it curled enticingly around her slender neck. Her mouth, as sweetly lush as he'd remembered, parted in a smile that entreated him to cast aside each and every one of his hard-won scruples.

"Damn it, Meg," he murmured, "you are the most beautiful woman I've ever known. I can barely keep my hands off you, but I promised myself—"

"Ransom, I'm not asking you to keep your hands off me. After all this time, I confess that I very much want to have them on me." Her laugh was light, uncertain.

He groaned. "No . . . not until we talk."

Meg came close to him. "We have the rest of the night to talk." She lifted her arms and put them around his neck, burying her face against his shirt. "Right now I need you to convince me that you really mean it when you say you love me."

"You doubt it?"

She looked up at him. "I do when I've thrown myself at you like a wanton and you're still talking about coffee and problems. Please, kiss me, Ransom."

His arms came about her waist like a vise. "If I start, lass, I won't be able to stop. We'll end up in that bunk in the corner there . . ."

Meg spared the narrow bed a swift glance. "That bunk looks fine to me," she whispered, and began unlacing his shirt. "I've missed you so."

Something in her touch sparked an answering hunger in Ransom, and he relegated to the future all thoughts of anything but loving her. Having made that decision, he discovered he hadn't the time or patience for a gentle wooing. His mouth found hers in a searing kiss, and then they were tearing at each other's clothing, consumed by an overwhelming passion that had smoldered for too long without being brought to flame.

Meg kicked her way free of her gown and petticoats and, wearing only her chemise, fell upon the bunk, reaching out for him. As soon as his own clothes had been stripped away, he lay down beside her and, without further words, covered her eager body with his. Pushing the loose-fitting undergarment to her waist, he grasped her hips and joined the two of them with a single deep thrust. Meg cried out in pleasure and clung to him, covering his throat with sweet, fevered kisses. He lowered his head to kiss her breasts through the soft cotton of the chemise, his mouth driving her to wondrous distraction. Their bodies strained together, creating a rhythm that sent them higher and higher, into a realm where they were cognizant only of the bliss they could give each other and, by doing so, give themselves.

In only moments, they were lost in shattering fulfillment, her soft cries of ecstasy mingling with his harsher ones. Breathing heavily, they lay locked in each other's arms, savoring a satisfaction neither would ever again take for granted. Love seemed sweeter for nearly having been denied them.

Later, as the cabin grew cooler, Ransom rose from the bed to stoke the fire in the small iron stove, and Meg watched him with worshipping eyes. Superb in his nudity, he moved with a casual grace that touched her. How had she ever survived the last weeks without him?

Ransom slipped back into the bunk, pulling the sheet and blankets over them as he drew her back into his embrace. With a sigh of repletion, she rested her head on his shoulder and snuggled close to his warmth.

"I don't believe I'm actually choosing to live in this foul country," Ransom idly remarked. "The weather is colder than a mermaid's—"

"You're going to . . . live here?" Meg interrupted.

"Yes, I mean to make Wolfcrag—and Scotland—my home. If you have no objection, that is."

"Of course I have no objection. But Ransom, I'd never ask that of you. I know how much you dislike it here. I'd be willing to go back to Devon with you."

He ran a hand through her hair, letting the ebony strands curl around his fingers. "No, we're staying here. Somehow, stark hills and gray seas seem to have taken my fancy." He kissed her ear. "And now that you've shown me such a delightful method of keeping warm, I believe I will be quite happy."

"But what about Rogue's Run?"

"It's no longer my concern—I've sold it. That's where I got the money to repay Clarice and Hale. And we should be able to live very respectably with what's left . . . as long as I keep a good, firm hand on the purse strings."

Ignoring his mild taunt, Meg pushed herself into a sitting position. "You *sold* your home?" she cried. "Ransom, no! You can't have done that!"

"But I did, love. To my father. And for a handsome sum, I might add."

"But I know how much you loved that estate," she murmured, tears welling in her eyes. "Oh, Ransom, what have I done to you?"

"Meg, listen to me. Selling Rogue's Run was my own idea. One week alone there and I knew it meant nothing anymore. It was empty without you — worthless." He raised himself on one elbow. "I once thought I was only happy in Devon, but you showed me I was wrong. Now I know I will be content with you, wherever we live. So don't cry for something that's really no loss."

She touched his face. "But I am so truly sorry. You've given up so much for me."

"Ah, yes," he growled, suddenly pulling her back down beside him. "Loneliness . . . unhappiness . . . self-pity!" He kissed her, deeply and ardently. "I love you, Meg."

"And I love you," she replied, smiling and crying at once. "Forever. No — much longer than that!"

The ship rolled gently, tugging at its moorings. Overhead the lantern swung, its light dancing erratically on the beams of the ceiling. Soft snores sounded from across the room, where Satan slept peacefully by the glowing stove. But Ransom and Meg were aware only of each other as they laughed and whispered throughout the long, blissful night.

# Chapter Twenty-two

"It's about time the two of ye decided to come back," Revan MacLinn grumbled as Meg and Ransom stepped into the Banqueting Hall from the secret passageway. "I've been waiting since the crack of dawn."

Meg glanced at the man beside her, her face coloring. Ransom merely smiled, dropped the seabag he carried, and put an arm around his wife's shoulders. "Did you want something?" he asked casually.

MacLinn's eyes narrowed. "Ye're damned right I did," he barked. "I wanted to make certain my daughter came to no harm." His brows drew together. "Harm that wasn't of her own choosing, that is."

Meg tried to deny the smile that threatened. "I'm fine, Father. I'm sorry if you've been worried."

"Oh, Fletcher and the others explained matters," he admitted. "And after the way your husband deserted you, Meg, it's probably best he handled his homecoming the way he did. Had you come to Wolfcrag first, laddie boy, you might have found your important parts ripped off and fed to the hounds."

"Father!" Meg scolded, shocked. "Behave yourself. Ransom, ignore him."

"It'll be my pleasure," Ransom informed her.

"Ignore me after you've answered a few questions," MacLinn suggested.

"What questions?"

"Are you staying this time?"

Ransom's arm tightened about Meg's shoulders and he gave her a slow, sweet smile. "I am."

"Good. I wouldn't want to be forced to disembowel my grandchildren's father, ye ken."

"Now, Father, if you're going to continue to bait Ransom—"

"Ah, let the lad speak for himself, Meggie. Do you want him to hide behind your skirts forever?"

"I've never—" Ransom began, only to be interrupted by the older man.

"What happened to Spottiswoode?" he demanded.

"Once he'd made his testimony to the king and signed the document absolving Meg of any guilt in the burning of his home, he was paid for his land." Ransom grinned broadly. "Two days later, he left London for the Continent—in the company, I was told, of one of the most notorious lightskirts in the city."

Forgetting himself, MacLinn smiled back. "Ah . . . he'll have a high old time, until his money runs out. Speaking of lightskirts, what became of Clarice Howard? Did ye bed her on the way back to England?"

*"Father!"*

"Now, don't take that tone with me, lass. You want to know as much as I do. Admit it."

Meg shook her head, but her intensely gray eyes lifted to her husband's face. Disregarding MacLinn's avid interest, Ransom took Meg's hand and raised it to his lips. "I won't pretend Clarice didn't offer," he affirmed, "but I swear to you that she could have pranced naked through the camp each night and I'd never have noticed her. My mind was still in Scotland, love."

"And how did Clarice take that?" questioned MacLinn.

"As well as could be expected, I suppose. And anyway, the first week we were in London, she took up with a handsome young rake she met at the gambling tables." Ransom winked at Meg as he kissed her hand a second time. "She assured me he was only a temporary balm for her shattered heart."

"Hmmmph," MacLinn snorted. "What about my pardon from the king? Is it genuine?"

"As long as you don't overlook any of the stipulations."

"But if I do," MacLinn crowed, "am I not correct in thinking that it'll be your fine English arse in peril?"

"My fine English arse, as well as your own fine Scottish one." Ransom grinned widely. "Let's just say it will benefit both of us to lead an exemplary life from now on."

MacLinn frowned. "Could I start being exemplary week after next, perhaps?"

"Why do you ask?" Ransom queried, certain of only one thing: he probably wasn't going to care for MacLinn's answer.

"As you may recall, my dear stubborn Cathryn ran away from me to stay with her kin in the border country. I've been patiently waiting for her to rue her decision and come home, but now it seems I will have to take matters into my own hands."

"Has something happened?" asked Meg. "Have you heard from them?"

"Oh, I've heard, all right," MacLinn stated. "Late last evening a messenger arrived from Briarthorn . . . with a request for a goodly sum of money. Her own damned relatives have decided to hold her and the boy hostage."

"Oh, no," moaned Meg. "Are you going to pay?"

"I wouldn't honor such a bargain—even if I had the money."

"Then what are you going to do?"

MacLinn smiled coldly. "We have no choice but to go to Briarthorn and steal them back."

"We?" choked Ransom. "What do you mean . . . *we?*"

"You'll have to go along, lad. How else will you be able to keep my fine Scottish arse out of trouble?"

"My God," intoned Ransom. He fixed his wife with a droll look and asked, for at least the dozenth time, "What have I gotten myself into?"

"Ye'll find out soon enough," MacLinn promised. "In the meantime, just keep telling yourself that it's all in the name of love."

"Hsst, lad—up there!" Crouched in the foliage at the edge of the forest, Owen MacIvor pointed toward a window high in the castle tower just across the river. " 'Tis your fair Cathryn, is it not?"

Revan MacLinn joined him, gazing upward. The woman had pushed aside wooden shutters to stand at the window for a long moment, looking out. "Aye, there's no mistaking that tartan shawl she's wearing. Seems we were right to figure they'd keep her in the top of the damned tower."

"Shall we signal her?" Ransom asked, coming to stand beside his father-in-law. "It might help if she knew we had come for her."

"Help?" MacLinn shot him a wicked grin. "Ye've got a lot to learn about Highland women, lad. How will it help if she doesn't want to come with us?"

"But her own kin are holding her hostage."

"Aye, but she ran away from me in the first place. She might not care to come back to Wolfcrag."

"So you'll take her back against her will?"

"Nay, she'll have her choice," MacLinn promised grimly. "But I want my son back, whether or no. The bastards have kept him from me long enough."

"How do you intend to get them out of there?" inquired Meg, materializing from the shadows. "We know the place is well guarded."

"Skulking about in the woods for the past two days has told us that," Ransom agreed. "With no more men than we brought, we'll never get through the front gates."

"Have a little faith, laddie." MacLinn rubbed his bearded chin. "The important thing is, we now know where they're keeping Cathryn. Since there's been no sign of Alex, we'll just have to hope they're together or that he's close by."

"So you do plan to storm the place?" Ransom asked, perplexed.

"No, we'll have to go up the wall."

"Up the wall?" repeated Ransom, turning his head for a second look at the vertical stone walls of the small castle.

MacLinn chuckled. "No sense doing this the easy way."

"Is that why we brought the grapple from my ship?"

"Aye. Now, I'll climb that tree nearest the tower, then toss the grapple through the window of Cathryn's chamber. We can lower her and Alex on the rope while Meg waits in the boat below."

"We're fortunate the room is at the back of the place," observed Owen. "If we wait until dark, we should be able to snatch them and be away before we're seen."

"It sounds risky," commented Ransom.

"Have ye any better idea?" asked MacLinn. "We can't just march up to the front gate and demand their release, ye ken."

"But what happens if they see us?"

"Lad, every Lowlander I've ever met was arrogant and narrow-sighted. The Campbells have set two guards at the only entrance to the castle, so naturally they think they've got all the protection they need. If we act quickly, doing something unlikely, we'll be back in the high country before they even know their hostages are gone."

"For all our sakes, I hope you're right."

Meg and the others kept watch from their camp hidden in the forest surrounding Briarthorn Castle, but as daylight ebbed, there was no sign of any activity. They saw Cathryn come to the window several times, gazing out in what appeared to be a wistful manner, but they made no movement to gain her attention. Hours later, as soon as the autumn moon was high in the sky, Revan MacLinn gave the order to put their plan into action.

Yates and Beale, who had chosen to return to Scotland with their captain, had fairly begged to be allowed to join the rescue party. Now they were given the task of striking camp and saddling the horses in preparation for a hasty departure. Meg and Owen slipped downriver to steal the rowboat kept for the use of the castle's residents. The deep, swiftly flowing waters of the river, which had been diverted to form a moat for the castle, presented a barrier that could only be broached by way of the drawbridge or by boat. It had taken most of a day's surveillance to scout out the hidden rowboat, but stealing it under cover of darkness was fairly simple.

With the last member of the group, Rob MacLinn, left on the riverbank to keep watch, Meg and Owen rowed the rescuers across the river. Revan MacLinn, grumbling about the weight of the iron grapple he carried, darted across the lawn to the huge beech tree that stood alongside the castle. Hidden by its shadow, he began the arduous climb upward. Ransom stayed in the boat with Meg, and together they watched as MacLinn swung the grapple outward and upward, hoping to get it inside the window of Cathryn's bedchamber. He missed the first attempt, and the iron hook clanged against the stone wall.

Meg gasped, clamping a hand over her mouth. Ransom dropped an arm about her shoulders and gave her an encouraging hug. "It's close to midnight, Meg. Everyone will be asleep."

"They'd have to sleep like the dead not to hear that," she whispered.

"Have a little faith," Ransom scolded, unconsciously using one of her father's favorite phrases.

MacLinn swung the grapple again, and this time the hook disappeared through the open window, landing inside the room with a dull thud. He dropped the rope and shimmied down the tree.

"Time for me to go," Ransom murmured. "Wish us luck."

Meg gave him a lingering kiss. "Please be careful," she said.

"Don't worry." He stepped out of the boat, then turned back. "Promise me something, Meg—if anything goes wrong, promise you and Owen will row this boat back to shore, collect the others, and get the hell out of here. Don't try to come to our aid . . . swear you won't."

"I swear it," Meg replied, gray eyes wide and solemn.

Ransom's white teeth gleamed in a broad smile. "I'm getting better," he declared. "At least I'm starting to *suspect* when you're telling a lie."

Meg grimaced and stood to give him another kiss. "Just be careful and I won't need to worry about rescuing you."

Revan MacLinn stood waiting for him, the end of the dangling rope in his hand. "You took long enough," he growled.

"Sorry. I had to say goodbye to Meg."

"Spare me the details." MacLinn tested the rope by giving it a hard yank. The grapple held. "It seems stout enough. I'm going up."

"Have a care," warned Ransom. "I can't understand why no one has come to the window yet. That hook landed with enough noise to wake a corpse."

"I know, and that worries me, too." He touched the dirk strapped to his leg. "Have ye a weapon?"

"Yes."

"Then let's be off." MacLinn began slithering up the rope. About halfway up, it started to sway; each time he advanced, his body was slammed against the unrelenting stones. Standing on the ground, watching, it seemed to Ransom that Meg's father would be beaten half to death before he ever reached the top of the tower. Eventually, however, Ransom saw the Scotsman heave himself over the window sill and disappear inside.

Not waiting for a signal, Ransom grasped the rope and began hauling himself upward. When he was only a few feet from the window, he heard the unmistakable sounds of a scuffle. Swiftly, he hurled himself across the sill in time to see two dark figures go rolling across the floor. He caught the gleam of MacLinn's dirk in the firelight, then heard an astonished exclamation.

"Alex?"

"Father! Father, is that you?"

"Aye, it's me. Give over, will you, lad? You've grown brawny in your absence from Wolfcrag."

Father and son rose from the floor to throw themselves into each other's arms.

"When the hook came through the window and awakened us," Alex explained, "we didn't know who or what to expect. I sent Mother into the garderobe to hide—"

"And jumped on me without even a weapon at hand," MacLinn finished proudly. "Good thing I halfway expected it of ye, or I might have done in my only son."

Ransom's eyes had grown accustomed to the darkened room. They took in the rumpled bed, the pallet on the floor. "I take it you and your mother were the only ones in the room," he said.

Alex nodded. "Over a week ago, Mother's uncle declared us

hostages and locked us in here. I'm glad you've come—I've grown to hate this cursed place!"

"And your mother?" MacLinn asked evenly.

"She hates it, too. She only wants to go home."

"Then fetch her, and let's get out of here."

Alexander crossed the floor to the garderobe. "I think," he said with a wide, mischievous grin, "that you're going to be surprised."

Before either of the men could determine his meaning, the youth led his mother from the toilet enclosure. Cathryn was dressed only in a long white nightgown, her red hair unbound and flowing well past her shoulders. When she saw her husband, she stopped in midstep, lingering uncertainly in the center of the chamber, her hands resting protectively over the huge mound of her belly.

"Jesus!" swore Revan MacLinn, nearly staggering with shock. "Oh my God, woman . . . what ails ye? Is it . . . are ye suffering from some sort of tumorous growth?"

Alex laughed aloud, causing Cathryn to toss her head indignantly. "If it's a tumor," she snapped, " 'tis of your making!"

Ransom clapped a hand on MacLinn's shoulder. "I think your wife is telling you that you're about to be a father again."

MacLinn's amber eyes blazed with some fierce emotion. "Is that the way of it, Cathryn?"

She nodded. "Indeed it is." She came toward him, her formerly graceful walk obscured by an ungainly waddle. "And the midwife here at Briarthorn insists I must be having twins."

"How long have you known?" MacLinn ground out. "Did you know when you left Carraig?"

"Yes, I knew."

"Why didn't you tell me?" he roared.

"Best keep your voice down, MacLinn, or we'll have visitors," Ransom cautioned.

"I tried to find an opportunity," Cathryn said, "but you were too busy with your silly battle training to pay me any heed. And then, when I decided not to let you endanger Alex's life, I knew I'd have to leave . . . so I didn't dare tell you."

"You're a deceitful woman, Cathryn MacLinn," he accused.

"The years we've longed for more children . . . and then the miracle occurs and ye don't even bother to tell me." He towered over her, fisted hands resting on his lean hips. "This is my babe, is it not?"

Cathryn's outraged gasp echoed loudly. "Why, you . . . you . . ." She raised a hand and applied it smartly to her husband's cheek in a stinging slap. "How dare you?"

Ransom moved quickly, planting himself between MacLinn and his wife. He didn't know precisely what action the man would take, but he knew MacLinn wouldn't let the attack go unanswered. For an instant, MacLinn's amber eyes glinted dangerously, and then, bit by bit, his expression cleared. He threw back his head and laughed.

"Stand aside, lad," he ordered, "and let me kiss my runaway wife. I promise not to strangle the wench."

Ransom did as he was bid, watching with amusement as MacLinn pulled Cathryn into his arms as best he could and proceeded to kiss her heartily. When he had her breathless and laughing, he drew back and murmured, "Catriona, don't ever leave me again."

"I don't intend to," she said with asperity. "And certainly not to run to my horrible family for protection."

"Speaking of Mother's family," interjected Alex, "shouldn't we be going?"

"And we do have a dilemma here," added Ransom, with a significant look at Cathryn's well-rounded contours. "Our original plan isn't going to work."

"No," MacLinn agreed. "I came here expecting to whisk my sylphlike bride away in my arms – and *now* look at her. Will she even fit through the window?"

Cathryn punched his arm in mock anger. "There's no time for insults," she chided.

"Insults?" echoed MacLinn. "It wasn't an insult, love. I think ye look beautiful."

"But can she slide down the rope in her condition?" queried Ransom. "We've got to think of something."

"Alex, you go on down and alert your sister to the problem," ordered MacLinn. "In the meantime, Ransom and I will figure out some way to lower your mother."

Ransom made certain the grapple was firmly caught beneath the stone sill before allowing the boy to descend. Then he turned back to let his eyes roam the chamber once again, breaking into a smile as they came to rest on a high-backed wooden chair. "I have an idea. We'll lash Cathryn to the chair and lower her to the ground that way."

Cathryn's eyes widened, and MacLinn gave her a comforting squeeze. "It'll be safer than me trying to carry you, love. We'll make sure the chair is secure, and I'll be as close to you as I can."

"But will the rope be strong enough to hold me?" Cathryn asked.

She turned her frightened gaze on Ransom, who nodded and said, "It will," all the while praying he was right.

"Put on your cloak and slippers . . . and a pair of gloves to protect your hands from the rope," MacLinn said. "We dare not waste another minute."

"But my belongings—what about them?"

"There's no time, love—you'll just have to buy new things when we get home. We'll go to Inverness before winter sets in." All the while MacLinn was talking, he was urging his wife toward the chair, which Ransom had dragged to the window. At the last moment, she balked.

"There is one thing I have to take," she announced stubbornly. "Something I've kept hidden from the first day I came here—and a good thing I did, too." She pointed to one of the bolsters on the bed. "Ransom, sewn into that cushion you'll find a large purse containing most of the money I . . . stole from my husband."

"Well, I'll be damned," muttered MacLinn. "And to think I'd forgotten all about it."

Ransom seized the cushion from the bed and hurried to the window. "We'd better take cushion and all," he said, and tossed it over the sill. "Now, Cathryn, seat yourself."

"We'll have to use bedsheets to tie her to the chair," MacLinn said. "We won't have enough excess rope otherwise."

They helped the heavily pregnant woman into the chair,

tore the sheets off the bed, and ripped them into strips to lash her to the back and seat.

"You'll have to go on down, MacLinn," Ransom said. "You'll need to be on the ground to assist Cathryn."

"You go down – I'll lower her."

"Are you sure you can lash the chair properly?"

A frown was etched onto MacLinn's forehead. "Do you think ye can do it any better?"

Ransom nodded. "I'm a sailor, remember. And that's what sailors do – tie knots."

"Will you be strong enough to hold her?"

"She'll be as safe as a babe in a cradle."

Cathryn patted Ransom's hand. "I trust you implicitly." She turned a dazzling smile on her husband. "Both of you. If I didn't, I'd take my chances staying here with the Campbells rather than risk my babies' lives."

"Good God, woman, MacLinn growled. "Stop speaking of *babies!* I'm gray with fright just thinking there's two of you. I canna deal with the thought of three – "

"It will be fine, Revan."

MacLinn's face was still grim, but he leaned forward to give his wife a kiss. "I'll be waiting for you on the ground, then. I love you, Catriona."

"And I love you," she whispered as she watched him throw a long leg over the window ledge and reach for the rope.

"Don't worry, I'll keep an eye on the grapple," Ransom said. "As soon as you're down, signal and I'll send Cathryn."

In a short time, MacLinn had reached the grass below, and Ransom hauled in the loose end of the rope to start forming a sling to hold the chair. Then, after testing each and every knot, he carefully lifted Cathryn and the chair onto the window ledge. Cathryn's face became ashen as she contemplated the long drop, but she raised her chin bravely and grasped the rope in her gloved hands, firmly refusing to look down again.

After wrapping the excess rope around his waist, Ransom began easing the chair out the window as slowly as he could. The slow coil of the rope around his body chafed and burned, and the muscles in his arms quivered with the strain, but he ignored everything but thoughts of the woman in his care. It seemed a breathless eternity before the chair reached Revan MacLinn's outstretched hands.

Ransom watched from above as MacLinn freed his wife from her bonds. His jaws were aching from being so tightly clamped, his ears ringing with the effort to hear signs of activity elsewhere in the castle. As soon as the rope was unsnarled, he seized it and stepped off the window ledge. Dangling precariously along the castle wall, he relished the feel of the bracing wind and the promise of solid earth beneath his boots once more.

As he dropped the last few feet onto the lawn, he thought about making a promise to himself that this would absolutely be his last wild and reckless escapade—but then he admitted the foolishness of such a declaration. All of his life among the MacLinns was going to be an adventure, and there was simply nothing he could do . . . but enjoy it.

Meg was waiting with open arms as he scooped up the cushion containing Cathryn's fortune, dashed across the grass, and cast himself into the rowboat.

"I'm so proud of you," she whispered into his ear. "This night you've proven yourself a hundred times over. If you didn't really love me, you'd never have risked so much for my family."

Her lips were warm and worshipping as she moved them over his, and it was with very little surprise that Ransom realized he would gladly repeat the night's activities just to earn another such reward.

Suddenly, he felt a powerful hand clasp his shoulder. "Laddie boy," came MacLinn's voice out of the near-darkness, "I've been thinkin'. Seems to me ye must have been born a Highlander and somehow, as a bairn, got stolen by Devonshire gypsies." The hand increased its grip, then was withdrawn. "Welcome home, son."

The horses were waiting as the boat bumped ashore, and it took only a moment for everyone to find a mount. Revan MacLinn insisted Cathryn ride with him—they'd go slowly, he announced, and stop at first light to purchase a wagon in which she could ride with more comfort.

The riders paused on the river bank to shout the MacLinn battle cry, just to let the guards know who their midnight visitors had been. Ransom heard himself joining in, his throat straining with the glorious call. Then the little band turned their horses toward the Highlands and the secluded mountain fortress that awaited them.

# Epilogue

*Christmas Night, 1770*
*Wolfcrag Castle, Scotland*

The bedchamber was almost stiflingly warm, redolent with the pungent scents of pine and bayberry candles. Cathryn MacLinn lay against the pillows of a big four-poster bed, holding her newborn son in her arms. Perched on the edge of the bed beside her, her husband was gingerly cradling his new daughter.

Dressed in black, the rugged Highland outlaw looked massive compared to the tiny white-blanketed bundle he held. The expression on his bearded face was a comical mixture of awestricken pride and masculine helplessness. Gently, he stroked the ebony curls atop the baby's head, then smiled at Cathryn.

" 'Twould seem the midwife at Briarthorn was right to suspect twins."

"I knew there were two all along," Cathryn murmured. "I just didn't know the wee scamps would choose to be born on Christmas Day." She sighed wearily, happily. "I hope we didn't ruin the holiday for everyone."

"Ruin it?" exclaimed Meg from the foot of the bed where she stood within the circle of Ransom's arm. "You made it the most perfect Christmas ever!"

"Except for me," spoke up Dr. MacSween from his seat near the fire. Della, his wife, was massaging his shoulders with a patient smile. "I hope you don't plan to do this again, Cathryn. I'm simply too damned old . . . and the excitement is more than my poor heart can take."

"Don't try to make my daughter-in-law feel guilty," said Margaret MacLinn saucily. "If she and my son decide to have more children, I'll be more than capable of doing your job." She grinned at Meg and Ransom. "All you did was order Mairi to bring boiling water and cloths. Then you paced up and down the floor, muttering, until the bairns were born. Cathryn did all the real work, while Revan mopped her brow and gave her a firm hand to hold. You, Dr. MacSween, are a fraud!"

"Nevertheless, Mother," MacLinn laughingly scolded, "we have to give the good doctor some credit. He was there to catch the children when they made their entrance into the world. I was shaking too hard to do it myself, ye ken."

"See there," declared MacSween in triumph. "Someone knows my worth."

"Why are the babies so ugly?" interjected Alexander, peering over his father's shoulder. "And so small?"

"Alex, you wretch," cried Meg. "They're not in the least ugly. Why, they're the most beautiful things I've ever seen. And babies are supposed to be small."

"Maybe so," Alex said doubtfully, "but what good's it going to do me to have a brother? It'll be years before he's big enough to ride a horse or hold a sword."

"Revan," warned Cathryn, her eyes gleaming with amusement, "I think you need to have a chat with your oldest son."

MacLinn heaved a hearty sigh, to the entertainment of everyone in the room. "Alex, what your mother's saying is that we're no longer warriors, we're farmers. But," he added hastily, sensing the protest his son was about to make, "ye needn't worry. At your age, you'll soon find other, more interesting matters to be concerned with." He gave the boy a wink.

"Revan! You're incorrigible!" Cathryn made a face at him. "I shudder to think what kind of father you'll be to these two."

"I'll be a damned good one," he vowed.

Cathryn reached out to take his hand. "Yes, I think you will," she murmured.

"Have you decided what to name the twins?" inquired Della MacSween. "Everyone in the castle is making wagers."

"They'll never find names that we all agree upon," remarked Margaret MacLinn. "The poor bairns may have to name themselves when they're old enough."

A chorus of disapproval sounded, and the room echoed with lively debate as each one insisted on his or her favorite names.

The din might have been alarming to a stranger, but Ransom calmly looked on, filled with a sense of contentment. He'd long since been accepted into the family and, when he pleased, could shout and argue with the best of them. But tonight his mood was too mellow—he was pleased to simply observe. Silently he counted his blessings, realizing he'd never known happiness such as he'd enjoyed since his return to Scotland.

He glanced down at his wife, marveling anew at his good fortune. Sometimes he felt he'd been only half-alive before the night they met, and though they'd come through near-disaster, survival was sweet indeed.

Meg tilted her head to give him a cocky smile. "Something tells me you're not the least interested in naming my new brother and sister," she said in an undertone.

"Naming babies isn't exactly my forte."

"Oh?" she teased. "Then . . . what is?"

His blue-green eyes sparkled. "Madam," he said, with mock affront, "need you ask?"

Rosy color glowed on Meg's cheeks. "Not really. I believe I recall. Of course, you could renew my memory."

"Gladly, but would you be interested in a walk on the parapets first? I have a sailor's yen to look up and see the stars."

"It'll be cold up there," Meg warned.

He smiled broadly. "But I know a wonderful way we can warm ourselves."

With final wishes for a happy Christmas, they bid the other family members goodnight and, ignoring the knowing smiles, left the room. As they were making their exit, the next group of visitors—Hale Dickson, Fletcher, and Mairi—were arriving, bearing gifts and congratulations.

Ransom and Meg stopped to don woolen cloaks, then climbed the narrow staircase to the roof of the castle. The night was still and calm, the sky adorned by thousands of stars, glittering like bits of ice floating in a sea of blackness.

Meg stepped to the high stone wall to gaze down at the ocean, which moved sluggishly, as though half-frozen by the glow of the December moon. Ransom closed the distance between them, putting his arms around her and pulling her back against him.

With a contented sigh, Meg remarked, "It was a splendid Christmas, wasn't it?"

"Mmmm," he agreed, bending his head to breathe in the heathery scent of her hair. Strands of black silk caressed his mouth as he kissed the top of her head. Meg's hair had grown nearly to her shoulders, and though she often teased him that she intended to cut it again because long hair was a nuisance, he was aware she didn't mean it. It was a source of amazement to her, he knew, that he took such pleasure in her beauty—she was still convinced she looked more like a lad than a lady. Ransom gloried in her ingenuousness and never wasted an opportunity to express his bold admiration.

"I'm so pleased about the message your father sent," Meg said, leaning her head against his shoulder. "To think he's returning Rogue's Run to you as a wedding gift! That must make you so happy . . ."

"Not as happy as the fact he actually found some concern in his soul for those people living in the village," Ransom commented. "Leaving them behind was the only real regret I had about selling the estate. I never would have expected my father to take such an interest in their welfare."

"Why do you suppose he did?"

"I'm not sure. No doubt Edmund had a great deal to do with it. He and I had a long talk before I left—maybe I finally swayed him to my way of thinking. I know we communicated as brothers, for once in our lives."

"Ransom, I have an idea. When it's warmer, let's take your ship and sail to Devon. We can spend some time at Rogue's Run and do . . . well, other things."

"What other things?" he queried, amusement in his voice.

"I'd like to meet your family—especially your father. I intend to set that man straight on a few things." She turned in his arms, her face earnest. "Ransom, it's time the rift between you two was healed, and I believe he's made the first move by giving back Rogue's Run."

"I agree. And, my darling, if anyone can bring my father around, it's you." He laughed, his breath steamy in the cold air. "But wouldn't you miss your own family?"

"Of course, but we won't be gone forever. And if we should decide to live part of each year in England, they can come to visit." She gave him an impish smile. "You might even present them at court!"

"That'd be something for the history books, I'd wager."

Meg stifled an unexpected yawn. "Indeed."

Ransom kissed her parted lips. "You're tired, love."

"Yes, it has been a long day."

"But a happy one." He scooped her into his arms and held her securely against his chest. "Now *I* have an idea," he stated. "I'll carry you down to bed."

Meg wrapped her arms around his neck, pulling his face to hers for a soft, sleepy kiss. "Let's leave the windows open tonight so we can smell the sea," she suggested in a whisper.

"But it's so cold . . ."

She kissed him again, lingeringly. "I think we're both aware of ways to keep warm."

Smiling, Ransom hugged her tightly. "You know, I believe Yates and Beale were right all along—you *are* a witch." His eyes caressed her lovingly. "At any rate, you've completely bewitched me."

Meg touched the golden earring he wore. "A witch and a pirate," she whispered. "Aren't we a fine pair?"

Ransom's rich laugh rang out. "Aren't we, though?" he murmured, warming her with his kiss.

A sudden wind began to stir, keening and wailing as it

swept along the battlements, scattering a handful of lacy snowflakes down upon them. But neither Meg nor Ransom noticed, for they were basking in the glorious sunshine generated by two loving hearts.

Wolfcrag Castle dominated the ice-encrusted shore, its immense towers rising from the huge boulders that formed its base. Ancient and indestructible, it had patiently endured, awaiting the day its walls would echo with the voices and footfalls of those who rightfully belonged there. That time was at hand—at last, the MacLinns had come home.